BEVERLY JENKINS

*313   313 515
0670*

WILD SWEET LOVE

AVON BOOKS
An Imprint of HarperCollinsPublishers

This is a work of fiction. Names, characters, places, and incidents are products of the author's imagination or are used fictitiously and are not to be construed as real. Any resemblance to actual events, locales, organizations, or persons, living or dead, is entirely coincidental.

AVON BOOKS
An Imprint of HarperCollins*Publishers*
10 East 53rd Street
New York, New York 10022-5299

Copyright © 2007 by Beverly Jenkins
ISBN: 978-0-06-116130-8
ISBN-10: 0-06-116130-6
www.avonromance.com

First Avon Books paperback printing: May 2007

Avon Trademark Reg. U.S. Pat. Off. and in Other Countries,
Marca Registrada, Hecho en U.S.A.
HarperCollins® is a registered trademark of HarperCollins Publishers.

Printed in the U.S.A.

10 9 8 7 6 5 4 3 2

For Angel

WILD SWEET LOVE

PROLOGUE

Teresa July was riding across the flats of Arizona Territory like she had demons on her heels because she did. Pinkertons, bounty hunters, local sheriffs, and U.S. Deputy Marshals had combined forces to finally put a stop to her bank robbing. She supposed she should be flattered that the authorities thought they needed thirty men to bring her in, but she didn't have the time to crow. Her destination were the craggy foothills ahead in the distance. Once there, she knew she could elude them because she'd hidden out in the area many times before. The hills, however, were a pretty far piece away.

The big powerful stallion beneath her continued to eat up the distance, but they'd been riding hard for miles and Teresa could feel the horse tiring. She bent low and shouted encouragement. "C'mon, Cloud! C'mon!"

Shots rang out, the sound loud over the horse's thundering stride, and she prayed she didn't get shot in the back. Her own firearms were in her holster. She didn't have time to shoot back, she was too busy riding.

The hills were getting closer, but so was the posse.

In her mind she could feel their hot breaths on her neck. Perspiration was pooling on her skin beneath her black leathers. If she didn't make it there ahead of them, she'd be in a jail before sunset, and she wanted to avoid that.

The shots were coming hot and heavy now, and she and Cloud were moving as one. Teresa loved to ride. Being set on a horse's back was one of her first memories. No matter the circumstances, riding thrilled her, even when she was riding for her life.

The earth-hued foothills rose into sight. She looked back at the herd of men and grinned. She was going to make it. "C'mon, big boy! C'mon!"

Teresa and Cloud had been running from the law together for a long time, and the black stallion knew sanctuary when he saw it. He gave her all he had. An exhilarated Teresa threw back her head to shout the victory cry of her Black Seminole ancestors, but was immediately silenced by the sight of the ten mounted men waiting for her up on the rock face. They'd appeared out of nowhere. Panicked, she hauled back on the reins, sending Cloud in a circle in a desperate attempt to find an escape route. But there was none.

Riders were charging from the right and the left, and the posse behind was closing in. The men in the hills had their rifles drawn and were close enough to pick her off like a jackrabbit. She sighed with resignation. After successfully eluding this particular group of men for months, and others like them for years, she'd finally been run to ground. She couldn't go forward, nor could she go back. As the net closed in on her, she gave Cloud an affectionate bittersweet pat.

"Guess it's over, boy. We had a great run, though, didn't we?"

Faced with defeat, she dismounted and removed her gun belt. After tossing it aside, she leaned back against Cloud, folded her arms and waited for her captors.

Later, when the sun set, she was behind bars, just as she'd predicted.

Chapter 1

Summer 1895
Outside Philadelphia, Pennsylvania

Scrubbing sheets on an iron washboard, Teresa thought about her capture. Although it had taken place three years ago, the memory felt like both yesterday and a lifetime. She wondered how Cloud was faring up in Kansas with her brother Neil and her sister-in-law Olivia. Did the stallion miss her as much as she missed him? Because musing on the past brought on a sadness she refused to acknowledge, she turned her attention back to the sheets she was supposed to be washing and stuck her red raw hands down into the hot lye-laced water.

The sheets piled on the ground beside her were waiting their turn on the washboard, and it would be dark before they were all done. But being a Black Seminole, she didn't mind the work; the necessity of living a hard life was in her blood. What she did mind was that she was in prison in Pennsylvania. Because she'd chosen to stay on the wrong side of the law instead of turning herself in, as her brother had, Hanging Judge Parker wanted to teach her a lesson. He'd sentenced her not to a prison in her beloved West, but here, up North, where she'd had to suffer through cold, mean winters, was too far away for family to visit her, and where she knew no one.

Teresa wiped the sweat from her brow and looked out at the other women in the yard. There were about fifty of them, and they too were hanging laundry and standing over wooden barrels. They'd been sent here for everything from stabbing their husbands to picking pockets. All were dressed in the same faded and worn blue sacks that passed for gowns, and prisoners wearing shoes outnumbered those without.

Teresa transferred the wet clean sheets to the female prisoner operating one of the many ringers, then returned to her own vat to start on the next sheet. Today's batch of linens had come from one of the area's hospitals. Tomorrow's would be from the fancy Philadelphia hotels. Washing and hanging sheet after sheet, day after day, was mindless, backbreaking work, but at least they were outside. In the winter the prisoners were forced to stay indoors, which bred fights, petty thievery, and sometimes madness.

By late afternoon she was tired, as they all were, and there was nothing to look forward to when the day ended but a plate of beans and salt pork that would be, and had always been, dinner. As a result, most of the women were thin and listless. Teresa doubted she'd ever again fit the leathers she'd worn here. Her once vibrant midnight skin was gray, her chopped-off hair matted and as full of lice as everyone else's.

"July!"

Teresa turned. It was Mrs. Cassidy, a burly brown-skinned matron whose sour expression had never changed in the three years Teresa had been in residence.

"Warden wants to see you."

Being summoned could be related to anything from a death in the family to punishments for infractions, real and imagined. Teresa wordlessly dried her hands and followed the matron across the field to the buildings a few feet away.

The warden was a White man named Burns. He rarely ventured out of his office. Teresa had only seen him twice before.

He looked up at her, but his face gave nothing away as to what this grand summoning might be about. "You're probably wondering why you're here."

"Yes, sir."

"It's about that fight last month."

The fight had been between a surly prisoner named Ethel and the only matron in the place who seemed to care at all about the inmates, a woman named Doreen. When Ethel had jumped Doreen, Teresa jumped Ethel.

"I submitted a request to the prison board," Burns said.

Ethel had been sent to another facility, and Teresa was certain they were about to do the same to her. She waited, steeling herself for the blow to come.

"The board has decided to give you credit for your time served as a way of rewarding you for coming to the aid of the matron."

Teresa blinked and her legs wobbled for an instant.

She took a deep breath to steady herself, then met the man's emotionless blue eyes.

"This means that in two hours you will be free to leave here in the company of a charity representative who helps women like you readjust to the outside. You will be her ward for the next year. Any infractions and you will be returned here to serve out the rest of your five-year time. Is that understood?"

Teresa was so moved she couldn't speak, so she nodded.

"Is that a yes, July?"

"Yes, sir."

"Mrs. Cassidy will help you get prepared. Good luck, July."

"Thank you, sir, and thank you to the board."

"Don't make me regret this decision."

"I won't. I promise."

Two hours later she walked out of prison and over to a wagon waiting by the side of the road. An elderly Black man held the reins. "You Miss July?"

She nodded.

"I'm Mr. Boswell, I'm here to take you to Mrs. Nance. Crawl in the back."

Teresa complied and made herself as comfortable as she could amidst the straw and farming implements in the wagon bed.

"We got about an hour worth of traveling."

She didn't care if the journey took six hours. She was free! "Mind if I sleep?"

"Not a bit."

A weary but happy Teresa closed her eyes, and before he even pulled away from the prison walls, she was asleep.

* * *

Teresa didn't realize she'd slept through the entire ride until she was jostled awake. Her slumber had been so sound that it took her a few moments to shake off the bleariness and focus on the stern brown face of the woman who was gently shaking her shoulder.

"Come," the woman said. "Mr. Boswell needs to get back to town."

Teresa grabbed the small bag holding her personal belongings and pushed herself up off the straw strewn wagon bed. Ignoring the stiffness in her legs, she slowly made her way to the ground, then dusted herself off. "Much obliged, Mr. Boswell."

He nodded, repeated the same gesture to the woman at Teresa's side, then he and his horse-led wagon rambled off down the cobbled street.

"This way," the woman directed.

Teresa wasn't offended that the well-dressed lady hadn't introduced herself. If the woman turned out to be the wife of Satan himself, she wouldn't have cared; all that mattered to her now was being out of jail and never going back.

The house was a fine two-story brick with pointed green roofs and gables up top. The short metal fence around the perimeter was also dark green, and the shrubs and trees inside the fence shaded the house from the sun and the street. A neat cobbled walkway led up the steps to a wide sitting porch and the front door.

Inside, Teresa looked around the fancy front parlor furnished with a blue brocaded sofa and matching chairs. A large mirror hung over the big stone fireplace, and an ornate chandelier, complete with fat white candles, hung from the ceiling above her head. Whoever owned the place lived well. Paintings of landscapes hung on the elegantly papered walls, and plush carpets covered the floors. Real well.

"Miss July?"

Teresa turned and saw that the woman's sternness remained. "Yes, ma'am."

"I'm Molly Nance. You'll be staying here in my home."

"I appreciate you taking me in." She had been expecting a small room in a crowded boardinghouse somewhere, not this small, elegant place.

"Just so you'll know, the last prisoner I took in ran off with everything of value she could carry."

Teresa refocused her attention. "Sorry to hear that. Was she caught?"

"Yes, and taken back to prison, but my things were never found."

Teresa didn't like hearing that. "Well, ma'am, I only stole from railroads and banks. Since you're neither, you're pretty much safe."

The quip melted Molly Nance's sternness a bit. "Then you and I should get along well."

"I'm hoping so."

"Come. I'll show you your room, and where you may bathe. I should have some clean clothing that you may wear until we can get you properly outfitted."

Teresa dearly wanted to scratch. The prison lice that had tagged along were plaguing her something fierce. Not wanting to embarrass herself by scratching like a dog with fleas, she bit down the urge and followed Mrs. Nance through the house.

They passed a formal dining room with a polished, dark wood table surrounded by carved backed chairs. There were carpets on the floor, there, too and more framed landscapes hung from the green papered walls. She caught a glimpse of a room filled with books that also housed a large black piano. Reading had always been one of her favorite pastimes. She wanted to go inside and explore the book titles, but thought it best she keep up with Mrs. Nance for now.

They entered the kitchen. Teresa marveled at the large cooking stove and other modern appliances. She wondered if all back East houses were this well equipped. It certainly wasn't the norm where she hailed from, or at least it hadn't been when she was sent to jail.

A tall, middle-aged woman wearing a black dress and white apron entered through the kitchen's back door. She was carrying a wooden crate filled with groceries and other items.

Mrs. Nance did the introductions. "Emma Bailey, this is Teresa July. Emma's the cook here."

"Pleased to meet you, Miss Emma."

Emma set the crate on the counter by the sink, then nodded a short reply. "You're the outlaw woman."

"Yes, ma'am."

Emma didn't look real friendly. Teresa wondered if she was comparing her to the last prisoner.

The cook told Teresa plainly, "Make sure you treat Mrs. Nance with respect. Not everybody will take in a jailbird like you."

There was a challenge in her voice and eyes, but Teresa bit back the urge to verbally retaliate. "I know that, so I'm real beholden to her."

Emma studied her for a moment longer, then asked, "You hungry?"

Considering the woman's no nonsense manner, the question was unexpected. "I am, but I'm more interested in a bath right now." Lord, she wanted to scratch.

"Come back after you're done," Emma said. "For the next couple days we'll feed you something light. Takes time for your stomach to get back on real food." She asked then, "Is there anything you don't like to eat or can't eat because it makes you sick?"

"Not that I know of."

"All right." And she began unloading the crate on the counter.

"Thank you," Teresa said in parting.

"And Teresa?" Emma called out.

"Yes, ma'am?"

"Welcome."

Touched by the unexpected kindness in Emma's tone, Teresa nodded, then followed Mrs. Nance down the hallway.

As they climbed the stairs to the upper floors, she wondered if she could be dreaming. First, her sentence had been commuted, and now she seemed to be in a household with fairly decent folks. If this was indeed a dream, she prayed she wouldn't wake up until after she had her bath.

"This will be your room."

It was small and plainly furnished, but there was a grate in the wall to keep her warm during the fierce winters, and a glass-paned door that led outdoors. Simple white eyelet curtains adorned the windows. The yellow quilt on the big four poster bed looked soft to the touch. All in all, it was the finest room Teresa had ever had the privilege of calling her own. "This is real nice, ma'am."

"I'm glad you approve. The bathing room is down the hall. Come. I'll show you."

Having washed up with either a basin or under a pump all of her life, Teresa found the newfangled indoor plumbing impressive. "So I just turn this handle if I want hot water, and this one for cold?"

"Yes. The boiler only holds so much hot water, but there's usually enough to take care of your needs."

Teresa wondered if this indoor plumbing was common here too. Thinking about the folks out West and their lack of amenities brought to mind her family and how they might be faring. It made her heart ache, so she stopped and paid attention to what Mrs. Nance was explaining. "There are soaps and salts in that basket over there. I'll bring you some orange oil for your hair and a comb and brush."

Teresa touched her short hair. She'd kept it cut during her incarceration, hoping to head off the lice, but it hadn't mattered. The only way to escape the little beasties would have been to shave her head completely bald, something the matrons refused to allow.

When Mrs. Nance left, Teresa stood in the quiet room, looking around at the white cabinets and the large claw-foot tub. She couldn't remember the last time she'd taken an actual bath. In the prison, they'd made do with hip baths and the long-handled pump in the yard behind their barracks. Walking over to the ivory colored tub, she placed the wooden stopper into the drain hole and turned the handle for the water. The sight of the clear stream spewing out filled her with delight. Holding her hand beneath the flow, she felt the temperature grow warmer. Grinning like a child at the fair, she stripped off her faded prison gown and watched the water rise with sparkling black eyes.

Across town, Mrs. Nance's only child, Madison, stood before the mirror in his bedroom and adjusted his tie. The former gambler, now a banker, was dressing for Paula Wade's twentieth birthday party. He knew Paula was a vain, social climbing nitwit, but had promised to attend, and he always kept his word. The party wouldn't begin for another few hours, but he was attending to his attire now because he wanted to stop by and check on his mother first. She had taken in yet another prisoner, and he wasn't pleased. In light of the theft by the last convict she'd opened her door to, he thought he had good reason to be distrustful. His mother had a crusading heart of gold, and he would not stand for it to be broken again.

In the hardscrabble world where Teresa grew up, fancy soaps and bath salts were usually reserved for sporting women and elegant ladies like her beautiful sister-in-law, Olivia. Women like herself, who robbed trains, slept in bedrolls on the ground, and ate beans out of a tin plate while hunkering next to a fire, rarely had the time or the inclination to soak in claw-footed tubs. But as she playfully raised her leg and watched the water slide down her foot and off her ankle, she decided she could grow to enjoy this. The warm water surrounding her, coupled with the sweet smells of the salts and her extreme relief at being free of the penitentiary was so relaxing, she wanted to lie there forever.

A soft knock on the door broke her reverie.

"Teresa? Are you all right?"

"Yes, ma'am. Doing just fine."

"I placed some clothing in your room along with the orange oil."

"Appreciate that. Thanks."

"You're welcome. Emma has some soup waiting for you when you're done."

"Tell her I'll be there directly."

"All right." And she was gone.

Eventually, Teresa left the tub and dried herself on a soft bath sheet. Wrapping herself in it, she padded barefoot back to her room and dressed in the muslin undergarments and plain white blouse and brown skirt lying on the bed. After putting the orange oil on her now clean hair, she picked up the hairbrush and walked over to the small mirror hanging above the fireplace mantel. As she raised the brush and looked at her reflection, she stopped. The painfully thin face of the woman staring back at her belonged to someone she didn't recognize. There was age in her features that hadn't been there before. Her dark skin was dull, lifeless, and the cocky eyes of her youth were now somber, older.

It had been three long years since she'd had access to a mirror, and seeing herself for the first time made her want to cry, but she didn't because she knew it wouldn't change things. By not taking Hanging Judge Isaac Parker's offer back in '88 to turn herself in and do her penance working for the railroads, she'd brought the resulting consequences down on her own head. Now, here she stood, three years older and a lifetime smarter. She began to ply the brush, and swore on the memories of her Black Seminole ancestors that she would never run afoul of the law again. The price had been too dear.

After going downstairs and consuming a steaming bowl of Emma's vegetable soup, Teresa excused herself from the kitchen table and headed back up, so exhausted that each step she took was a chore. It was almost as if her mind had finally allowed itself to acknowledge the physical toll the years of imprisonment had extracted, which up till then she had refused to do. To have surrendered to the fatigue of working sixteen-hour days scrubbing floors and doing laundry in vats filled with lye would have been to show defeat. She was Black Seminole, descendant of a people who'd fought the United States government for thirty years. A people who on the Great Trek had walked from Indian Territory to the Texas-Mexico border. Surely she could survive being in jail. And she had. But now, as she neared the top of the stairs, it seemed she had nothing left. A newborn prairie dog pup had more strength.

Deciding to take a seat on the stairs and close her eyes for just a minute, then get up and finish the walk to the bedroom, Teresa sank down onto the step. Laying her head against the carpeted edge, she closed her eyes.

When Madison entered his mother's house, he found her seated on the chaise in the parlor. She had her nose in a book, her favorite pastime. Upon seeing him, she set it aside and greeted him smiling. "My, don't you look grand."

He walked over and planted an affectionate kiss on her soft cheek. "I'm on my way to Paula's birthday dinner." His black and white evening wear had been tailored by one of the city's finest, and the lines showed off his tall, lean form. The elegant silk topper in his hand added a crowning touch.

"How is dear Princess Paula?"

The sarcasm made him smile. Paula Wade's desire to be his wife was no secret. "Doing well, I suppose. I haven't seen her in a few weeks."

"Tell her I send my regards."

"Stop lying, Mother, before lightning strikes the house."

"Am I that obvious?"

"Transparent as a plate of glass, I'm afraid."

"Then I shall try and do better next time."

Madison loved his mother's wit. "Did your charge arrive?"

"She did."

"May I meet her?"

"As long as you don't lecture her on her conduct, yes you may."

"I just want to introduce myself."

She was skeptical and didn't bother to mask it.

His mustache twitched with humor. "I know we disagree on her being here, but I'll be polite. I promise."

She didn't look convinced. "I'll go up and see if she's awake. She was rather tired when she arrived." His mother got up then, and exited, leaving him alone.

Madison's promise to her notwithstanding, he was still opposed to her having a prisoner in her home. The fact that this newest project wasn't the average everyday female felon, but the infamous, train-robbing hellion Teresa July only added to his concern. Newspapers all over the nation had chronicled her exploits, then her capture, trial, and imprisonment. Being informed by his mother a few days ago that the outlaw woman would be her ward for the next twelve months made him want to throw up his hands.

Emma's entrance into the room brought him back to the present. The worry on her face was plain. "What's the matter?"

"Your mother needs you upstairs."

Hoping the July woman wasn't already causing trouble, Madison hurried to the stairway.

There was no trouble, just his mother standing at the top of the stairs. Lying at her feet was a sleeping dark-skinned woman wearing a simple skirt and blouse.

"Poor thing," his mother said. "She was even more weary than Emma and I imagined. Will you pick her up, dear, and carry her to the room?"

Madison was taken aback by the request, but upon realizing her suggestion was the only solution, he gently scooped the outlaw up and held her against his chest. Following his mother, he entered the room and softly deposited the sleeping woman on the bed.

His mother covered her with a lightweight quilt. "Sleeping, she looks very innocent, doesn't she?"

Madison had to admit that she did. Looking at her now, a person might find it hard to believe her capable of all the bedlam she'd been convicted for. But he knew looks could be deceiving; she'd been sentenced for a reason.

"I was expecting a much larger woman," his mother said, keeping her voice low so as not to wake her charge.

Madison agreed. If the press were to be believed, Teresa July should have been Amazonian in size. Instead, she was of average stature and painfully thin. Faint traces of the scented soap and salts she must have used in her bath drifted up to his nose from the fabric of his coat. "Is the parole board going to let anyone she's here?"

"Other than the chief of police and the mayor, no. And they prefer the papers not find out either, at least not right away. They feel she'll adjust better if she isn't badgered by busybody reporters."

Madison could hear July's soft snores. If the press found out she was here, there'd be no peace. "I still don't think this is a good idea."

"I know you don't, dear, but I can make a difference in her life."

Madison's sole concern lay with his mother's safety. Changing the July woman's life didn't matter to him one whit.

"Let's let her sleep," his mother said.

Molly slipped her hand into the crook of his arm and he escorted her out.

"I appreciate your concern," she told him. "Miss July and I will do well, I can feel it, so you go celebrate with Paula and I'll return to my book."

"Which is?"

"A fascinating tale called *The Time Machine*, by Mr. H. G. Wells. I purchased it at a bookshop in London last year. It's all the rage. It's about a man who builds a machine that takes him back in time."

"Interesting."

They were now downstairs and standing by the open front door. It was time for him to depart, so he placed a quick peck on her cheek. "I'll stop in and meet your ward tomorrow. Let's hope she and the silver are still here."

Molly playfully pushed him toward the door. "Out. Let's hope Paula Wade doesn't have you fit for a nose ring by tomorrow."

"Touché, Mama." And with a grin he departed.

Outside, Madison climbed into his carriage and headed the horses up the residential street. His mother's parting quip had been rooted in truth. Were it up to Paula Wade, he'd have a ring in his nose large enough for a circus bear to perform in. But he'd told her on several occasions that he had no intentions of marrying, and so far he didn't see himself changing his mind.

The only woman with the beauty and wit to propel him to the altar had been the lady gambler Loreli Winters. To his disappointment, she'd fallen in love with a Kansas pig farmer named Jake Reed and was now happily living with him, their son, Jacob, and Jake's twin nieces, Bebe and Dede. Granted, Loreli was almost a decade older than he was, but he hadn't minded the difference in their ages. To him, the irrepressible gambler represented the kind of spirited, independent woman he'd envisioned spending his life with. He didn't resent the happiness she had found with Reed, but he had yet to meet another woman with the same joie de vivre.

Paula Wade was a beauty too, but she had no interests outside of shopping and gossip. Nothing on earth would have compelled her to read Mr. Wells's *Time Machine*, unless there was a new hat in the balance. She could tell you all about the newest fashions, but nothing about the myriad issues facing the race or the nation.

The birthday party was being held at the home of Paula's aunt and uncle, Harold and Daphne Carter. The street outside the place was filled with carriages and fancy buggies of all kinds. It seemed everyone in town was in attendance. Harold Carter had been a business associate of Madison's late father, Reynolds, and ran a very successful teamsters service. Based on the many luxurious coaches lining the curbs, many of Carter's well-heeled customers must have been invited to the celebration, along with Paula's own set of friends. Madison planned to stay only long enough to be polite, then excuse himself for the drive over to the club owned by his childhood friend Ben Norton. Once there, he intended to while away the remainder of the evening playing cards and enjoying himself.

First, however, he had to survive the crush of the people inside. In his attempt to work his way through the throng, he nodded a greeting to those he knew. Everyone had on their best dress. The women were in expensive gowns, and their husbands were nattily attired in formal evening wear. Uniformed waiters holding trays aloft moved expertly through the crowd, offering drinks and small pastries. Rebecca Constantine, a friend of his mother, greeted him with the sly smile usually reserved for a woman twenty years her junior. "Good evening, handsome."

He shook his head at her antics. "Evening, Mrs. Constantine. You look very lovely."

"Lovely enough for you to ravish in a dark secluded corner somewhere?"

She was one of the most audacious women he knew. "No, ma'am," he laughed. "Besides, what would your husband Miller say if he heard you propositioning me this way?"

"Since he's deaf as a mailbox, probably not a word."

"You are incorrigible."

"As long as I live." She smiled at him from beneath enough rouge and paint to outfit a convention of circus performers, but because he'd known her most of his life, he didn't find it strange. Instead, he placed an affectionate kiss on her cheek and promised to visit with her again later.

After some searching and a few more stops for conversations with people he knew, he finally located Princess Paula and her aunt and uncle, holding court in the solarium. The room had been outfitted with enough flowers to fill Mother Bethel AME, but because of all the people, the fragrance of the blooms had to compete with the scent of heat and bodies.

Paula's brown eyes lit up with delight when she spotted him. Rising from her chair and showing off the beautiful lemon yellow gown seamstresses must have been working on for months, she walked over to greet him. "You finally made it. I was worried."

"I promised I'd attend, didn't I?"

"Yes, but you can be so unpredictable sometimes." She grabbed his hand and led him over to her aunt and uncle. Madison had known Harold Carter and his wife Daphne almost as long as he'd known Rebecca Constantine. Although Harold Carter and Reynolds Nance had been business associates and friends, their wives had never gotten along. Daphne considered Molly a snob, and Molly thought Daphne a social climber with too much money and too little sense. Paula was Daphne's niece, and although she hailed from Memphis, she'd been living in Philadelphia for almost three years.

Madison shook Harold's hand and greeted Daphne with a polite smile.

"So glad to see you," Daphne gushed. She was brown-skinned and had a freckled face. The gown she was wearing, while fashionable and expensive, would have fit her very well ten years ago, but because she was as vain as the day was long and apparently refused to consider the reality of how much she actually weighed now, she looked like a sausage in a casing.

He withdrew the small jeweler's box from the inner pocket of his suit coat and handed it to Paula. "Happy Birthday."

Her eyes went wide. "Is it what I've been hoping for?" she asked in her pronounced southern accent.

With Daphne gazing on eagerly, Paula opened the lid. When she saw the locket nestled inside, she didn't bother hiding her anger. "This was supposed to be a ring, Madison Nance."

"Oh, really?" he drawled, wondering just how ugly a scene this would turn out to be. The guests within earshot were staring and whispering.

"This is my birthday celebration, and I hoped you'd come to your senses so we could announce our engagement this evening too."

Madison hated being the subject of gossip and knew this incident would be talked about for weeks to come. "I've told you my feelings on the matter many times. Why would you believe I'd changed my mind?"

You could hear a pin drop in the crowded solarium.

Paula had never been one for logic, and true to that spirit, said, "Because I'm twenty years old. How much longer do you think I'm going to wait for you to ask me?"

He shook his head at the ridiculousness of this encounter. Rather than give the gossips more fuel, he said, "Happy Birthday, Paula," then turned to walk out.

"Madison Nance! If you leave, I'll never speak to you again!"

Sarcastically hoping she'd keep her word, Madison kept going until he was outside in the fresh night air.

Chapter 2

When Teresa woke up in bed that next morning, the room was unfamiliar, but after looking around at the starched white curtains and the sunbeams dappling the floor and the walls, everything came back to her and she relaxed and she laid back with a smile. The fact that she couldn't remember coming to bed didn't worry her, because she was not in prison anymore. Her release hadn't been a dream. In spite of being thousands of miles away from home, and mandated to be under Mrs. Nance's guidance for the next year, her life and prospects were infinitely brighter than they'd been at this same time yesterday. Speaking of which …

She turned her attention to the small clock on the fireplace mantel and bolted upright when she saw the time. Was it really one in the afternoon! Mrs. Nance probably thought her to be the laziest of lazybones after sleeping away the day. Alarmed, Teresa threw aside the quilt, then realized she was still wearing the blouse and skirt she'd donned after last night's wonderful bath. Puzzled, and deciding maybe she did need to find out how she came to be in the bed after all, she walked down to the bathing room to take care of her needs. She didn't have any other clothes to change into, but even though wrinkled, what she was wearing beat her old prison gowns, hands down.

Emma was in the kitchen when she walked in, and all the cook said by way of greeting was, "Mrs. Nance is in the library."

Teresa was as hungry as a barn full of cowboys, and the aroma of whatever was cooking on the stove made her mouth water, but when Emma didn't offer up any samples, Teresa and her grumbling stomach left the kitchen to seek out Mrs. Nance.

The library room was filled with more books than Teresa had ever seen. She stopped at the sight of them all, and didn't realize she was staring around in wonder until she heard Mrs. Nance say brightly, "Good afternoon, dear."

Teresa tore her attention away from the hundreds of volumes neatly arranged in elegant wooden bookcases and immediately apologized for her tardiness. "I'm sorry for sleeping so late, Mrs. Nance. I really am. No idea what came over me."

"It's called fatigue," Mrs. Nance quipped sagely. "Frankly, I'm amazed you're awake now. Did you sleep well?"

"Like a dead man, and I don't remember climbing in bed or why I slept in my clothes. Sorry about that too," she said, looking down at her wrinkled skirt and blouse.

"No apologies needed, and we'll see to fresh clothing momentarily, but you don't remember going to bed because you fell asleep on the stairs."

The memories drifted back. "Oh, yeah," Teresa

said, though still confused. "But how'd I get to the room? Did you sleepwalk me there?"

"No. My son Madison carried you."

"Oh really?" Teresa wasn't sure she liked the idea of some stranger carrying her around while she was out cold like a drunk in an alley. "I didn't know you had children."

"He's my only. He's thirty-seven now. Used to be a gambler, of all things, but now he's a banker."

A gambling banker. Teresa found that interesting because Mrs. Nance seemed far too proper to have raised a gambling man. "Does he live here?"

"No. He has his own place. He stopped in last evening to meet you, but as I said, we found you asleep."

Teresa wondered if the gambling banker approved of his mother taking a former bank robber into her home, but then the sight of all the books recaptured her attention. "Have you read all of these?"

"Proud to say I have. Do you read?"

"Yes, ma'am. Used to be one of my favorite things to do. My mama Tamar insisted my brothers and I learn. She said it would help our futures."

"She sounds very wise. Is she still with us?"

"Far as I know. She lives in south Texas near the border with Mexico."

"Would you like to send her a telegram to let her know where you are?"

"Tamar can't read, but I'd like to send one to my brother out in Kansas."

"Your brother Neil?"

Teresa was surprised Mrs. Nance knew his name, then decided she shouldn't be. Newspapers all over the country had printed many stories on the adventures of the train robbing, bank robbing Julys over the years.

"We can send word to him if you'd like."

Teresa nodded. Neil would be glad to hear from her, and doubly glad to learn she'd been given an early release.

Mrs. Nance fetched some paper, and Teresa wrote her brother a hasty note.

"Emma will take it to the telegraph office later on," Mrs. Nance said. "A messenger will deliver the reply soon as it's received."

Pleased to have that taken care of, Teresa returned her attention to the books. She couldn't believe Mrs. Nance had read them all.

"Feel free to read whatever interests you, Teresa."

Embarrassed to have been caught staring again, she nodded. "That's real kind of you." Then her voice took on a more serious tone as she asked, "What kind of work do you want me to do so I can help out around here? I'm good at cleaning. I could do your rugs and your windows. I'm a pretty good cook. Emma will have to show me how to work the stove, of course, and where she keeps everything, but on her days off, I could do the cooking."

"We'll talk about that tomorrow. Right now, let's work on getting you fattened up and rested up."

"But Mrs. Nance—"

"Are you hungry?"

"As a bear after winter."

"Emma was making corn chowder earlier. Smells like it might be done."

Teresa was hungry but wanted to continue the discussion about her role in the household. Apparently, Mrs. Nance planned to stick to her guns because she was already leaving the room. Teresa gave the books one last fond look, then hastened to catch up.

When Mrs. Nance entered the big dining room, she took a seat at the polished table, but Teresa hesitated. She didn't think it her place to sit and eat in this fancy room. "I'll go eat in the kitchen with Miss Emma," she said.

"Sit down, Teresa."

"But—"

"Sit, dear."

The firm patience on Mrs. Nance's face made her reluctantly comply, but once seated, Teresa tried to press her case, "Mrs. Nance, I—"

"This is where you will be taking most of your meals from now on, at the table, like a lady."

Teresa blinked. "Excuse me?"

For a moment Mrs. Nance studied Teresa intently. "When you were young, what did you most want to be when you grew up?"

"Part of my brothers' gang."

Mrs. Nance dropped her head and chuckled. Composing herself again, she asked, "Wasn't there anything else? Something a bit more lawful?"

Teresa thought. "Wanted to be a schoolteacher at one time. When the government closed down the school, our teacher left too, and for a while I taught the young ones. I enjoyed it, and Tamar said she was real proud of me, but riding with my brothers was all I ever wanted to do."

"Understandable. It must have been very exciting."

"Oh yes indeed."

"But you can't rob trains or banks anymore, dear, so, what do you wish to do with your life?"

Teresa went silent while mulling that over, then shrugged. "I don't know."

"Well, that's why you're here, so you can figure it out."

"But I don't know if I have anything else in me to be." It was an honest answer, but she knew Mrs. Nance was on the mark. She had already sworn off outlawing, so she needed a legal way to make a living. "What do you think I can be?"

"Anything you put your mind to. Any woman with the gumption to be an outlaw already has a leg up on ninety-nine percent of the female population. We're raised to be scared of our own shadows. There should be more like you."

Teresa found that declaration surprising. For all of Mrs. Nance's proper ways, she liked her thinking.

Emma entered the room then, pushing a short wheeled tray. On top was a covered, green soup tureen and bowls that matched. Beside them were spoons, fine linen napkins, and short lead crystal glasses monogrammed with an elaborate N. Teresa stood, thinking to help Emma set the table, but the cook's sharp look sat her back down. Frustrated, Teresa let herself be served as if she were the Queen of the May and not a poor Seminole from southern Texas. She'd never been waited on this way before, and the experience made her downright uncomfortable. "I'll help wash the dishes, Miss Emma."

"Not in my kitchen you won't. That's my job. You keep Mrs. Nance company. I'll keep you both fed."

On that note, Emma and the cart exited the room. Teresa looked to Mrs. Nance, who smiled sympathetically and said, "Pass me your bowl."

The corn chowder was good. Emma had thinned her portion with a little watered down cream to make it easier for her stomach to digest, but Teresa didn't mind. After eating tasteless prison rations for the past three years, Emma's cooking was heavenly. "She's a real good cook."

"The best I've ever had."

"How long has she been with you?"

"Over twenty years. She was in her early thirties when she came to work for my mother."

"Does she have family?"

"Not blood, no. Madison and I consider her a member of our family, though. She held me up when my Reynolds died a decade ago."

"Sorry for your loss."

"Thank you."

Teresa wanted to ask how long the two had been married, but thinking that more questions might remind Mrs. Nance of her sorrow, she focused on finishing her chowder instead.

After eating, she and Mrs. Nance went upstairs to ferret out a wardrobe for Teresa from amidst the donated clothing and goods Molly kept stored in various trunks and crates in a hall closet. Teresa didn't mind the prospect of wearing castoffs because anything was better than the sacks she'd worn in prison. Besides, until joining up with her brothers' gang, she'd worn nothing but charity clothes anyway. Growing up poor and Seminole, the only thing she and her family had in abundance was courage.

"I've a few more things in my bedroom," Mrs. Nance said.

And what a beautiful room it turned out to be. Teresa looked around at the lovely pale blue wallpaper and saw that the bedding, draperies, and upholstered furniture were of similar tones. She was certain that Olivia would fall in love with a room like this one, but the space was a tad too ladyish for her. The nice plain room she'd been given suited her just fine.

Teresa took her new wardrobe to her room and placed the items in the armoire. Mrs. Nance came in with a couple more pieces, and Teresa put them away too.

"Once you start putting your weight back on," Mrs. Nance said, "we'll get you in some new clothing."

"That isn't necessary. The things you've already given me are fine."

"But I'm a seamstress by trade and haven't sewn in years. Outfitting you will give me a chance to re-sharpen my needles. Do you sew?"

Teresa snorted. "Me? I can tighten a button or stitch a tear in my leathers but that's all. My sister-in-law is the seamstress."

"Sewing is a very good skill to have, so we'll add it to our list."

"What list?"

"The one I'm making of all the things you need to learn in order to be able to provide for yourself, and to make yourself more rounded."

Teresa's skepticism was plain. "Really?"

"The parole board will be sending a representative over to check on you periodically, and we need to be able to show them you're making progress in your rehabilitation."

Teresa supposed that made sense, but she didn't have to like it. Keeping her voice even so as not to hurt Mrs. Nance's feelings, she asked, "What else is on this list?"

"Let's see. Deportment. Table etiquette and table settings. Music appreciation. Flower arranging. Cooking. Cleaning. We'll add more as we go along."

Other than the cooking and the cleaning, Teresa didn't see much value in the list. What good would deportment or music appreciation do her out West, but she didn't argue, because no matter the task, she'd learn it, even flower arranging, if it meant having the parole board's blessing to head home.

A sudden yawn claimed her, and Mrs. Nance nodded sympathetically. "I want you to rest. Go down and get something to read if you'd like. I have to go over to the church to help with the preparations for tomorrow's service. I'll be back in a few hours."

"I can't just sit around reading all day. You must have something I can do."

"Not that I can think of at the moment, so rest. You may think you've regained your strength but I'm pretty sure your body knows otherwise."

Teresa sighed with frustration.

"I promise to take you up on your offer to help out."

"I'm holding you to that."

"I'm sure you will. We'll talk when I return."

After Molly's departure, an irked Teresa flopped down on the bed. Looking up at the ceiling, she wondered how to get Mrs. Nance to stop treating her like a hot house plant, but before she could concoct a plan, her eyes drifted closed and she was asleep.

Madison was grim when he left the meeting at Bethel AME. He and twenty other prominent men had come together to form an organization that would speak to the problems and issues faced by Philadelphia's citizens of color, but for four hours they'd done nothing but argue. The heated debate stemmed over which tact to take: Conservative or Radical. All over the country the same battle was being waged. Men like Madison and Dr. N. F. Mossel, founder of Douglass Memorial, the city's only Negro hospital, were considered Radicals because they favored continued political agitation, even though the Jim Crow laws made their efforts seem futile. The Conservatives, led nationally by Tuskegee Institute founder Booker T. Washington, favored what the Black press had dubbed "accommodation." The Conservatives preached that since segregation and Jim Crow were the law of the land, the race should forget about calling for justice and equality, and concentrate instead on self-sufficiency, farming, and learning a trade. The Conservatives touted their approach as being the only way the Negro would earn the right to the protections offered by the Constitution. The Radicals thought that hogwash.

Madison hoped he and the others could iron out their differences soon because there was much to address. The schools were underfunded, the owners of public facilities continued to draw the color line, and in the South lynchings were becoming a macabre national pastime.

As he drove away from the church, he put the meeting out of his mind and headed to his mother's house with the hope of meeting an awake Teresa July. From reading newspaper stories about her, one would think that she was as wild as a mountain lion and twice as cunning. In her heyday, she'd ridden with the remnants of the notorious Dick Glass gang, and supposedly robbed her first bank at the tender age of fifteen, an age when most of the well-raised young women in his mother's circle were contemplating more law abiding endeavors like marriage or furthering their education. Admittedly, she hadn't appeared very ferocious when he carried her to the room last evening; in fact, sleeping, she'd seemed downright tame. He could still feel the weight of her in his arms and recall the scents she'd been wearing. He shook off the memory because in reality she was a very dangerous woman, and if she harmed his mother, he'd personally see to it that she returned to prison for a very long time.

He also wanted to stop in and tell his mother about Paula's party. More than likely the gossip about it was making the rounds, and he preferred that she hear the facts from him than from someone relating what they'd heard thirdhand. Lord willing, Paula would now set her sights elsewhere and leave him the hell alone.

When Teresa awakened for the second time that day, she shook her head in wonderment; she'd never slept so much. After throwing some water on her face and taking a brush to her short hair, she went downstairs to see if Mrs. Nance had returned. Not seeing her in the parlor or the library, Teresa entered the kitchen. Emma was there peeling potatoes.

"Is Mrs. Nance back?" she asked.

Emma shook her head. "Should be soon, though."

"Oh."

Teresa watched Emma and the potatoes. "I'd ask if I could help with dinner, but you'll probably chew my head off, so I'm going to the library and get a book."

Emma glanced up from her peeling and studied Teresa for a long moment. "Did Mrs. Nance say you could touch her books?"

"Yes, ma'am, and that I could read one if I found anything to my liking."

"Go on, then," Emma replied, waving the knife in her hand. "Just make sure you don't bother anything else."

"I won't."

Teresa entered the library with a reverence worthy of a cathedral. As much as she enjoyed reading, she'd never owned a book in her life, but here she was surrounded by hundreds of them. Some were thin, others fat; some had red bindings, while others had titles printed in gold. She doubted the gold was real, but the realization that there were people in the world who cached books the way she and her brothers had cached loot was new for her. Out West, libraries were common in some of the larger towns, but she didn't know anyone who had a library in their home.

She toured the room, stopping to open a book here and there. One that piqued her interest right away was *Journey to the Center of the Earth* by someone named Jules Verne. She wasn't certain if Jules was the name of a man or a woman, but the title intrigued her so she held onto it. Then she saw *Black Beauty*, by Anna Sewell. Thinking it might be a story about a woman of color, she took it down and leafed through it for a moment. Realizing that the book was in fact about a horse, she didn't know whether to be disappointed or not because she did love horses. Replacing it, she moved on to *The Prince and the Pauper* by Mark Twain, *The Adventures of Sherlock Holmes* by Arthur Conan Doyle, and *Clotel: Or the President's Daughter* by William Welles Brown. Next to Clotel stood another book by Mr. Brown, and it had the longest title she'd ever seen: *The Black Man, His Antecedents, His Genius, and His Achievements*. She vowed to come back to that one later, but for now she just enjoyed being in the room.

"What are you doing in here?" The voice was male, harsh and accusatory.

Teresa turned around slowly. Standing on the threshold was a very handsome man. A mustache accented his full mouth and he was tall, lean, and wearing a nice suit. Because the brown eyes viewing her with such suspicion and hostility were twins of Mrs. Nance's, Teresa guessed this was the son, Madison.

In that same hard voice, he snapped, "I asked, what are you doing in here?"

"Picking out a book." She sized him up. About six feet, three inches tall, and rude.

"Why?" He came into the room, and while waiting for her to answer, made a point of taking a long, silent look around the interior.

Teresa had always been careful not to assign reasons to people's actions without knowing their real intent, but she got the distinct impression that he was trying to determine if there was anything missing. When he seemed satisfied that nothing was amiss, he turned his attention back to her. "Can you speak?"

"Sure."

"Why do you have that book?"

She thought he had the right to be suspicious, after all, she was the dreaded Teresa July, but she didn't have to like his attitude. Looking down at the book in her hand, she shrugged, then drawled, "Oh, I don't know. Guess I'm just trying to decide how big a book I'll need to overpower Emma and run off with the silver. Think this one will do?" She held it up for him to see.

His eyes blazed a silent response.

Smiling coolly, Teresa turned back to the bookcase. "Name's Teresa July. You must be Mrs. Nance's son."

"Where is she?"

So much for polite introductions, Teresa thought, then took down a copy of *The Strange Case of Dr. Jekyll and Mr. Hyde,* by Robert Louis Stevenson and leafed through it for a few seconds before replacing it. "She's helping out at the church," she finally replied. "Emma says she should be back any time now."

"She left you here unsupervised?"

"Imagine that. Guess she's not worried about me stealing anything. Boy, will she be surprised." She looked his way and took in his tightly set jaw. Even mad, he had the good looks and manner of both a gambler and a banker. The women probably fluttered like moths to a flame when he came around.

"I was against my mother taking you in."

"Really? Why?" Teresa already knew the answer, but she was still simmering from his rudeness and wanted to get his goat.

"Because I don't want her taken advantage of."

"And what if I said I agree?"

"You're pretty combative, aren't you?"

"And you probably prefer your women a lot more docile. Docile women don't make the newspapers."

With her book in hand, Teresa walked to the door. His tall frame blocked her exit, but he stepped aside. Looking up into his cool eyes, she stopped. "Thanks for carrying me to bed last night. Nice meeting you." And she left the room.

Madison watched her go, not pleased with this first encounter with the lady outlaw Teresa July. Contrary to Miss Wild West's statement, he didn't prefer his women docile, but he didn't like smart-mouthed ones either, especially living with his mother.

Back upstairs in her room, Teresa put the book on the nightstand and wondered how much influence Madison Nance had over his mother. Was it enough to influence her continued stay in the Nance home? In her youth, she had never worried about the consequences of being flippant or crude or smart-mouthed. Anyone taking offense could always challenge her to step outside. Prison changed that—somewhat. She'd learned early on that talking back to the matrons or complaining about the conditions got you nothing but a hard way to go.

She'd been denied food, beaten, and forced to sleep outside in the cold for so many nights that first year she'd almost died of pneumonia. Now, wiser but no less spirited, she wondered if the pretty boy downstairs would go tattling to his mama about her less than deferential responses. Although Madison Nance looked to be more of a man than that, one could never tell.

In the end, she decided that if Mrs. Nance decided she had to go, she'd leave this nice room and the lady's nice house without a fuss. Being here had been like stepping into a fairy tale, but because she knew women like herself weren't allowed in fairy tales, she'd take this one day, store it away in her heart, and move on.

Downstairs, Madison was indeed tattling, but on himself. He'd told his mother about his run-in with her charge and how it ended. "I suppose I jumped to conclusions."

"Sounds like she put you in your place, though."

"She did indeed, and I must tell you, I wasn't pleased."

"That's because every female you've ever known has licked your boots instead of boxing your ears."

A smile crossed his handsome face. "Quite true, but you understand why I was suspicious of her actions?"

His mother nodded, "I do. She did steal the railroads blind, but she has promised me those days are over, and I intend to take her at her word."

Madison didn't hide his skepticism. "You're going to take the word of a train robber?"

"It's better than taking the word of a tinhorn," Teresa drawled as she entered the book-lined room. She didn't see Mrs. Nance's surprised smile, she was too busy glaring at her son. She reckoned that if she were going to be asked to leave, she'd better get her licks in now.

Chapter 3

Madison studied the feisty woman with the flashing black eyes and didn't know whether to be angry or laugh. "A tinhorn."

"Yes. Where I hail from, it's what we call cheap flashy gamblers."

Madison decided he was angry.

Mrs. Nance hid her startled laugh beneath a feigned coughing spell.

Teresa turned her way. "I figured he was down here tattling, so it's okay if you want me to move out."

"Move out? What are you talking about?"

"I thought you'd be mad at me for sassing him earlier—you being his mother and all."

"Of course not."

Madison's exasperation flared, but she ignored it. "I'm certainly not going to lie, Madison," she told him. "Of course I'm not upset. It's not often someone in a skirt sets you back on your heels, and frankly, I'm enjoying it."

"When your gems turn up missing, there'll be no crying allowed."

Teresa gritted out, "If you accuse me of wanting to

steal from her one more time, the only person crying will be you."

Madison had had it, but before he could give her the verbal lashing he felt she so richly deserved, she tossed back sagely, "And I've never known a pretty boy who could take a punch."

He thundered, "You're threatening me?"

Ignoring him, she said to his mother, "I'll let you all finish your visiting. I'll be in the kitchen." And she left the library without a backward glance.

Teresa marched into the kitchen and plopped down into a chair at the table. Emma took one look at her cross face and asked, "What is the matter?"

"Do you like Mrs. Nance's son?"

"Of course. Madison is a fine man. He and his bank have helped many people here in Philadelphia. He's kind and upstanding."

"Must be an acquired taste—like eating alligator."

"Alligator?" Emma was thoroughly confused.

Teresa waved her off. "Never mind."

"You and Madison have a row?"

"Yes ma'am. He thinks I'm going to steal everything in the house that isn't nailed down." Before Emma could comment, Teresa declared emotionally, "Does he know how grateful I am that his mother took me in? I could be living in a cramped, nasty boardinghouse somewhere fighting rats for a place to sleep, instead of being here where it's so nice. I'd shoot myself if I ever stole from her."

She was too busy simmering to see the small smile on Emma's face. But then Emma said, "I know it's almost time for supper, but do you think a small piece of peach cobbler might turn off the steam pouring out of your ears?" Teresa's mood brightened.

"I think it might," she replied. And once she got a taste of the still warm cobbler, she forgot all about Madison Nance's smug attitude, and his nice brown eyes.

"That certainly went well," Mrs. Nance declared after Teresa's icy exit.

The glower on Madison's face told all. "Did you hear her threaten me?"

"I did."

"What kind of woman does that?"

Mrs. Nance's eyes were shining with mirth. "Apparently the kind that hails from where she's from."

"This isn't funny, Mother."

"Sure it is, dear, and I'm hoping to have a front row seat for the second act."

Madison couldn't believe she'd actually threatened to punch him. "You're determined to have her here."

"Oh yes. More than ever. Tinhorn." Unable to control herself, his mother chuckled.

Madison had never met such an ornery woman in his life. He preferred the sleeping version of Teresa July. "She's going to be trouble."

"No. She's a young woman raised under extraordinary circumstances who tried to make the best out of what she knew."

"By robbing banks? Surely, you aren't condoning that now too?"

"Of course not. But darling, who would you be had you grown up in her circumstances instead of being the coddled son of your well-to-do father and adoring mother?"

He didn't respond.

"Your father was the guiding hand in your life. Hers were her brothers. She told me all she wanted to do when she grew up was to ride with them. What would you have wanted to be had you been her?"

Madison got the point even though he didn't care for it. He knew Teresa July was Black Seminole and that the once proud people had been brought low by the U.S. government. The fact that she hadn't had the advantages he'd enjoyed growing was a given too. But ... "As always, Mother, your argument rules the day, but if she threatens me again, I'm going to paddle her train robbing little behind."

"That might be easier said than done. Remember what she said about your face."

His scowling features showed he wasn't amused. Admittedly, he knew women found him attractive, but he'd never had a woman mock him because of it.

"I imagine the house will be a lot more lively with her around," his mother was saying. "And we've probably only seen the tip of the iceberg. What a warrior she is. Makes me want to rob a few trains myself."

The mental image of his mother holding up a train was such a ridiculous one, he couldn't hide the humor it brought to his eyes. "Don't even think about it."

"I'd never do something so foolish, but I'll bet it would be exciting."

"Not as exciting as seeing your name splashed across the front of the *Tribune*." He moved his hand to highlight the imaginary headline. "'Society Matron Molly Nance—Jailed for Bank Robbery.'"

Grinning at his play, she said, "Speaking of foolishness. Tell me about Princess Paula's birthday temper tantrum. I heard a few whispers at the church this afternoon that after you walked out of the party, she spent the rest of the evening crying in her room."

He rolled his eyes then told her the tale.

When he finished, his mother wasn't pleased. "I hope you aren't feeling remorseful. You never told the silly girl to expect a ring, or did you?"

Madison found her pointed question amusing. "No, Mother, not in any shape or form. I took her to the ball last year as a courtesy to the Carters. Who knew she'd attach herself to me like shoe black on boots?"

"Maybe the gossip will be enough to send her back to Memphis. Are she and that wretched aunt still bothering you at the bank?"

"No, I put a stop to it months ago." The women were trying to make a habit of coming into the bank wanting to chitchat or get his opinion on Paula's newest hat or gown. By the third visit in two days, he'd stopped being polite.

"Let's hope the twit takes her hunting elsewhere," his mother said.

"Or maybe we can sic your houseguest on her. She's spoiling for a fight."

"I'd purchase a front row seat for that bout. Can you imagine?"

"After meeting July, yes I can." If she truly represented femininity out West, he felt sorry for the men. Having to put up with all that sass and bad attitude probably drove them all to drink. His mother's voice broke his musing.

"Would you do something for me?"

He replied genuinely, "Whatever it is."

"I know you and Teresa got off on the wrong foot, but would you give her the benefit of the doubt for now? I think she could be such a fine young woman with the proper training."

Madison thought pigs would fly first. "Mother, not even you can turn that wildcat into a swan."

"I believe I can."

"Then you have my sympathies because you have your work cut out for you." In his mind's ear he could hear Teresa's western-accented voice threatening to make him cry. He silenced it forcibly.

"I'll wager five double eagles I can have her so polished in six months every eligible man in Philadelphia will be calling on her."

Madison shook his head at his mother's unfailing optimism. "If you just want to throw your money away, I can recommend plenty of worthless stocks for you to purchase."

"One hundred dollars, tinhorn. You in or not?"

He enjoyed the determination on her face and the sparkle of challenge in her eyes. Being a gambler, he never turned down a bet, and she knew it. "I'm in, but don't expect me to return your eagles when I win."

"You just be ready to pay up when you lose."

Their twin smiles met.

His mother asked, "So we have a deal?"

"Yes, we do."

She nodded, confident she'd be victorious in the end.

Madison was just as confident Teresa July would have her pulling out her hair by week's end.

Teresa didn't say much during dinner. What with all the different forks and plates, and Emma bringing in courses and taking them away, she was at sixes and sevens trying not to show just how ignorant she was of proper etiquette. She was smart enough to watch Mrs. Nance, though, so when Molly picked up a fork, Teresa followed suit.

She was well aware that the tinhorn was watching her, but she did her best to ignore him. It was difficult however. She'd never been around a refined man before. The outlaws, bank robbers, and gunslingers of her world rarely had polished manners, never wore nice suits except for weddings and buryings, and for sure knew nothing about eating at a fancy table. They also didn't wear cologne that smelled of spices and smoke, being more partial to the scents of horses and sweat. Where she hailed from, refined men were often viewed as effeminate, weak, but Madison Nance, with his sardonic brown eyes, appeared to be neither. She had to admit that he was handsome as all get out, but it would take more than his pretty face for her to like him.

Madison was indeed watching Teresa. Her efforts to conceal her unfamiliarity with the cutlery were admirable but obvious. Having been raised in his parents' home, he'd learned proper etiquette at an early age. What had she learned at an early age? he wondered. Unable to answer that question, he took in her patchy skin, wan figure, and chopped-off hair. He still didn't believe his mother would have her ready for society in six months, but if she did manage it, the men would come flocking strictly for the novelty July represented. Anyone looking for a beauty would have to search elsewhere.

"Is there a fly on my nose?" Teresa asked him.

His reverie broken, Madison asked, "Excuse me?"

"You're staring."

"My apologies."

Teresa went back to her cobbler but wondered what he'd been thinking about while staring at her that way.

Molly asked her son, "So how did the meeting go this afternoon?"

He shook his head and forked up some cobbler. "Not well. We couldn't come to agreement on anything. There's going to be a convention next week in Boston. Ida Wells and other radicals will be speaking on the lynching epidemic in the South. The local conservatives don't think anyone from Philadelphia should attend."

"Are you going anyway?"

"Of course, and while I'm there, I'll be looking over a shipyard some of my investors are interested in buying."

"How long do you plan to be away?"

"Two weeks, give or take a few days."

"What lynching epidemic?" Teresa asked.

Madison studied her silently, and was about to ask how she could not have heard of the lynchings, but then remembered that she'd been in prison. "Nearly two hundred people have been lynched in the past two years," he told her, "and those are only the documented deaths. It's anyone's guess as to how high the numbers really are."

"Things have gotten that bad?"

He responded somberly. "Yes, they have."

Teresa found that upsetting. "What's the President and the Congress saying?"

"Nothing."

"Any of us still in Congress?"

Madison was both surprised and impressed by her question. Was there an intelligence beneath all that bad skin and vinegar? "Only one. George Murray from South Carolina."

"My people stopped looking to the government for help a long time ago."

"From what I hear, you had good reason."

"We'd have been better off putting our trust in a nest of rattlers."

Mrs. Nance said, "We also lost old Fred Douglass, back in February, if you didn't know."

"I didn't."

Molly added, "His personal life was a scandal, but the race couldn't have had a better champion. He will be missed."

After the meal, Teresa asked Mrs. Nance, "Do you mind if I take a walk out back?"

"Go right ahead."

"Thanks." Giving Madison a quick, uncertain glance, Teresa left them at the table.

Madison watched her go. The fading notes of her scent were left behind, the same fragrance she'd been wearing when he carried her to bed last night. It smelled faintly of oranges, and seemed way more familiar to his nose than it should have been, considering the few times he'd come in close contact with her. Pushing that disturbing admission out of his mind, he pondered instead the effect of their fighting on his mother. "I suppose if she's going to be a guest here," he said, "I ought to try and get along with her."

"I'd appreciate that, Madison. I really would."

Madison sighed and finished his dessert.

Teresa stepped out onto the small sitting porch attached to the back of the house and looked around. Out in the yard, she saw a covered gazebo trimmed with gingerbread and shaded by a stand of oaks. Its latticed sides were threaded through with the long, leafy canes of the rosebushes growing around it. The wooden bench inside beckoned invitingly, so she went to answer its call. The sun had set and dusk was rising. As she walked toward the gazebo, the tall grass plucked at her skirt, making her wish she were wearing her leathers, especially when a few mosquitoes snuck beneath the hem to take bites out of her bare legs above her shoes. Swatting at the beasties, she took a seat. She spied a few other houses off in the distance, but none were close enough to impinge on her privacy.

The quiet was relaxing; the breeze an added bonus. The summer day had been hot, but with the approach of evening, the air had cooled. Once again she wanted to pinch herself to make sure she wasn't dreaming. Evenings in the prison were never serene like this. Never. She sat back and let herself be soothed by the sounds of wind rustling the grasses and the birds calling lyrically from the trees.

Just as she got comfortable, Madison Nance

stepped out onto the porch. Teresa watched him approach the gazebo with his fine fluid walk and tailored brown suit. Even though she thought him the best looking man this side of the divide, she was not pleased by his interruption.

"Did you come to make sure I wasn't stealing the roses?"

His brown eyes blazed. "No. I came to say good evening."

"How kind of you."

"Look, Miss July, my mother's not going to be happy if we fight every time our paths cross, so I've come bearing an olive branch."

"And that means what, exactly?"

"A truce."

"Ah. Never heard that one before." Teresa studied him. "So how's this truce going to work?"

"We agree to be civil."

"Sounds fine to me, but you sure you can hold up your end? I am a thief, you know."

"You're determined to make this difficult, aren't you?"

"Nope. You're the one with your nuts in a wringer."

His jaw tightened. "That's not something a lady says."

"Good thing I'm not one, then, isn't it?"

Madison wanted to turn her over his knee. She was the most maddening, cocky woman he'd ever had the misfortune to meet. "Do we declare a truce or not?"

She shrugged. "Sure. I can be civil, if you can."

"Then we have an agreement and I'll take my

leave." He gave her a terse nod. "Have a good evening, Miss July."

"You too, Mr. Nance."

He turned away and walked back across the grass. As he entered the house, she stuck out her tongue, then settled in to watch the moon rise.

The next morning was Sunday, and since Mrs. Nance had already informed Teresa that they would be going to church, she looked through her clothing for a dress to wear. She wasn't much for churchgoing. The missionaries she'd encountered in her youth had spent more time berating her people for having so-called savages for ancestors than sharing the Christian message. She finally settled on a simple high-collared dress. It fit reasonably well once she put it on. In the mirror, she could see that the olive green cotton was shiny with age and the gray cuffs were frayed, but it was clean, so she shrugged off her reflection and left the room.

When Teresa came downstairs, Mrs. Nance took one look at her and said, "We have to get you some new clothing. That dress is in a lot worse shape than I thought."

Teresa looked down at herself. "It's fine, Mrs. Nance."

"No, it isn't. The sooner Emma fattens you up, the sooner we can begin sewing. Go back upstairs and see if there's something nicer in your armoire."

"That's not necessary. I'm fine, really."

Mrs. Nance was all spiffed up in her stylish Sunday dress, gloves, and hat. She looked like the society lady that she was. Teresa didn't mind the differences in their clothing, though. Dresses were not her attire of choice, so it didn't matter to her that the one she wore was old.

"All right," Mrs. Nance said. "Soon as Madison arrives, we'll leave."

Teresa was surprised. "He's going with us?" Truce or not, she was not looking forward to the gambling banker's company.

"Of course, dear. Madison is a member of Mother Bethel too."

Another surprise, but Teresa had a question. "I know that AME stands for African Methodist Episcopal because there are AME churches back home, but why is the one here in Philadelphia called Mother Bethel?"

"Because it was the first AME church established in the nation."

While they waited for Madison, Mrs. Nance told Teresa about Richard Allen, Mother Bethel's founder. "To make a long story short, one Sunday, Mr. Allen and two of his friends were worshipping at St. George's—a White Methodist church. In the middle of prayers the men were asked to remove themselves because they weren't praying in the pews relegated to Blacks. Mr. Allen and the church's White elders had been having disagreements for years over the race's inclusion in the congregation, so when Mr. Allen was asked to leave, he did so permanently and formed his own church."

"When was this?"

"Around 1787. Mr. Allen—or Bishop Allen, as he became after being ordained—was one of the first prominent leaders of our race, and Bethel was our first real institution."

Teresa was impressed. "Back then my people were still living in Florida. I wonder if they knew about Bishop Allen and his church?"

"It's possible."

Madison's arrival brought an end to the short history lesson. He was impeccably dressed in a black vested suit and snow white shirt with a fashionably round collar. To Teresa, he looked both wealthy and important, but he was still an ass.

"Are you two ready?" he asked.

His mother nodded.

Madison scanned Teresa with a critical eye. The dress was obviously one of his mother's charity finds. The color was faded, and the crease above the hem showed it had been let down more than once. It fit her thin frame, but that was the only positive. The straw boater on her head covered up the bad hair and made her look like a country girl from the Deep South. He could already hear the snide comments that were surely going to be whispered behind her back by the congregation's cattier female members.

Teresa saw the disapproval in his eyes and took it personally. "Am I too ill dressed to be seen with you?"

Madison didn't sugarcoat his response. "Frankly, yes. Don't you have something better she can wear, Mother?"

"I tried to get her to change but she says she's content."

Teresa replied coolly, "If my attire isn't suitable, I can always stay here."

"Oh no," Mrs. Nance countered. "Church attendance is mandatory in this household."

Madison told the outlaw, "I'm just trying to save you from rude comments."

"Thanks, but I can save myself."

Even though Madison didn't care for her, he'd been genuinely trying to spare her feelings by asking her to change clothes, but all he'd gotten for his trouble was sass. Convinced that his mother's plan to turn this prickly pear into a lady was doomed to failure, he escorted the two women from the house.

On the ride to Mother Bethel in Madison's fine carriage, Teresa divided her time between ignoring him and trying not to act like a rube as she took in the hustle and bustle in the city's busy streets. None of the cities back home were as large as Philadelphia and she'd never seen so much vehicle traffic in her life. There were beetle-shaped streetcars that ran on tracks laid into the streets, carriages and delivery wagons pulled by large-chested horses. People were everywhere. Having lived her life against the quiet open spaces of the West, she found the cacophony of noise deafening and the tall brick buildings eye popping. Mrs. Nance's voice drew her attention.

"Teresa, the parole board doesn't want the press to know you're in town until you get settled in because of all the hubbub it will probably cause. I plan to introduce you as a distant family cousin. Do you have a name you'd like to be known by for the time being?"

"Sure, I'll be Tamar. Tamar August."

Molly chuckled. "Very clever."

Madison thought the play on her last name clever

as well, but kept it to himself. He doubted the outlaw wanted any compliments from him, and after butting heads with her this morning, he wasn't of a mind to offer any—truce or not.

They arrived at the brick-spired church a short time later, and there was a slew of carriages and nicely dressed Black people outside. For a woman who'd never met a situation she couldn't face down, Teresa was uncharacteristically nervous. She knew she lacked polish. Back home she'd never needed any, but she wasn't at home now, and she didn't want to embarrass Mrs. Nance by saying or doing something uncouth.

"I'll try not to embarrass you, ma'am," she said.

Mrs. Nance patted her hand. "You'll be fine."

The genuineness in July's tone gave Madison pause. There were obviously parts of Teresa July that he hadn't seen. Not that he cared one way or the other, but he was pleased she understood that any untoward actions could reflect on his mother.

He found a place to park and came around to help the ladies down. His mother was first. When it was Teresa's turn, she stuck out her hand and he took it in his own, noting the warmth of the flesh, how perfect her hand seemed to fit, and the rough, callused feel of it. He was oddly struck by that, and found himself slowly turning her hand over to scan the toughened skin of her palm.

Teresa wondered what he was about. She wanted to yank her hand back because she thought he was going to make fun of her unladylike calluses. She was also shaking like a leaf. Not wanting him to know how rattled he was making her, she asked impatiently, "Are you done?"

"No." Fueled by unknown forces, Madison moved the pad of his thumb gently over the calluses at the base of her fingers, then looked into her eyes. The silent contact was charged, electric, and something neither of them could name uncoiled and came alive.

Teresa didn't know what was happening, but the softness of his touch against her skin and the curiosity in his blazing gaze made her go all strange inside and her heart beat way too fast.

"Come on, you two. Let's go inside."

Molly's words broke the connection, and they shook off the encounter as if emerging from a dream. Madison slowly relinquished his hold on Teresa's hand, and they followed Molly to the church door.

Teresa spent the entire service conscious of Madison seated beside her on the pew. The church was crowded, and although there was a decent amount of space between her body and his, he sat much closer than she wanted him to be; so close that the heat of his body floated against hers like warmth rising from a stove in winter. Telling herself that it was just a hot day and in reality the heat was emanating from all the bodies inside the church didn't work, and more important, there was nothing she could do to take charge of the situation. Jumping to her feet and demanding in a loud voice that he and his heat move over was out of the question. Mrs. Nance would probably be so mortified that she would make her leave her house. Teresa didn't want that, so she silently endured the situation and tried not to think about Madison's thumb moving gently over her bark-rough palm earlier, and the way her breath caught from his touch.

Madison was as aware of Teresa as she was of him. No matter how hard he tried, he couldn't stop thinking about her callused hand. Not only had he no explanation for his actions earlier, but the idea that he had been somehow moved by her was disturbing. He didn't like her, and she certainly didn't like him. As the service ended and they stood for the recessional hymn, his eyes strayed her way. Nothing about her appealed to him as a man; she was skinny as a street hound, smart-mouthed, and it was a toss-up between what made her look worse, the dress or the hat. Yet there was something going on inside of him that seemed intent upon looking at the woman underneath and that disturbed him as well.

After the service, the congregation gathered outside to greet each other and socialize for a few moments before heading home. As planned, Mrs. Nance introduced Teresa as a distant cousin, and she was greeted warmly.

They meandered through the congregation, stopping here and there, and no matter how much Teresa tried not to, her eyes kept straying to Madison. While Mrs. Nance talked with a group of her friends, she surreptitiously watched his black-suited form moving through the crowd as he shook hands with the men and received hugs from some of the older women. The younger women he stopped to speak with had stars in their eyes when he moved away, and Teresa shook her head at their mooning.

Mrs. Nance broke into her observations, asking, "Do you see Madison? We should be getting home."

He was a short distance away, having a conversation with a beautiful woman dressed in blue. He was smiling, and the lady was too. "He's there," Teresa replied.

"Ah. I see him now. That's Millie Cummings he's with. A few years back I thought maybe she'd be my daughter-in-law, but nothing ever happened. She's a nice girl."

Who, by the looks of her, probably had nice soft hands, Teresa thought sarcastically, remembering the way he'd looked at her own rough-skinned hand.

Teresa watched Madison and the young woman say their good-byes, then he walked over to where she and his mother stood waiting. "Millie's invited me for dinner. You don't mind if I skip out on you this Sunday? She's leaving for Atlanta in the morning to take care of a sick aunt."

"Of course not. Enjoy yourself."

He then turned to Teresa. "Do you mind?"

She didn't blink. "Yeah, I do. Who are me and my callused hands going to fight with at the table?"

Her reply made him study her and her black eyes closely. "You think I was poking fun at your hands?"

"Weren't you?"

He shook his head and said truthfully, softly, "No. Their condition caught me off guard. My apologies if my actions were upsetting."

Admittedly, they were upsetting to her, but not in the way he thought. Even now her palm tingled with the memory. "My hands are the way they are because of who I am," she explained quietly. "They've chopped wood, set bricks, and done a hundred other unladylike jobs both in an out of jail. My right is also my gun hand. It's supposed to be tough, not soft like Millie's."

"Who said anything about Millie?"

"You did when you asked me if I minded you having dinner with her."

A silent Molly watched them with great interest, but thought it wise that they leave now, before the discussion disintegrated into the argument that always seemed to follow whenever they were together. "Come, children. I'm ready to go home."

On the drive back, Teresa saw very little of the scenery. She was too busy trying to figure out what it was about Madison Nance that rubbed her the wrong way. But had no answer.

Behind the reins, Madison was thinking the same about her.

When they reached the house, he pulled the carriage to a stop out front, and Molly said, "Thank you for the chauffeuring, Madison. Have a good visit with Millie."

He set the brake. "Let me help you down."

He came around to offer his gentlemanly assistance. As before, his mother was first, but when it came time for Teresa, she shook her head. "I'm fine. I don't need any help." She didn't want her hand to catch fire again.

She stepped down and avoiding his eyes, moved past him and left him and his mother talking by the curb. As she neared the front door, she took a hasty look back and found him watching her. The odd sensations caused by his silent gaze made her stumble. Cursing silently, she composed herself and entered the house.

Standing by the buggy, Madison smiled.

Chapter 4

Following Monday morning's breakfast, Mrs. Nance said to Teresa, "I promised I'd find you something to do, and I have. Come with me."

A grateful Teresa followed her into the room next door to Mrs. Nance's bedroom. Teresa stared around the interior, slack-jawed. The place was a mess. There were fabrics, threads, ribbons, dress forms, and every other kind of item connected to sewing. The room was a riot of color, and so crammed full of stuff, it took her a moment or two to see the twin sewing machines hidden beneath all the clutter.

"This is—or was—my shop," Mrs. Nance said. "I'd like to be able to sew in here again, but as you can see, I can barely turn around without tripping over something."

Bolts of colored fabric were stacked against the walls, and the floor was littered with pins, paper patterns, and ribbon snips. Teresa had been expecting physical work like washing windows or scrubbing floors, not this. "Mrs. Nance, I don't know the first thing about cleaning up a sewing room."

"But I do, and between the two of us, it shouldn't take long."

Teresa was skeptical, but she and Mrs. Nance dove in. Items that were damaged or no longer usable were piled outside in the hallway. The stack grew so high that Teresa went to retrieve the empty rubbish barrels from the back porch.

After the first barrel was filled to the top, Mrs. Nance instructed her to take it outside and set it by the road so it could be emptied by the rubbish man, who was scheduled to come by the next day.

Carrying the heavy barrel down the stairs, Teresa got her foot wedged in the hem of her skirt and almost fell downstairs. After cursing the skirt and righting herself, she moved on.

Back upstairs, Mrs. Nance had unearthed a trunk filled with a beautiful array of silk fabric. Seated on a short stool, she was going through the trunk with such melancholy eyes that Teresa asked, "What's wrong?"

"Oh nothing," she sighed. "I've just been saving this silk for years."

Teresa walked over and squatted next to her. "Why?"

"For Madison's wife."

Teresa was shocked. "You didn't say he had an intended."

"That's because he doesn't."

Teresa didn't understand. "I'm confused."

"Don't be, dear. The contents of this trunk represent the dream of a silly old woman who wants a daughter-in-law. I had hoped to one day be able to sew for her, but it doesn't look like my son will ever marry."

"Why not?" Teresa already had an answer. His

tendency to be overbearing and arrogant didn't make him an ideal catch at least in her mind.

"Can't find the right woman, I suppose."

"Has he been looking?" She thought about Millie Cummings and wondered why he hadn't married her.

"He's had various lady friends over the years, and many—like Millie—set their caps for him, but none of the relationships led anywhere. Lately, there's been a very disagreeable young woman named Paula Wade running after him. I'm glad he's not giving her the time of day, but I think my son is more interested in accumulating greenbacks than a wife."

"If this Paula isn't real likable, maybe going after greenbacks is better."

"I agree. I'd hate to have her in the family, but there doesn't seem to be anyone else on the horizon. If I don't get some grandchildren soon, I'll be too old to spoil them."

Teresa was amused. "I'm sure it'll all work out, ma'am."

"I do hope so."

"Does he know about this trunk?"

"No, and I don't want him to. He'll think it's silly."

Teresa thought the sentiment behind the silk quite sweet and that Mrs. Nance would make a wonderful mother-in-law. She couldn't imagine any woman crazy enough to marry Madison Nance, though, but kept that opinion to herself.

They went back to work. There was soon enough discarded items to fill the second rubbish barrel. This time, Teresa managed to get the barrel outside without the hem of her skirt flinging her down the stairs.

She'd just put the barrel down next to the other one when a fancy black carriage drove up. The gray horse appeared old and tired, but the young Black man driving looked real proper in his blue livery with big gold buttons. On the seat behind him were two women; one young, one not. They were fashionably dressed in the fancy gowns and veil-draped, wide-brimmed hats city women sported.

Aided by the driver's hand, the women stepped down. The older woman's blue gown fit like someone had forced twenty pounds of potatoes into a ten pound sack. "Are you with Mrs. Nance's household?" she asked Teresa.

"Yes."

"Please run and tell her that Miss Paula Wade and Mrs. Daphne Carter are here to visit. Thank you."

The tone was the dismissive one used for servants, and Teresa wasn't pleased at all. She assumed the young woman was the same Paula Wade trying to rope Madison, but she had no clue as to who Mrs. Carter might be. Because the older woman could be a close friend of Mrs. Nance, and Teresa didn't want to offend her benefactor, she turned and walked back to the house without being rude. Dressed in her too large skirt, second-hand blouse, and well-worn brogans, she supposed she did look like the help.

Just then Mrs. Nance appeared on the porch. She was carrying a broken dress form.

"Guests," Teresa told her, taking the form from her mentor's hands.

Upon recognizing the two women coming up the

walk, Mrs. Nance sighed unhappily, "More like, pests."

Teresa grinned. She was liking Molly Nance a lot.

Carrying the form out to the street, she heard Mrs. Nance say behind her, "Daphne and Paula. To what do I owe this pleasure?"

"We were in the area," Mrs. Carter trilled, "and thought we'd stop and visit."

"I really hadn't planned on entertaining callers today, but please, come in."

Teresa decided to reenter the house through the back door in order not to disturb the women's visit, but when she entered the kitchen, Mrs. Nance was there, putting small cakes on a platter and grumbling beneath her breath, "Apparently, proper etiquette has gone out of the window. You do not show up at someone's door just out of the blue."

"Is this the same Paula Wade you told me about earlier?" Teresa asked.

"Yes. The other woman is her aunt Daphne." Mrs. Nance opened the icebox and took out the pitcher of lemonade Emma prepared each morning. "If they want fancier refreshments, they are free to seek it elsewhere."

Teresa picked up the tray of cakes from the counter. "You go on ahead. I'll bring this and come back and get the lemonade."

"Thank you, dear. Now give me a moment to plaster on my smile and we'll go."

Hiding her amusement, Teresa followed Mrs. Nance to the parlor.

As Mrs. Nance took a seat on the settee and began to make small talk, Teresa set the tray of cakes down on a small table, then went back to the kitchen to retrieve the lemonade.

Teresa returned and had no sooner placed the pitcher down when Paula Wade said in the same cool tone her aunt had used earlier, "Just a small portion, please. Sweet drinks don't go well with my skin."

Teresa looked her up and down. The girl was beautiful, but Teresa didn't like her attitude or her smugness, so she poured just enough lemonade in the glass to wet the bottom. "Here you go."

Teresa turned to Mrs. Nance, "Would you like some too?"

Molly's amusement was plain. "Yes, dear."

Paula was staring at the minuscule portion in her glass as if she were frozen in place. She swung her attention to Teresa, now pouring for Mrs. Carter.

Teresa met Paula's icy stare. "Problem?"

"Well yes. I'd like a bit more, please."

"You and your skin sure?"

Paula's eyes narrowed. "Yes, we are."

Teresa poured until the glass was half full, then set the pitcher down. The aunt was shooting daggers her way, but Teresa ignored her. "Do you need me for anything else, Mrs. Nance? If not, I'll head back up to work."

"Have a seat please, dear. We can finish later."

"But—"

Mrs. Nance responded with that look, so Teresa sat.

Daphne Carter said haughtily, "I know you consider yourself very progressive, Molly, but our visit is with you, not with your servant."

"She's a cousin, Daphne. Her name is Tamar. Apologize."

Daphne startled. "I'm sorry. She doesn't look—"

Molly's brittle gaze stopped Daphne in mid-speech.

"My apologies," she offered Teresa hastily.

"Thanks."

Mrs. Nance's voice was wintry as December. "You and I never pay social calls on each other, Daphne, so there must be a reason for this interruption of my day. My son, perhaps?"

Teresa had no idea Mrs. Nance could be so lethal. She wanted to cheer.

"This was all my idea, Mrs. Nance," Paula confessed in her Memphis-accented voice. "We stopped by the bank so that I could tell him how sorry I am for embarrassing him at my party, but his secretary refused to announce us. I was hoping you'd intervene on my behalf."

"Hasn't Madison told you that he doesn't wish to be pestered while working?"

"Well, yes, but—"

"Did he say this to you in a foreign tongue?"

"No ma'am, it was in English."

Teresa hid her laugh with a faked coughing fit. "Sorry," she offered, napkin covering her mouth.

Mrs. Nance's interrogation continued. "Then why do you persist, Paula?"

"I just want to say I'm sorry."

"Ah," Mrs. Nance replied knowingly. "Then I shall let him know you stopped by and apologized. I'm sure that will be sufficient."

The girl whined, "But I want to speak with him personally."

Mrs. Nance didn't bother hiding her irritation.

Daphne quickly placed a quelling hand on Paula's arm. "I'm sure you'll see him soon, niece. Now, let's leave Mrs. Nance and her cousin to enjoy the rest of their day." She stood, and the surly-faced Paula grudgingly followed suit.

Daphne said to Teresa, "It was a pleasure meeting you, Tamar."

"Same here."

Her niece said nothing.

Mrs. Nance walked them to the door, and after their exit, closed it firmly.

Teresa drawled, "Interesting pair."

"Not half as interesting as they think," she replied, then did a mincing imitation of Paula. "'No, ma'am. It was in English.'"

Teresa's laughter erupted.

"Simpering little nitwit. No man in his right mind will marry that girl. Come on, let's see how much more we can get done upstairs before luncheon."

They accomplished quite a bit. By the time Emma came up to announce that lunch was ready, the room was in much better order. It was not finished by a long shot, but at least the floor could now be seen.

At about three that afternoon, a messenger from the telegraph office arrived. Mrs. Nance gave the young man a few pennies for a tip, then handed the envelope to Teresa, who tore it open and read:

WE ARE SO PLEASED WITH YOUR NEWS. WILL WRITE TO YOU SOON. WE LOVE YOU VERY MUCH. NEIL AND OLIVIA.

Tears stung her eyes. Dashing them away with the back of her hand, she wished she didn't have to wait another year to see them again.

Mrs. Nance appeared to have read her mind, and said in a soft voice, "You'll see them soon. The year will pass quickly."

While incarcerated, Teresa hadn't allowed herself to even think about being reunited with her family because it was too painful, but now, as three years of pent-up emotions rose up and grabbed her, she thought her heart might burst. "Do you mind if I go sit in my room for a spell?"

"Go right ahead. I'll let you know when supper's ready."

"Thanks," she whispered.

Upstairs in her room, Teresa sat down on the bed, clutched the telegram close to her heart and let the tears run unhindered down her cheeks.

The First Community Bank was founded by Madison and a small group of investors three years ago because the White-owned banks downtown eschewed the savings of the poor people in the city. The banks' reasons were both racial and economic; they saw little value in maintaining accounts that held the five dollar savings of a domestic worker or the twenty dollars belonging to a hotel doorman.

Traditionally the race avoided banks anyway. Many folks preferred to secret their savings in mattresses, pillowcases, or in the city's well-run benevolent societies. The failure of the Freedman's Bank during Reconstruction had wiped out the hard-earned savings and pensions of its Black investors, leaving them with nothing. Now they were wary of financial institutions of any kind.

That wariness had even applied to Madison's establishment. Trying to convince people that their money would be safe had been difficult at first, but he'd found salvation. The fifty-five Negro churches in and around the city had over twelve thousand members and took in roughly $94,000 a year in income. Madison and his staff had spent months, and in a few cases years, wooing the various reverends and pastors in an effort to convince them to commit their funds to the bank for safekeeping. In the end, some had, but others had not.

He was grateful for those who had because their funds allowed him to make loans in the community to small businesses and entrepreneurs who were given short shrift by the downtown banks. Across the nation, the number of banks owned by men of color could be counted on one hand. Most were modest operations like First Community, but all served a noble purpose.

"Thank you, Mr. Nance," the heavyset woman seated on the other side of his desk said with heartfelt emotion. He'd just approved the loan she'd applied for to buy the house next door to her home. She planned to lease out the space to supplement the income she brought in as a hairdresser. He had loaned money to her before, and she'd always repaid her notes in a timely manner, so Madison considered her a good risk.

"Glad I could help you, Mrs. Randana. Now you can begin advertising for tenants."

"I already have a couple in mind. He's a waiter,

and she takes in wash. I met them through my church. You've given me a blessing that I can now pass on to them. Thank you."

He nodded and stood to escort her out of his office. They walked to the front door, and after thanking him again, she left smiling.

Martin Tate, Madison's secretary, was seated at his desk set up outside of Madison's office door. After her departure, he said with a grin, "Mrs. Randana is going to wind up owning half the Seventh Ward if the city isn't careful. Isn't this her fifth house?"

"Yes, it is. She's a good landlord. We could use more like her in the Seventh Ward."

Tate, a recent Howard College graduate, was efficient, hardworking, and smart. Madison, who prided himself on the ability to quickly compute numbers in his head, was often left in the dust by the speed of the younger man's mind.

Madison looked at the watch attached to his vest. "We may as well close up for the day. It's past four. I'll see you in the morning."

"Have a good evening, sir."

After Tate's departure Madison straightened his desk then grabbed his hat and headed for the door. Two new accounts had been added today. The downtown banks would sniff at such small pickings, but he did not. Each new account helped keep his doors open.

Outside, the hustle and bustle of the Seventh Ward surrounded him. The Seventh was the traditional home of Philadelphia's Negro population. It held their homes, businesses, triumphs, and tragedies, but the ward was changing. Folks with the economic means were slowly moving away and into wards of the city that had been closed to the race when Madison was growing up. Left behind were the poor and those who had no plans to move, like Madison, his mother, and other descendants of the Seventh's original settlers. Crime was rising, and young men unable to find employment because of Jim Crow and a lack of education and training were loitering in doorways, drinking and shooting dice. Portions of the neighborhoods were now slums, but the Seventh continued to be vibrant and alive. There were still more Negro business owners there than anywhere else in the city, and most residents were employed and owned their own property. Madison's years as a gambler had been lucrative ones; he could afford to live anywhere, but he chose the Seventh because it was his home.

He was just stepping into his buggy when someone called his name. He turned and saw Dawson Richards, a ward boss for the Republican Party, walking toward him. Always impeccably dressed, the handsome mulatto had come to Philadelphia from New Orleans a few years ago, but in that short time had risen to the top of the party's ladder by ruthless intimidation. Now however there was a broad smile on his face.

"How's business, Nance?" he asked.

"No complaints," Madison replied.

Richards's ties to corruption and illegalities made him a pariah among the honest Negro men of the city, but invaluable to the political machine that employed him because of the impressive numbers of voters he and his henchmen were known to command.

"I hear your bank's doing rather well."

"Is there something in particular you wanted to discuss, Richards? If not, I need to get home."

"Just wanted to let you know that the party could use an influential and respected man like yourself."

"Neither of which I would be once my name became linked to the party's, so thank you, but no thanks."

"Who watches your bank at night when it's closed? Crime being what it is in the area, I'd hate to have something happen to your building."

Madison met the man's hazel eyes. The unveiled threat didn't sit well. "That would be a pity, wouldn't it? But I don't worry about it, and neither should you. Should something damaging happen, I've associates in the wards who'd make it their life's work to find the perpetrators and teach them the error of their ways."

Richards stilled.

Madison got into his buggy and took up the reins. Satisfied that his point had been made, he said, "Good evening, Richards." And without waiting for a reply, he drove off.

Madison made his way through the thick traffic and tried to curtail his anger. Before leaving for Boston tomorrow, he'd make arrangements to have the building watched after hours. If someone so much as dropped a piece of paper in front of the door, he wanted to know about it. Whether Richards had been bluffing or not, he didn't have the luxury of ignoring him. Too much was at stake. His customers were counting on him to safeguard their savings, and he took that trust seriously.

With his plan formed, Madison put aside Richards's threat and set out for his mother's house. He wanted to say good-bye before his trip tomorrow, and hoped to finagle dinner out of her too. Yesterday's meal with Millie Cummings had been disastrous. Millie had many skills, but none related to the kitchen. He hadn't eaten anything of substance today, and as a result he was starving. Paying his mother a visit meant having to see Teresa July too, and he wondered which Teresa she'd be today. Whichever personality she presented, he hoped she remembered they were still under truce, because he was in no mood for her sass.

Teresa finished writing her letter to Olivia and Neil and placed it in the envelope. Both the writing paper and envelope were scented, but she was sure Olivia wouldn't mind. Emma had offered to take the envelope to the post office when she did her errands tomorrow, so Teresa left her room to take it downstairs. Not finding Emma in the kitchen, she went in search of Mrs. Nance, who was in the parlor talking with her son.

When Teresa entered, he stood up. No man had ever done that before and it threw her, but she managed to keep her voice even. "Evening, Madison. How are you?"

"Well, and you?" His brown eyes held her black ones.

"Can't complain."

He had on yet another brown suit, this one as impeccably tailored as the others. She looked at his generous mouth with its tempting mustache and wondered if it was possible for him to be better looking than he'd been yesterday. She decided to chalk it up to her imagination, but the palm of her right hand began to tingle, bringing back their encounter outside the church.

Rattled even more, she turned away from his amused but steady gaze and gave her attention to Mrs. Nance. "Um, here's my letter. I didn't see Emma in the kitchen, but she said she'd post it for me tomorrow."

"She has the evening off. Just set it there on the mantel and I'll make sure she takes care of it."

Teresa placed the envelope on the mantel and turned to leave the room and escape the disquieting power of Madison Nance, only to have his mother say, "Please stay and join us, Teresa."

She didn't want to, but having no legitimate reason to turn down the request, she sat.

"I was just telling Madison about the progress we're making upstairs on the sewing room."

Madison got the distinct impression that Miss Wild West was as aware of him as he was of her and that she had no idea what to do about it. Surely she couldn't be an innocent? "Do you sew, Miss July?"

Teresa snorted. "Not a stitch."

"Might be a good time to learn," he pointed out, wondering why he felt drawn to her when he didn't even like the woman.

Not sure what was happening either, Teresa pulled away from his assessing eyes. "Your mother thinks so too. Maybe if I do learn, I can make me a pair of leathers. I'm not real comfortable in these skirts."

"Why not?"

"I keep getting my foot caught in the hem. Skirts may be okay for other women, but this getup's not real practical for someone like me."

"You didn't wear skirts out West."

"Of course not. You can't walk the top of a moving train wearing one of these. All this fabric blowing around get you killed."

Mrs. Nance looked confused. "Walk the top of a train?"

"Yes. Sometimes, to sneak up on the conductor, we'd run along the top of the train so he wouldn't know we were coming."

"While it's moving?"

"Yes ma'am. It's pretty hard to do that these days, though. Trains move so fast now, it's hard to catch up to one and board it like we used to."

"Isn't that dangerous?"

"Can be. I fell off one a few years back, busted my arm. First time I walked a train I was scared to death, but by the third or fourth time, it was fun. Got to be good at it too."

The sincerity of her boast made Madison shake his head and contemplate what he might do with the one hundred dollars he was surely going to win from his mother. No way was she going to turn this train walking cowgirl into a lady.

"What's wrong?" Teresa asked him.

"Nothing. Just astounded."

"You must lead a pretty bland life if you find me astounding."

Madison saw the challenge twinkling in her eyes. "You don't have a shy bone in your body, do you?"

"Last time I checked, no."

Teresa's heart was beating too fast again. Hastily turning away, she found Mrs. Nance viewing her with a secretive smile.

"Something wrong?" Teresa asked.

"Just pleased you two appear to have gotten past your differences."

"We haven't, but we declared a truce so you wouldn't be upset by us going at each other."

"Thank you for taking my feelings into consideration."

"You're welcome."

Madison was still trying to analyze why she was beginning to intrigue him so. As he'd noted yesterday, he certainly didn't find her physically attractive, but he enjoyed spirited women and maybe that was the reason.

Teresa knew he was watching her, and she was as uncomfortable as a spinster in a whorehouse. Why a suit-wearing, back East banker she didn't even like would be making her go all strange inside was not a question she had an answer for.

"So, Teresa," Mrs. Nance said, "if I may be so rude to ask, did you really rob your first bank at fifteen?"

Teresa was glad to move her mind away from Madison. "Yes, ma'am, and I was more scared than I was the first time I walked a train."

"Really?"

She nodded. "I did it so my brothers would let me join the gang. They told me the only way they'd let me join was if I robbed a train or a bank. They were hoping the condition would scare me off. They didn't want me doing what they were doing, said it was no life for a girl, but I wanted to ride with them so bad my teeth ached."

In his head, Madison heard his mother's question echo: *What would you have wanted to be?* "So what happened?" he asked.

"Found a little town outside of Denver, went in and announced I was robbing the place. I was shaking so bad my gun went off and I plugged the wall behind the teller. The poor man thought I was shooting at him so he gave me every coin they had."

"How much did you get?"

"Four dollars and thirty-six cents." The memory was an amusing one. "Me and Cloud hid out for a few days, then went looking for my brothers."

"And Cloud is?"

"My stallion. He'd ride me into hell if I asked him. Had him since he was a foal … " Her voice trailed off and she stared out, silent and unseeing for a few long moments. "Miss him."

Madison and his mother shared a look.

Pulling herself away from the past, Teresa asked Madison with a false brightness, "Are you still heading out to Boston?"

"Yes, tomorrow." The remnants of pain lingering in her eyes touched him. "I stopped by to tell Mother good-bye and to see if she'd feed me dinner tonight. I'm starving."

His mother drawled, "After you tossed me over yesterday for a younger woman? I'm not sure I will."

"I accepted Millie's invitation strictly as courtesy, Mother. To say that Millie can cook is like saying frogs can play poker. I had overdone corn bread and underdone roasted chicken. I could only guess at the origins of the rest of the burnt offerings on my plate. Any man marrying her will need to hire a cook."

"And here I thought she was such a lovely girl," his mother replied.

"She is, if you're not hungry."

Teresa had no idea why she was pleased to hear that the soft-handed Millie Cummings had flaws, but she was.

"So, now you're here begging me to feed you?"

"On my knees if you'd like, Mother."

It was a side of him Teresa hadn't seen. Who knew he had any humor in him at all, let alone this dry wit?

But in the end, Molly acquiesced, as everyone knew she would, and they all sat down at the dining room table to enjoy the leftover ham, vegetables, and yeast rolls from Sunday's dinner.

Afterward, Mrs. Nance announced, "I have some letters to write, so Teresa, you can wash up the dishes, and Madison, you may dry. He can show you where the soap and the dish tub is kept."

Teresa would have preferred to handle the task alone, but having no choice, she cleared the table and headed to the kitchen.

For the first few minutes they worked silently. To Teresa, the kitchen felt small and the air in the room warmer than it should have been even on a summer evening. She wanted to attribute it to the hot dishwater she had her hands in but knew it was a lie.

"Cat got your tongue?" Madison asked as he dried a plate and placed it atop the others that would be going back into the china cabinet in the parlor.

"No. Just got nothing to say."

"Ah."

Teresa washed and then rinsed a glass. "Is Millie your mistress?"

Madison stopped. "I thought you had nothing to say?"

She shrugged. "Now I do."

"And the reason for asking such a personal question?"

"Because I'm nosy. You can answer or not."

She had a swagger in her Madison had never seen in a woman before. Ever. "She was at one time but isn't anymore. Anything else?"

"Nope." Teresa went back to her washing. For unknown reasons, his answer pleased her as well.

Once the work was done and everything was put away, they left the kitchen to see if his mother was done with her letters. She was seated at the writing desk in her bedroom.

"We're done, Mrs. Nance. I'm going to finish straightening out those ribbons now."

"Thank you, Teresa. I'll be in to help in a moment."

Teresa turned to Madison. "Have a good time in Boston."

"I'll see you when I return."

She gave him a tight nod and left them alone.

Madison was still pondering the conundrum of Teresa July when his mother asked, "You two didn't fight, did you?"

Madison answered truthfully, "No."

"Good, go easy on her. I believe she's carrying a lot of hurt inside. Did you see the way she looked when she talked about her horse?"

He had, and the memory of her sadness rose unbidden. "I did." She appeared fragile one minute then rock hard the next.

"How awful it must be to be in a strange land so far away from everyone and everything you love."

"True, but the courts don't give out bags of peppermints for crimes like hers."

"Must you always be so cynical?"

"It's not cynicism. It's truth. You and I both had stock in some of the railroads she robbed."

Outside the door, Teresa was eavesdropping. She'd wanted to hear what, if anything, they had to say about her after her departure. Mrs. Nance's support touched her heart. Madison's words evoked different emotions. He was right, she had deserved her sentence, she just wished he'd stop enjoying it so much. *Damn tinhorn!*

After Madison's departure, Mrs. Nance joined Teresa in the sewing room.

"What kind of child was Madison growing up?" Teresa asked.

"Stubborn and incorrigible," Mrs. Nance said with a laugh. "If there was a line to cross, Madison would find it, just to see what was on the other side. When he was fourteen, he spent the entire summer confined to his room. The only place his father and I allowed him to go was to church."

"Why?"

He and his best friend Benjamin Norton were

picked up by the police during the raid of a gambling hall. They were supposed to be attending a night watch at Bethel."

"Really?" So the tinhorn wasn't as holy as he appeared.

"Most of the gray hair on my head was put there by my son. Between the gambling, the carousing, and the women, my husband and I didn't think he'd live to be twenty-five. I'm glad he's turned his life around, but he was a handful."

Later, ready for bed, Teresa doused the lamp and snuggled beneath the bedding. Lying there in the dark, the memory of Mrs. Nance's earlier words rose: *I believe she's carrying a lot of hurt inside.*

Yes, she was hurting, something powerful. After reading Neil and Olivia's telegram, she wondered how they were doing, what they were doing. Had they talked to her half brother Two Shafts, and was he enjoying the home he'd built in the mountains? Did her mother Tamar still walk the earth or had she crossed over to the realm of the Ancestors? Teresa was indeed in a strange land, and her loved ones seemed a lifetime away.

For a few moments the pain of the separation began to rise but she beat it back. Pining wouldn't solve anything, she still had a year to go; so she turned over in the bed and made herself more comfortable under the fresh smelling sheets. Closing her eyes, she slept.

Elsewhere, in another room, Madison doused his light. He was packed and ready for tomorrow's trip. Lying in bed in the dark, he thought about Teresa July. His mother was right. He had spoken cynically.

In the gambling days of his youth, he'd walked on the edge of the law more times than he cared to admit, so it was hypocritical to be so judgmental now. Making a mental note to get to know Teresa better when he returned from Boston, he turned over and closed his eyes.

Chapter 5

For the rest of the week, Teresa and Mrs. Nance worked on the sewing room. When they were finally done and had every pin, bobbin, and ribbon in place, they both stood back and admired the now clean and organized space.

"We make a very good team," Molly declared.

"Yes we do. Are you going to go back into business?"

"Yes, and you're going to be my first customer."

"I don't need any clothes."

"Teresa, you're wearing hand-me-downs. Every woman needs new clothes. Skirts, blouses, gowns."

"Gowns?" Teresa frowned. "Why on earth would I need a gown?"

"For social outings."

Teresa had no intention of attending any social outings, but Mrs. Nance seemed so entranced by her plan that she didn't have the heart to argue. Then again, Mrs. Nance had been so wonderful and caring, Teresa knew she would probably don a potato sack and dance a jig in the center of town if the lady asked her to.

So for the next two weeks, Teresa stood for fittings

and Mrs. Nance sewed. Using her Singer sewing machine, she ran up enough blouses and skirts to keep Teresa well dressed for the time being. She decided to wait until Teresa's weight evened out before taking measurements for gowns. She wanted them to fit perfectly when the fall social season began.

They'd not heard from Madison. His mother wasn't worried about that, but every now and then she'd muse aloud about missing him. Teresa held no such feelings, or at least told herself that she didn't.

In addition to getting Teresa outfitted, they also began tackling the list of things Mrs. Nance thought she needed to master in order to have a successful rehabilitation and to make her more of a lady. Every morning, Teresa was required to scan the newspaper and read to Mrs. Nance the most interesting item she came across. Before going to jail, the only time Teresa picked up a newspaper was to see if any new bounties had been placed on her head and how much reward money was being offered for her capture.

Reading to Mrs. Nance showed her that there was a lot more going on in the country and around the world than she thought. A man named Eugene Dubois was in Europe showing off an old skull he'd dug up. He'd named the thing *Homo erectus* but the papers were calling it "the ape man of Java." Another man, James Edward Keeler, had somehow figured out that the rings around Saturn didn't rotate together, and a Russian scientist named Konstantin Tsiolkovsky believed that in the future, liquid fuel would be used to send vehicles up to the stars. Teresa shook her head at that.

She was also required to read the slew of Negro

newspapers that Mrs. Nance subscribed to in order to keep up with the state of the race and the ongoing national battle between the Radicals and the Conservatives led by the powerful Booker T. Washington. As far as Teresa could tell, Washington was winning hands down. From the *Cleveland Gazette* to the *Washington Bee,* he was criticized for his opinions and leadership, but when President Grover Cleveland needed the names of men of color to appoint to jobs, he consulted Washington. White charities that wanted to give to Negro causes funneled their funds into the programs and schools he designated. For now, the nation considered him the chief spokesman for the race, and all the Radicals could do in response was fume.

Learning to sew was harder than learning to walk a train, however. Teresa didn't have the necessary patience. For the past few days, she'd been practicing sewing seams with little success. Instead of the small, tight, uniform stitches Mrs. Nance had started the seam off with, Teresa's finishing stitches were oversized, out of line, and loose.

Mrs. Nance was now studying her work silently. Teresa knew it wasn't very good, but felt the need to defend herself. "What difference does it make if they're not tiny like yours? The two pieces of fabric stay together."

Mrs. Nance peered down at her through the sewing spectacles perched low on the bridge of her nose, silently letting Teresa know she wasn't buying the excuse.

"Suppose going back to prison hinged on you being able to sew a decent seam?"

Teresa's lips thinned.

Mrs. Nance waited.

Grumbling, Teresa took the fabric from her mentor's hand and ripped out the stitches. Cursing silently, she picked up the threaded needle and started over. Again.

Thanks to Emma's cooking, Teresa was starting to flesh her out, and the more she ate, the more Emma prepared. Teresa knew she wouldn't be restored to her former self overnight, but by the end of those first two weeks, when she looked at herself in the mirror, her reflection was no longer frightening. She'd stopped resembling a fledgling now that her thick black hair was growing out, and her ebony skin was beginning to reclaim its luster.

At breakfast that morning, Mrs. Nance said to her, "My friend Rebecca has a horse farm. Would you like to go riding? I know you must miss it."

Teresa's smile lit up the room. "How soon can we leave?"

"Whenever you're ready."

An hour later they were on their way. Mrs. Nance was behind the reins of the buggy, and they were soon traveling down a quiet country road.

Teresa relished being out of doors. "I'm still getting used to how green everything here in the East is. Back home it's all browns and reds."

"Is it beautiful?"

"Oh yes, ma'am, but it's a different beauty than here."

"How so?"

"The beauty here is lush. Back home it's stark, almost harsh, but it's beauty just the same."

"I'd like to visit the West someday."

"I'd get a kick out of showing you around. Ever seen a desert?"

"No."

"In the spring when the cactus blooms, it's enough to take your breath away."

"Then I shall be sure to see the desert when I come."

The horse farm of Miller and Rebecca Constantine had been in their family for over a hundred years, and was situated on five hundred acres about an hour's drive outside of the city.

"Rebecca and I have been friends since childhood," Mrs. Nance told her. "She's smart, opinionated, and very eccentric, and I love her like a sister."

"Never had a friend like that."

"Good friends can help you through the rough patches of life, and Rebecca has always been there to offer a hand when I needed one."

They were entering the fenced-in property and when Teresa caught her first glimpse of some of the Constantines' fine-looking stock, she found it hard to contain her excitement. There were comely mares, proud stallions, and knobby kneed foals. The sight was so moving, tears stung her eyes. She discreetly dashed them away.

"She and Miller breed racehorses for the wealthy planters in Kentucky," Mrs. Nance was saying. "Some of the richest men in the country buy from the Constantine farms."

Off to her right, Teresa saw a young man on a long striding stallion that reminded her of Cloud. Watching the horse and rider eat up the ground before disappearing from sight made her hands itch to hold a pair of reins. She prayed the Constantines had a suitable mount.

The woman who stepped off the wide porch of the large white house to greet their arrival had enough paint on her face to be a circus clown. Unlike Mrs. Nance, who wore her graying hair pulled back into a fashionable knot that rested demurely on her neck, the woman now waiting for them to get out of the buggy had on a red wig that matched the rouge on her cheeks.

Mrs. Nance made the introductions. "Rebecca Constantine ... Teresa July."

Rebecca threw open her arms and gave Teresa a big hug. "Welcome, my dear. You've no idea how long I've wanted to meet you. I've followed your adventures in the paper religiously. Here in the East we can't get enough of the Wild West."

Teresa had been so busy taking in the woman's makeup, she'd failed to see the leather trousers Rebecca was wearing. Unlike the black pairs Teresa had worn back home, Mrs. Constantine's were brown. Teresa liked her immediately.

Noting Teresa's scrutiny, Rebecca asked, "Do they look authentic?"

"Yes, ma'am, they sure do."

She clapped her hands with glee. "Oh, wonderful. I was hoping they were at least close to the genuine article."

"Right on the money."

Rebecca grinned. "Come inside, you two. Molly, thanks for bringing her out. What a great way to start my day."

Sharing a smiling, they followed Rebecca inside.

Once they were settled into the parlor, Rebecca brought in some refreshments, and while they drank punch and ate little cakes, Rebecca asked Teresa, "Is Molly treating you well?"

"Yes ma'am. Just like kin."

"Good. Molly is known for her generous hospitality."

"Why thank you, Becky," Molly said, then asked, "Where's Miller?"

"He went up to the convention in Boston."

"So did Madison. Ida Wells Barnett is supposed to be speaking. She's doing us ladies proud with her fiery attacks on the lynchings."

"That she is. I was so impressed when she spoke here last year. What a crowd she drew."

Teresa asked, "Who is she?"

"One of the most progressive women journalists in the country," Molly informed her, "and she's a woman of color."

Rebecca added, "So progressive the bigots in her home town of Memphis burned her out and she was forced to flee. A few years before that she sued one of the transportation companies there for their Jim Crow practices, and won."

"Then lost after the company appealed, of course, but she's a true crusader."

"Sounds like my kind of woman," Teresa said approvingly.

"Ours as well."

As the women continued to talk about Ida Wells, Teresa discreetly scanned the windows for a glimpse of more horses.

Noticing, Mrs. Nance apologized, "Teresa dear, I'm sorry. You didn't come with me to listen to two old hens talk politics. Rebecca, she needs a horse so she can go riding."

Rebecca brightened. "Well, Molly, why didn't you say so? Come, Miss July, I have the perfect mount."

And the stallion Hannibal was perfect, Teresa thought as the two of them thundered across the countryside. According to Mrs. Constantine, Hannibal had won many races down in Kentucky, but now that those years were behind him, he was back with the Constantines as a stud. Teresa was in heaven atop the powerful animal. Rebecca had sent one of the young grooms along to make sure she didn't get thrown or lost, but Teresa didn't need a duenna. She was certain the stallion would know his way back to the barn when it came time to return home, so she urged to Hannibal to show her his stuff and they soon left the groom behind.

She rode and rode and rode. Tired of cursing her skirt, she rolled up the hem until the yards of fabric were around her waist and tucked it into the waistband. Her legs encased in black cotton stockings were now free and she was able to ride the way she preferred.

The horse seemed to be enjoying the adventure as much as Teresa. She knew horses well enough to sense how much Hannibal loved to run, so she let him have his head. Since he knew the terrain better than she, all she had to do was lean low and let him carry her where he wanted, and when she saw where they were headed, she yelled with joy. The land ahead was flat as the Kansas plains for as far as she could see. The evenness of the terrain meant Hannibal could go all out, and when she felt his powerful muscles bulge against her knees, she knew that's what he was about to do.

Teresa was ecstatic. This was the closest she'd come to riding since she and Cloud were brought down by the posse back in Arizona. All she could hear was Hannibal's thundering hooves and her own breathing.

It crossed her mind that while she was out here riding, she could turn the animal west and head home. It would be hours before anyone guessed what had happened. The old Teresa wouldn't have thought twice about it. She'd have stolen this fine animal from Mrs. Constantine and thumbed her nose at Mrs. Nance's many kindnesses because the ends would have justified the means; home was the only place she wanted to be, and she knew instinctively that this beautiful horse could get her there. But she was a different Teresa now, and the idea of sneaking off and breaking Mrs. Nance's heart in the process didn't sit well. Not to mention the crow Molly would have to eat when her son found out. Teresa refused to give him the satisfaction of telling his mother, "I told you so!" Vestiges of the nineteen-year-old hothead she used to be were alive and well, but they'd been tempered by the maturity forced upon her by incarceration, so she shook off thoughts of escaping home and enjoyed the ground-shaking ride.

"We'll I'll be. Would you look at that!"

Driving the buggy, Madison turned his head in the

direction Miller Constantine was pointing and saw a rider bent low over a fast moving horse.

"Why, that's Hannibal," Miller exclaimed. "Who's that riding him? Doesn't look like one of my grooms."

Madison could see the horse and rider heading toward the road the buggy was on and traveling at a tremendous pace.

"What's he wearing on his legs?" A confused Miller turned to Madison as if seeking an answer.

"I've no idea."

As the horse and rider approached, the men were unable to take their eyes off the pair.

"Whoever he is, he's riding like a bat out of hell," Miller added in a voice laced with admiration and excitement. "Look at that form."

By now the horse was on the road, only a few yards behind the buggy and closing fast. Madison had to admit the rider and horse did appear to be fused. As the rider's features became clearer, his jaw dropped. *Teresa July!*

"Why, it's a girl!" Miller gasped.

Sure enough, as the horse drew closer, Madison got a good look at the rider's face and it was all the verification he needed. *Why in the hell is she riding around with her legs bared that way?*

As she and the horse hurdled by, her face was such a study of gleeful concentration, Madison couldn't tell for certain if she even saw him or not. He, however, had no difficulty spying the shapely legs encased in the dark stockings, and the startling sight of her comely behind moving up and down as the horse headed away from the buggy and up the road.

"Let's go, Madison! I want to find out who she is!" Miller urged.

The tight-jawed Madison already knew her identity, so he slapped down the reins and got the buggy moving again.

Teresa righted her clothing when she got within sight of the house, and after dismounting and giving the spirited stallion a grateful hug, she turned the reins over to the waiting groom, then joined the smiling Rebecca and Molly on the porch.

"How was it?" Molly asked.

An ecstatic Teresa sat down on the lip of the porch and stretched out flat on her back. "Wonderful. Miss Rebecca, I believe I'm in love with Hannibal."

"You'll have to fight the mares for him, dear."

Teresa chuckled. "What a prized animal. I see why he won all those races. He can fly like the wind."

Molly said, "We were concerned when the groom returned alone."

"He was slowing us down. Hannibal and I didn't need hand holding."

Then Teresa met Molly's eyes and confessed, "I have to admit that once we took off, I did play with the idea of stealing Hannibal and heading home, but I didn't want to disappoint you. Not after all you've done for me."

Molly and Rebecca shared a look.

Teresa added, "Thought about you having to eat crow for your son too. Didn't want that to happen either."

Molly's feelings were in her eyes. "I appreciate that, Teresa. He'd never let me live that down."

"I know."

When a buggy pulled up in front of the house, Teresa sat up, and Rebecca said, "Speak of the devil. Here comes Madison and Miller now." She hurried off the porch to greet her husband, while Madison pulled Miller's luggage out of the back of the buggy.

Teresa suddenly remembered the buggy she and Hannibal passed back on the road. She'd been too busy enjoying herself to pay any attention to the occupants. Had it been them? Had Madison seen how unladylike she'd been riding? It was a pretty safe bet he had if he'd been in that particular buggy. It was also a safe bet that he hadn't approved.

Miller stepped up on the porch and greeted Molly with a smile before asking his wife, "Who was the girl riding Hannibal?"

Rebecca gestured to the now standing Teresa. "Miller meet Teresa."

"That was you?"

"Yes, sir."

The silent Madison was taken aback by the startling change in her physical appearance. She was downright beautiful.

Miller went on, "You were riding so well, thought you were a man with some kind of black stuff on your legs."

Molly's forehead creased with confusion. "Black stuff?"

Madison, studying Teresa with his arms folded, drawled, "Yes, Mother. Your charge was riding across the countryside with her skirt hiked up and her legs out."

Molly swung surprised eyes Teresa's way.

"Tattletale," Teresa groused. "You ever tried riding a horse in a skirt?"

"No, but well brought up ladies do it all the time."

"Since I am neither, why should I care?"

"Next time you're riding like a hellion," Madison countered, "try thinking about Mother's reputation, since you obviously don't care about your own."

"And you might think about minding your own damn business."

Mrs. Nance tried to nip the escalating battle in the bud. "Children. We're guests. You can fight when we get home. What happened to the truce?"

Teresa grumbled under her breath, "Tinhorn."

"I heard that."

"Good. Tinhorn!"

"Call me that again and I'll paddle your behind."

"Touch me and you'll wake up in the middle of next week. Tinhorn!"

He advanced, and before Teresa could react, he snatched her up against his chest, looked down into her furious eyes, and kissed her. Really kissed her. And he did it so well and so deliciously she forgot to sock him and melted right there on the spot.

When he turned her loose, her insides felt like butter.

"Now, I'm going home," he stated firmly. Nodding terse good-byes to his startled mother and her friend, Madison strode to his buggy, set the horse in motion and drove away. Only when he'd driven off did he smile. *That ought to give her something to think about.*

The still stunned Teresa watched him depart. Her lips were still stinging from his forceful kiss, but not in a bad way. She turned startled eyes to Mrs. Nance. "He kissed me!"

"Yes, he did, dear."

The irrepressible Rebecca asked, "Was it a good one?"

"Yeah!" But upon hearing herself, Teresa declared, "No!"

Mrs. Nance's soft chuckling didn't help matters.

Teresa seethed. "Next time I see him I'm going to kick his tail from here to Tucson!"

Miller was staring. "Do you have a last name, young woman?"

"Yes, sir. July. Name's Teresa July."

His eyes went even wider. "Teresa July! The outlaw?"

Teresa tore her eyes away from Madison's disappearing buggy. "Yes, sir."

"My lord. Molly, did you know that?"

"Yes, Miller. She's staying with me for the next year."

He looked as stunned as Teresa had after Madison's bold kiss. "No wonder you were riding Hannibal that way. Well, welcome to my farm!" And he stuck out his hand.

Teresa shook it. "Thanks, sir. Do you mind if I come out and ride once in a while?"

"Of course not. Come every day, if you care to. Do you know how famous you are?"

Rebecca took her husband by the arm. "Come on inside, Miller, before you forget you're married to me and propose to the girl."

Molly laughed. "We should get going. Are you ready, Teresa?"

She nodded.

"Becky, Teresa and I will be back in a few days."

"We'll be here. And Hannibal will be too, Teresa."

"Thanks, ma'am. Nice meeting you and your husband. Thanks for letting me ride."

"You're most welcome."

Teresa didn't have much to say on the ride back to Molly's, she was too busy fuming. Although she was doing her best to fight it, she kept recalling the heat and vividness of his kiss. She didn't even like Madison Nance, yet the power of his embrace had shaken her from the top of her head to the tips of her toes. She'd be the first to admit that she hadn't done a lot of kissing in her life, but none had ever seared her like his. The memory of its sweetness started her heart pounding all over again. She was counting on her bad mood to shoot it down, but it wasn't working.

"Are you all right, dear?" Molly asked.

"No."

"Still mad at Madison?"

"Yes."

"If it's any consolation, he looked as surprised as you."

"Tinhorn."

"Considering the results, you might want to refrain from calling him that."

Teresa muttered unladylike beneath her breath.

"I don't understand it. Madison has always prided himself on his mental control."

"Well, I don't, and I never have."

"That's evident," Molly pointed out with mild reproach.

Teresa sighed. She supposed she had let the hothead parts of herself take over. "I didn't mean to embarrass you in front of the Constantines. I'll apologize next time I see them."

"That's acceptable. I'm sure Becky didn't care. She was probably as stunned as I by Madison's actions. It was interesting, I must admit."

Teresa began grumbling again, but had nothing more to say.

Madison let himself into his home and dropped his luggage at the door. First things first, he walked over to his finely made liquor cabinet, withdrew a bottle of aged scotch, and splashed some into a glass. Draining it, he poured another, then sat down and slowly swirled the contents of the glass in his hand.

Kissing Teresa July had not been planned, but at the time it was either throttle her or kiss her, so he chose the latter, because he'd never laid on a woman fueled by violence. Admittedly, he'd been in a bad mood when he arrived at the Constantines'.

The convention had been a disaster. The arguing and heckling that preceded and followed each of the speakers became maddening, and then to be told by the train conductor that the only car available for the trip back to Philadelphia for men and women of color was the cattle car had left him infuriated. He and Miller Constantine had opted to rent a buggy and split the cost. The trip took much longer than it would have by train, but they'd arrived home with their dignity intact, and just in time to see Teresa ride by dressed in her stockings.

He took a sip of the scotch. She needed to be fenced

in. The kiss had stopped her in her tracks, though; something that probably didn't happen often, he thought with a glint of humor in his eyes. He was willing to bet she was still fuming. The feel of her in his arms, the sweet taste of her mouth, were as memorable as the image of her leaning low over Hannibal's back with her lovely bottom moving rhythmically with the animal's gait. Had he found the answer to taming Miss Wild West? Maybe. He had to admit it was a novel approach, one he might want to try again should the situation warrant it, because truthfully, he'd enjoyed kissing her. He couldn't place the blame for his bad mood on that. More likely, the combination of her sassy mouth and surprising beauty were what sent him over the edge.

Madison drained the scotch, grabbed up his luggage and went upstairs to get some sleep. Guaranteed, there were bound to be fireworks when he saw Little Miss Outlaw again, but he was certain she wouldn't call him a tinhorn again unless she wanted to be kissed.

The next morning, Teresa came down to breakfast in a sour mood. She'd dreamt about Madison that night, and he'd been kissing her, again.

Molly glanced up from her newspaper. "You don't look like you slept well."

"I didn't, but I'll be fine." She helped herself to the bacon, oatmeal, toast, and eggs.

An amazed Molly asked, "Where do you put it all?"

Teresa shrugged. "I've been around men most of my life. Guess I eat like them too."

Amusement on her face, Molly set the paper aside and picked up her coffee cup. "I'll be doing charity visits most of the day. Do you want to come along?"

"I suppose I could." She would have preferred another visit to the Constantines' and a ride on Hannibal, though.

Apparently, the desire showed on her face, because Molly said, "First thing tomorrow, we'll ride out to Becky's so you can take Hannibal out again. Would that be all right?"

Teresa's smile told all.

In the dream, she had been wearing a fancy black gown. Madison had on an equally fancy evening suit. They were standing in what appeared to be Mrs. Nance's gazebo. It was dark, and they were kissing each other like there'd be no tomorrow.

"Teresa? Did you hear me?"

She shook herself back into the present. "I'm sorry. Daydreaming. What did you say?"

But before Mrs. Nance could reply, Emma walked in. "Mr. Weathers sent a note around saying he can't cut the wood today either."

Mrs. Nance sighed with frustration. "That man. Why do I put up with him?"

"Who's Mr. Weathers?" Teresa asked.

"The man I hired six weeks ago to chop some wood."

"Where is it?"

"Behind the shed in the back."

"I'll chop it. How much is there?" She stood. The idea of being able to do something physical to work off her irritation with Madison made Teresa eager to volunteer.

"Quite a bit, actually. Which is probably why Mr. Weathers keeps sending notes of apology."

"Can I see it?"

"Certainly."

Behind the shed there was enough wood to keep Teresa busy for days to come. "Where do you want me to put it when it's chopped?" she asked.

Mrs. Nance gave her instructions, then told her where to find the axe. "Are you sure you want to do this?"

"Mrs. Nance, if I don't do something to work off all this energy, I'm going to burst. So please, you and Emma go on about your day, and this will be my chore until it's finished."

The women nodded, and Teresa went to change her clothes.

Madison could hear the axe ringing as soon as he stopped his buggy in front of his mother's house. Glad that Weathers had finally shown up to do what he'd been hired to do, he went around the back to speak to the man, and to see how the work was progressing. Seeing Teresa swinging the axe instead slowed his steps. She brought the blade down precisely and expertly. Her familiarity with the chore was apparent, and when she looked up and saw him, she paused.

"'Morning," he said, continuing toward her.

"You're pretty brave walking over here while I have this in my hand." She raised the axe again and brought it down with a powerful swing.

"Then I'll stand out of range."

"Smart man." And she split another log.

"Where's Mr. Weathers?" Her beauty had not been a figment of his imagination yesterday. Her hair was growing out thick and black, and there were no mistaking the lush curves beneath the old clothes she was wearing.

"He sent his apologies." She freed the blade from the wood. "I volunteered to take his place."

Teresa wiped the sweat off of her brow with the rolled-up sleeve of her blouse and studied Nance. She'd always been a vivid dreamer, and the one last night had left her not only with the memory of the kiss, but with the spicy scent of his cologne. This morning, he looked fine as always. She wondered why he hadn't married. She raised the axe. "Why haven't you married?" she asked, and lowered the axe. It rang out against the silence.

Accustomed to her blunt and sometimes nosy questions he replied easily, "Haven't found a lady to my liking."

"Then there's your problem—you're looking for a lady." Her axe sank into another large log, then she worked the blade free. "Back home, men don't go for ladies like the ones I've seen here. They want women who can ride and rope and shoot."

"Women like you?"

"Oh, hell no. I'm never getting married."

"Why not?"

"Getting married means falling in love, and falling in love makes you loco."

He chuckled. "What?"

"My brother Neil fell in love, then turned himself into the law. Nothing I could say would change his mind. Shafts and I even offered to help him escape before his trial, but he wouldn't hear it. Damnedest thing I ever saw."

"So, no falling in love for you?"

"Nope. Never."

She began chopping again. Watching, Madison found her so fascinating, he couldn't have moved if he'd wanted to. "So you think I should look for a wife on the other side of the Mississippi."

She shrugged, then brought the axe down. "Depends. If you want a woman who can't drink lemonade because it rubs her skin the wrong way, then look around here."

"Rubs their skin the wrong way?"

"Paula Wade said she didn't want a lot of lemonade because sweet drinks disagreed with her skin."

"You met Paula? When was this?"

"Few weeks back. She and her aunt came around to visit your mother."

His mother hadn't said anything about a visit. "What did they want?"

"Paula wanted to apologize to you for something that happened at a party?"

He nodded. "Her birthday party."

"Your mother said she'd pass the apology on, but Paula said she wanted to do it face-to-face. She left mad."

He shook his head. "Glad I missed her."

"She didn't make a real good first impression. Talked to me like Emancipation had never happened and her daddy was the master."

Madison knew that both of Paula's parents were former slaves, but in spite of that, she persisted in looking down her nose at those she considered herself better than. It was yet another reason he didn't care for the Carters' niece. "So, should I apologize for my actions of yesterday now, or would you rather just take the axe to me?"

Earlier, Teresa had wanted his head on a platter, but sharing this easy conversation had done much to cool her temper. That and the fact that she could still feel his mouth on hers. "An apology will do."

"My deepest apologies, then. No idea what came over me. Tired from all the traveling, I suppose."

"Probably," Teresa said, again feeling the dream rise but quickly shaking it off. "Just don't let it happen again."

"Don't worry."

She wasn't sure she liked his tone. "You hated kissing me that much?"

He studied her for a long moment. "Truthfully, no. Found it rather nice."

She wasn't sure how to take his response or the amused glint in his brown eyes, so she looked away.

Madison had decided to answer her question truthfully. The memory of the brief kiss was a pleasing one. Even now he found himself staring at her full, ripe mouth. Recalling her seconds-long surrender was stirring. "Why'd you ask?"

"Just curious."

In the silence that crept up between them, Teresa's dream rose again, and in her mind's eye his lips were slowly burning kisses over the curve of her shoulder. Her head was thrown back, her eyes closed. Moving back into reality, she found him watching her, and her heart began beating like a war drum. Speaking more calmly than she felt, she told him, "I should get back to work."

"Of course."

But he didn't move, and neither did she.

For a moment they took each other in, and the air between them crackled like the onset of a summer storm. Finally, she resumed her chopping. When she next looked up, Madison was gone.

He had gone into the house to talk to his mother.

"Shouldn't you be at the bank?" she asked.

"Thought I'd stop by and see you on my way."

She didn't look as if she believed a word. "Have you seen Teresa?"

"Yes, saw her chopping wood out back."

"She's not real happy about that kiss."

"I apologized."

"Good. Madison, you are my son and I love you, but I also know how you are with the ladies. Teresa is not here to become another notch on your bedpost. If your intentions are honorable, that's another thing."

"Understood," he replied, not sure how he felt about his mother's warning. After all, he was a grown man, and Teresa a grown woman.

Molly looked skeptical but didn't add anything else on the matter. Instead she said, "I'm on my way to the church. Since you're here, can you drop me there on your way to the bank? I'll take the streetcar back."

"I'd love to."

Chapter 6

After leaving his mother at the church, Madison headed to the bank. Thoughts of Teresa continued to dog him. Common sense said no man with the sense God gave a goat would be attracted to such an outlandish woman. He understood being attracted to her spirit, but she lacked the ladylike qualities he'd always been partial to in the women he'd pursued in the past. Teresa had no polish at all, yet he couldn't get the feel of her or the kiss out of his mind, and as insane as he knew it might make him sound, he wanted to do it again; this time leisurely, so he could take the time to explore her and taste her in depth. Would she bring that fire to a man's bed? That question grabbed him, and he forced his mind to a halt before he could contemplate an answer. The jury was in. He'd lost his mind. He'd gone from kissing her to fantasies of bedding her. Again he asked himself why, and the answer was: She intrigued him way more than he cared to admit.

Madison spent the first part of his morning talking to his secretary, Tate, and getting caught up on what had transpired during his absence. According to Tate, a dozen new people had opened accounts, and all expected loan payments had arrived on time.

Tate added, "And the night watchman you hired has had nothing to report so far."

The man's name was Solomon. He'd been a pugilist at one time in his life, and had come highly recommended by his friend Ben Norton. No news was good news, Madison liked to think. Maybe Richards had been bluffing all along, but he planned to keep Solomon around just in case.

"There were a few fires while you were away. A small hat shop over on Pine and a grocery a few doors down."

Madison didn't like hearing that. As the president of the Seventh Ward Negro Business Association, he knew that all businesses, large and small, were vital to the ongoing economic health of the ward. "Was anyone injured?"

"No, but the fire department is investigating. They think the fires were deliberately set."

"Arson?"

"Apparently. The hat shop was torched first and the grocery two nights later."

"Sounds like a topic for the association meeting tomorrow evening. Maybe someone has more information. When were the fires?"

"Last week."

Madison mused over what he'd heard. "Okay. Anything else I need to know?"

"No, sir. That's all.

When Mrs. Nance returned from church later that afternoon, a very tired Teresa was seated in the gazebo. The wood she'd cut earlier was neatly stacked inside the barn.

Molly joined her on the bench. "How'd the chopping go?"

"Just fine. I probably won't be able to lift my arms in the morning, but the activity felt good." She figured it would take another couple of days to get it all done, but she enjoyed the way the work made her muscles sing. Over the past few weeks, in addition to all her lady lessons, she'd been doing yard work, beating rugs, and mopping floors, but none of those chores made her feel this good.

"Tired you out, did it?"

"Yes, ma'am. Legs are as sore as my arms."

"You did too much."

"Probably, but I'll live. How were things at the church?"

"Good. We ladies are trying to start a social hour for the city's unmarried domestics. Many are young and with no family in town. We hope bringing them together on their days off will foster some friendships and offer them an opportunity to let their hair down."

"Sounds like a good idea."

"I think so too. If it's successful, we may do it on a regular basis." Mrs. Nance then changed the subject. "Madison said you two spoke?"

"We did."

"Did you settle your differences?"

"I suppose. We didn't fight, if that's what you're asking, so I guess it went all right." Teresa tried not to think about what he'd said about kissing her; she still had a hard enough time keeping last night's dream out of her head.

"Glad to hear it. As you've probably guessed, my son is very successful with women, but I reminded him that you are not here to become one of his conquests."

Teresa was embarrassed. "I appreciate that."

Molly patted her affectionately on the arm. "Good. Now go up and soak yourself in the tub so you won't be stiff later. No more wood chopping today."

"It's the middle of the afternoon."

"And so?"

"Never took a bath in the middle of the day."

"Today you will. We are fortune enough to have hot water whenever we like. Take advantage of it."

Teresa smiled. "If you insist."

Molly's eyes were bright. "I do."

After her bath, Teresa went downstairs. As she cut through the kitchen where Emma was preparing dinner, the cook said, "A crate came for you. It's by the front door."

Puzzled, Teresa thanked her then went to investigate.

Sure enough, a large crate sat by the door. The post label on the top showed it had been sent by her sister-in-law, Olivia. Mrs. Nance fetched a crowbar, and Teresa pried off the top. The first thing she saw was folded black leather. Excited, she snatched it up, shook out the folds, and the sight of the leather trousers made her crow, "Hallelujah!" She did a little jig and held the leathers against her heart. "Olivia, I love you!"

A further search turned up two pairs of boots, both new; some men-cut flannel shirts that she could have used that morning while chopping wood; a small vel-

vet box that held all the ear bobs she'd had to leave
behind when she left for prison; three pairs of Levi's
denims; and other articles of clothing like socks, ban-
dannas, and nightgowns. At the bottom of the crate,
wrapped in one of Olivia's monogrammed tea towels,
was Teresa's Colt. Beneath it lay her gun belt and a
box of cartridges.

She picked up the gun. The familiar sight and
weight of it in her hand brought on bittersweet
memories. Moved, she placed a soft kiss against the
shiny barrel, then looked over at Mrs. Nance, who
was now very quiet and still. Teresa wrapped the gun
up again and handed it and its ancillary items to her.
"You should put these away somewhere. I'll get them
back when the time comes for me to head home. And
if it's all right with you, I'd like to get some target
practice in every now and again. Never know when I
may need to protect myself or you, and right now, my
gun hand's pretty rusty."

"I'll place them in the safe."

Teresa nodded. "That's fine."

"Why would she send a gun?"

"Because it belongs to me and she knows that
eventually I'll be coming home. A woman traveling
alone is not always respected."

"I see."

Teresa looked into Molly's eyes. "Please don't think
I'd ever turn it on you, because I never would. Ever."

"Thanks for the reassurance."

"You were worrying, I could tell."

"I was."

"Well, don't. You've treated me like kin. Julys
don't shoot their kin."

Mrs. Nance smiled. "Come, I'll show you the safe."

"I don't need to know where it is. Probably make you more comfortable if I don't. I know it'll make your son feel better."

Molly studied her for a long moment. "You're a rare individual, Teresa."

"No ma'am. I'm just a July."

Madison was reviewing a loan application from one of the churches when Tate stuck his head in the door. "Mr. Watson is here. He's anxious to speak with you."

"Send him in." Charles Watson had been a good friend of Madison's father, Reynolds. In the seventies and eighties Watson had owned one of the city's finest catering businesses. Now, because of Jim Crow and America's fascination with French cuisine, his business and the businesses of other prominent Negro caterers handled mostly segregated affairs.

"I'm being threatened," Watson said as he entered the office, the look on his burly gray-bearded face conveying his anger.

"By whom?"

"Bunch of young hooligans from a ward club down the street."

Madison gestured him to a seat. "Did they threaten you personally, your property, your family?"

"All of those unless I sign up with the protection service they say they're offering because of last week's fires."

"When was this?"

"Last night just before I closed up."

"Did you report it to the police?"

"Yes, and was told they can't do anything until a crime is committed."

"Had you seen these men before?"

He nodded. "Yes. They're usually hanging around the doors of the club when I open in the morning and when I close up at night. Most of them are Richards's toughs."

"Have you spoken to him?"

"Yes, but of course he claims to have no knowledge of the men or the scheme, but everyone knows that those yahoos don't spit on the street without his approval."

Madison recalled his own conversation with Richards. Ruffians of all races were in the employ of the city's political bosses. With monies provided by the party, the gangs bought votes and ferried in ringers to the voting polls. The men were usually the shiftless and dishonest from the underbelly of society. "Has anyone else been offered this so-called protection?"

"Most of the owners near my restaurant have all been approached. Many are afraid. Me, I'm just angry."

"Let's talk about this at the meeting tomorrow night, and in the meantime I'll do some asking around."

"I know Dawson Richards is involved. I can smell it."

"I agree. Nothing happens here without his knowledge. Nothing."

"I let him know that I'll not be run out or burned out, not without a fight."

Madison nodded grimly. Men like Watson were having a hard enough time trying to make ends meet without their livelihoods threatened by members of their own race.

After Watson's departure, Madison put Tate in charge of the office and left to make some inquiries on Mr. Watson's behalf.

The Fifth Ward, known for its pimps, hustlers, gamblers, and prostitutes, had been a home away from home during Madison's youth. He'd spent many a night at the clubs and pool halls there, as had many wealthy White men drawn by the edginess of the atmosphere and the prostitutes they could easily dally with on the side. Many of those same gentlemen won and lost fortunes in the cribs and back rooms of the Fifth Ward, and even now, ten years later, the steady stream of Whites seeking adventure continued to flow.

As in most of the city's slums, be they the neighborhoods of the Negro, Irish, or Italian, the streets were lined with houses in disrepair, laundry was strung between light poles, and in the evenings the doorways and stoops were filled with crowds of loitering men playing dice and drinking, while rouged women offered tumbles for whatever you could pay. In early afternoon, like now, the night crowd wasn't on the streets yet, so the children were free to play, the elderly could visit the nearby grocers, and women could sweep debris from the walks in front of their homes.

Madison parked his horse and buggy in front of the house he was seeking and gave a few coins to a young man nearby to keep an eye on it until he returned. A knock on the door was soon answered by an obviously sleepy Irene Garner.

"Madison," she said with a welcoming smile. "Come in."

Even though the drapes were drawn on all the windows, there was enough light filtering inside to show that the place was well furnished. Quality furniture, landscapes on the walls, carpets on the floors. By day it could have been any tastefully decorated row house in the city, but at night it was one of the most well-known gambling clubs in the ward.

Irene had obviously just gotten out of bed. The thin wrapper she held closed made it easy to see she was nude underneath. "Can I get you a drink?"

He shook his head. "No, just need to see Ben."

"Must be important to get you down here during the day. Or at least it better be. He just went to bed a couple hours ago."

"It is. Can you get him for me?"

She nodded. Irene was Ben Norton's woman and had been for ten years. She was the madam for the prostitutes Ben supplied for the high rollers who filled his club each night from the moment the doors opened until whenever closing rolled around.

Ben came out a few minutes later. At six feet four inches tall and almost three hundred pounds, he filled the room. They shared an embrace.

Ben took a seat on one of the embroidered back chairs. "What brings you to my little corner of paradise at this ungodly hour?"

"To see if you've heard anything about the fires set in the Seventh last week. Authorities think it might be arson."

"I heard about the fires but nothing else."

"There seems to be a protection scam spinning

off the fires too. Charlie Watson was threatened last night."

"The caterer? What is he, almost seventy years old now?"

Madison nodded.

"He catered my sister's sixteenth birthday ball. Remember?"

"I do." Ben and Madison had grown up together, and in their youth were best friends. Ben's father was a prominent minister in those days. When he died of a heart attack five years ago, Ben's mother had forbidden Ben's presence at the funeral, holding him and his lifestyle partly responsible for his father's demise.

"Does Mr. Watson know anything about the men?" Ben asked.

"He says they hang out at the local ward club."

"Richards's thugs?"

"I'm pretty sure they are."

"Do you want him killed tonight or tomorrow?"

Madison chuckled. "Let's wait until the facts are in."

"I say we do it tonight, then if we find out he's not, he can be held up as an example to wayward youth anyway."

"Like the ones we used to be?"

"Exactly." Ben grinned. "I'll put some feelers out on this arsonist business and get back to you. Can't have that bank of yours burning down. Some of my money's in it. Obviously, Richards doesn't know that you know the people you do, or that at one time you were one of those people."

"Obviously."

"But now you're all cleaned up and respectable. Well, somewhat. Still giving the society ladies hell. Any of them serious candidates for the title of Mrs. Mad?"

Teresa July's face floated into his mind. He quickly shooed it away. "No."

"You need a woman, Mad. Can't go through life doing nothing but counting your dividends—you're as old as I am. Irene was and is the best thing that ever happened to me. Something to be said for having someone in your life you can be honest with and will overlook your faults."

"And we know that you have many," Madison tossed back.

Their bond to each other was strong.

Ben countered, "Almost as many as you. So find you a woman."

"Yes, Pa. Can we get back to Richards?"

Ben's face soured at the name. "Disliked him since the very first time he came down here. Walked in, throwing his weight around—demanding this and that—then had the audacity to think he could leave without paying his bill. Told me, as the new ward boss he expected everything to be gratis. You can imagine my reply."

Madison could.

"I'd just as soon send somebody over to pour kerosene on that big fancy house the party purchased for him."

"Let's see if we can nail him first, then you can burn his house."

"All right. I'll play fair for now, but you're taking all the fun out of this."

"I know. One of us has to function as the conscience."

"I miss raising hell with you."

"I miss those days too, but not enough to go back."

"Well, you know me, in for a penny, in for a pound. I'd never be able to make it on the other side, not after all this time." Ben's voice dropped to a serious tone. "Have you seen my mother?"

"Saw her at the post office about a month ago. She's aging but doing well. I've been keeping an eye on her for you. Mother goes over and visits with her regularly."

"Good." Ben quieted then, and Madison knew his friend was thinking back. He hoped that Ben and his mother would one day reconcile. Ben had taken the death of his father pretty hard, and Madison knew how much he loved his mother.

"I'll let you get back to sleep. There's going to be an association meeting tomorrow. If I hear anything else, I'll let you know."

"Okay. How's Solomon working out as the night man?"

"The bank's still standing, so thanks for the recommendation."

"Any time."

Madison stood and Ben stood as well. They embraced each other with the mutual affection of old friends, then stepped apart.

Ben said, "If there's any dirty work to be done on this, let me do it. My reputation can stand it, yours can't, at least not anymore."

"We'll see. I haven't been in a knock-down, drag-out in a long time. Might be fun."

Ben shook his head and laughed. "Go back to the bank. See you soon."

"I'll be in touch."

As he drove away, Madison was glad to have Ben as a friend and on his side.

It was now the middle of July. Teresa was all but settled into her new life. She and Molly were getting along well. Madison, the Kissing Bandit, hadn't stopped in for a few days and that suited her just fine. She was nearly back to her old weight, her hair was growing in, and she wore her denims, boots, and work shirts more often than not. All in all, life was good. For it to be perfect, she'd have to be back home, but knowing that would come around soon enough, she had no complaints.

At least not until Mrs. Nance decided the time had come for them to make her a few gowns. By the second day of the project, Teresa was tired of all the fittings and fussing. She prayed the half-done gown she was wearing now would be the last of them. She couldn't deny the beauty of the midnight blue silk, but the sharp pins holding it together were like bees stinging her arms, waist, and chest. No matter how she maneuvered herself in an effort to avoid them, the pricks continued to bedevil her mercilessly.

"You have to stand still, Teresa," Mrs. Nance gently cautioned while placing more pins to create seams for the gown's flowing skirt.

"Sorry, but the pins are like hell fire."

"A lady doesn't say 'hell,'" she admonished while folding the length of silk across the bottom of Teresa's ankle to estimate where the hem should be.

"Then I'm glad I'm not a lady."

"You could be if you tried."

"Only if I can still belt on my Colt."

Mrs. Nance's amusement was obvious. "You are truly an original, Miss Teresa July." Still adjusting the fabric, she looked up. "Can you lower your arms for just a moment. I want to get the true drape of this hem."

When Teresa complied, the partially finished bodice she'd been holding together slipped to her waist, showing off the thin white silk camisole she was wearing beneath. She'd made the simple undergarment herself.

"Turn slowly."

The pins were placed one by one, and when Mrs. Nance was finally satisfied, she said, "Good. Now, let's—"

The sudden opening of the sewing room door followed by the unannounced entrance of Madison caught both women by surprise.

"Mother, I—" Then he stopped. The sight of Teresa standing in the center of the room wearing nothing above the waist but an arousing silk confection rendered him momentarily speechless. Her well-formed bare arms and shoulders were unlike the soft-skinned beauties he was accustomed to stroking. The female outlaw appeared to have been delicately sculpted from a living piece of ebony stone so vibrant his hands tingled with the need to caress her skin. He ran his eyes over the tantalizing hollow of her throat, and unable to stop himself, the rounded tops of her veiled breasts. Only then did he meet her eyes and see the fiery displeasure blazing there.

Hand on her hip, she drawled, "You should pick up your eyeballs before they get stepped on."

Madison's jaw tightened and he turned his back. "My apologies," he ground out, mad at himself for the social blunder, and mad at her for being the cause. Behind him, he could hear the rustle of silk, and he wondered if she was removing the gown. The thought made him mentally speculate what the rest of her might look like were he the one easing it off of her. His manhood stretched in response and he cursed silently.

His mother said in a voice tinged with censure, "You may turn back, Madison. She's decent."

Madison had a feeling Teresa July would never be decent in his eyes again, and that only added to his mood. When he turned back, he saw that her sculpted beauty was now safely hidden beneath a tightly belted green satin robe, but the fire in her dark eyes continued to smolder.

His mother asked, "What can I do for you?"

Trying his best to keep his vision focused on his mother and off of Teresa July, he spun his mind to remember why he'd come to see her. "Just stopped in to say hello. And to let you know that I saw Ben Norton a few days ago. He sends best wishes."

"That's nice of him. How is he?"

"Fine. Just fine." He swung his eyes in Teresa's direction and saw that although some of the heat had left her gaze, a simmer remained.

His mother said, "Rebecca and Miller are having the August first picnic a few weeks early this year. Her birthday is August third and he's taking her to Chicago to see her sister as her gift."

"So when's the picnic?"

"Saturday. Can you come?"

"I've an early meeting with someone that morning, but I should be able to make it out there around noon."

"Good. Teresa and I will see you there."

He looked Teresa's way. "Again, my apologies."

"Thanks."

And Madison departed with the image of Teresa burned permanently into his memory.

When the British Parliament abolished slavery in the West Indies on August 1, 1834, U.S. Blacks in the North embraced the day for the hope it gave to the three million captives enslaved in the South. It was now a traditional day of celebration for America's Negroes.

The festivities usually consisted of rallies, parades, speeches, and, in churches like Philadelphia's Mother Bethel AME, commemorative services and night watches were held. Over the years, other dates were added to honor the race's milestones. In Washington, D.C., Black folks honored April 16, the date Congress abolished slavery in the District in 1862. It was usually marked by a large parade complete with military bands, fraternal societies, and mounted marshals. In its heyday during the 1880s, the processions were a mile long and included five thousand people of all colors, classes, and distinctions. The August 16 parade was so highly regarded that in 1884, when the route took it by the White House, then President Chester A. Arthur stood in review.

Molly was explaining all this to Teresa on the ride

to Miller and Rebecca Constantine's annual August first picnic.

"Never knew about any of that," Teresa said in response to the short history lesson. "In Texas they celebrate Juneteenth."

Molly nodded while she drove. "I've heard of it. Supposedly the news of the Emancipation didn't reach Texas until June nineteenth, 1865."

"Do they still have the big parades here in the East?"

"No, for three main reasons. One, people began questioning why the race should celebrate anything associated with the dark days of slavery, a debate still going on today, as you well know by reading the newspapers."

Teresa did.

"Two, the cost of the parade permits were skyrocketing, and three—hooligans."

"Hooligans?"

"Yes. Instead of the tasteful, proud parades we had in the past, where people knew how to conduct themselves and wanted nothing to mar the race's image, the events began to attract a less genteel crowd, shall we say. Drunks on rickety wagons, people in garish cheap clothing. Bands of rummed-up youth from the countryside wandering the parade route assaulting people, and murdering the English language, as one editor so baldly put it. It was appalling. One year, the parade in Washington even had a group of young men dressed up as minstrels. In blackface!"

Teresa could hear the disgust in Mrs. Nance's voice.

"Our young people born after slavery have no attachment to the past. For them our holidays were nothing more than an opportunity to leave work, carouse and drink. It's sad for the race and for our future." She looked Teresa's way. "As you can probably guess, I'm very passionate about the subject."

"Nothing wrong with that. By the time Jim Crow gets done pecking us to death, passion may be all we have left."

A whole slew of buggies and wagons were parked along the white fences that lined the road to the Constantines' place. After she and Molly found a place in the line to park, Teresa could smell meat roasting and hear fiddlers as they walked onto the grounds. Happy voices floated on the air, and Teresa admitted to being more than a little excited. She hadn't been to a party in a long while and was looking forward to some fun.

Rebecca Constantine, wearing more face paint than usual and a simple but elegant blue skirt and matching shirtwaist, met them at the gate with a smile. "Welcome, you two. Teresa, you are getting more beautiful every day. Living with Molly is agreeing with you."

Amused, Teresa nodded. "That, and Emma's cooking."

The grinning Rebecca turned to Molly. "Shall I introduce her as your niece, Tamar?"

"Yes. Let's keep the ruse going."

"All right."

The women walked out to join the rest of the invited guests. Teresa had no idea the gathering would be so large. People were spread out over the grounds talking and visiting, while others sat on blankets under the trees. Children were chasing a rooster that suddenly turned and charged, sending them running and squealing with laughter. A group of men gathered at a horseshoe pit were pitching shoes and having a good time. Domino players were slapping bones, while spectators stood around smiling and waiting for a turn to play. Molly and Teresa each picked up a tumbler of the ice cold lemonade waiting on one of the food tables that was fairly groaning from all the covered dishes placed on them.

As they walked, Teresa met more of Molly's friends—a Mrs. Mitchell, who, Molly informed her later, was one of the two female undertakers in town. She was then introduced to a Mrs. Fletcher, one of the teachers at the famous Philadelphia Institute for Colored Youth. Teresa met a host of other women and their husbands, who all smiled kindly at her and welcomed her to the city.

Leaving Molly to visit with her friends, Teresa wandered over the grounds, enjoying the sights and soaking up the atmosphere. She paused at the horseshoe pit and joined the small group of men and women watching the tosses.

"Well, hello," said a frosty female voice. It was Paula Wade, decked out in a fancy green walking suit complete with bustle.

Teresa nodded.

Paula said, "Everyone, this is Mrs. Nance's niece. What's your name again?"

"Tamar. Tamar August." She received a few skeptical looks from some of the younger women, but there was a decided interest in the eyes of their young men.

Teresa didn't pay any of it any mind. "Can I toss?" she asked at the end of the game.

The winner, a portly brown-skinned young man in a striped blue shirt and white trousers, looked her up and down. "Shouldn't you be cutting the pies or something? Girls don't throw shoes."

"They do where I come from."

He paused. Smiling, he looked to his friends for a moment, then said, "Oh really, and where in the *South* might that be?"

The girls, including Paula, giggled at the veiled insult.

"Texas."

He studied her.

"So, can I toss or not?"

He shrugged. "Sure. Shouldn't take but a minute to put you down."

Teresa gave him a cold smile. "Since you're so sure of yourself, let's make it more interesting. How about one of you boys over there walk off another ten paces in the pit and replace the spike there."

Her opponent stared. Teresa picked up a pair of the shoes from the dirt and tested the weight. "What's your name?" she asked him.

He stuttered, "Alvin. Alvin Porter."

"Okay, Alvin. Alvin Porter."

One of the young men walked off the ten paces, moved the spike, and pounded it into the dirt with a mallet lying in the grass next to the pit.

Alvin gestured and said coolly, "Ladies first."

"Thanks."

Teresa wished she had on her denims instead of a skirt, but it couldn't be helped. She did have on a pair of her new boots, however, and they helped her set her feet in the soft earth of the pit. Bending at the waist, she sighted the spike with the open ends of the horseshoe, then pitched it. It sailed the distance, hit the spike and rattled around it until it hit the ground.

Alvin and his friends were wide-eyed.

"Your turn."

He stared as if she'd just sprouted wings. Paula and her lady friends appeared stunned, but everyone else was watching with eager interest.

Someone called out, "Hope you didn't bet the farm, Porter."

Laughter followed the remark, and Porter looked none too pleased. He threw the shoe, and it landed just south of the spike's original location. Teresa had been chopping wood, she was fit and strong. The doughy Porter didn't look as if he'd had any exercise outside of raising a fork to his lips.

Evidently word had spread about a girl tossing horseshoes because as Teresa lined up her second try, there were many more people looking on, including Molly and her lady friends. Her second throw was a duplicate of the first. The sound of metal striking metal rang out as it hit the spike, rattled around it, and landed on top of its twin. Loud cries of amazement and encouragement came from the spectators. Pleased, she stepped aside.

Teresa didn't know if the game was scored the same way it was back home. She figured it wouldn't matter if her tosses bested his. And they did, again and again.

Finally, someone hollered, "Game to the lady!"

Cheers went up from Molly, her friends, and

many of the older men and women crowded around the grassy edges of the freshly dug pit. Paula Wade looked put out, as did the girls with her. Loser Alvin Porter's jaws were as tight as the lid on a jar of home-made preserves.

Teresa asked, "How about another?"

"No. I have an appointment to meet someone at home. I'm already late."

"Ah."

Then, from behind her, she heard, "Never send a boy to do a man's job."

The familiar voice was as much a caress at it was a challenge. Turning, she stared up into the handsome face of Madison Nance. In his hands were horseshoes. In his eyes, mischief.

Chapter 7

"Are you challenging me?" she asked, all the while wondering why seeing him made her feel so good inside when she didn't want it to.

"Yes, ma'am."

He was close enough for her to feel the heat rising off his tall lean body and to pick up the faint scent of his now familiar cologne. "Challenger goes first."

He was staring down with such intense amusement, she swore she knew what he was thinking. Just in case she was right, she beckoned him down and whispered in his ear, "If you kiss me in front of all of these folks, so help me I'll crack you over the head with this horseshoe."

Eyes twinkling, he replied with a soft whisper of his own, "Then I'll wait until later."

Teresa's knees almost gave way.

Although no one else had heard the whispered exchange, the interaction was plain. People were smiling as if they knew something Teresa didn't, but Paula Wade's anger was all over her doll-like face. "Is that really your cousin?" she asked.

Madison was lining up his shot. "Anyone tell you different?"

Because Paula couldn't say yes, she folded her arms across her chest and remained silent.

Madison flung the shoe. He used a side-arm motion, similar to the way Teresa's brother Shafts threw, and just like Shafts, the shoe caught the spike, circled it and hit the ground.

"Not bad," she said, "but watch this." Mentally cursing her skirt because it was in the way, she sighted, leaned in, and sent the shoe tumbling end over end to the spike. Ringer. Flashing Madison a superior look, she stepped aside so he could take his second shot.

He did, and matched his first. Ringer.

In order to tie him, Teresa had to hit one too. The pit spectators were quiet and the atmosphere was tense. They watched as she held the shoe in front of her and focused on the stake. She swung her arm back then stepped into the throw. Everyone's eyes followed the shoe as it turned end over end in the air, and when it hit the spike and landed on top of Madison's shoe, a cheer went up.

They battled. Ringer after ringer. Game after game.

At one point Madison stopped to remove his blue seersucker suit coat because of the heat of the day, but Teresa would have none of it. "If I have to throw in this skirt, you have to keep that coat on."

Her female rooters soundly agreed.

Teresa then added saucily, "But if it's getting too warm for your city blood, you can always surrender."

"Not on your life. Only person surrendering will be you, my sweet cousin."

Teresa blinked. Was he flirting with her? It certainly felt that way, and the wild beating of her heart was threatening her focus. She wondered if he was purposefully trying to distract her in order to win, and decided he was. Ignoring the sensations evoked by him watching her, she flung the horseshoe in her hand toward the stake for another perfect throw.

They matched each other point for point for another ten minutes. In the end, Teresa lost not because of skill, but because she stepped on the hem of her skirt as she made her toss and the subsequent stumble sent her and her throw awry.

Her supporters groaned.

Cursing mentally, she picked herself up, dusted herself off. She wasn't the type to use excuses, so she coolly gestured for him to take his turn.

Since Madison had no skirt to foul his throw, when he hit another ringer, the game was over. The men cheered loudly.

Teresa knew the game had been fair and were it not for her damn female clothing she could have pitched with him for another hour and probably won. Her shoulders were going to be mad at her later, she thought, because she hadn't thrown shoes in years. But having grown up with her brothers, she loved a good game, no matter what it was, and she'd enjoyed competing against him. She stuck out her hand.

Madison looked down at it. He only knew one woman who shook hands like a man, Loreli Winters, and now he knew two. He grasped her hand, smiled and said, "We can have a rematch whenever you like."

Teresa noted how warm his hand felt holding hers. "Only if I'm wearing trousers or you're wearing a skirt."

He laughed, then took the two glasses of lemonade his mother handed him before she and the other ladies went to get the meal started. He handed one to Teresa.

She took a long swallow then sighed softly with satisfaction. "Thanks. I need to find some shade. I'm roasting. How do women wear all this clothing and not keel over from the heat?"

"Many of them don't," he said, amusement lifting his mustached lips. He looked around the grounds. "I see an empty bench under that tree. How about we head there and cool off?"

Teresa could see people watching the exchange between them. Paula Wade and her gang were among them, and she ignored them as she walked with Madison across the grass.

They sat down. The shade felt good, and the lemonade was a blessing.

"You throw horseshoes pretty good," he said.

"For a girl?"

"No, for anybody. Calm down."

She smiled over her raised glass. "Started pitching shoes soon as I could lift them, and since my brothers were always bigger and stronger, I've never beat them."

"If it hadn't been for that stumble, we might still be going at it."

"No *might* to it. We would be."

"I'd've won eventually, though."

She cut him a look.

He responded. "Bigger. Stronger."

She rolled her eyes.

They went silent for a few moments while the

picnic played in front of them like moving pictures. The children had claimed the horseshoe pit, and sure enough some of the girls spurred on by Teresa's performance were challenging the boys.

Madison watched them for a moment. "You've started something. Now, all the little girls will be wanting to horn in."

"Nothing wrong with that. I'd rather have them pitching horseshoes than acting prissy like Paula and her friends." She turned to him, "And I liked the way you answered Miss Paula's question about us being kin. Very clever."

"Why thank you. It's about time you started noting some of my better qualities."

"First time I've seen one."

He threw back his head and laughed. Holding her eyes, he went silent for a moment and studied the face that had been haunting him since the last time he'd seen her in that indigo gown. "You're something."

Feeling the attraction arching between them like heat lightning over the desert, she shrugged. "I'm just a little country girl from out West."

Neither of them moved until he reached out and very slowly traced a finger down her ebony cheek. When he leaned down, she knew he was about to kiss her but couldn't have moved if she'd wanted to. The kiss was as mesmerizing as he, the sweetness of it far more powerful than the one he'd given her last time. This one awakened her inside, made her lean closer so she could respond, and he did the same, cupping her neck with his hand to pull her even closer as the kiss deepened.

She said softly, "We shouldn't be doing this."

"I know."

But like adolescents finally allowed to be alone, they kept at it, learning, exploring, soaring. She finally backed away, her breathing coarse, her eyes closed, and leaned back against the bench to catch her breath and restore her sanity. Moments later she opened her eyes and found him watching her. She held his eyes, wondering where this might lead, if anywhere.

"So," he said quietly.

"So," she echoed. "What brought this on? A month ago you wanted me chained in the cellar."

He chuckled softly, "A month ago I didn't know what a fascinating woman you'd turn out to be."

"I'll take that as a compliment."

Teresa had always considered old friend Griffin Blake to be the handsomest man in the country hands down, but not anymore. Madison Nance made Griffin look like the back end of a mule. Madison's strong jaw, the brown eyes. To be truthful, she was attracted to everything about him, from the neatly cut hair, to the thin mustache framing his full lips. Most of the eastern men she'd met were only a few inches taller than she, but Madison rivaled her brothers in height, and she liked that aspect of him as well.

But she'd be willing to bet her new boots that he wasn't looking for anything more than a roll in the hay from her. If he had expected the little country girl to be dazzled by the big city boy's attentions, she was, but it didn't mean she'd misplaced her brain. He probably had more notches on his headboard than she'd had Wanted posters and she didn't see herself as being one of the stories men tell each other when they get together and whiskey's in the room. "Thanks for the kiss," she said genuinely, "but you should probably be saving them for that bride you're looking for."

Wanting to feel her silky skin again, Madison ran a finger down her cheek. "You didn't like my kisses?"

His touch gave her sweet shakes, "Liked them fine, but there's no future in it."

He met her eyes. "Why not?"

"Because this is probably just a game for you."

"I think I'm insulted."

"You shouldn't be. Men are who they are. Been around them all my life."

"And you think you know them?"

"Like the back of my hand, and to prove it, I'm going to ask you a question. And you have to answer truthfully."

"Okay."

"Could you see yourself falling in love and then marrying a woman like me?"

His stunned silence put a bittersweet smile on her face.

She stood. "See, it is a game. I'm going to go get something to eat."

She walked away and left him sitting there.

For the rest of the picnic, Teresa made a conscious effort to avoid Madison. On a few occasions she saw him watching her from afar, but he didn't approach, and that suited her just fine. She wasn't looking to be tumbled then tossed aside when the next pretty face rode up, because as loco as it sounded, she was developing feelings for him.

On the ride home, she was so quiet, Molly asked, "Are you all right, dear?"

"Yes, ma'am."

"You and Madison didn't have another fight, did you?"

She shook her head. "No."

Molly turned to look in her face, and Teresa gave her a small smile in return. "I'm okay, really."

"Okay, but if something is bothering you and you want to talk, I'm here."

"Thanks," Teresa said genuinely.

That night, as she sat alone in the gazebo watching the moon and thinking about the day, the memories of the kiss returned. She supposed she had no one to blame but herself for asking Madison if he could see himself falling in love and then marrying a woman like her. She knew they were from worlds as different as night and day. And more important, as she'd noted many times, women like her didn't belong in fairy tales. With that in mind, she sat there a bit longer, taking in the clean night air, then said good-night to the moon and the stars and went inside to bed.

Seated in a chair on the balcony attached to his bedroom, Madison studied the moon. Teresa July was on his mind and had been since she'd put him in his place. Her question had been far more weighty than he'd expected, and the quick flash of sadness he saw cross her features in response to his silence was not something he'd soon forget.

Could you see yourself falling in love and marrying a woman like me?

Truthfully, no. Men of his class did not choose paroled prisoners as wives. Successful businessmen usually allied themselves with women who'd be an asset;

women who could run a household, entertain friends and clients, and be elegant and graceful at both. Men from elite families did not consider horseshoe throwing, train robbing, or wearing a gun belt qualities they were looking for in the potential mother of their children. Yet, she intrigued him so much he wanted to see her right then.

Teresa July.

To make matters worse, she was more beautiful each time he saw her. If he didn't know better, he'd swear she was using an old Seminole spell to enthrall him. He'd had trouble putting the brakes on his attraction when she'd had butchered hair and dry ashy skin, so how in the world was he supposed to ignore her now that she'd filled out so temptingly and her black hair had grown long enough to pull back and frame her stunning ebony face? The prominent cheekbones, the full luscious mouth, the ink black eyes ... Sooner or later such beauty would attract attention and the men would came calling, a certainty he found troubling.

As she'd pointed out, he'd wanted her chained in the cellar. But now he wanted her chained to his side until he learned everything there was to know about her. That she was unconventional was an understatement, and it was that aspect of her personality that ensnared him the most because she appealed to the unconventional sides of himself. During his early twenties, he and Ben had only three pursuits in life: cards, women, and scotch. They'd sit at tables with the scions and captains of industry one night, and be in a whorehouse playing with pimps and hustlers the next.

For five years the two best friends—one Black the other White—gambled, drank, and whored their way from Philadelphia to Havana and back. They'd shot their way out of rigged games in Washington, D.C., and jumped out of windows, clothes in hand, to escape enraged husbands more than once. They'd been handsome, articulate card sharps who gave no quarter. In light of their adventures, they were lucky to be alive, but now, he sat musing over a woman who challenged him where women like Paula had bored him to death. Maybe that's what's been wrong with me? he thought. Society dictated that when a man settled into being an adult, he would place his oat-sowing days behind him and concentrate on attaining a successful life, and he'd done that. But did that successful life have to be dull and lifeless like his had admittedly become? He worked, played cards at his club and at Ben's occasionally, then went home. He visited his mother and occasionally took a select few women to the theater or a concert, women who invariably bored him with their addle-headed prattle about hats and who was seeing whom, but he slept with them.

When Ben had told him he couldn't spend his life alone counting his dividends, he'd wanted to disagree, but maybe Ben was right. What happened to the Madison he used to be? When had the fire in his life been extinguished? Yes, he was passionate about the fate of the race and planned to keep storming the gates, but what about passion in his personal life? He'd flirted with Teresa today during the horseshoe game, something the old Madison had done instinctively but the present version hadn't done consciously in quite some time. Who was there to flirt with? Paula? The daughters of his mother's friends? Yet with Teresa, he'd slipped back into his old persona so effortlessly he hadn't realized it, and it felt good. Their verbal jousting and charged encounters seemed to have freed him from the lethargy he'd unknowingly buried himself beneath.

So, what to do? No, he didn't want to marry Teresa July, any more than she wanted to marry him. But he did want her company, her wit, her sass. He wanted to take her for rides in the park, escort her to the theater, maybe even take her to see Ben. He wanted to show her the city and, yes, make love to her—no sense in denying that—but that wasn't his main focus. Just being in the glow of her radiant and captivating personality was enough, because it seemed that she was drawing him back into the light.

Teresa woke up the next morning with her arms and shoulders stiff and sore. It took a moment for her to figure out why, then the horseshoe contest came back, which in turn brought back memories of Madison, the kissing, and the aftermath. Deciding she wasn't going to think about Madison Nance today, she got out of bed.

She had the paper open and was reading to Molly about a cereal food coffee called Postum that was invented and being sold by a man named Charles W. Post when Emma came in and said, "There's a gentleman in the parlor wanting to call on Teresa."

Teresa spit out her coffee.

Molly smiled. "Really? Who?"

"Matthew Mitchell, the undertaker lady's son."

Molly looked to Teresa. "What do you think?"

"I don't think my parole allows me to have gentlemen callers."

Molly waved that off. "Silly girl. Go change your clothes. Who knows, you may like him."

Teresa doubted it. "Mrs. Nance, I genuinely don't—" The look on Mrs. Nance's face told all, so a reluctant Teresa got to her feet. "Okay. Miss Emma, tell him I'll be there directly."

Emma nodded and left.

Not happy, Teresa went up to her room to change out of her leathers. Dressed in more traditional female clothing, she went back down to meet the undertaker's son.

He was three inches shorter than she and had bad skin. He stood when she entered the parlor, but when she stuck out her hand, he seemed startled. Catching himself, he gave her hand a quick shake.

Teresa waved him to a seat.

Thanks," he said, seemingly unable to take his eyes off her. "I was at the Constantines' picnic. Not sure you remember seeing me."

"I do."

"Really?" He seemed pleased and excited.

Teresa sighed mentally. She sensed it was going to be a long morning. "So what do you do?"

"I work with my mother. She's an undertaker."

"Ah."

The parlor became so silent she could hear the clock ticking on the mantel. Finally, he asked,

"Uh, where are you from? I heard you tell Alvin Porter you were from Texas. Was that true?"

"Yes. My family lives near the Mexican border."

"I hear Texas is full of bloodthirsty Indians. Have you ever seen any?"

Teresa studied him for a moment. "Where I come from, the bloodthirsty people call themselves Americans."

He seemed puzzled by that, and Teresa mentally rolled her eyes.

"You impressed a lot of people at the picnic," he told her. "Heard quite a few men said they were interested in courting you. Thought I'd try and get here first. You know, the early bird getting the worm, and all that."

She cocked her head at him.

As if he'd heard himself, his eyes widened and he said hastily, "Oh, no. I wasn't implying that I ... that you ... " He hung his head. "You probably think I'm an idiot."

She smiled at his contrite, embarrassed manner. "No. How old are you, Matt? May I call you Matt?"

"Oh, yes, Miss August. Please do. I'm twenty-one."

"I see. Do you know that I'm twenty-six, almost twenty-seven?"

Surprise filled his eyes and he scanned her as if looking for gray hairs. "No."

"So, I don't think we're equally yoked, agewise."

"Twenty-six? Really?"

Teresa nodded. "Almost twenty-seven." She hoped it would be enough to deter any interest he may have been harboring, but just in case, she added, "And I'm an Indian. Black Seminole to be exact."

He jumped to his feet as if he'd suddenly sat on a

hot poker. His eyes were wide as saucers. "What!"

She nodded. "Yep. One of my brothers is half Comanche."

The eyes popped even wider. "Why, the Comanche are supposed to be the most savage—" he stopped, then cleared his throat. "I suddenly remembered that I have an appointment with a grieving family. I—have to go."

"I understand."

If he could have bolted from the house, he would have. Instead he made as hasty a retreat as he could to the door and still be polite. "Nice talking with you, Miss August."

"You too, Matt."

And he departed as fast as his legs could carry him.

Sighing, Teresa closed the door and looked down at her skirt. Next time, she'd just keep her leathers on and save herself the trouble.

She was on her way back upstairs to change when Mrs. Nance walked out of the library. "What happened to Matthew?"

"He remembered that he had a grieving family to attend to."

Molly searched her face. "Did you scare him off, Teresa?"

"I think he scared himself. Especially when I told him my brother was half Comanche."

Molly shook her head. "Teresa."

"Mrs. Nance, he said he'd heard Texas was full of bloodthirsty Indians. Besides he's only twenty-one. He'd do better spending time with someone like Paula."

Molly sighed. "Well, do you want to go with me over to the church this afternoon?"

Teresa had been helping out with the weekly afternoon teas the Bethel Ladies had been putting on for the young domestics, and she found the volunteering oddly satisfying. She'd never done charity work before, but before she could answer the question, the door pull sounded.

"Now, who could this be?" Molly wondered aloud.

It was Madison. He kissed his mother on the cheek. "Good morning, Mother ... Teresa."

Teresa tried to deny the way her body fluttered when he walked in the door, but she couldn't. "Madison."

"What brings you here?" Molly asked. "Why aren't you at the bank?"

"Declared today a holiday," he said, his eyes on Teresa.

His mother appeared shocked. "You? A holiday?"

"I may even take the rest of the week. All work and no play has turned Madison into a very dull boy, so I came over to see if Teresa cared to see the city."

Teresa blinked.

Molly turned her way. "I think that's a fine idea. I have to go over to the church, and I'd planned to take her with me, but no sense in the both of us being cooped up inside on such a lovely day."

That morning, Teresa had vowed not to think about Madison, so she definitely wasn't keen on the idea of being in his company. "I think I'd rather help you and the ladies at the church."

Molly shook her head. "Thanks, but that won't be

necessary. Go on with Madison and have some fun."

That said, she went back into the library, leaving Teresa standing in the foyer with Madison.

"So," he said.

"So," she echoed.

"Are you ready?"

"No."

He smiled. "Come along anyway. I promise to be on my best behavior."

Teresa was drowning in his eyes, but she didn't believe him for a minute.

"I promise, we'll have fun."

She didn't believe that either, but Mrs. Nance hadn't left her a choice. "Okay, let's get this over with." Striding by him without another word, she walked out into the sunshine.

Madison shook his head and followed in her wake.

When they were seated in his carriage before he picked up the reins he said, "I'd like to apologize for my rude behavior at the picnic. I wasn't trying to hurt your feelings."

"You didn't." That was a lie, of course, but she certainly wasn't going to acknowledge the truth. "I asked you a question and you answered honestly."

"Suppose we turn that same question your way. How would you answer?"

"I told you before, I don't plan on marrying."

"Then we're of a like mind."

"I suppose." Except her feelings were involved and his plainly were not.

"Would you say we get along well when we aren't fighting?"

"I would."

"Then how about we agree to simply enjoy each other's company?"

"No games?"

He shook his head. "No games."

"No kissing?"

"Only if you ask."

She rolled her eyes and her smile crept out. "I thought you were going to be on your best behavior?"

"I am, but you're a beautiful woman, Teresa, and as you so sagely pointed out, I am a man. No getting around that."

Their gazes held. He wanted to trace his fingers over her mouth. She smelled the faint spicy scent of his cologne.

Feeling herself succumbing to his silent spell, she said, "Drive, Nance."

"Yes, ma'am."

With the tension between them lightened, Teresa relaxed and settled in for the ride.

The first part of the tour took them to Seventh and Lombard, the area of the city that gave rise to Philadelphia's first Black enclave. "This is where everyone's grandparents and parents lived initially," Madison said. "No matter your station or class, home was here in the blocks between Eighth, Pine, Sixth, and South."

He went on to explain that many of the city's Black residents were native Philadelphians descended from the original slave captives who were brought in 1684. "Back in the 1840s and 1850s, Philadelphia was home to the largest number of free Negroes in the country, but as you can see, this is a slum area now. Some of the streets over in the Fifth Ward are much worse, but this is a slum nonetheless."

Teresa wasn't accustomed to seeing so many people and so many derelict houses packed so densely. Back home, there was also tremendous poverty, but at least the dwellings weren't stacked against each other like the row houses they were driving by. She noted the groups of men loitering on corners, and raggedly dressed children playing in the streets. Signs touting pool halls, political clubs, and gambling establishments seemed to be on every other storefront.

"Most of the poor here are immigrants from the South who came north after the war to escape the violence and look for a better life."

"Doesn't look like they found it."

"No, they didn't. There are very few opportunities. When we go uptown you'll see all the new construction going on, but not a company will hire us. Not even to sweep. The steel industry is booming too, but only one private company, Midvale Steel, hires workers of all colors and pays everyone equal wages."

He then pointed out the spot where the famous Philadelphia Institute for Colored Youth stood until the decaying condition of the neighborhood forced the Quaker-run private school to move to Bainbridge and Ninth in 1866. "I graduated from ICY," Madison told her proudly. "The principal, Mrs. Fanny Jackson Coppin, is an Oberlin graduate. She speaks five languages, including Sanskrit."

"What's that?"

"An ancient language of India."

Teresa had no idea why someone in Philadelphia would need to speak Sanskrit, but kept the question to herself as he began to recite the names of some of the school's famous students.

"Dr. Rebecca Cole, the first female of the race to earn a medical degree from the Women's Medical College. Richard T. Greener, the first man of the race to receive a degree from Harvard. The institute's first graduate, Jesse Glasgow continued his education at the University of Edinburgh."

"Where's that?"

"Scotland."

"Really?"

He nodded. "And in 1875 the first Negro to get a Ph.D., physicist Edward Bouchet, became one of the teachers."

"That's a lot of firsts."

He grinned. "Yes, it is."

He drove to his bank. "This is my bank."

It was a nondescript building, a simple storefront, but Teresa was impressed nonetheless. She'd robbed a fair amount of banks in her time but never personally knew anyone who owned one. He parked and they went inside. He introduced her to Tate, his young scrub-faced assistant, then she looked around. The interior was small. Madison had an office but Tate did not. There were a few tables where customers could sit and fill out their slips but little else in the way of furniture.

"Where do you keep the money?" she asked curiously. She didn't see any safes and the place looked too small to hold a vault.

"Hidden," he replied with a grin.

"Clever, Nance. Real clever."

But she was smiling.

"Ready to see the main city center?"

"Yes."

Outside, he began walking away from where they'd parked the buggy. Teresa looked at the buggy. "Where are you going?"

"To the streetcar."

She hurried to catch up with him. "Streetcar?"

"Ever ridden one?" he asked.

She shook her head.

"Then you're in for a treat," he said, but even as he did, he thought that the treat was having her by his side.

Chapter 8

When the beetle-shaped car with its antennae stopped for them, Teresa, trying her best to not act like a rube from the country, let Madison get on first. He dropped the fare into the box and she followed him down the aisle. They found two empty seats in the middle of the car just as it began moving again.

Teresa was impressed by this modern convenience. When Madison explained that the car was powered by the electricity it drew from the wires skimming its antennae, she was amazed.

She was further amazed by all the wondrous sights she took in. The Pennsylvania Railroad Station, with its multispired clock tower, was by far the largest building of its kind she'd ever seen; Congress Hall, where the United States Congress met when Philadelphia had been capital of the nation; and the truly magnificent Masonic Temple on Broad Street looked to her gaping eyes more like a castle than a church.

He took her to Market Street, where the trolley line turned around, and pointed out the buildings sporting painted signs for everything from shipping and cigar makers to painless dentistry. She learned the street was named Market because it originally held the stalls where farmers sold produce and meats to the city's residents.

And just as he'd noted earlier, construction seemed to be going on everywhere, from the waterfront to Penn Square, but she saw not one man or woman of color working on any of the sites.

For the rest of the day, they alternately walked and rode the streetcars until everything became for Teresa one big wonderful blur. She had her first taste of Irish corned beef, and then grinned like a happy kid when Madison purchased a cool dish of ice cream for her. She had to admit, he'd been right, it was fun, the most she'd had since being sent to jail, and as he drove her back to Mrs. Nance's late that afternoon, she realized they hadn't argued about anything at all. "Thanks for a great day," she told him.

"You're welcome. Did you have fun?"

"I did."

"Told you."

"Yes, you did."

Their gazes met, and Teresa wondered how to make her rising attraction to him stop. Developing feelings for Madison made about as much sense as running naked through a stand of cactus, but they seemed to be barreling ahead no matter how many times she pulled the brake. He was so outside of her sphere. From his suit and tie, to the way he spoke and moved, he was as exotic to her as she probably was to him, but there was something about him that drew her like a thirsty woman chasing a desert mirage.

"Have dinner with me, tonight." Madison wanted to spend as much time with her as possible, and having dinner would keep her near.

Teresa drew in a long breath as his soft invitation rippled through her.

"I won't pressure you in any way. Just want more of your company."

The thirsty woman inside of Teresa wondered why she was even fighting this. She was a woman full grown. A man with his charm and sophistication would never enter her life again, so why not enjoy whatever the Ancestors had in store. "Do I have to get fancied up?"

Certain he'd never tire of her colorful speech, he replied, "I've never seen you fancied up."

"Last time I dressed up was at my brother Neil's trial. I was wanted by the law at the time, so to keep anyone from recognizing me, I rigged myself up like my sister-in-law Olivia does with a hat and a fancy dress. Sat right there in the courtroom with Hanging Judge Parker and the railroad lawyers and they never caught on." She added, "Of course, I had my gun belt and leathers on underneath, just in case."

"Of course," he chuckled.

"Why are you laughing?" she asked with a smile.

Madison was more enamored with every passing moment. "The wonder of you, that's all. You are one of a kind, Teresa July."

"I hope so. Don't think the world could handle two."

Madison didn't think so either but was glad the one and only was with him.

He pulled his horse and buggy to a halt in front of

his mother's house and set the brake. Neither of them moved, not wanting the afternoon to end.

"So, will you have dinner with me?"

"Yes."

Madison looked at the delicate arch of her brows and the long lashes fanning the midnight eyes and beat back the urge to trace a finger over her tempting lips. "Good," he responded in a voice far softer than he'd planned. "A caterer friend of mine owns a place where we can eat and hopefully not be disturbed." Because he wanted her to himself.

Teresa was as aware of him as she was of her breathing. "That sounds fine."

Madison caught a flicker of movement out of the corner of his eye. "Mother's standing in the doorway. We should probably go in."

Teresa nodded. Feeling as if she were awakening from a dream, she shook off the fog and let him help her down from the buggy.

"Did you have a good time?" Molly asked, opening the door for them.

"I did," Teresa said.

"Me too," Madison echoed. "Which is why I've asked her to have dinner with me this evening."

"Oh?" Molly responded, studying them both.

Teresa added hastily, "Unless you don't approve."

"Oh, no. I do." She looked between the two of them again, apparently pleased.

Trying to ignore the knowing look in her eyes, Teresa asked Madison, "What time should I be ready?"

He glanced down at the silver watch attached to his vest. "It's four now. How about eight?"

"Okay."

"I'll see you then." Madison forced himself to turn away from her compelling eyes and gave his mother a quick kiss on the cheek. "I'll see you later too."

"Good-bye, son."

Once he was gone, Mrs. Nance turned to Teresa and said, "Dinner?"

"Yes. We had a nice time, so we're having dinner. That's all."

"You sure?"

"Yes, ma'am."

"Pity. You'd make a fine daughter-in-law."

Teresa laughed. "Madison doesn't want to marry me any more than I do him, so don't start naming your grandchildren."

"An old woman can hope, can't she?"

Teresa's amusement showed on her face. "I suppose, but it isn't going to happen." Changing the subject, she asked, "Is there lemonade?" She was thirsty.

"Yes. Look in the ice box."

Teresa went to retrieve a cold drink, leaving a thoughtful-looking Molly behind.

Feeling refreshed after a shower, Teresa looked through the armoire for something to wear to dinner with Madison. She knew she couldn't wear her leathers so she chose a nice looking white blouse and a navy skirt she'd made in Mrs. Nance's sewing class. The waistband wasn't as evenly stitched as it could have been, but she doubted anyone would get close enough to see. She'd decided not to wear any of the fancy new gowns because she was going to be uncomfortable enough without being in uncomfortable clothing too, and she didn't actually plan on wearing any of the gowns unless she absolutely had to. Teresa truly appreciated Mrs. Nance's beautiful handiwork, but Molly was going to have to put a Colt to her head to make her leave the house wearing one.

Dressed, her hair done, and nothing left to do now but wait for him to arrive, Teresa went downstairs.

To her surprise, Madison had already arrived and was in the parlor talking with his mother. The woman beneath the outlaw rose to the surface and left her feeling nervous and unsure. She knew how to rob banks, break horses, and make a smokeless fire, but she didn't know beans about having dinner with a fancy man.

When she entered the parlor, he smiled and said softly, "You look nice."

Molly nodded her approval as well. "I especially like the ear bobs. Where'd you get them?"

Teresa's fingers unconsciously strayed to the filigreed silver discs hanging from the delicate wire in her earlobe. "Neil and Shafts got them for me in Mexico City."

"They're very lovely."

A glance Madison's way found him watching her, and her attraction for him radiated inside. She thought he looked very handsome in his dark suit, white shirt and tie, and she was so nervous she had a hard time breathing normally.

"Shall we go?" he asked.

She nodded. "I guess."

So he escorted her out to his buggy, helped her in, and they drove away.

Teresa didn't know what to do about her nervousness. This was all so new to her. She looked his way and wondered if there was a more handsome man anywhere. Were he to ever meet her brothers, she wondered what they'd think of him. Knowing them the way she did, she was sure they'd tease him mercilessly for being city born, for being a banker, and for being with her. It was a good thing the imagined meeting would never take place, because she'd probably have to shoot them to make them leave him alone. Then again, Madison impressed her as a man who could take care of himself, so maybe bullets wouldn't be needed.

When they entered Charles Watson's small restaurant, Madison was not pleased to see Republican Party ward boss Dawson Richards waiting ahead of them to be seated. Standing with him was Paula Wade, of all people. The silly girl had no business being with someone so sinister, and he wondered if her aunt and uncle approved. He kept the displeasure from his face, however; he had no intention of letting Richards or his companion spoil his evening with Teresa.

As both couples waited for the maître'd' to return and show them to a table in the moderately filled dining room, Richards noticed them for the first time, Madison nodded a terse greeting, and noted Richards's obvious interest in Teresa.

"Nance," Richards replied to Madison's nod, showing off his perfect, pearl white teeth. "I don't believe I've met your lovely companion."

"Tamar August ... Dawson Richards," Madison said.

Without knowing a thing about Richards, Teresa sensed the predator lurking beneath the man. The reptilian light in his mulatto eyes gave him away. "Pleased to meet you."

Paula seemed to be doing her best to pretend Teresa wasn't there.

"Texan?" Richards asked, smiling delightedly upon hearing her accent.

She nodded.

"I was born in Louisiana. Are you a visitor to our fair city, or do you reside here?"

"Visiting."

"Ah."

Paula seemed perturbed by his inattentiveness, and gave Teresa a cold stare, which she ignored.

Tearing his eyes from Teresa, Richards said to Madison, "The party is having a fund-raising ball in a couple of weeks. I'd like for you and Tamar to be my guests."

"No thank you."

His eyes flashed. "Maybe the lady would like to answer for herself."

"No thank you," Teresa echoed.

Tight-lipped, Richards looked between the two of them. "Pleasure meeting you, Tamar."

"Same here."

The smiling maître d' returned then and led Richards and the stony-faced Paula to a table.

"Is he as big a snake as he looks?" Teresa asked.

"Bigger," Madison replied.

People were afraid of Dawson Richards because of the power he yielded over everything, from jobs and housing to the city permits needed by businesses.

People who crossed him suddenly found their jobs eliminated or their stores shut down for code violations. Landlords had their occupancy permits voided on trumped-up violations, and on every other corner in the Seventh were thugs who functioned as his intimidators and his eyes. Madison didn't fear him, however. He'd been his own man with his own property and fortune for many years. He wasn't beholden to Richards for anything.

The maître d' returned, and it was their turn to be seated. Greeting them with a smile, he took them through the main room past the other diners. Teresa could see the interest, especially Dawson Richards's, but she ignored the stares.

They were shown to a white-clothed table nestled in a corner at the back of the establishment. There were a few other tables positioned around the space, but none were occupied. The shadowy setting, both intimate and private, kept them from being viewed by the prying eyes up front.

Madison helped her with her chair, something no man had ever done for her before, but Teresa bore it graciously. The heat of his nearness wafted over her back and neck for a prolonged moment, then faded as he moved away to take his seat across the table. The maître d' informed them that their waiter would arrive shortly, then politely excused himself to return to his duties.

Content now that they were seated, Madison asked, "Comfortable?"

Teresa nodded, then confessed, "I've never had dinner with a man like this before."

"Really?"

"Nope. Spent my meals with outlaws and cowboys."

"This is better, I hope?"

"Much," she admitted, and it was. But her nerves were still jumbled, so she took a deep breath and tried to act as if this was just another meal.

The owner of the restaurant, Charles Watson, dressed in the white coat of a chef, came over to their table. "Evening, Madison."

"Evening, Mr. Watson. How are you?"

"Fine, fine."

"I'd like to introduce Tamar August. She's staying with Mother on her visit to the city."

"Nice to meet you, Miss August. "Heard you throw some pretty mean horseshoes."

Teresa dropped her head, then said with a smile, "I should have won."

"Heard that too."

Teresa liked the burly, gray-haired gentleman instantly.

Madison asked him, "Any more visits from our friends?"

"Nope. Things have been real quiet."

Teresa wondered what he was referring to but wasn't rude enough to ask.

Madison replied, "Good. Let me know if you do."

"Sure will." Pausing, he turned to Teresa. "Miss August, nice meeting you. Enjoy your visit."

"Nice meeting you too, and thanks."

He left them, and a young male waiter stepped up to take their order.

Once that was done and he'd departed, they settled back to wait. Madison studied her, enjoying her beauty, and said, "Tell me something I don't know about Teresa July."

She thought for a moment. "Well, let's see. My middle name is Angel. Not many folks outside of my family know that."

"Angel?"

"Yes. My mother said when I was born she looked in my eyes and knew right off I'd be a hellion, so she and my grandmother added Angel to my name, hoping it would temper my personality."

"Did it work?"

She chuckled, "What do you think?"

Madison's smile lit his face.

She turned the tables. "Tell me something I don't know about you."

He thought for a moment too. "You already know I think you're stunning."

Teresa's heart sped up in response to his words and smooth tone. "Yes."

"And that I'm being on my best behavior so you won't sock me, shoot me, or hit me over the head with a horseshoe."

She couldn't hide her humor. "I'm noticing. Now, be serious."

"Okay. I always wanted a sibling. How about that?"

"Did you?"

"So much so that when I was about seven, one of my friends told me that babies came when parents went to the market together, so every week I begged my father to go with Mother when she went to Market Street, but he never would."

Teresa chuckled softly. "Did you ever tell him why you wanted him to go?"

"No, but I did tell Mother."

"What did she say?"

"Nothing. She kissed me on the forehead and laughed until she had tears in her eyes."

Teresa enjoyed the story. "For all it's worth, when I was growing up you could have had any of my siblings. Take your pick. Being the only girl, the boys went out of their way to make my life miserable."

"How many brothers do you have?"

"Four. The twins, Neily and Shafts—short for Two Shafts—then there's Harp—that's short for Harper— he owns a saloon up in Montana, and Diego, the youngest of the boys. No one knows where Diego is—if he's living or with the Ancestors. Been a decade since we saw him last." Her voice trailed off as she thought about the brother she loved the best. "He and my pa got into an argument one night, and Diego jumped on his horse and rode away. Never came back."

"I didn't mean to stir up sad memories."

She shook her head. "It's okay. Just wonder about him, that's all. He and I were closest because we were the babies. Miss him something powerful even after all these years."

Once again Madison had to readjust his preconceived notions about her. When they first met, he was so intent upon being disapproving, it never occurred to him that beneath the dangerous reputation might dwell a woman with feelings. The cold-eyed outlaw portrayed in the press did not mesh with the striking ebony temptress seated across the table. He was pleased to be learning the truth.

Their dinner arrived, and while the waiter put down all the plates, glasses, and covered dishes containing their food, Teresa contemplated Madison. Who knew that when she walked out of the penitentiary she'd wind up here, having dinner with a man like him? In her former life, men like him were strictly prey, because he looked like he'd have a fat money belt. Instead, he'd turned into a companion, and their day together had been memorable. During their tour of the city, she'd asked him a hundred questions or more, and he patiently answered them all, never once making her feel dumb or uneducated. He'd been kind and considerate, something she never would have believed him capable of the day she first met him in his mother's library.

"Penny for your thoughts," he asked.

"Just thinking about how well you and I seem to be getting along."

He looked into her eyes. "Are we?"

"Yes."

"Then let's try and make it last for a while."

She nodded. "I'm in."

They began the meal. The late evening had by then melted into night, the darkness in the restaurant held back by the soft glow of gas lamps in the sconces on the walls.

Madison had another question. "Did you leave a beau behind out West?"

"Heavens no. Me? A beau?" She shook her head. "The closest I ever got to a beau was on those rare nights I needed an itch scratched. Once it was done,

I pulled on my leathers and went on my way."

Madison spit wine and grabbed up his napkin.

Chagrined, Teresa said, "I wasn't supposed to say that, was I?"

"No," he said, wiping his mouth and eyeing her with a mixture of disbelief and humor. Recovered, he asked, "Those *rare* nights weren't really that passionless, were they?"

She forked up a piece of the succulent chicken and shrugged. "It's an itch. Passion doesn't have anything to do with it."

Madison paused and assessed her for a moment. "Is that really what you believe?"

"Sure." When she noticed the puzzlement in his gaze, she asked, "What's the matter?"

"If this is too personal a question, you may sock me, but have you ever had a man make love to you, and I mean truly make love to you."

Her brow furrowed. "If you're asking me that, then I guess my answer is no."

The male in him was delighted. "Really?"

"You sound like a pleased mountain lion."

He moved his vision over her slowly, taking in the succulent mouth, the vibrant eyes, and asked with a hush, "You've never had a man take his time kissing his way across your skin, touching you here or there while your breath stacked up in your throat?"

Teresa swallowed.

"Never had a man give you more pleasure than you could hold, then have him pleasure you again, and again?"

Her eyes slid closed for a long second. "No."

Beneath the table, Madison was hard as granite.

He wanted to do to her exactly what he'd described because he already knew how fervently she'd respond. To learn that she'd never been properly loved only added more fuel to an inner fire that had been rising since the first day they met.

Teresa wasn't sure how she'd ended up in this conversation, but her tightened nipples and awakened core were making it difficult to focus. "I suppose you'd like to be the one to show me what you mean?"

"I'm not going to lie, of course I would, but that isn't why I asked. Your answer was so unexpected, I was simply curious."

"I see." He looked cool as a fall rain, but Teresa knew better. His desire was plain, and it was kindling her own.

For the rest of the meal, the subtle heat between them rose. Every time she looked up, his eyes were waiting for her, silently tempting her to come out and play. She resisted as best she could because she instinctively knew that if she allowed him to show her the passion he'd talked about, she'd never be the same, but the thirsty woman inside her stood up and questioned her stance once again. That inner woman didn't care about ramifications or repercussions, real or imagined. She wanted to *know*.

"So, where do you want to go?"

Madison eyed her over his raised wine goblet. "Go?"

"If I was back home, we'd meet behind a building or find a barn somewhere."

He stared. "What are you talking about?"

"This passion thing. I want to try it."

He set his goblet down. "You want to try it," he echoed skeptically.

She nodded. "Yeah. You can get your itch for me out of your system, I can get mine out of my system, and we can go on about our business."

Madison was floored. "Teresa, making love is not—" He stopped because he didn't know what to say. "A barn? Really?"

"Why pay for a room? For the little bit of time it took, it never made sense."

Speechless, he sat back against his chair.

"What?"

He shook his head. "Just amazed. Behind a building? Teresa, you are worth so much more than that. A woman like you—I'd make love to you until sunrise."

"Why? It takes five minutes, tops."

He dropped his head and chuckled softly.

"What, Madison?"

"Nothing. Tell you what," he said quietly. "How about we go back to Mother's and sit out in the gazebo and talk about this."

Teresa shrugged. "Sure."

"Are you done eating?"

"Yep. It was very good. Thanks for bringing me."

"You're welcome."

On the ride back to Mrs. Nance's through the dark streets of the Seventh Ward, Teresa looked his way. *I'd make love to you until sunrise.* Had he been serious? She could count the number of times she'd been with a man on the fingers of one hand, and none of those encounters had lasted until sunrise. The longest might have been fifteen minutes. Invariably, at the start, she'd be as hot as a mare for a stallion, but somewhere in the middle of the act the man would be so busy puffing and rutting, she'd lose interest and wind up just lying there until he finished. Sunrise? If Nance took that long with a woman, did it mean he didn't know what he was doing? She couldn't see that being the case, so why talk about sunrise? She supposed she'd have to wait until they got back to the gazebo for an answer, but sunrise? She didn't understand it at all.

Mrs. Nance greeted them upon their return. "Did you enjoy yourselves?"

"We did," Teresa told her.

"There's cake in the kitchen if you didn't have dessert. Me, I'm going to bed. Madison, please lock the door behind you when you leave."

"I will. Pleasant dreams."

She smiled and left them alone.

In the silence that descended over the room, Teresa felt the heat simmering in his eyes touching her, stroking her. "Do you want cake?"

"Not really. You?"

She shook her head.

Madison knew what he did want. "Then come outside with me."

Teresa sensed that agreeing would open a door she might not be able to close again, but having been fearless her entire life, she nodded.

It was a warm night as they walked side by side to the gazebo. The breeze played across her face and whipped at the fabric of her skirt. The heat and wind reminded her of nights back home, nights too hot to sleep when she'd jump on Cloud and ride. Her yearning for home rose with such swift sharpness, she forced it back down and looked up at the stars and moon instead.

Inside of the gazebo's latticed walls they took a seat on the stone bench. His presence beside her was as vivid as the wind and the nocturnal symphony of the crickets playing around them. She gave him a quick glance, not sure what she was supposed to do.

Madison reached out and gently lifted her chin so he could see her features in the moonlight. Into view came the eyes and the curve of her lips. Lowering his head, he brushed his lips across hers. "You're a beautiful woman, Angel," he husked out. "Don't ever let a man treat you as if you're not."

He kissed her then, and the intensity spread through her like a slow tide of fire. Until meeting him, she'd no idea kisses could be this powerful or the sensations so overwhelming. As the passion rose and the kissing intensified, she slid her hand to the back of his neck to bring him closer. He complied, increasing the play of his mouth on hers; teasing her, wooing her, gathering her against him. They relished the contact of their flush bodies just as much as they did the tastes of each other.

He left her mouth to blaze a trail of kisses over the shell of her ear and husked out, " I want to touch you, Teresa … "

Her body rippled in response to the heated plea, and when his hand toured slowly over her thin blouse to caress the breasts beneath, she groaned with a reaction fed by delight. *"Dios."*

Smiling, he kissed her full mouth again, nibbling her succulent bottom lip, all the while knowing this one night wouldn't be long enough to love her the way he desired; no night would ever be. "This is passion," he whispered while his experienced hands plied her nipples and made her draw in ragged breaths. "And this is passion ... " Leaning her back against the bench, he nibbled at the tightened buds through the fabric of her blouse. Her body arched like a Seminole bow and the sensations pierced her with arrows of desire.

Teresa didn't care that he was opening her blouse, and in her present state would have gladly assisted him, except she couldn't summon the mental ability to remember how. The fog of desire was so enveloping, the only thing she knew for sure was that he definitely did know what he was doing, and that she was damn glad. The blouse lay in open halves, and he put his hot mouth against the vee of her breasts then blazed a trail over the lace of her camisole. The feel of the night breeze on her bared throat competed with the heat of his breath and kisses, and he won hands down.

"This is passion," he echoed as he pulled down the top of her camisole and circled his tongue around her berried nipple until her gasps of pleasure sounded loud in her ears. The circling and tonguing, enhanced by his plucking fingers, followed by his bold sucking, turned her gasps into responsive groans, and no, she'd never had a man love her this way. *Ever.*

Madison thought her nipples as tempting as pieces of sensual candy, and he strove to draw as much sweetness from each tight dark morsel as he could.

The male in him wanted to open his trousers, free his manhood, and place her atop it now, but he wouldn't, not tonight. Without protection he'd undoubtedly get her with child, so he'd have to be content with tonguing her, sucking her, and touching her instead.

The sight of her bared breasts in the shadowy moonlight made him so hard he brushed his mouth over them, saying, "After tonight, your nipples will harden every time I look at you."

Teresa didn't doubt the boast. She was on fire. Her hips were rising and her core was damp and pulsing. His kisses were like manna from heaven, and his hands—moving purposefully over her back and bared breasts—divine. When his palm moved down and began to glide over her skirt-covered thighs, her head dropped back and he placed kisses on her bowed throat. She didn't protest when her skirt began inching up. The warmth of his touch against the skin of her thigh made her suck in her breath. She felt storm-tossed and disconnected from everything around her except him, and because she was so new to both passion and a man who adored her, when he slipped his caresses lower and eased his fingers against that damp and pulsating spot, she came with a long cry. The orgasm buckled her and swept her up. He covered her vocal reaction with his mouth, savored the kiss-swollen lips while his fingers continued their lazy dallying.

The orgasm impeded her vision and her sense of place. She knew she was outside in the night air and that he'd just treated her to the most sensual experience of her life, but that was all. In reality, it didn't matter; only her pleasure did. "You're real good at this," she admitted softly, "damn good, but then you already know that."

The soft smile on his face answered her question, and she leaned up and kissed him without shame. "Again, please ... "

"Yes, ma'am." Delighted, Madison knew he would pleasure her a hundred times and more if she asked, so he recaptured her mouth and showed her just how happy he was to oblige. Humid kisses were joined by exploring hands that readied her nipples for more conquering and teased the honeyed gate between her thighs. Her skirt was rucked up around her waist and she parted her legs willingly to the heated palms moving so boldly over her drawers. He dragged them down, and she lifted her hips to facilitate their removal. He set them aside and her legs were scandalously bare to the night wind and his sensual explorations. Madison teased the wet flesh at her core, and she groaned, then purred and let him do whatever pleased him because she and that woman inside her had become one. Now, she understood *sunrise*. Now, she knew what it meant to have a man kiss his way across her skin so slowly and expertly the breath stacked up in her throat, and how it felt to have her nipples inside of his mouth and his fingers inside.

"*Dios,*" she husked out again in response to his long-boned fingers entering her flesh. If he pleasured her until summer's end, she'd wantonly want more, more kisses on her lips, more of his mouth surrounding her nipples, more of his fingers ... "Oh," she groaned heatedly.

The fingers impaling her so wickedly were moving with a lazy, delicious rhythm that made her hips rise in responsive tempo. She felt like an exotic instrument that only he could play. He knew just how to coax her into crooning and sighing, knew how to keep her nipples ripe, while his fingers continued to guide her body in the ancient dance of lust.

"Think how it will be when it's me filling you instead of my hands," he said. "Sunrise won't be long enough."

She came again, keening and twisting and not caring how she looked, or that she was slippery with her own essence. Her being was centered on the sensations rattling her from head to toe and on the man with his hand between her thighs.

Madison wanted her like a condemned man wanting a reprieve. His manhood was demanding completion, but he reminded himself that it couldn't be. She didn't need an unexpected child and neither did he. A younger Madison would have thrown caution to the wind and played the percentages, but he was too old for that now. Were she to become pregnant, his honor would demand that they marry for the good of the babe, and that had disaster written all over it. So even as he watched her respond to the fading orgasm, he fought down the overwhelming urge to replace his fingers with something harder and far more substantial.

When he withdrew his fingers and gently brushed the coat of dampness against the fabric of her rucked-up skirt, she sighed with a pleasure tinged by satisfaction. Leaning down, he put his mouth to hers then righted her camisole and skirt. He then did up the buttons on her blouse.

He was nearly finished by the time she came back to herself. "What are you doing?' she asked softly.

"Buttoning you up again."

"But, aren't we—"

"No."

"Why not?"

"Because I'm not ready to be a father."

"Oh."

He smiled at her in the dark. "So, did you enjoy the passion thing?"

"You know I did," she replied without shame. He'd made her see stars. "Now, I understand what you meant during dinner, and you're right about sunrise not being long enough."

Madison liked hearing that. He did his best to ignore the way he ached for her, though it was difficult. Lord, she was passionate. Uninhibited too, to his delight. She was more responsive than he ever imagined.

Teresa leaned up and kissed him sweetly. "Can you be prepared next time?" She wanted all of him, and she didn't care how unladylike that made her be.

"Next time?" he asked, running a worshipping finger down her night-shrouded cheek. "There's going to be a next time?"

"Oh yes," she whispered confidently. "I don't think there's any question."

He chuckled, "You're right. There will be, and as soon as you'd like, but let's make it in a bed."

A clap of thunder broke the silence and the wind picked up. A storm was rolling in. They ignored it for the time being; kissing each other was far more important. "Guess we should go," he eventually told her softly.

Teresa didn't want to. She wanted the kisses and his loving to have no end. "Guess so."

He took her hand and led her across the grass for the return walk to the back porch and inside the house. They walked to the front door. In the echoing dark silence of the house, they heard the thunder sound again. Madison gently pulled her against him one more time because he couldn't get enough. He looked down into her sparkling midnight eyes. "Good night, angel."

Their final kiss was filled with the wild sweet passion they both felt. "'Night, Madison."

With one last look back at him standing in the darkness, Teresa departed and floated up the stairs to her room.

Chapter 9

Teresa awakened the next morning to dark clouds and the sound of raindrops hitting the windows. Her thoughts slid back to last night and her body echoed with the remembering. Madison had a touch as magical as a shaman's and the double barrel orgasms he'd wrung from her were vivid proof of his skill. She could only imagine the heights he would have taken her to had he been prepared to complete their tryst. Shaking her head at her shamelessness, she placed the blame for her outrageous musings at Madison's door, then left the bed to wash up and head downstairs to breakfast.

When Teresa walked by the parlor on her way to the dining room, she saw a White man she'd never seen before sitting and talking with Mrs. Nance. Not wanting to disturb them, she tried to tiptoe by without being seen, but upon hearing Mrs. Nance call her name, she stuck her head in the door. "Yes, ma'am?"

"Teresa, this is Mr. Singleton from the state's Prison Board."

She nodded his way. "Good morning." She hoped her inner wariness wasn't reflected in her tone. She supposed she shouldn't be surprised by the visitor's presence, Mrs. Nance had warned her that a person from the board might come around to check on her progress. That he might be here because the board wanted to reverse her release was the first thing that came to mind, though. Taking a deep breath to calm herself, she waited for him to speak.

"Come in and take a seat," he said.

The gray-haired man's chilly blue eyes revealed nothing. Casting a quick glance at Mrs. Nance, she took a seat.

"I'm here to evaluate your progress," he stated. "How are you and Mrs. Nance faring?"

"Fine. At least I think so."

She looked to Molly, who said, "I'm pleased to have Teresa here."

The man was writing on some papers. He asked gruffly, "No inappropriate behavior or language?"

Molly replied, "No."

"Any problems with morals?"

"None."

"Liquor?" His eyes speared Teresa.

"No."

"Has she had any contact with people you'd consider bad influences?"

"No."

He continued writing, then looked up and fixed his gaze on Teresa again. "Being treated well?"

"Yes, sir. Very well."

"What kind of things are you learning that'll keep you from turning back to crime?"

Teresa was glad she had an answer. "I can sew now. I also know how to run a household and use modern appliances. Mrs. Nance lets me read the morning newspaper to her, so I know what's going on in the world. I attend church at Mother Bethel, and volunteer there too." It was impossible for her to tell if her answers met with his approval or not.

"You know that any trouble will send you back."

She nodded. "The warden warned me the day I was released."

"Make sure you remember." Gathering up his papers, he stood. "Thank you, Mrs. Nance."

"I'll show you to the door."

Before exiting, he sent Teresa one last chilling look, then followed Mrs. Nance out of the room.

When Molly returned, Teresa drawled, "That was fun. Got the feeling that if I hadn't rattled off all that stuff you made me learn, I'd be on my way back."

"He was rather brusque."

"Knowing he's the one looking over my shoulder will definitely keep me on the straight and narrow." She could still feel his cold stare.

"Whatever it takes, dear. I told you all that lady stuff would come in handy."

Teresa agreed up to a point. She still thought learning to arrange flowers was a waste of time, but Mrs. Nance had insisted on her mastering that art as well. "How often do you think he's going to come around?"

"In the past, the parole board agents used to come every two weeks, but now they are so overworked and underpaid, we may see him again in a month's time or never see him again."

"I vote for the latter."

"Don't much blame you, but either way, your rehabilitation is coming along just fine. You're well on your way to becoming a lady."

Teresa wasn't sure she liked hearing that, but she appreciated the praise.

"I was praying you weren't wearing your leathers when I heard you in the hall. Had you not been properly dressed he might have held that against you."

Teresa blessed her skirt for the very first time. "Then I'm glad I was too. Not because of me but because I wouldn't want my actions to reflect badly on you for anything in the world."

"I appreciate that, Teresa."

"You're welcome."

Thunder boomed outside. It had been raining since last night.

"Doesn't look like there'll be any riding this morning," Mrs. Nance said.

"I know." Teresa was disappointed. She'd been looking forward to saddling up Hannibal. "Maybe tomorrow. Have you eaten?"

"No. I was just getting my coffee when Mr. Singleton arrived. Shall we go into the dining room?"

A thought occurred to Teresa then. What happened to her drawers last night after Madison removed them? She didn't remember having them on, or in hand when she went to bed last night. *Dios! Are they still outside!*

"Are you all right, dear?"

Teresa's attention snapped back to Mrs. Nance. "Um, yes, ma'am. I was daydreaming somewhere again, I guess."

"You sure? You looked ill for a moment."

"I'm fine."

Mrs. Nance didn't appear convinced but didn't press the matter.

Following her to the dining room, Teresa looked out of the windows at the pouring rain and prayed she'd have a chance to go out and search the area by the gazebo before someone else found them.

Last night, Madison had driven halfway home when he remembered that Teresa's drawers had been left on the ground in the gazebo. Turning the buggy around, he'd quickly driven back to retrieve them. Now, with his morning cup of coffee in hand, he glanced over at them folded neatly on the fireplace mantel in his bedroom. What a woman. Just thinking back made his manhood rise, and neither it nor he could wait to take her fully.

Banishing thoughts of her and her tempting loveliness for a moment, he swung his mind back to another interesting encounter he'd had last night. A few hours after his return home, Ben had stopped by. Accompanying him had been a young woman he'd introduced as Charlotte Richards—Dawson Richards's wife and the mother of his children. Madison had been surprised to say the least. Ben learned of the woman's existence through contacts he had in New Orleans. Madison had hoped the feelers Ben said he would put out on Richards would produce fruit, but he never imagined anything as damning as a wife and children, especially not a wife and children Richards had deserted. According to her story, before being approached in New Orleans by Ben's friends, she'd no idea where her husband was residing or if he was even alive. He'd left Louisiana two and a half years ago to look for work, promised to write, give her his location as soon as he settled, and send money for her and his children. She never heard from him again.

Madison took a sip of his coffee while the rain continued to come down outside and shook his head over Richards's shabby treatment of his family. While his wife and children were struggling to make ends meet, Richards was in Philadelphia getting fat on bribes and living in a mansion like a Medici prince.

Getting up, he walked to the window and looked out at the gray day. With his blessing, Ben planned to arrange legal representation for Richards's wife. She'd come north with her marriage certificate and the certificates that documented the births of the Richards children so there would be no question as to the validity of her claim. As far as Madison could tell, Dawson Richards had two choices. He could pay Charlotte to go away and remain silent, but considering how furious the woman had been upon hearing how her husband now made his living, Richards would be lucky to have carfare left when she finished suing him for abandonment. Or the ward boss could opt for the second choice—meet her in court and risk airing his dirty laundry for the whole city to see. Madison smiled. Either way, Richards was damned. The Republican Party certainly wasn't going to applaud when news of Charlotte's existence came to light. Hopefully, they'd toss him over for someone with a cleaner reputation.

To set that process in motion, Madison gave Ben the name of an old friend who could duplicate Charlotte's documents. The man had served time for forgery. Although he had gone to jail and paid his debt to society, he could be counted on to produce quality copies of whatever one needed. Even better, he was discreet.

As soon as the copies were completed and the originals placed in a bank vault Ben kept downtown, Madison planned to mail one set of documents to the party and the other to the local newspapers.

Madison set his cup down and stepped onto the balcony. The spray of the rain brushed his face, but it was a warm muggy day and the rain was warm as well. The arsonist they were hunting hadn't been found yet, but the search was ongoing. With all of the merchants in the area asking questions, and with his and Ben's people doing the same, Madison knew it wouldn't be long now, unless the person had left town. At the last meeting of the association, the members had voted to offer a reward to anyone who came forward with information that led to an arrest. He hoped that would up the pressure.

In the meantime, he could do nothing but wait, wait, and think of Teresa. He went back inside, left the door open to catch the breeze, and walked to his closet to get dressed and start the second day of his holiday from work.

As he made final adjustments to his tie in the mirror, his attention strayed to Teresa's folded drawers lying so innocently on his mantel. Grinning at the prospect of returning them to her for a most sensual price, he gave his short-cut hair a quick brushing then left the house.

He didn't get far. Standing by his carriage under an umbrella held by a drenched but ape-sized underling in a shabby coat was Dawson Richards. "'Morning, Nance."

From under his own umbrella Madison returned the greeting, adding, "What can I do for you, Richards?"

The ward boss flashed his predator smile. "I'm growing impatient with your continued refusals to support the party."

"And?"

"So, I've decided to push you a bit."

Madison waited silently.

"What would your bank customers say if they knew one of the country's most violent criminals was within a hand's reach of their hard-earned deposits?"

Madison held his temper in check. "And this violent criminal would be whom?"

"Don't play ignorant, Nance, it's beneath both of us. You know that there's little going on in the ward that escapes me. And if something does, I have friends downtown to alert me."

"So, what are you proposing?" Madison had no intentions of capitulating, and how Richards found out about Teresa didn't matter now that the cat was out of the bag. What did matter was that Madison didn't care if every bank customer on his ledgers withdrew their funds. No way would he lend his name or influence to further Richards's corrupt ambitions.

"I'm proposing that you come out in support of me for City Council and I'll keep quiet about Miss July. I assume that was her with you at Watson's."

"Assume whatever you like, Richards, but the answer is still no. You'll have to excuse me. I'm late."

The ape with the umbrella made a move to step forward, but the pistol suddenly in Madison's hand

and aimed at his large chest made the big man blink, then stop.

"Are you going to let me pass or do I shoot your boss?"

Richards's eyes widened with alarm, then he calmed himself. "You wouldn't shoot me on a public street."

"You sure of that?" Madison waited. The gun never wavered.

Richards saw the calm purpose in Madison's eyes and he growled. "Let him pass."

"Thank you."

"This isn't the end, Nance," Richards threatened. "I'm sure the newspapers will be interested in knowing there's a criminal in their midst."

Madison thought about Charlotte Richards. "I'm sure they will."

Without a further word, he got into his carriage and directed his horse up the street without looking back.

When Madison had been an adolescent, Harold and Daphne Carter moved to the Thirtieth Ward, where the residents were far removed both socially and economically from their racial brethren in the Fifth and Seventh wards. The houses there were grander, and not interspersed with political clubs, loitering men, or gaming houses. These were the homes of what researcher W.E.B. Dubois called the race's "Talented Tenth."

Madison left his horse and buggy at the curb and went to the door. The Carters' blond maid, a recent Swedish immigrant, ushered him in and directed him to the parlor while she went to get her employers.

Madison had asked her to announce him to both Carter and his wife. Only because of his father's ties to Harold had Madison come, otherwise he wouldn't have cared beans about Paula and Dawson Richards, but the men had been friends, and Madison saw it as his duty to share what he'd learned about Richards's Louisiana past.

The Carters entered the parlor with the hard-eyed Paula in tow. He stood out of respect and shook Mr. Carter's hand while the ladies took seats.

Harold, gray-haired and thin, asked, "What brings you here, Madison? Though it's always good to see you."

"I've come about Dawson Richards being out with Paula."

"Dawson is a fine man," Paula stated haughtily.

"He's also married."

Daphne Carter, wearing yet another too snug gown, shouted, "What!"

"I've met her and seen her marriage certificate."

Paula snapped, "You're lying. You're just trying to stir the pot. You don't want me, but you don't want anyone else to have me either."

"That's not true."

Harold said to his niece, "Now, Paula—"

Daphne didn't look as if she believed Madison either. "Dawson is one of the most prominent men in Philadelphia. If he was married, the papers would have said so."

"In a few days they probably will."

"I refuse to believe it," she snapped. "This is nothing more than sour grapes on your part, Madison Nance."

He ignored her tirade and directed his words to her husband. "Because you were my father's friend, I felt it was my duty to tell you the truth. If you choose not to believe me, that's your choice, but I've met my obligation. I'll leave you all to your day. Thank you for seeing me."

Madison made his departure and walked back out into the rain. He figured Paula would run and tell Richards about his visit first thing, and that suited him just fine. On the heels of the encounter by the bank, he was certain Richards thought he had him by the short hairs, but the ward boss now had problems of his own.

By late morning it had stopped raining and Teresa was walking around the parlor, balancing a book on her head. It was one of the items on Mrs. Nance's list. She wanted Teresa to not only talk like a lady but to walk like a lady as well. Teresa, on the other hand, liked her walk just the way it was, but in order not to hurt the woman's feelings, she played along.

Molly asked, "Can you waltz, Teresa?"

Teresa turned her head so quickly the book plummeted to the floor. She stooped to pick it up. "No, ma'am."

"We must get you some lessons. If you're going to be the belle of the ball this autumn, you have to be prepared."

"Belle of what ball?"

"Many of the associations have their anniversaries and fund-raising balls in the fall, and it will be good practice for you to attend a few of them."

"Why? There's no call for waltzing where I hail from."

"Who says you have to go back out West? You may find a compelling reason to stay here in Philadelphia."

Teresa shook her head. "That won't happen."

"You sound so sure."

"I am. There's too much noise and too many people. You can't see the sky for the buildings. There are no tortillas or mescal. You can only ride horses outside the city. I won't be staying. That's a promise."

"Oh."

Teresa heard her dejected tone and sighed in response. "I'm not trying to hurt your feelings. You're one of the best things that's ever happened to me, but my life is on the other side of the Mississippi, and that's where I'll be heading soon as I'm allowed. I'm sorry."

"You have no reason to apologize. I was just hoping ... "

Teresa saw the melancholy smile. "I was born under an open sky. Plan to be buried that way. I'm okay with not being able to rob trains anymore, but if I stay here, I'll shrivel up and die."

Molly nodded solemnly. "I understand. I won't broach that subject again, but I will not give up on sanding down those rough edges of yours. You are a beautiful, smart woman, and you should have the poise and grace to go with it."

"If you say so."

"I do," Molly stated firmly. "So, place that volume on your head. Shoulders back. Begin."

Teresa resumed her walk around the parlor. When the door pull sounded, she said, "I'll get it." With the book perfectly balanced, she walked very gingerly to the door. Bending slowly, she grasped the cut glass knob and opened the door.

Madison took one look at the book on her head and said softly, "I'm told you're missing a pair of drawers."

Teresa's book hit the floor. Retrieving it, she cut him a look. "You are incorrigible, do you know that? And yes, I am missing those drawers. Do you have them?" She had never asked a man if he had her drawers in his possession, and it made her feel strangely heady inside.

"I got halfway home last night and suddenly remembered where you'd left them."

"Where *I* left them."

"Yes, you."

His eyes were working her over something fierce. Seeing him made the day seem suddenly brighter, and as he continued to hold her gaze, last night came back in all its lusty glory. The memory made her nipples tighten in response, just as he'd boasted they would. "So, do you know where they are?"

"On the mantel in my bedroom."

Her knees went weak, and as if he knew that, his mustache lifted teasingly. "Figured better there than in the grass by the gazebo. I can't imagine how you'd explain their presence to Emma or my mother."

Teresa couldn't either.

Molly walked out to the foyer then, and upon seeing her son, a smile crossed her face. "Why, Madison. Hello."

"Hello, Mother. How are you?" He prayed she hadn't heard anything.

"Fine. Come on in. I was just telling Teresa about the fall balls."

Madison saw Teresa roll her eyes in response. "Are you planning on attending?" he asked her.

"Your mother thinks I am, so I guess the answer is yes."

"Do you need an escort?"

Molly said, "Why, that's a fabulous idea, thank you, Madison."

Teresa noted that she hadn't agreed to have him as an escort, but thought the idea a good one too.

They all went to the parlor and took seats.

Molly said to Madison, "How's the day been so far?"

He shrugged. "I stopped by to see the Carters."

"Whatever for?"

"Dawson Richards is squiring Paula Wade around town."

"Is Daphne that desperate to find the girl a husband that she'd entertain that scoundrel as a candidate?"

"Apparently, but after learning Richards is married, she may change her mind."

"Married?" a shocked Molly said. "To whom?"

He took a few moments to tell her the story.

When he finished Molly shook her head. "What a dastardly deed. Three children, too? Now that's going to feed the gossip mills. Maybe the scandal will make him resign."

"I'm hoping so. He's been involved in some pretty shady doings around town recently, and it would be nice if he could be brought down."

Teresa asked, "What exactly does he do?"

Molly replied, "Besides supporting the criminal element, not much."

Madison smiled at his mother's assessment. "He's a ward boss for the Republicans, which means he's responsible for getting the vote out on election day."

Molly said, "By bribing and bringing in wagons filled with people who don't live in the ward. In some of the poorer areas he and his hooligans buy votes with dollars, whiskey, and even cigars."

"Is that legal?"

"Of course not, but it's how politics are conducted these days, no matter the race, party, or city for that matter."

Madison further explained, "The few civil jobs available to us are only given to those who are loyal to the party. Granted, some of the men are qualified, but they sold their souls to obtain the positions."

Molly added, "No one minds any member of the race getting ahead, but we do mind the criminal element that tags along."

"Meaning?" Teresa asked.

Molly said, "Most of the loiterers you see in the doorways and in front of the political clubs are on the party's payroll. When there's no election, they have no money, so they commit crimes. But as soon as one of them is arrested, their bosses—like Richards—come down and immediately post their bail. Few if any are ever convicted."

"And this is the man who was at the restaurant yesterday?" Teresa asked Madison. "The one who wanted us to come to his dance?"

"Yes."

Teresa knew he was a snake, but now had an

idea of just how low to the ground he slithered.

Molly shook her head. "And apparently he's calling on Paula Wade. I hope Harold will put his foot down. I don't like Daphne at all, but Harold is another matter. He and Reynolds were best friends. I'd hate to have him gossiped about."

"Which is why I went to tell them about Richards' wife," Madison said.

"How did they respond?" Molly asked.

"Not well. Paula accused me of not wanting any other man to have her."

"She's as silly as she is pretentious," Molly declared. "I hope that aunt of hers will come to her senses, but I wouldn't count on it. Are you still on holiday?"

"I am. All week."

"Good, because tomorrow Emma and I are going to Cleveland to see my cousin Willa. We'll return Saturday evening. I spoke to the parole board representative this morning. Teresa's not allowed to leave the state, but Mr. Singleton said as long as Teresa is monitored by someone trustworthy, he saw no reason why I can't go for a visit."

Teresa stared. Mrs. Nance hadn't mentioned making a side deal.

Madison made her back up. "The parole board agent came by? Why?" He assumed the board hadn't decided to rescind Teresa's parole, otherwise his mother would be upset.

"Yes. A Mr. Singleton. He came over to make sure Teresa was still on her rehabilitation path. He wasn't very friendly, but after she relayed all of the things she's accomplished, he seemed satisfied and left."

Madison was confused. "What things?"

"Things like sewing," Teresa said, "volunteering at the church. I left out the table setting and flower arranging."

He was pleasantly surprised.

His mother said, "Don't tell me you haven't noticed how refined she's becoming."

Madison had to admit he'd been too busy being bowled over by her beauty and her kisses to pay much attention to the results of his mother's tutoring. He supposed he was in danger of losing the five eagles riding on their bet, but he didn't really care.

"Now, Madison, if you have other plans this week, I can delay my visit. I just thought that with you being off it would be the perfect time for me to visit for a few days."

Madison was holding Teresa's eyes. "No. No plans." He got the distinct impression that his mother was playing matchmaker.

She turned Teresa's way. "You don't mind Madison looking in on you while I'm gone?"

"No, ma'am." Teresa sensed Molly was starting to name her grandchildren again. Apparently, they were going to have to revisit the subject. However, her leaving for Cleveland would allow her and Madison a good two and a half days to take care of the business they weren't able to complete last night. His heated gaze said he'd come to the same conclusion, and her nipples tightened in response once more.

"Then it's settled," a pleased Molly pronounced. "Madison, if you could get us to the station in time for the eight o clock train, that would be wonderful."

"I'll be here."

His mother smiled and stood. "I'm going to tell Emma to start packing, and I'm heading upstairs to do the same. Do me one last favor?" she said to her son.

"What is it?"

"Give Teresa waltzing lessons while I'm away. It's on her list of things to learn."

Teresa folded her arms. Her silent response spoke volumes.

Madison saw her reaction and smiled. "With pleasure."

Molly left them to take care of her preparations for the trip, and once they were alone, Teresa asked him, "Is it just me, or is your mother trying to hitch us together?"

"I think she's playing matchmaker too."

"We both know that isn't going to happen, correct?"

"Correct."

"I don't need any ties, and neither do you. Just as soon as my parole is over I'm heading west."

The idea of her leaving disturbed him, especially if he was destined to never see her again, but he knew any attempts to talk her into staying would be fruitless. "With that understanding, what would you like to do tomorrow?"

"Other than go riding at the Constantines', I've no idea. How about you decide."

"Okay." What he wanted most was to take her home and spend the next three days initiating her fully into what she called "that passion thing." After last night's vivid sample, he was finding it difficult to keep from dragging her to him and kissing her until she whispered *"Dios."* Pleased that he'd have her all to himself, he waggled his eyebrows playfully. "I'm sure I can come up with something entertaining for us to do."

"I'm sure you can."

In their eyes were embers of last's night's heated tryst. Teresa could still feel his kisses on her skin, and Madison's memory lingered on the beguiling sight of her half naked in the moonlight.

"You're making me warm looking at me that way."

"Good," he told her, his eyes glittering with desire. "Until Mother returns from her trip, making you warm is going to be one of my major goals."

Teresa's eyes closed in response to his sensual boast. "You're real good at this passion thing."

"Yes I am."

"Modest too." Her blood was racing and the warmth was slowly spreading through her senses.

Emma entered the parlor then. "Teresa, there's a man at the back door. Says he's from a newspaper in Kansas. Wants to talk to you."

Shaking off her Madison-induced spell, Teresa asked with confusion, "From Kansas?"

"That's what he said."

She looked to Madison. He shrugged.

"Okay," she said. "I'll bite."

She threw Madison a puzzled look before she left the room, but he threw her a bold wink in response, making her warm all over again.

Chapter 10

Teresa stepped out onto the back porch. The eager face of the young man from Kansas looked very familiar, but placing him was a different matter.

"Hello, Miss July," he gushed, eyes bright, sounding as if he were having difficulty containing his excitement.

"Hello," she replied kindly. "I know we've met somewhere before. I just don't remember where."

"Henry Adams, Kansas. Name's Tom Kelly. I interviewed you for the *Nicodemus Cyclone* after that big shootout with the bounty hunters at the Liberian Lady saloon in Henry Adams, a few years back."

"I remember now. How are you?"

"Much better now that I've found you. I came all the way to Philadelphia just to see you."

Teresa could see Molly, Madison, and Emma crowded in the doorway, listening. "How'd you know I was here?" she asked.

"Once you sent that wire to your sister-in-law saying you'd been released, the news spread through the Great Solomon Valley like wildfire. Letter to the parole board took care of the rest. Told them I wanted to use you as an example for a story I was writing on how crime doesn't pay."

"Excuse me?"

"No, no," he said hastily, seeing the challenge in her eyes. "That's not what I'm really going to write about. I lied to them because I didn't think they'd give me your whereabouts if I said folks back home just wanted to hear how you were doing."

Teresa was touched. "Folks have been asking after me?"

"They have. You cast a mighty long shadow for a lot of years. You and your brothers kept folks entertained with your exploits. Would you mind if I asked you some questions? I promise not to take up a lot of your time."

"Not at all." She turned to Mrs. Nance. "Can we use the parlor?"

"Of course."

Teresa knew the press would find her sooner or later, so a newspaper from back home might as well get in the first shot.

For the next hour, she and Tom Kelly sat in the parlor talking, laughing, and talking some more. He brought her up to date on some of her old companions and acquaintances.

"Cherokee Bill's in jail at Fort Smith," he said. "He tried to break out a few weeks back and a guard was killed. Word is he's going to hang."

Teresa shook her head. "What about Tom Root and Buss Luckey?" Years ago she had ridden with the two Black outlaws in a gang headed by a White man named Nathaniel "Texas Jack" Reed.

"Far as I know, they're in jail at Fort Smith, Arkansas, too. They robbed a train down in Indian Territory last November and a deputy was killed when the law tried to apprehend them."

"Judge Parker still around?"

He nodded. "Heard he's not well, but his court is about to be dissolved. Rumor has it he's pardoning most of the people he locked up. Cherokee Bill's trial may be one of his last."

Teresa didn't see herself being pardoned. Parker had sent her to prison to teach her a lesson. She wondered how many outlaws, criminals, and bank robbers Hanging Judge Isaac Parker had seen in his life on the bench. Too many probably. Members of her family were included in those numbers. "Have you seen my brother Neil or my sister-in-law Olivia?"

"Your brother's been working for the trains out in California. Came home about a month ago. Saw your sister-in-law just before I left." He reached into the inside pocket of his suit coat. "She asked me to deliver this letter."

Tears stung her eyes as she took the envelope from his hand. "Thanks. Is she well?"

He nodded. "And still mayor. Got herself reelected a few weeks back."

Teresa thought that good news. She'd been real skeptical about Olivia when they first met. Teresa didn't like her because she'd held Olivia responsible for Neil wanting to turn himself into the law. Over time, however, they'd become the sisters both women had wanted growing up. She put the precious letter into the pocket of her skirt, and the interview continued.

Meanwhile, outside the parlor door, Madison was pacing. When his mother passed him on her way to the kitchen, he said, "They've been in there for over an hour."

"He's from her home, Madison. They probably have a lot to talk about."

"But why is it taking so long?"

She gave him an affectionate pat on the shoulder. "You sound like an impatient child. Emma's making lunch. Go get some. Teresa will be done when she's done." She moved on.

It was good advice, he realized. He also realized he had no idea why Teresa being in the room with the reporter was causing him to react this way. When had he become so possessive? Not sure he wanted to go down that slippery slope, he headed for the kitchen.

After the interview, Teresa stood on the front steps and watched Tom Kelly drive away. Talking with him had been fun, but the knowledge that he'd be heading west in a few days left her melancholy. She wanted to go home so badly she could taste it. The desire to feel the hot wind on her face, to sleep under the stars and see the mountains against the horizon all rose up at once, and she had to fight hard to keep from succumbing to the ache in her soul.

"Are you okay?" she heard Madison ask quietly behind her.

She shook her head. "Nope. So can you go back inside and leave me to myself for a few minutes?"

"Sure," he said softly.

She heard the door close and sighed. When she was younger, her brothers would always tease her if she cried, so she'd learned to do it only when alone. She needed that privacy now, and as she wiped away the tears gathering on her cheeks, she'd never felt so alone.

Teresa was quiet for the rest of the day. Madison could have chosen to do any number of things since he wasn't going to the bank, but he hung around because he was concerned about her. His mother and Emma were concerned as well, but nobody tried to get Teresa to talk about what she was feeling or took offense at her mood. Instead they left her alone and hoped she'd work through her sadness.

After dinner, Madison was about to suggest a ride in the park when Emma came into the parlor with a stunned look on her face. "The front yard is full of newspaper reporters," she said. "I mean, they are shoulder-to-shoulder."

Madison and Teresa moved quickly to the window, and sure enough out front saw enough reporters and men carrying cameras to cover a presidential election.

Madison said, "What the hell—"

His mother asked, "Teresa, do you think Mr. Kelly told the Philadelphia papers where to find you?"

"He said he was going to try and sell the story, but I thought he meant out West."

Madison was fairly certain this was Richards's doing and he was not pleased. "I'll go out and see what they want."

When he stepped outside, he was peppered with angry questions.

"Mr. Nance, is it true that Teresa July is living here?"

"Mr. Nance, who gave the okay for such a dangerous woman to be released here?"

"Mr. Nance, as a banker and a son, aren't you concerned that this outlaw may turn on your mother and rob your bank?"

"Isn't your mother concerned having such a desperado on the premises? What's her church think about this heathen outlaw in our midst?"

"Mr. Nance!"

"Mr. Nance!"

Madison had never dealt with such chaos in his life. The angry questions continued to be shouted at him and the camera flashes were blinding. And watching them trample his mother's flower beds and lawn infuriated him.

Inside, Teresa felt bad for him. It was she they wanted. The angry questions matched their angry faces. They were riled up and probably wouldn't leave until she made an appearance. "I need my Colt and my gun belt," she said to Mrs. Nance.

"What on earth for?"

"So they'll take their cameras away and leave you and Madison in peace. It's me they want to see, Teresa July the outlaw, so I'm going to give her to them."

Mrs. Nance stared.

"Please, Mrs. Nance. You aren't going to have any flowers left, and Madison looks ready to throw some punches. I'm going to go change. I'll meet you back here."

"Teresa?"

"Get my stuff." She took off running.

Teresa dragged on her leathers. She knew how to handle the press, she'd done it her entire outlaw life. Reporters had loved her and her brothers out West. If she didn't go out there and charm them there was no telling what they'd print and she didn't want them dragging the Nance name through the mud. After all they'd done for her, it wouldn't be fair.

Madison had just opened his mouth to tell a reporter to get the hell out of his mother's flower beds when the screen door behind him opened and Teresa drawled, "Hello, boys!"

The reporters all but fell over each other to get a closer look. Flashes went off like July Fourth fireworks, and the din of male voices shouting to be heard filled the air.

Madison turned to her and his jaw dropped. She was wearing a tight-fitting suit of black leather. Around her waist was a gun belt studded with cartridges. The Colt stuck in the belt was big and sported a white mother-of-pearl handle. On her feet were black-heeled boots. A black flat-crowned hat hung down her back from a string around her neck. When she walked by him and stood on the step below him all he could see was the way the snug leather clung to her legs and accentuated the curves of her hips. He had never been rendered speechless by a woman before, but couldn't have made a sound if his life had depended upon it.

The press made up for his silence. Teresa took questions, posed for pictures, and showed them her Colt, adding with the patented July grin, "Make sure you tell your readers the Colt is only for your pictures. Parole board doesn't want me carrying, and I'm trying to play by the rules."

The men laughed and more questions were shouted her way. They wanted to know the name of her horse. Had she seen her brothers? Did she like Philadelphia?

By the time she called out, "Last question, boys," she had them eating out of her hand. Some of the reporters wanted to arrange one-on-one interviews to be conducted in the weeks ahead, and Teresa agreed.

The reporters hung around for a little while longer, writing down her colorful quotes and taking more pictures. When they'd finally gotten their fill, they put away their pens, packed up their cameras, and left en masse.

A tired but happy Teresa entered the house, went into the parlor, and collapsed in a chair. Mrs. Nance was smiling with surprise. "They loved you!"

Teresa's eyes were sparkling. "Yes, they did, and I had fun."

Madison could not get over her attire. When she walked by him and into the parlor, the snug black leather fit her so alluringly he had to fight himself to keep from easing up behind her and filling his palms with her luscious looking behind. He had never seen anything like them. "Is that how you usually dress out West?"

"All the time. This pair's new," she explained and running her hand over her leather-sheathed thigh. "They're still a little stiff, but the more I wear them, the more they get broken in."

Molly stated confidently, "I'm going to make me a pair."

Madison stared at her, shocked.

His mother countered, "Rebecca has some."

He started to chuckle. "You're pulling my leg, right?"

"No. They're brown. Aren't they, Teresa?"

"Seen them with my own eyes."

Madison looked to the heavens, but not for long because Teresa's outfit kept grabbing his attention. All he could think about was pulling those leathers down and showing her how much they aroused him.

Teresa wondered if Molly could see the heat in her son's eyes. Teresa certainly could. Each time he glanced her way, the intensity grew, making Teresa remember the slide of his hands on her skin. Beneath her short-waisted leather coat, her nipples were ripening to his silent call. Farther south, her core was blossoming as well.

Madison managed to look away from Teresa long enough to ask his mother, "What time do you want me to fetch you in the morning?"

"A bit before seven."

He nodded. "That should get us there in plenty of time."

Being around Teresa was making his manhood harder and harder. To avoid embarrassing his mother and himself, he thought it best that he leave. The anticipation of having the lady outlaw all to himself for the next few days only added to his arousal, as did anticipating removing her leather trousers, so he said, "I'm going to head home. I'll see you both in the morning."

Molly nodded. "Okay."

"See you, Madison."

Lying in her bed later that night surrounded by the darkness, Teresa reviewed her day. And what a day it had been. Tom Kelly. Madison. The newspaper reporters. Madison. A buoying letter from her sister-in-law, Olivia. Madison. Madison, Madison,

Madison. He filled her thoughts. Having never been taken with a man before, the feelings he evoked were overwhelming. She knew that some of what she felt was fueled by plain old-fashioned lust, and she would make no apologies for being woman enough to acknowledge that. But why did her life seem brighter when he was around? Why did his smile make her heart swell, and why, when he wasn't around, was he becoming all she could think about? It was curious. Something was going on between them, and she liked it, but she wasn't sure she was supposed to.

The next morning, she rode with Madison, Molly, and Emma to the train station. In spite of the early hour, the huge edifice was filled with noise and people hurrying to catch their trains. She was fascinated by all the different races, languages, and manner of dress, but to someone accustomed to wide-open spaces, the press of the crowd was stifling and the din of hundreds of conversations in tandem with the shrill whistles of the departing and arriving trains deafening.

When the time came for Molly and Emma to depart, Teresa gave them both strong hugs. "Have a safe trip and a good time, " she said genuinely.

After receiving parting hugs from Madison, they boarded. Madison and Teresa waited on the platform while the train's whistle sounded. When the locomotive slowly began to make its way down the tracks, they waved at Molly in the window, then walked back out into the sunshine to where he'd parked his buggy.

As he merged into the heavy morning traffic of buggies, streetcars, and delivery wagons, he asked,

"Would you like to get some breakfast? Mr. Watson's place is open."

Teresa liked the old gentleman and his food. "That sounds good."

Because they had to drive back to the Seventh Ward, it took some time, but they kept glancing at each other and smiling. Content on the seat beside him, she asked, "So what do I have to do to get my drawers back?"

He grinned, shrugging. "Oh, I don't know. Been thinking on it, though."

"Well, you can't keep them. I don't have that many pairs."

"Understood." The idea of hanging on to them like an erotic trophy had crossed his mind, but he didn't tell her that. "I'll come up with something."

There were quite a few vehicles parked near Mr. Watson's place, and it took Madison a few moments to find a place to put his. The only spot available was in front of one of the political clubs, and he pulled in there. Because of the early hour, the political club was still closed, so he felt fairly safe in believing the horse and buggy would be still there when they returned.

The inside of the storefront restaurant was much more crowded and lively when they entered, but when the diners noticed Madison and Teresa waiting to be seated silence fell over the place and everyone stared at them. A confused Teresa turned to Madison, who appeared just as puzzled. Out of the back came Mr. Watson. Walking toward them, he grinned and began to applaud. Soon, others joined in, and the sound rose. By the time he reached them, folks were cheering and tapping silverware against their water glasses.

The noise seemed to shake the windows, but neither Teresa nor Madison had any idea what it meant.

Then Watson called out in a loud voice, "Ladies and gentlemen! Mr. Madison Nance and the very lovely Teresa July!"

The crowd roared so loud, Teresa felt like the President.

Madison grinned. "You're famous."

"I know, but this is embarrassing."

"May I show you to a table," Watson said, gesturing elaborately.

"Please," Teresa said, hoping the din would die down. Folks were smiling and clapping and standing up. She half expected this kind of reaction from a room full of men, but there were women on their feet applauding and smiling as well. She was amazed.

Mr. Watson led them to the same table they'd had on their last visit, but this time the other tables were all occupied, so there'd be no intimate privacy. In fact, all of the people nearby looked on with bright smiles.

Once Teresa and Madison were seated, Mr. Watson said to her, "I knew there was something special about you the moment I laid eyes on you."

"Mr. Watson, please—"

"No, let me finish."

Teresa nodded.

"Folks here in the East have been real taken with all the outlaws and gunfighters out West. Things in the newspaper about this one and that one. The stories are exciting and make everything about the West seem bigger than life. Then you and your brothers come along. Robbing banks is wrong. I know it and you know it, right?"

Teresa nodded, reluctantly.

"But you were Black. Now, we had outlaw stories in our own papers that were just as hair-raising as the White ones. We'd shake our heads with disapproval every time you all robbed something, but that didn't mean we couldn't be as excited as the Whites were about reading about their kind." He asked her, "Does that make sense to you?"

"Sure."

"Especially now that you've paid your debt to society and did your time. The community is real tickled to have you here, Miss July, so welcome to Philadelphia."

"Thanks."

"Did you see yourself in the papers this morning?"

"No."

Watson sent a waiter to his office, and the young man returned with a stack that he placed on their table. Sure enough, there she was, posed in her leathers and smiling. Madison leafed through a few of the others until he saw pictures of her, and true to Watson's claim, all the editions, both Black and White, seemed elated by her presence in the city. One White paper promised its readers more pictures, another promised future detailed interviews, while still another promised to find out if it was true that she ate raw skinned squirrels for breakfast and slept outside in a tepee. Madison shook his head. Teresa notwithstanding, he wondered if the city newspapers would offer this much coverage to the upcoming antilynching march his business association and some of the other Black organizations planned to have.

Teresa and Madison gave the waiter their orders, and when their food arrived a short time later, they ate their meals while the other diners scrutinized their every move, especially Teresa's. She became self-conscious about how she was handling her cutlery, how she reached for her water glass, and if she was chewing like a horse. The last thing she wanted was folks gossiping about her manners, because that would undoubtedly reflect back on Molly Nance, so she tried to comport herself in a way that would make her mentor proud.

"How're you doing?" Madison asked.

"I feel like a two-headed calf at the fair."

He chuckled. "They're just interested, that's all."

"I know, and I guess I should have expected it, but I didn't. Not all this—newspapers, folks clapping and whistling, Mr. Watson bowing and scraping."

"It's probably going to be this way until the papers find something new to embrace, so for the moment, you're it."

"I guess." Teresa never sat anywhere where she couldn't see the exits, but Madison was seated with his back to the room. When she looked up and frowned, he asked, "What's wrong?"

"That Richards fella is coming up behind you. Looks mad too."

Madison didn't turn around. He knew that by now Dawson Richards had probably heard from Paula that he knew he was married and probably wasn't pleased. Not that Madison cared. He tended to think they were just about even, but the other shoe still had to drop on Richards. He'd stopped by to see Ben yesterday, and Charlotte had already engaged a lawyer who planned to take his payment from the settlement she was sure to receive.

Sure enough, when Richards reached their table, he snapped, "I ought to take a buggy whip to you."

Madison put down his coffee cup and looked up. He said drolly, "And good morning to you too, Richards. You seem upset."

"How dare you tell Paula and the Carters I'm married. My personal affairs are none of your concern."

"You aren't married?"

"Of course not!"

"That isn't what Charlotte claims."

He looked startled.

"You know Charlotte, don't you?" Madison asked. "Lives in New Orleans. Mother of your three children."

Richards's eyes blazed with fury.

Madison kept up his cool recitation. "I talked to her a few weeks back. She's having trouble keeping food on the table. She's here in town, I hear, and talking with a lawyer."

Because Richards had grabbed everyone's attention with his holier than thou entrance, he now had a diner full of Black folks taking in every word of the conversation.

Madison continued, "Thanks for sending the press to my mother's house. Hope you're ready for your interviews. Someone, and I'm not sure who, plans to send a copy of your marriage certificate to the city papers. I didn't see anything in today's edition, but there's always tomorrow, or the day after."

In response to that shocking news, the diners began to whisper. Madison and Teresa noticed it, and so did the livid Richards.

"I'll get you for this," he promised.

"You're threatening me in a room filled with people. Surely you're smarter than that."

It was obvious the ward boss didn't know what to do. Had he been a child, he would have been sputtering, he was so angry. "I'm a dangerous enemy, Nance."

Madison shrugged. "I'm sure you believe that."

Teresa had never seen this cold, confident side of Madison before, and she was impressed. She hoped Richards wouldn't be harebrained enough to start a fight in the middle of the restaurant, but she waited to see how the confrontation would play out.

Mr. Watson walked up and asked Richards, "Is there a problem, Mr. Richards?"

Richards, his eyes never leaving Madison, said, "No. I was just leaving."

"Good," Watson said. "I'll walk you out."

He growled, "I know where the exit is." Giving Madison and Teresa one last angry glare, he turned and strode away.

"Well now," Teresa said, "nothing like a little anger to spice up your breakfast."

Madison smiled. Charles Watson did too, then returned to his kitchen. As Teresa and Madison went back to their meals, the restaurant was abuzz.

"I didn't know there was steel beneath that city boy suit," Teresa said.

Amusement was in his eyes. "There are lots of things you don't know about me."

"So I see. I like it, though."

"Do you?"

"Yeah. Thought you were soft when I first met you."

"I noticed that."

"No offense, but the way you dressed and talked—where I come from that spells S-O-F-T."

He chuckled. "And now?"

"Now? I think Richards might want to think twice about crossing you."

"You are as smart as you are beautiful."

She laughed. "So where are we going after we leave here?"

"You mentioned wanting to go riding, am I right?"

She grinned. "Can we stop by your mother's so I can put on my leathers?"

Madison silently cheered, but kept that to himself. "Sure. That's no problem at all."

"Will you ride with me?"

Will you ride me? was his mental response, but he buried that, too. Instead, he nodded. "I have some old clothes I keep at Mother's house somewhere. That'll save us having to make a stop by my place as well." He looked her way and saw she was smiling. "Why the smile?"

"Just thinking about your mother wanting her own leathers."

He shook his head. "She is something." His tone turned serious "And your coming to stay has been good for her. She's always done the charity work and been active in the church, but she hasn't had the spark she used to have before my father passed."

Teresa saw the feeling in his eyes.

"Now, she's sewing again and talking about balls and wearing leathers. I'm very grateful."

Teresa was touched by his words. "She's a real special lady. And I like a man who cares about his mother."

"Most of us only get one, so I have to take care of her, especially with my father gone."

His unabashed devotion made her think of her brothers and her mother Tamar. They'd fetch her from the grave if she asked them to.

"Are you ready to leave?" he asked.

She nodded.

Madison paid the bill, then escorted her to the door. Calls of good wishes and "Welcome to Philadelphia" heralded their departure. A smiling Teresa gave the diners a wave good-bye, and with Madison by her side, stepped out into the sunshine.

Chapter 11

It didn't take long for them to change clothes, but leaving the house became another matter. Seeing her enter the parlor clad in her leather trousers and a faded blue work shirt, Madison wanted to linger over her for a passionate moment or two, and Teresa could clearly see the desire standing in his brown eyes. Never shy, she walked over and stood close. This was the first time they'd been alone together in the empty house. "Penny for your thoughts."

He circled an arm around her waist and pulled her to him. "I've been waiting to kiss you all morning."

"And I've been waiting to be kissed all morning. Where've you been?"

His grin was infectious. "Sassy woman. Let's see if I can't give this mouth something else to do."

So he did, and the soft but potent kiss pierced her with its power. Tongues mated beguilingly, hands roamed lazily, and she was instantly entranced. She loved the solid feel of his body against her own, loved his cajoling kisses, and had no defense against the heat they planted in her blood. They both knew they had no future, but at the moment neither cared. Until time came for them to part ways, they planned to fuel each other's passions, then live their separate lives filled with the memories of what they'd once shared.

At the moment they were sharing ever deepening kisses. Her hands fed on the strong muscles of his arms and back. His hands tingled against the leather encasing her warm, saucy behind. She rained possessive kisses on the edge of his strong jaw, soaring with the thrilling sensations. He soared too, seeking her mouth while he expertly undid the buttons running down the front of her old shirt. The worn cotton was almost as soft as the dark silken skin that he knew lay beneath.

Madison pushed back the halves of her shirt and ran glowing eyes over her black silk camisole. He placed his lips against the hollow of her throat, then slid down the straps. He paused at the sight of the length of gray silk circled around her upper torso. The material wasn't very wide. It hid her nipples from view but not the soft mounds of the tops of her breasts. The sight was as erotic as it was arousing. He glanced a fingertip over the shrouded nipple. "What's this for?"

The feather light movements of his finger against the sensitive tips was deliciously distracting. Teresa had trouble forming speech but finally managed to say, "I bind myself when I ride. It's more comfortable."

Without a word, he tugged down the silk and covered the freed flesh with his large hand. He watched her eyes as he played with the hardened point, loving the way her long lashed lids fluttered closed in rapt response. Fueled by her, he lowered his head and took the black berry into his mouth. Her body shimmered.

He treated her to a series of brazen licks before covering the damp nipple with his mouth once more. His hand moved to the other breast and prepared it for its own sensual feasting, and when he was satisfied that it was ready, he made love to them both.

In the silence of his mother's house, Madison dallied and teased. He was hard as a rock and wouldn't be able to ride a horse for a week if he didn't stop this soon, but he couldn't. She was too gorgeous, her breasts too tempting and her mouth too sweet. This opening prelude had bewitched him, fired him. He was only a few passionate moments away from finding someplace to lay her down, ease the leathers from her legs, and make wild sweet love to her the way he'd been craving. He wanted her madly, but not here in his mother's house, at least not the first time. "We need to go."

"You're the one holding us up ... " Teresa couldn't see. Desire had her vision so cloudy she didn't even know where she was.

"It's these beautiful breasts of yours. They won't stop whispering my name." To prove his point, he bit them gently, then raised himself so he could watch her face while his palm moved over the buds to make sure they stayed tight and ripe. "You have to close your shirt, Teresa."

He bent down, circled his tongue around the twin treats, and she crooned. She couldn't have complied with his heated request if someone held a Colt to her head; his wicked feasting had her throbbing and pulsating everywhere. "Madison ... "

He captured her mouth again. "What, angel?" His lips moved down and branded the edge of her neck.

"We should get going."

"I know." Reluctantly, Madison stepped back. The desire in his eyes matched hers. He did up her buttons, kissed her soundly one last time, then walked with her out to his buggy.

Rebecca Constantine and her husband Miller greeted Madison and Teresa warmly. "We saw you in the papers, Teresa. Guess the jig is up?" Miller said with a twinkle in his old eyes.

Teresa nodded. "Looks that way, but everybody's been real nice."

Rebecca asked Madison, "Did Molly and Emma get off okay?"

"Yes, they did, so Teresa and I came out to go riding."

Miller said, "Help yourselves. Hannibal's been waiting on Teresa. Gotten so he doesn't like anybody else riding him."

Sure enough, when Teresa entered the barn, the stallion lifted his head and nickered a greeting. She walked over and gave him a hug and an affectionate pat. "How are you, boy? Been missing me? I sure have missed you."

While the grooms accompanied Madison to find him a suitable mount, Teresa took down the tack she'd been using on her visits and led the big animal out into the sunshine. "Wish I'd raised you," she said to Hannibal. "Then we wouldn't have to use this saddle. Cloud and I rode bareback most of the time. You'd like Cloud. You two would probably fight over the mares, but he's a good horse and so are you."

After throwing on the saddle and tightening all the

cinches, Teresa stuck her boot into the stirrup and lifted herself to the saddle. Reins in hand, she turned Hannibal and they trotted over to meet Madison, mounted on a brown stallion named Toussaint, who was almost as large as Hannibal.

Leaving the paddock area, the two riders took a leisurely stroll down the paths that led to the open land. Madison couldn't remember ever having a more enjoyable morning. Being under the open sky alone and carefree made the rest of the world feel miles away. Here, there was no Richards, Jim Crow, or anything else to keep him from concentrating on the thing he wanted to focus on the most—Teresa. She rode beside him confident and at ease. That she was an excellent horsewoman was evident in her posture and manner. She and Hannibal moved as if they were joined, bringing to mind the image of a beautiful female satyr.

Teresa was also enjoying the lazy pace. She looked up and saw a blue jay, its wings spread against the sky. When he cawed, the sound echoed across the silence. "This is real nice," she said to her companion. "Sometimes it's good to ride by yourself, and other times it's good to be with somebody."

"I'm enjoying your company as well."

Teresa's attraction to him rose. "You ride much?"

He chuckled to himself. "Not as much as I'd like."

She could see the double meaning in his eyes and her body began to call. "Never had a man try and seduce me while I was riding."

"No?" he asked with mock innocence. "Then you've probably never had a man ask you to unbutton your shirt so he can see your nipples in the sunshine."

She almost lost her seat. "No."

His grin was so playful and so male, it made her dizzy.

"And no, Mother doesn't know about this side of me either," he offered, his mustache twitching with amusement.

Teresa was wearing one of the well-worn flannel work shirts sent by Olivia in the crate.

"Open your shirt, Angel, and let me pleasure you while we ride."

Her breath was stacked up in her throat, and under his blazing eyes, she slowly granted his request.

Madison watched boldly as she worked each button from its hole. The movement of her fingers and the sight of her dark flesh being revealed as the fabric opened wider and wider made him steel hard.

Then she was bared. Her nipples, dark as onyx jewels, were open to the sunshine and to his touch. The horses slowed and Madison reached over and toyed lazily with first one and then the other.

Teresa lost all touch with time. His fingers circled, squeezed, and gently plucked. Her breathing increased, as did the warmth in her blood.

"Lean this way ... "

And when she did, he took the nipple into his mouth and she groaned with welcoming pleasure. He took his time making sure she stayed ripe and hard, filling his hands with her soft weight while he dallied and feasted. When he seemed satisfied that her buds would answer only to him from now on, he drew away, leaving her hard and damp underneath the sun.

"Now, we can go on with our ride," he whispered.

Only instinct prompted Teresa to pick up the reins; everything else was in a fog.

They rode farther into the open wilderness of the Constantines' property. Still echoing from his pleasuring, Teresa wondered what other shameless courses he would put her through. In reality, she couldn't wait.

They rode for nearly an hour, and during the journey he made a point of stopping every now and then to open her shirt to make sure her nipples hadn't forgotten him. She was so dazed she didn't know where she was.

They eventually rode down an embankment and stopped beside a small stream hidden from view by the thick trees lining the bank. They dismounted, and while the horses bent to drink, Madison fit himself gently behind her. Placing a kiss on her neck, he swept his hands up to capture her breasts inside of her still open shirt, and Teresa melted like water into sand. She could feel the pressure of his manhood against her hips, and she slowly moved against him, mare to his stallion, as he teased her back into arousal. Unashamed to show how much she desired him, she removed her boots, then undid the snaps on the placard of her pants. She turned to face him then, and he met her mouth with a kiss that set them both on fire. Still loving her, he worked the leathers down her hips. When he touched bare ebony skin, he stopped, then looked down with amazed and heated eyes. "Where are your drawers?"

Grinning, she skimmed the leathers the rest of the way down and off. "You don't wear drawers beneath leathers, city boy," she said seductively. "They make you a bunched-up mess."

Watching her stand there naked from the waist down, her nipples teasing from within the old shirt, Madison could have come right then and there. Instead he moved a hand between her sculpted thighs and tantalized the damp vent until she crooned. Taking a moment to remove his own boots and pants while she undid the buttons of his shirt, he looked around and spied the wooden bench a few feet away. He would have preferred this first coupling to have been in his bed, but he couldn't wait. He wanted her now.

Teresa had never made love with a man sitting down before, but after he placed the rubber on his manhood and she eased herself down onto the sheathed hard prize, the feel of him filling her made her want more.

"Like that?" he husked out.

"Oh, yeah," she whispered, leaning in to reward him with a kiss for the wanton pleasure. His possessive hands on her hips guided her slowly at first, letting her become accustomed to his size and girth, and then the rhythm began. Her positioning gave him ample access to her breasts. While he brazenly enjoyed her, their bodies instinctively increased the pace. Soon, his lust-fired strokes became focused and true, and the mare rode her stallion scandalously in response to the hands guiding her up and down and back and forth. Her orgasm exploded. His did too. He gripped her silken hips roughly, and thrusting like a man gone mad, his hoarse shout of completion mingled with her sharp cries as they soared into paradise.

Teresa came back to herself cuddled against his

sweat damp chest, head against his shoulder. Raising her head, she looked down into his eyes and saw her future. The strange sensation scared the hell out of her, shaking it off, she tenderly touched his cheek with her fingers, then gave him a long meaningful kiss.

Madison didn't want to move ever. He wanted his entire world to center on the woman sitting so shamelessly in his lap. He gathered her in again and held her close.

They had to leave, however, so they parted the seal of their bodies, shared a few more poignant kisses, then got into their clothes.

Riding back, they kept flashing each other silly grins. It had been a long time since Teresa had been so happy, and Madison felt like a giddy adolescent. They both sensed something special forming, but neither could give it a name. Lust was involved, but it was more than that.

He said, "There's a show tonight at the Academy of Music. Would you like to attend?"

She shrugged. "Sure. What kind of show?"

"Madame Sissieretta Jones, and R. Henri Strange. The papers call him 'America's Greatest Colored Tragedian.'"

"What in the world is a tragedian?"

"He recites Shakespeare. Usually the tragedies."

"I see."

He reached into the pocket of his trousers for the handbill he'd brought along for her to see.

She unfolded the announcement and scanned it. A company called the Afro-American Amusement Company was putting on the show, and in addition to Madame Jones and R. H. Strange, there were other performers and amusements listed, including a pie eating contest and a Tom Thumb wedding. "Sure, I'd love to go. Sounds like fun."

"You'll have to wear one of your fancy gowns," he warned.

Teresa blew out a breath of frustration.

"I promise it will be worth it."

She didn't know if she believed him, but said, "I'm holding you to that."

"I don't doubt that at all. What time does it say the event starts?"

Teresa searched the wording. "Nine. Nine to midnight."

It was nearly noon now, and Madison's stomach rumbled in complaint. "I'm hungry. How about you?"

"Starving." She handed him the concert handbill. They'd ridden out two hours ago, and the early breakfast at Mr. Watson's seemed like yesterday.

"How about we stop and get something to eat on the way back, then I'll drop you at Mother's and return for you around seven-thirty or so."

"That's fine, but you don't have to spend any money for lunch. I'm sure Emma has something stored away I can fix."

"You cook?"

"Almost as well as I ride."

"And you do ride well."

The heat in his gaze made her say, "I've never met a man quite like you. Madison Nance."

"And I've never met a woman like you, Teresa July."

"Good, maybe you'll remember me for at least a little while after I leave for home."

Madison knew it would be much longer than that. She sat Hannibal as if she'd been born to ride, and back on the bench she'd ridden him just as well. Feeling his manhood swell in response to the lusty memory, he focused his mind elsewhere lest he wind up searching for another hidden spot so he could have her again. "Race you back!"

He kicked the horse into a gallop. As he and Toussaint pulled away, her outraged cursing made him laugh.

"You cheater!" Teresa and Hannibal took after them. The big stallion hadn't had a good run all day and he was ready to fly.

It took them a quarter of a mile to catch up, but when they were neck and neck, Teresa looked over at the grinning Madison. She urged Hannibal to increase his speed, and he complied with a powerful stride that inched them past their opponent. Now out in front, Teresa shouted, "Eat dust, city boy!" She threw back her head, gave the Seminole victory cry, then she and Hannibal roared off, leaving the laughing Madison and his mount behind.

A groom was leading Hannibal back to his stall when Madison rode up. Teresa was standing against the side of the barn with her arms folded lazily. "Took you long enough."

He dismounted and handed the reins to another Constantine groom. "What was the sound you made back there?"

"Seminole victory cry. Learned it from my grandfather, one of the old chiefs."

"Very memorable."

"Guess you never heard a Cherokee gobble either, then?"

He chuckled. "No."

"You need to come West. All kinds of things to learn and see."

"Maybe I will," he said, enjoying her smile.

Rebecca walked up. Both Madison and Teresa noticed she had on her leathers. "Teresa, I adore these," she said. "They don't hinder my movements. I can ride and not be snagged by branches and brush, but I have to ask you something. Privately."

"Sure. How about we step over there." Giving Madison a smile and a shrug, she followed Rebecca to a spot a few feet away, and asked, "What's your question?"

"How do I keep my drawers from bunching up?"

"You don't wear any," Teresa told her frankly.

The eyes in Rebecca's overly painted face widened. She whispered, "Really?"

"Yes, ma'am."

She seemed to think on that for a while, then brightened with delight. "Oh, wait until I tell Miller." Rebecca went silent, thinking, then giggling like a young girl, declared, "I do hope Miller took his heart pills this morning. Thank you, Teresa!" And she hurried off.

Teresa laughed so hard she slid down the barn wall to the grass. Madison, watching Rebecca quickly moving across the grounds, had no idea what had transpired, but as soon as Teresa could speak, she told him, and his howl of laughter filled the air.

Still amused, the two of them retrieved the buggy.

Not wanting to disturb whatever Rebecca and Miller might be up to inside the house, they drove off without saying good-bye.

Madison made a stop at a diner near Molly's home and brought the food with them to the house, where he decided it might be fun to have their meal outside. He found an old blanket and they spread it out on the grass by the gazebo. He unwrapped the corned beef sandwiches and gave Teresa one of them, and she set it on a small plate. But before eating she stared curiously at the small brown disks lying on a bed of paper he set on the blanket between them.

"Ever had Saratoga chips?" he asked.

Shaking her head, she picked one up. It was warm, and she bit into it. It was crisp.

"They're sliced fried potatoes," he explained, grabbing a few for himself and placing them on his plate. "A Negro chef from Saratoga, New York, invented them back before the war, or so the legend goes."

Teresa thought they were very good, and a wonderful salty complement to the sandwiches.

While he ate, Madison tried his best not to stare, but because the memories of this morning's tryst completely filled his mind, he found it difficult. The remembrances of her uninhibited response to their lovemaking coupled with the tastes and scents of her were as vivid now as they'd been then. He ran his eyes over Teresa's full, tempting lips, her sparkling black eyes, and the thick sweep of her lashes and brows. He now knew that she applied the same indomitable spirit to making love that she applied to life, and he was honored to be the man she'd chosen to teach her passion.

When they finished eating, Teresa walked him back through the house to the front door.

"I'll be back for you later," he said, raising her chin and staring down into the face he wanted to memorize for eternity. He kissed her with a slow thoroughness that made her see stars, then with a smile, left her standing dizzy in the foyer.

Teresa took a long, hot scented bath, and Madison filled her mind. The memory of him asking her to open her blouse was powerful enough to knock her out of the saddle all over again. After making love to him, she could now answer unequivocally the question he'd put to her earlier—no, she'd never been properly loved back home, but now she had.

When it became time for her to get ready, she looked through the armoire for something to wear and decided on the fancy midnight blue gown Mrs. Nance had finished a few weeks back. Next to her skin, she wore a thin black camisole with insets of lace. The blue silk corset, trimmed with a thin black ruffle and patterned all over with small red and black flowers, came next. Instead of the whalebone that she would never have worn, the corset's support came from thin flexible strips of what Mrs. Nance called watch spring steel. It was pliable and offered her both the comfort and support she'd need to fill out the top of the low-cut gown. Pulling on a pair of matching blue silk drawers with short blousy legs, she carefully slipped into the silky, black lisle stockings and tugged on the garters that were needed to hold them up.

Dressed now, she studied herself in the mirror. Even though the gown was not her choice of preferred attire, she liked how she looked. With her hair gleaming and pulled back, and a hammered gold disc hanging from each ear, she thought she'd cleaned up well. Granted, there were probably going to be women in attendance decked out in more expensive gowns and wearing a chest full of jewels, but none were going to be escorted by Madison, so she figured she'd drawn the best hand.

He arrived a short while later dressed handsomely in formal black evening attire complete with silk top hat. He looked her over with approving eyes. She turned around slowly so he could see all and his approval grew. "You're stunning."

"Been called a lot of things but never stunning."

"Stunning, lovely, sensual."

"Behave now," she said with mock warning. "You don't get to take off my clothes until later."

He laughed, his desire rising in response to her delightful frankness. "Then we should probably leave, because in my mind I've already removed your dress and I'm opening your corset."

The searing words put a wobble in Teresa's knees. "Out, Nance!" she commanded, pointing. They made sure the lamps were doused, locked the door behind them, and departed.

A hired cab with a uniformed driver up front waited at the curb. Confused, she turned to Madison, who said easily, "Thought I'd spend the ride concentrating on you instead of a horse's rump."

He helped her in, and after joining her on the seat, signaled the driver, who started out.

The Academy of Music was located on Broad Street. Modeled after La Scala in Milan, Italy, it was known as the best acoustical theater in the nation. Its doors had opened in 1857, but it didn't allow all Black productions to use the facilities until 1876.

As the cab joined the slow moving line of hacks, carriages, and buggies trying to get to the front of the theater, Teresa could feel the excitement in the air. The paved walks leading to the theater were filled with people dressed up in their evening finery. They all looked so dignified. She had never seen anything quite like it. There were wealthy people of color out West, but not in the numbers she was witnessing.

As they inched closer to the theater, Madison pointed out the well-heeled hotels spread out along the block: The Windemere, Bellevue, and Stratford, with their fancy windows and doors, were finer than any place she'd seen back home. Teresa was having trouble deciding where to look. The streets, awash in the electric lighting, also new to her, gave the night a rosy glow. She felt like a little girl at the fair.

Looking over at Madison, she found him watching her. "Sorry I'm not more sophisticated," she told him.

"You've nothing to apologize for. I'm enjoying watching the excitement in your eyes."

She appreciated his kindness and wondered if she'd ever meet another man as special as he. Her attraction was growing into an attachment, she realized, that would be hard to shake when she returned to Texas if she weren't careful. Offering him a soft smile, she went back to seeing all she could.

Still watching her, Madison wondered what he was supposed to do with the feelings rising inside him. He wasn't foolish enough to think he could make her stay past her appointed time, but when that day came, would he know all there was to know about the compelling Teresa July? He didn't think so. She was the type of woman a man needed a lifetime to fully explore.

When they finally reached the theater's front doors, Madison paid the driver, then he and Teresa made their way to the end of the line that snaked down the street. As they passed those already in line, she was recognized—no doubt because of the pictures in the daily newspapers—and could hear her name being whispered excitedly. A few people even called out to her. Grinning, she called back, saying hello.

They were polite enough not to impede her progress, but some of the newspaper photographers were not. They bade her and Madison stop so they could take pictures for the next day's editions. Rather than cause a scene, Teresa agreed, then she and Madison moved on.

Chapter 12

The theater's interior took Teresa's breath away. The places out West calling themselves opera houses may as well have been privies when compared to the Academy of Music's grand hall. The ornate balconies and velvet seats were eye popping and the chandelier jaw dropping.

It's made of crystal," Madison told her. "Fifty feet in circumference and sixteen feet in diameter, according to this program."

She and Madison were in what he called a proscenium box, which she found out was the fancy name for the box seats between the curtain and the orchestra pit, and in her opinion the best seats in the place. She could see everything from their pricey perch.

"How much does it weigh?" she asked, staring in awe at the massive chandelier. "If our seats were down there, I'd spend all night looking just up to make sure it wasn't falling down. Something that big could kill a person."

He chuckled. "Says here it weighs five thousand pounds, and there are 240 gas burners inside."

Teresa shook her head in amazement, then turned her attention to the people filling up the seats on the floor below. Once again she had never seen so many well-dressed folks. They were streaming in all gussied up, and the hall was buzzing with the muted sounds of hundreds of different conversations. She was seated right up against the ornate wall that made up the front of the box, and she supposed that to all of the sophisticated city people in the boxes nearby, she looked like a country rube, but she didn't care. She didn't want to miss a thing.

Madison watched her with affection. She was definitely enjoying herself. He could see some of the people seated in the other boxes observing her with smiles. They apparently recognized her and seemed to be enjoying her excitement just as much as he. And she looked beautiful in her fancy midnight blue gown. He recognized it as the one she'd been wearing the day he came into the sewing room and was told to pick up his eyeballs from the floor, but tonight he could look at her to his heart's content. His mother's favorite designer was the English-born Charles Frederick Worth, and she fashioned her patterns to mimic his. The gown Teresa was wearing, with its deep alluring neckline and feather-capped sleeves, had skirt panels shot through with metallic threads and a long flat trail. The dress was designed to hug the wearer's waist and emphasize the bust, which it did very well. She was the most distinctively dressed woman in the place, and he was proud to say she was with him.

"Well! I'd no idea we'd be sitting with a known criminal."

Teresa and Madison turned to see Paula Wade and her escort, Dawson Richards, taking the seats behind them in the box. The snippy comment had been Paula's.

"You could always sit someplace else," Teresa told her.

"Dawson paid eight dollars for these seats. I'll just pray we're downwind."

Teresa shook her head at the woman's audacity but didn't take the bait. Instead she glanced at Madison, who said to her, "You can shoot her next time."

"I'll hold you to that."

Strangely, the tight-lipped Richards had nothing to say. Madison wondered if his silence stemmed from the rumors flying around about his wife's lawsuit. In truth, the reason didn't matter, because he didn't care.

Putting Paula out of her mind, Teresa sat mesmerized through the show. It opened with W. I. Powell, billed as the "Celebrated Baritone and King of Fun," then out came R. Henri Strange. He recited scenes from *Othello* and *Richard the Third*. Teresa hadn't a clue as to what he was talking about, but he sounded very eloquent, so when he left the stage to thunderous applause, she too clapped vigorously and made a mental note to ask Mrs. Nance if she had any Shakespeare plays in her library.

Next came jugglers, a buck and wing contest that had the audience clapping with the music, and two little children outfitted as bride and groom in a Tom Thumb wedding.

However, it was Madame Sissieretta Jones, who brought down the house. From the first note, Teresa understood why she was called the "Greatest Singer of Her Race." Displaying the seventeen medals she always wore on her gown whenever she performed, she held the audience in the palm of her hand. Singing everything from spirituals to the operatic arias she'd performed all over the world, her voice filled the concert hall like an angel's. The dark-skinned beauty, born in Portsmouth, Virginia, could have been a July, Teresa thought with a smile, taking in the woman's coloring. According to the program, she'd sung for three different Presidents and was managed by Major J. B. Pond, who also managed Mark Twain and the Reverend Henry Ward Beecher. Teresa was so impressed by Madame Jones's voice, she could have listened to her sing until Christmas, but the hour long performance had to end at some point, and when it did, the appreciative crowd jumped to their feet, shaking the building with their deafening applause.

The evening over, Teresa took a last look around the hall so she could commit it to memory. She never wanted to forget the night. Gathering up her wrap and the empty handbag that matched her dress, she and Madison waited in the crush of people leaving. Paula and Richards were standing directly in front of them, close enough for Teresa to see that the texture of Paula's kitchen did not match the nearly straight hair on the rest of her head. Teresa's long black hair had come from her mixed heritage of African, Spanish, and Seminole ancestors; Paula's had come from a wig store.

Paula looked back at her, and wrinkling her nose, began to fan the air elaborately with a gloved hand. "Dawson, if we don't start moving soon, I'm going to swoon from prison stench."

Before she could put Paula in her place, a beautifully attired older woman standing near her said pointedly, "Miss July, please don't judge we Philadelphians by this graceless visitor from *Memphis*."

The offended Paula flashed around as if to offer a stinging retort, but the woman wasn't cowed. She looked Paula dead in the eyes and said haughtily, "The only stench I smell is the one emanating from someone being squired around by a married man."

Tittering greeted that blast from the woman's guns. Teresa wanted to cheer as a stony Paula turned back around. Everyone could see the rigid set of Richards's back, his fury over the public put-down obvious, but he didn't utter a word.

Seemingly satisfied that the issue of who was who and what was what had been handled, the woman then asked Madison, "How's your mother, Madison?"

Barely containing his smile, he replied, "She's fine, Mrs. Fitz, just fine. She's in Cleveland visiting family."

"Tell her I asked after her, would you please."

"Yes, ma'am."

Mrs. Fitz turned to Teresa. "Have Molly bring you around for tea when she returns, Miss July. I'd enjoy having you visit my home."

"Yes, ma'am. I will. Thank you."

She nodded like the grande dame that she was, then tossed Teresa a tiny wink.

On the ride through the night, Teresa sat with Madison's arm around her in the back seat of the cab.

She couldn't believe the wonderful evening. Once again she felt like a woman in a dream, and she definitely didn't want to be awakened.

"Did you have a good time?" he asked.

"Oh yes." She looked up at him in the shadows of the cab's hood. "Thank you very much."

"You're welcome."

Teresa smiled and cuddled closer.

Madison tightened his hold, enjoying her nearness. "I had a good time watching Mrs. Fitz fillet Paula too."

Teresa chuckled. "So did I. Did you see the look on Miss Paula's face? She wears a wig, you know."

"Do tell?"

"Yep. Fake as my uncle Graham's wooden teeth."

Madison laughed. "You do have a way with words."

"Thanks." Teresa was content, more than she'd ever been in her life. "So, where are we going now?"

"Thought I'd steal you away for a while and take you to my place."

"Hmm," she replied with smiling interest. "Your place?"

"Yep."

"I think I like that idea."

"Do you?"

Their eyes met in the dark. She whispered, "I do."

He traced a possessive finger along the curve of her breasts above her gown, then said slowly, "If I kiss you and touch you the way I've been wanting to all night, the cabbie's going to get an eyeful, so hold onto that look in your eyes until I get you home."

Teresa resonated from the touch and the power in

his tone. Personally, she didn't care about the cabbie, but she knew that in Madison's world propriety was taken seriously. Being the gentleman that he was, he was likely concerned about damage to her reputation and didn't want the cabbie boasting to his cronies about what he'd seen. Filled with anticipation over what the rest of their evening would hold, she added yet another positive attribute to the growing list of things that made Mrs. Nance's handsome, seductive son one of a kind.

The cab pulled up in front of a row house in one of the better sections of the Seventh Ward. Madison paid the cabbie, then escorted her inside.

He had a nice place, Teresa noted, looking around. It lacked the grandeur of his mother's home, but the carpets, upholstered furniture, and framed paintings on the wall reflected a man who had taste and made a good living. "I like this," she said as they entered his small parlor. The dark wood and heavy furniture exuded a distinct masculine air, and so did he, she noted, placing her wrap and handbag on a chair. Her nipples were already up and ready, her skin craving that first vivid touch.

"Would you like something to drink?" he asked.

"What do you have?"

"Lemonade. I can make us coffee? Boil water for tea?"

"Coffee, if it's not too much bother."

"It isn't." Madison wanted her so badly, he had to force himself to stand where he was. He was certain that if he moved any closer, the coffee would be forgotten.

Teresa didn't need Second Sight to glean his thinking. The heat in his eyes was as plain as the heat reflected in her own. "We could always have the coffee later," she suggested softly.

"I suppose we could," he said, crossing the room to where she stood. He gently pulled her against him and their gazes locked in the silence of the dimly lit parlor. He lowered his mouth to hers, and the sweet intensity sent Teresa's world spinning. She put her arms around him, wanting to bring their bodies even closer. Hands began roaming in a quest to explore, and hers were as active as his. She loved placing her lips against his jaw, loved running her palms along the strength in his upper arms, loved the hard warmth of his desire pressed ardently between their flush forms. This man and this man alone had taught her more about passion than she ever thought possible. His lips on her neck were like flames, his hands moving over her breasts stirring. When he kissed his way across the skin above her gown, she crooned for him. With her breath coming in short, soft gasps, there was nothing she wanted more than for him to love her like she knew he could, so when he swept her up in his arms, she didn't protest. Instead, she fed herself on his kiss and let him carry her, fancy gown and all, up the dark staircase.

Teresa had no idea what his room looked like. All she knew was that the bed he'd sat her on felt large and soft and that he was standing above her. Reaching out, she moved her hand purposefully up and down the hard velvet part of him that had given her so much pleasure earlier in the day, then squeezed him until he pulsed, before skimming a savoring hand over its length again. She stood slowly, her touch never leaving him, and said in a low voice, "I think I should take off this dress."

A spiraling Madison agreed. His eyes were closed, a testament to the searing level of lust her touch had caused. When she removed her hand to see to the task, he was bereft.

As she removed the dress, the silk rustled in the quiet.

"Hand it here," he invited. "I'll place it over the chair."

After doing that, he took a moment to light a lamp, the low wick giving off just enough light for them to see each other.

And what Madison saw when he looked her way stole his breath. The black corset, with its tiny flowers and accenting lace trim, barely covered her nipples. Her drawers had also been removed in the dark, and she was standing before him wearing nothing but the corset, her stockings, garters, and black velvet high button shoes. Just like this morning, he could have come right there and then, but he held on. He planned to enjoy her like a boy with new toys on Christmas morning, and he was sure it would take a long time.

To that end, he rejoined her by the bed, then bent his head to brush his lips over the arousing hills of her breasts. "I like this," he whispered. "You should wear these more often."

Draping an arm low on her back, he brought her forward so he could kiss her in earnest while he circled a worshipping hand over the flare of her soft, warm behind. A fleeting touch between her thighs affirmed that she was as ready for him as he was for her, and he felt his manhood swell in response. While he undid the hooks of her corset, he fed himself on the passion blazing in her eyes.

Once the loosened corset panels hung free, her creased and wrinkled camisole was the only barrier between his lips and her skin, one he conquered easily when he took a shrouded nipple into the heat of his mouth.

Teresa groaned with the pleasure. He languidly played and dallied until she was ripe as summer blackberries, then he bit them gently before repeating the glorious process again. The hand between her legs had to be the most magical touch east or west of the Mississippi, and she was soon crooning in response to his delicious wizardry.

Madison could have touched and teased her until eternity. Every taste, feel, and scent of her fired his need. She was responsive, uninhibited, and so brimming with passion, he kissed her down onto the bed so he could show her just how much she moved him.

And he took an inordinate amount of time doing so. His kisses worshipped her from the hammered gold hoops in her ears, down her throat, then paused to sample her lush breasts. His fingers found her vent damp and wet. When he slid a bold finger inside, her hips rose erotically and she purred. She'd wanted him to show her passion, and he was doing his best to make sure she received as much as she could stand.

By the time he slid his sheathed man root into the place she most wanted it to be, Teresa was so scandalously hot, he could have been stroking her in the center of the stage at the Academy of Music and she wouldn't have cared. *Lord have mercy!* Feeling him filling her, riding her, and making sure her nipples stayed wet and taut, sent her soaring toward orgasm, and when it burst, she screamed long and loud. As she twisted and shuddered, she sensed him raise her hips and begin to pump in and out with such lust-fed fury that her body arched her like a bow. For the next few minutes cries and growls and the sound of the bed squeaking resonated in the room. A thunderous release claimed him. He tightened his hold and kept thrusting as his head fell back and he yelled out his joy .

Moments later he pulled her in against him. With their shattering completions still echoing inside, they breathlessly wondered if they'd ever be whole again.

But they didn't lie quiet for long. They were too tempted by each other, too eager to retrace their climb to passion's peak. She rode him this time, just like she'd done this morning on the bench. After that second orgasm tore through her, he had her turn over and kneel against the large wooden headboard, and he took her from behind.

Teresa found the positioning splendidly intoxicating. He could kiss her throat, tease her breasts, and ply that little citadel of flesh at the gate of her thighs, all while stroking her deliciously. The rhythm quickened, the plying increased, and soon she was crooning and coming and fairly swooning in response to the force of his hard thrusts as his orgasm sent him flying over the edge too.

This time when they were done, neither could move. Their eyes met across the bed and they shared a mutual smile of satisfaction and affection. He reached out and languidly entwined his fingers with hers. Teresa tightened the hold, relishing his nearness, and wondered how in the world she was going to be able to leave this man when the time came for her to return to her life out West.

Rather than worry about it, she decided to just enjoy the moment. Her lips were kiss swollen, her thighs stroke swollen, and she was filled with the remnants of his spectacular loving. Who knew that the rude and distrustful city boy she'd first met in his mother's library would make love like he'd been given a Gift, and that she would be thanking her lucky stars for being the beneficiary. *Dios, he was good!*

"Penny for your thoughts," he said softly, turning his gaze her way.

"Just thinking how very good you are at this passion thing."

Tickled, he replied, "I've never had any complaints."

"I'll bet you haven't."

"You're a fast learner, though."

"It's easy when you have a good teacher."

Later, after they showered and dressed, Madison drove her home. The sun was just coming up and the streets were all but empty. They'd had such a good time they wanted to do it again.

He walked her into the house and gave her a parting kiss. "There's a ferry that offers moonlight cruises on the river. Would you like to go tonight?"

"Can I wear my leathers?"

He smiled and shrugged. "Why not? Who knows, your celebrity may earn us free passage."

"That would be fine because you've been spending an awful lot of money on me. I've been keeping a tab because I want to pay you back eventually. Were those seats at the Academy really eight dollars?"

"Yes. And you may as well forget about the price. I won't be taking any money from you, now or in the future. Are you trying to insult me on purpose?" he asked, holding her close and looking down at her.

"No, but you shouldn't be footing my bills."

"Teresa, paying for your meals and taking you to the theater won't put me in the poorhouse. I might not be as rich as Andrew Carnegie, but I can afford Saratoga chips."

"Just accustomed to paying my own way. That's all."

"When you go home, you can go back to doing that, but while you're here, you're my guest."

She gave him a reluctant, "Okay."

He placed a kiss on her forehead. "I'll see you this afternoon. Go on to bed. I'll lock the door behind me."

She nodded tiredly and left him standing in the foyer.

Madison waited until he heard her walking on the floor above, then, with a smile on his face, he took his leave.

Teresa awakened and peered bleary eyed at the small white porcelain clock on the bedside table: twelve-fifteen. For a moment her sleepy brain had difficulty determining if the time applied to afternoon or midnight, but the light in the room supplied the answer. Her first instinct was to burrow back into the bedding for a few more hours of sleep, but instead she sat up. The soft life she'd been leading since her release was not something she wanted to become accustomed to. By this time next year, Ancestors willing, she'd be home and life would be a struggle again, especially now that she had to find legal means to support herself. The last thing she needed was to believe that she was actually this woman she was pretending to be, because in truth she was a poor Black Seminole with a ramshackle three room cabin in Indian Territory that might or might not be still standing. In her world, there were no silk camisoles, no maids to make her meals, and no special men who made love to her until dawn. It was best she remember that.

The first thing Madison wanted to do when he awakened was see Teresa. After last night's memorable bout of lovemaking, he was as eager as an infatuated youth to share her company again, hold her again, kiss her again. His sleep had been so sound he didn't remember dreaming, but he was certain she'd been in his nocturnal world, tempting him with her smile and her sleek onyx body. Just thinking about her made his nature rise, so he put aside his desires for now and got up to start his day.

Because he didn't cook, he ate out most of the time, usually at Mr. Watson's place. When he entered that afternoon, Watson was on the register.

"Afternoon, Madison," Watson said.

Madison nodded. "How are you, sir?"

"Can't complain. Where's the lovely Miss July?"

"At Mother's."

"Pity. She lights up the day when she's around."

"That she does."

"Give her my regards when you see her again."

"I will."

He took Madison to a table. The lunch crowd had all but emptied out, leaving the restaurant quiet and slow. The workers were taking advantage of the lull, changing table linens, mopping floors, and eating at a few of the tables in a back corner.

After taking Madison's order, Watson asked, "Have you seen the *Tribune*?"

Madison hadn't. The eight page *Tribune* was Philadelphia's longest established Black newspaper, one of five published in the city.

A paper was retrieved and handed to him. On the front was a picture of a smiling Teresa in her stunning gown. The caption under the picture read:

LADY OUTLAW TERESA JULY VISITING THE ACADEMY OF MUSIC

All Madison could do was smile.

Watson said, "Now, turn to the second page."

Beneath a badly done pen and ink drawing of Dawson Richards was the caption:

PARTY BOSS DAWSON RICHARDS EMBROILED IN CONTROVERSY

Madison read further:

According to the State of Louisiana, party boss Dawson Richards is married to a Charlotte Baines Richards of Baton Rouge. If that is true (and we believe it is via an official document received by this editor), why is he squiring around the young women of this city? Has he forgotten his wife or simply mis-

placed her? Many of us have chosen to overlook the
questionable and allegedly corrupt tactics of Richards
and his associates on election day because he does deliver the votes needed by the former party of Lincoln.
However, the lack of morals shown by a man who has
seemingly abandoned his wife and three small children can not be overlooked nor ignored. This editor
asks, is there no one else in the city of Philadelphia
with the abilities and unstained morals to be party
boss for the Seventh Ward? Surely one exists, and we
demand that the party begin the search immediately.

Madison looked up into Charles Watson's pleased
face. "Well," he said with satisfaction. "That ought
to put Richards on notice."

"Let's hope so."

Although Madison had declared this week a holiday, he nonetheless swung by the bank on his way
home just to make sure the ship was still afloat.

Inside, there were no customers, which was not
uncommon for an operation as small as his, but he
nodded to the clerk behind the desk, then stuck his
head into his office.

"Hello, Tate. How are things?" he asked his second in command.

"Hello, sir. We had an interesting morning. A couple
of customers came in and closed their accounts."

Madison was confused. "Why?"

Tate shrugged. "They said there were better investment opportunities elsewhere."

"Who were they?"

Tate gave him the names of two very prominent
citizens.

Madison was at a loss. "Were we able to cover their withdrawals?"

"Yes, but if this is a trend, we may be in deep water."

Madison didn't begrudge people moving their money, but he wanted to know why, if he could. "I'll go around and speak to both of them before I return on Monday and see if I can win them back. In the meantime, any other dealings I should know about?"

"Nope. Everything's smooth."

Madison smiled. "Good. Well, tomorrow's Friday. Close up at three. I know you're anxious to get to Baltimore and see your intended."

"I am, sir, so thanks."

Madison departed. The withdrawals were baffling. Both customers were civil servants and had invested large sums with his First Community Bank. There had been enough funds to cover the losses, so staying solvent wasn't an immediate concern, but as Tate stated, if this was somehow the beginning of a trend, they could have trouble meeting their future fiduciary responsibilities, and that the bank couldn't afford.

Eager to get to the bottom of it, Madison hopped on the streetcar and rode downtown. One of the people who'd pulled out his money was civil service employee Wallace Bush. Few men of color worked for the civil service. Most of the jobs were party patronage jobs, and that thought brought Madison up short. Was Richards behind the withdrawals? Thinking it over, he was willing to bet he was. By being the chief supplier of names to the party for such jobs, he wielded a lot of power over the people who eventually took those positions. Was he exercising that power over Bush, one of the mayor's chief messengers?

Wallace Bush was a short little man with ears that should have been given to someone much taller. When he saw Madison approach his desk, he looked around frantically as if seeking a place to hide. They'd gone to school together at the Philadelphia Institute of Colored Youth, and he was one of the smartest individuals Madison knew, but he had met rabbits with more spine.

Bush immediately stood up. "Hey, Madison. The mayor needs me. Nice seeing you."

Madison gently grabbed hold of Bush's arm to keep him from fleeing. "This won't take but a moment. Why'd you take your money out this morning?"

That frantic look flashed in Bush's eyes again. "No real reason. My brother over in Jersey gets a better rate at his bank."

He tried to pull his arm away, still seeking to escape, but Madison held on. "Wally, we've known each other since we were eight. You don't have a brother in Jersey or anyplace else. You're an only child."

"Did I say brother?" He laughed nervously. "I meant cousin. My cousin."

Madison waited.

Wally sighed. "Okay. Truth is, party boss Richards told me if I didn't pull my money out, I'd lose my job. You know I can't afford to be out of work."

"I know."

"He's got it in for you, Mad. Wants to send you to the poorhouse."

Madison could see the other office workers staring at them with disapproval. "Okay, I'll let you go before there's trouble. Don't worry about the money. Do what you need to do to feed your family. I'll handle Richards."

"I'm sorry, Madison."

"It's okay, Wally. At least you told me the truth."

Madison left his childhood friend to his job, then stepped back out into the sunshine. He assumed Richards would be applying pressure to as many of his customers as he had influence over. A grim Madison had to give it to Richards. It was a novel revenge; too novel, in fact, because if it resulted in a run on the bank, he knew he would be out of business by the end of next week.

Chapter 13

Teresa was seated on the library's carpeted floor, engrossed in Shakespeare's *Taming of the Shrew,* when she heard the door pull chime. Irritated by the interruption because she wanted to read more about Kate and her nemesis husband Petrucchio now that they'd had their wild and crazy wedding, she got to her feet, went to the door and snatched it open. The sight of Madison standing on the other side of the screen instantly restored her mood. "Well, hello."

As soon as he stepped inside, he brought her in against him and greeted her with a slow, dizzying kiss that proved far more moving than any words might have been.

"I like the way you say hello," she said from within her fuzzy world. "How's the day been for you so far?"

"Been interesting, but everything else pales when compared to you."

"You sound like Petrucchio."

"Who?"

"*Taming of the Shrew.* He's the man Kate's parents paid to marry her."

"Ah. Shakespeare. You're reading Shakespeare now?"

"Wanted to know what that Mr. Strange fella was reciting last night at the Academy. Your mother has all the Shakespeare plays, but I don't know why I was surprised. She has every other book in the world, it seems."

"Strange was reciting from *Othello* last night. Did you read it?"

She shook her head. "The description said it ended with some man choking his wife to death. I can read about that back home, but the description for *The Taming of the Shrew* didn't sound too bad."

"Are you enjoying it?"

"It's a struggle to read but I'm getting most of it, and some of the jokes too."

"Good." Madison realized he was in danger of losing those two double eagles he'd bet his mother. Teresa wasn't exactly a lady yet, but Shakespeare? He was impressed.

"Are we still going on the boat ride?" she asked.

"Yep. Unless you'd rather stay home."

She studied his eyes. His meaning was plain and her nipples stood up. "Let's take the boat ride first. I've never been on a steamship before."

"Really?"

"Nope."

"Then by all means let's do that. Later, I've a bit more land-based entertainment in store."

Again Teresa wondered how she'd get through the rest of her life without him around. "I can't wait."

He stroked her soft cheek. "I wanted to come over

and see you as soon as my eyes opened this afternoon."

"You would have been welcomed. I wanted to see you too." Last night's lovemaking was still vivid, and no matter the future, she was enjoying her time with him.

"Well before this mutual admiration society turns into a mutual undressing society, we should go. They'll have box dinners for sale on the boat, so we can eat once we board."

"Sounds good." She rose on her toes to kiss him with as much potency as his kiss greeting her had held. "That's to give you something to look forward to later."

He grinned and let her go so they could leave.

As they caught a street trolley, Madison enjoyed the sight of her in the snug leathers, and so did the other male passengers, but only he knew that she didn't have a stitch on beneath them. In place of the leather coat that she'd worn for the photographers and the press the day they descended on his mother's house, she had on a high-necked, long-sleeve blouse instead, and her black boots. He found the mix of primness and sensuality arousing. Her attire made him eagerly anticipate being alone with her in the dark on the ferry ride. If the outing ran true to form, though, the vessel would be crowded and the chances for trysting in earnest slim, but he'd take what he could get. There would always be an opportunity for more kisses once they returned to shore.

There were quite a few people waiting at the Market Street dock for the evening's outing. Many in the crowd smiled Teresa's way as she and Madison got in line. In spite of Jim Crow, Philadelphia's Negro citizens enjoyed recreation just as much as their White counterparts. Church- and club-sponsored train and steamship excursions to Washington, Boston, and other cities along the eastern coast were common, especially among the elite who also had summer homes on the Jersey shore. The common folk unable to afford pricey trips or summer homes took day trips to picnic groves or caught the ferries to New Jersey that left every fifteen minutes from the same docks where Madison and Teresa were waiting near now. One particularly popular place in New Jersey was the amusement park at Gloucester where there were rides and swimming. Another was Stockton Grove in the Black section of Camden, but because Teresa couldn't set foot on the soil of any state other than Pennsylvania, because of the conditions of her parole, she and Madison were content with tonight's excursion down the Delaware River.

The White captain of the vessel recognized Teresa from the newspapers and happily offered her and Madison free admission, just as Madison had predicted. Now, standing by the rail with him by her side, she looked out over the ink black water that was dappled by the moonlight. She could smell the water. There was a wonderful breeze, and even though the sound of the boat's engine seemed magnified against the quiet, she was enjoying the journey. Courting couples made up most of the vessel's passengers, and everywhere one looked there were lovers holding hands or sneaking kisses in the shadows. She and Madison had managed to steal a few that left them both dizzy, but they were content with each other's company and the time alone.

Madison asked her, "What's the first thing you want to do when you go home?"

"Ride Cloud, and then find a good bottle of tequila."

"Tequila is a liquor, I'm assuming."

She nodded. "Mexican made, from the agave plant. Some people like it, others don't."

"But you do?"

"Is that disapproval I hear?"

"No."

"Liar," she chuckled. "We treat things differently out West, so let's drop this subject before an argument breaks out. It's too lovely a night to fight."

"I agree."

She looked his way and found his eyes watching her in the moonlight.

"What do you want to do after the tequila?" he asked.

"See my mother Tamar. Then visit my brother and sister-in-law in Kansas. I miss them all so much it hurts sometimes."

Madison couldn't imagine how hard it must be for her to be so far away from family and friends. Had the judge deliberately sent her east as further punishment for her crimes? He didn't know, but considered the sentencing fortuitous because if she hadn't been sent to Pennsylvania, the two of them would never have met, and he and his life would be poorer for it.

"You'd like the West," she said to him. "It's open and you can see the sky. The water's clear. Game's not as plentiful as it once was, but there's plenty left to keep you fed."

"I haven't hunted since I was young. My father and I would go all the time."

She looked. "You hunt?"

He shrugged. "Sure. Don't most men?"

"Just never thought about city boys having to put meat on the table. I assumed you all used butchers."

"Most people do, but when I was growing up people hunted."

"Interesting."

Madison wondered what the West looked like, and what kind of opportunities it might hold for a man like him. "Maybe Mother and I will train out and see you. I know she'd enjoy it."

"I'd love to show you around. We can see the mountains. I'll even show you how to shoot fish with a bow and arrow."

"What?"

"Many Native bloods fish with a bow and arrow like the Ancestors."

Madison had never heard of such a thing. "Does it work?"

"Of course," she said with a soft laugh. "Who do you think is going to bring back the biggest catch— somebody sitting on a bank praying the fish will visit the hook, or somebody with a bow who's standing in the water watching the fish and ready to pounce?"

"The person with the bow."

"Exactly."

"That has to be something to see."

"For us, it's how we fish. It's nothing special."

Madison was impressed. He wanted to go west just to see that. Fishing with a bow and arrow. He found that amazing. She was pretty amazing too. Everything about her, from her colorful speech to her take no prisoners attitude toward life, could make him follow her to the Great Wall of China if it meant staying by her side. She and his old friend Loreli Winters Reed were the only women he'd ever wanted to keep in his life, but the fates had other plans, it seemed. He was destined to give up Teresa just as he'd done with Loreli. Depressing thoughts, and he put them away. He'd have the rest of the year to enjoy Teresa's company. No sense in crying over milk that wouldn't spill until then.

They took a cab from the docks back to Madison's place. Unlike the vehicle they'd ridden in last night, this one had a privacy curtain that separated the driver from his passengers and shielded them from prying eyes on the street. When Madison drew the curtain closed, Teresa felt like she was in a cave surrounded by the black velvet darkness and by him. He lowered his mouth to her lips and gently invited her to come play. For the first moments, they let the sensations rise, feeding on each other, coaxing each other with nibbles and lazy licks. Their tongues mated, then danced, and hands began to reacquaint themselves with the length and breadth of arms and backs. He skimmed a hand down her spine then up to the back of her head and pulled her closer.

The heat of his mouth on her throat, and the hands squeezing and moving her breasts, elicited a soft moan. Her head fell back on the warm leather seat and she let it brace her as the storm intensified. His mouth burned her nipple through the thin white cotton of her blouse. As he took it in, then rolled his tongue around it, she arched so he could take more.

And he did, gladly, wantonly leaving the fabric wet and the nipple beneath hard as a jewel. He raised his head to seek her lips, his fingers moving over the damp circles, and whispered, "That's enough for now ... we'll finish when I get you home."

Teresa vaguely remembered leaving the carriage and walking up the steps to his porch and door. Her world was hazy from desire and the kisses and touches he'd gifted her with on the ride to his place, but the world became crystal clear when he ushered her inside, kicked the door closed behind him, and carried her upstairs. She never thought she'd enjoy having a man carry her, but knowing that once they reached his room he would really treat her made her smile.

He set her on her feet, then lit a lamp. She could see the heat in his eyes and again wondered why the room hadn't already caught fire. He came back to her and after kissing her until her knees melted into her boots, made short work of the buttons on her blouse, which she tossed aside. The heat in his eyes flared at the sight of the black silk binding her breasts, and he ran a rough possessive hand over its wound and tied length.

"Lord, woman," he whispered thickly. Tugging the taut silk aside, he took the freed nipple into his mouth and placed his hand on her back to bring her forward. Soon the silk was down around her waist and he was enjoying her fully with his lips and hands, and all she could do was stand there on shaking legs and try not to shatter.

Madison straightened and put his hands to work on the placard of her leathers. Her passion-lidded eyes reflected every touch, kiss, and caress he gave her, along with a blatant hunger for more. He dragged the trousers down her firm dark legs then placed a bold hand between her thighs. Her core was hot and flowing, so much so that he wanted to give her the most carnal kiss of all. "Lie down on the bed for me, Angel."

Complying, Teresa shuddered in response to his tone, words, and fevered touch. He pulled the leathers free. He touched that burning damp place and sat down on the bed beside her. His continued teasing made her spread her legs shamelessly, and when he lowered his head and flicked his tongue across the space, her hips lifted like a puppet on a string and she uttered a sharp strangled cry.

"Hold onto yourself, Angel, don't come yet ... "

He commenced the wanton conquering. The sensations were so staggering, she could hear herself gasping and whimpering. In spite of his caution, the orgasm was drawing near. She tried to master it, but all she could feel was his mouth, his wicked, wicked tongue, and herself starting to break apart. When he took the little pleasure bud into his mouth and sucked, then slid two long-boned fingers into her swollen breach, she came, screaming. He didn't stop. While she bucked and screamed and twisted he continued his erotic feasting; holding her hips so she couldn't get away, he branded her for eternity with a loving she'd remember for a lifetime. She'd never had so much pleasure in her life, and to keep him from stealing her soul, she growled and backed away, her hand covering herself to ward him off.

He grinned like a satisfied male. "Is that Teresa July running away?"

"You just stay over there," she warned with a laugh. She had no words for how well he'd loved her.

He took off his pants and said, "But if I stay here, you won't get this ... "

Teresa shifted her attention to the splendid-looking reward standing hard between his lean brown thighs, and she playfully beckoned him to her.

Grinning, he grabbed a pillow from the bed and slipped it between her hips. In answer to her curious look, he said, "You'll enjoy yourself better."

Teresa doubted anything could be better than what she'd experienced with him so far, but he was the *brujo,* and she the woman under his spell. With the length of him encased in rubber, he slowly worked his way inside. He was right, being lifted by the pillow did affect the feel, and as he pushed home, she purred sensually.

"I knew you couldn't resist."

And he was right. No woman in her right mind would say no to this, to him. The pillow gave her just enough height for him to feel him fully, and the dance began.

As the night lengthened, they lost track of time and themselves. He took her on the bed, on the chairs, and standing before the mirror so she could watch his hands teasing her breasts and sliding down between her thighs. He took her in the shower, then against the wall of the washroom. They took another shower, this time under tepid water, and he finally carried her back to the room.

While he stripped off the soiled sheets and quickly put on fresh ones, the boneless Teresa, throbbing and echoing, stood against the bedpost. When he finished, they laid down. He pulled her shower-fresh body in against him, kissed her one last time, then they both drifted off to sleep smiling.

It was Friday. Mrs. Nance and Emma were scheduled to return on Saturday, so Madison and Teresa knew they had one last day of uninterrupted and unsupervised time together.

"Wake up, lazybones."

Teresa turned over, and the sight of him sitting on the edge of the bedside put a sleepy smile on her face. "Morning?"

"More like afternoon."

"What time is it?"

"A bit after one."

Her earlier vow not to lie around like a lazybones and forget who she was had been forgotten in the aftermath of last night. He was dressed, she saw. "Are you leaving?"

"Nope. Just came back. I went and got us something to eat."

She raised up and pulled the sheet up to cover herself. "What a night."

"Indeed, it was."

The muscles in Teresa's back and thighs were tight. Her legs were sore and felt like they often did after a long hard ride across country, and she supposed their strenuous lovemaking qualified as that. As the old western saying went, she'd been ridden hard and hung up wet. But she had no complaints. Not one.

Teresa knew that the longer she stayed around him, the harder it would be to turn him loose. Common sense said to end this dalliance so that leaving would be easier when the time came, but the woman inside herself was selfish, and as long as he was near, she didn't care about the consequences, at least for now.

Madison had been around her enough now to know when she was thinking. He reached out and stroked her satiny cheek. "What's going on inside that head of yours?"

"Just thinking that a loving like last night might make it hard for a girl to leave."

"You could always stay," he countered quietly.

Her smile was bittersweet. She shook her head. "No. I couldn't live here. Too much missing."

He understood, but that didn't stop him from wanting to change her mind. "Friend of mine is having a birthday party tonight. Do you want to go?"

"Sure. What's your friend's name?"

"Ben Norton."

"Can I wear my leathers?"

"You really do prefer to wear them, don't you?" he said, amusement threading his voice.

"Yes. The leathers make me feel more like me. Dresses turn me into somebody else, somebody who's soft and maybe can't take care of herself. Does that make sense?"

"I suppose. Makes you feel vulnerable."

"That might be the word. I always feel like I need to have my Colt strapped on, and because I don't, I'm not comfortable."

"I'm sure Ben won't mind if you wear your leathers."

"What about you?"

He shrugged. "Me, I like you in whatever you have on—or not."

"The *not's* better, I'll bet."

"Oh, yes, ma'am."

Teresa enjoyed him so much. "So what time does this shindig start tonight?"

"Nine, ten. In the past, his parties have gone until dawn."

"What time is your mother due in tomorrow?"

"Four o'clock."

"Gives us plenty of time for one last night."

"Yes it does, so let's make it a good one." Unable to beat down his desire to touch her, Madison slid the edge of his finger over the point of her nipple poking the sheet. "Maybe Ben will even have some tequila."

Teresa's body began to coo. "I dare him, although the parole agent did ask about my drinking liquor."

He transferred his hello to the other nipple. "I don't think one night of fun will land you back in the pokey. Besides, Ben's friends are select and discreet. No one will give you away."

Teresa liked the sound of that. Since her release, she'd been a very good girl. It would be nice to have a chance to kick up her heels at least once during her confinement, even if it was for only a few hours. The rest of her thoughts had trouble aligning themselves because of Madison's touches. When he freed the sheet from her hand and tasted the nubbins he'd been preparing, she had trouble breathing evenly as well.

"I wonder how these would taste with orange marmalade?" he husked out.

Teresa rippled with a response that flooded her core.

"Think I'll find out." He bit her gently, then left the room.

When he returned with a small bowl of the orange sweet, he put a bit of it on his finger and with his eyes blazing placed the finger in her mouth. She took a few seconds to suck it clean, then he dipped up some more and coated first one nipple and then the other. He left her a moment to stand and remove his clothes, and when he joined her on the bed, he treated her to the most erotic afternoon she'd ever had in her life.

Madison took her home. When he returned that evening to pick her up, the sight of her in the flowing black gown surprised him. "I thought you were going to wear your leathers?"

The black gown with its full skirt was accented with midnight blue threads. The deep cut of the neckline offered a sumptuous view of the soft tops of her onyx breasts, while long black evening gloves graced her arms and hands. Once again she'd stunned him with her loveliness.

Teresa secretly enjoyed the approval in his gaze. "Thought I'd wear this. In certain circumstances, gowns are more convenient, shall we say?"

Madison grinned. "You're turning into a pretty naughty woman, Teresa July."

"I wasn't the one who brought marmalade to bed," she replied with knowing eyes. Just saying the word marmalade made Teresa's core pulsate.

"Is that a complaint?"

"Oh, no. I love your games."

"And I love that you like to play."

The heat began to arch, and they both felt it.

Madison said, "We should probably get going."

"I agree."

But he had to kiss her first, and she wanted to be kissed. After they'd shared enough kisses to hold them for a while, they left Mrs. Nance's house and walked down the path to his buggy.

The street outside Ben Norton's place in the Fifth Ward was so crowded when they arrived there was no place to park. Men and women dressed to the gills were moving up and down sidewalks toward the large row house, and Teresa was reminded of the scene outside of the Academy of Music.

To deal with the parking dilemma, Ben had hired men to be valets who would park the carriages and buggies a few blocks over. Every owner was given a ticket with a number so they'd be able to reclaim their vehicle when they wanted to leave. Madison placed the ticket inside of his suit coat and escorted the gown-wearing Teresa up the stairs and inside.

Ben's live-in woman, Irene Garner, met them at the door. Madison had to shout over the din in order to introduce her to Teresa. The downstairs was packed with celebrants.

Irene yelled, "Nice to meet you, Teresa. Saw you in the papers." Turning back to Madison, she added, "Take her upstairs. Quieter!"

Madison nodded. Taking Teresa's hand, he cut a swath through the crush and led her up the stairway to the second floor.

It was indeed much quieter there. He looked into the billiards room that was filled with cigar smoke and saw Ben hunched over the large table, cue in hand. Madison and Teresa waited until he made his shot, then entered the room.

"Mad. How are you?" Ben said, setting down his cue.

The two friends shared a warm embrace, then Madison made the introductions. Ben said to her, "I was wondering if he was ever going to bring you by. I saw you in the newspapers."

"Seems like everybody has."

"Not often we get someone as famous as you around here, so welcome. Make yourself at home."

Teresa eyed the pool table.

Ben asked, "Do you play?"

"I do."

"Let me finish whipping Clyde over there, and you can have the next game."

Teresa's smile was appreciative.

"In the meantime, you all head down the hall. There's a buffet and a bar. Help yourselves."

Teresa had a wonderful evening. She ate, played pool, watched Madison win a lot of money, then went back and shot some more pool. The men she beat were as surprised as Alvin Porter had been when she beat him at horseshoes, but none were as angry.

In fact, she ran into Alvin Porter, standing near the bar. She'd had a small glass of wine earlier and came back to see if the barkeep had found the bottle of tequila he swore was on the premises somewhere. No one ever asked for it, she was told, so he had to locate it. Locate it he did, and as he poured her a small shot, Porter, apparently still miffed about the horseshoes, sneered, "Is that the swill you drink out West?"

There were a number of men and a few women standing nearby, and they all went quiet in response to Porter's rude words. Teresa took a sip of her drink, and the familiar kick made her mentally sigh with satisfaction. "Yes," Teresa said, turning and finally responding, "but it's not for children."

He took offense at her jab and puffed up. "You calling me a child? I can outdrink you any day of the week."

"Oh, really?"

He looked her up and down. "Yeah."

The crowd started buzzing and people began angling for a better view.

Teresa asked him, "You sure?"

"Yeah I'm sure. Are you stalling because you're scared?"

"Not me."

"Then let's go."

Teresa shook her head at this foolish young man. "Okay." Tossing back the drink in her glass with one swallow, she told the barkeep, "Pour him one."

Madison was at the poker table when he heard a crowd of people roar. He looked up. Ben, seated at the table beside him, looked up too.

Irene came hurrying in and said, "Madison, you probably should come and get your lady, she's in a drinking contest at the bar."

Madison lowered his head to the table and bounced it against the edge a few times.

A laughing Ben tossed down his cards and backed his chair away from the table. "Come on, Mad."

Madison got up reluctantly.

With Ben behind him, Madison made his way to the front of the crowd just in time to see Teresa slam her shot glass down on the bar and demand, "Hit me again, barkeep!"

The mostly male gathering cheered as the grinning bartender splashed a brown liquor into her glass. She gave a cool smile to the red-eyed young man swaying on his feet, then tossed the drink back in one swallow before slamming the glass down again. The crowd roared.

"Your turn," she told her opponent, a hard challenge in her bright black eyes.

Madison recognized her opponent as Paula's friend, Porter. The young man was a boastful lout who had undoubtedly stepped on one of Teresa's outlaw nerves. He looked drunk enough to tip over with the touch of a fingernail, but he picked up his glass, hefted it, then promptly keeled over backward like a felled tree. As he hit the floor, the noisy celebrants erupted.

Teresa yelled over the din, "Barkeep, drinks on me for everybody!"

Madison was so stunned, he walked up and studied her. On the outside she didn't look drunk at all, but the sparkle in her eyes gave her away.

She drawled, "Well, hello, city boy. How are ya?"

He shook his head. "I'm well. You?"

"Doing real fine. Had to teach that little varmint a lesson. He actually thought he could outdrink me. Me!" she said, pointing at herself. "Teresa July. I have drank tequila for three days straight and swallowed every worm!"

Madison didn't have a clue what swallowing worms had to do with anything, and told himself he probably didn't want to know. He did know this demonstration of hers was going to be all over town by dawn, regardless of the discreetness of the guests, and his mother was going to throw a fit when she found out. He needed to get her home.

"You know something?" she said to him, grinning.

"What?" He couldn't stop his answering smile.

"I just ordered drinks around and I don't have a dime."

"I was wondering about that."

"Guess I'll have to rob somebody, huh?" She began laughing.

Madison shook his head at her antics. "I'll take care of it. Where's your wrap?"

He could see her mulling over the question.

"I don't think I have one." She turned to the bartender. "Do I have a wrap?"

He bent down behind the bar and handed Teresa her blue wrap and handbag.

"Guess I do. Thanks."

"Are you ready?"

"As a hog in heat."

Madison shook his head.

She linked her hand into the crook of his arm and he led her away. First, however, he had to endure the delay to their departure as every man in the place jockeyed to tell her good-bye.

"Good-bye, Miss July."

"See you again, Miss July."

"Hope to see you again, Miss July."

Madison's quelling look kept most of them at bay, but Teresa didn't seem bothered by all the commotion. When they finally got to the door, she held up her hand and called out, "See you next time, boys!"

And then Madison walked her back downstairs and out into the night.

Chapter 14

The valet took their ticket then left to retrieve the buggy.

As the slightly swaying Teresa and the outdone Madison stood by the curb, she said, "Haven't been drunk in a long time. Feels kinda good."

"Oh really."

"Yep. I'll probably be sick as a dog in the morning, but right now, I don't care."

While they waited, she started softly singing a song in what he assumed to be drunken Spanish. He didn't ask her to explain the song because he doubted she'd be able to tell him anything coherently.

Once the buggy arrived, he tipped the young man, poured her in, and drove toward his mother's house. There'd be no lovemaking tonight. He was taking her home.

They were just about there when she looked his way and said, "If you mother finds out about this, she's probably going to be very disappointed with me, isn't she?"

"More than likely. She's trying to turn you into a lady, and ladies don't have drinking contests."

"I keep telling you all, I don't want to be a lady. I just want to be me. Teresa."

He shook his head, "I tried tell her it would never work."

Teresa spun, eyes flashing, and Madison knew instantly that he should have kept the comment to himself.

"You don't think I can be a lady?" she asked sharply.

"You're the one drinking men under the table, what do you think?"

"I think you stink."

"And you're drunk as a skunk."

"I could be a lady if I wanted to be. How much do you want to bet?"

He chuckled at yet another bet on this subject. "I don't make bets with drunken women."

"Bet me, tinhorn!"

He looked her way. "No. If you want to fight, let's do it tomorrow when you're in your right mind."

"Just because I'm drunk doesn't mean I don't know what I'm doing."

He rolled his eyes heavenward.

"You're afraid you'll lose."

"From what I saw back there, my money's real safe."

By then they were in front of his mother's house. He didn't see any lights on.

"You think so?" she asked pointedly.

"I'm pretty confident. Yes."

"Well, you're wrong!"

Madison couldn't believe her stubbornness.

Leaving his seat, he went around to her side and put out his hand to assist her.

She ignored it. "Since you don't think I can be a lady, why are you trying to act like I am one. Get out of the way!" Snatching up her wrap and bag, she stepped down and sailed past him.

Jaw set angrily, he followed her to the door.

Her inebriation fouled her efforts to fit the key in the door, so he took out his.

She told him, "I don't need your help."

"No. You need a keeper."

"Just go home."

He forced his key into the lock and pushed the door open.

She entered and promptly tripped over the threshold rug. She would have fallen had he not caught her arm. She shook herself free.

"Go to bed," he told her.

"Don't tell me what to do!"

"Somebody needs to!"

"Well, it won't be you—tinhorn!"

"You're about two seconds from me paddling your drunken behind!"

"Touch me, and I will sock you so hard you'll think you're Paula!"

Mrs. Nance's voice rang out. "Stop it this minute! People can hear you in Pittsburgh!"

They stared over at her and Emma in shock.

Molly snapped, "Yes, I'm home. Emma and I came back early." She turned up the lamp, and the soft glow illuminated Teresa and Madison glaring at each other angrily. "Now, what is this about?"

Simmering, Madison crossed his arms. "I'll let her tell you."

Mrs. Nance turned. "Teresa?"

"He thinks I can't be a lady because I drank one of Paula's friends under the table."

"You did what?" Wide-eyed, she asked her son, "Where were you?"

"In the other room playing cards and minding my own business. The woman's a menace."

"I am not!"

Mrs. Nance studied Teresa for a moment. "Are you drunk?"

"As a skunk as your smug son so eloquently put it."

"Teresa?"

"I'm sorry, Mrs. Nance, but I couldn't let that little bug Porter sass me like that. He was the one who threw down the glove, I just picked it up. Had to defend my honor."

Mrs. Nance was staring at Teresa as if she'd never seen her before. Then she turned amazed eyes to her son.

"I'm going home," he said firmly. "If you want to fuss, I'll come by tomorrow. Right now, *I'm* in need of a drink." He looked over at Teresa. "Good night, Miss July."

"Good night," she threw back crossly.

Shaking his head, Madison left.

Mrs. Nance turned to Teresa and said frostily, "We'll speak in the morning. To bed, young lady."

"Yes, ma'am."

In the dream, Teresa was in her cabin cooking beans on her small iron stove. When she turned away, she saw her mother seated at the table. "Tamar?" she said. "What are you doing here?"

Tamar was dressed in the old way. Bright colors and feathers. "Your brothers are gathering. Time has come."

Teresa searched her mother's face and saw that she looked older than she'd been the last time they'd seen each other. "Time has come for what?"

"He will give me strong grandsons. Treasure him."

"Tamar?"

"My soul is almost gone but I had to see the daughter of my heart one last time. Stay with him, Teri. He has the silence inside that you need."

Tamar rose from her seat and began walking away. As Teresa stared, her mother looked back one more time, then disappeared into a sparkling mist.

Teresa bolted awake. She was shaking, and covered with ice cold sweat. *Is Tamar dying?* A sense of foreboding filled every inch of her body. She had to find out. She needed to send a telegram to Neil and Olivia right away. She glanced at the clock. Seven A.M. Mrs. Nance and Emma were probably up by now.

Teresa moved to stand, but the searing ache in her head was like a kick from a mule and it forced her to sit back down. Gasping, she placed her pounding head in her hands. *"Dios!"*

Too much tequila. Way too much tequila!

She had to get up, though. Even though her head was screaming, she had to move. She had to find out what was happening with Tamar. Grabbing hold of the bedpost, she pulled herself to her feet and immediately felt her stomach churn ominously. Groaning with distress and alarm, she plastered her hand over her mouth and only sheer will propelled her to race from her room to the washroom so she wouldn't foul Emma's carefully waxed floors.

Teresa had no idea how much time had passed

as she lay stretched out on the washroom floor. Her stomach seemed to be empty, but the misery had her by the throat. Her head was still pounding. Last night's drinking had been a mistake. She shouldn't have let herself be goaded into showing off. Now she was paying the price. Her mother may or may not have passed on to the Ancestors, and she was too hung over to see about it.

Some daughter I am.

She heard footsteps, then Mrs. Nance's surprised and concerned voice. "Teresa! What's the matter?"

"I have a Goliath-size hangover and I need to wire my family in Kansas."

Mrs. Nance knelt at her side. "Come, let's get you to bed. This is what you get, you know."

"I know." Teresa struggled to her feet with Mrs. Nance's help. She was unsteady at best and her head still felt like someone was inside knocking down walls with a sledgehammer. "*Dios,* my head hurts."

"Then I shan't fuss. This is a far better punishment."

They were slowly moving down the hall back to Teresa's room. "Will you send a telegram to Olivia for me?" she asked. "I think Tamar is dying."

Mrs. Nance stopped. "Why do you think that?"

"She was in my dreams last night. Said she wanted to see me one last time."

"Are you sure this wasn't the liquor?"

"Positive."

They were by the bed now, and Teresa crawled in. "Please, send a wire to Olivia and ask her. Please."

"All right, dear. I'll send Emma first thing. Let's get you comfortable first."

"No! I'm fine. Just send the wire."

Mrs. Nance nodded worriedly and hurried from the room.

Teresa didn't realize she'd fallen asleep until she was gently shaken back to consciousness. Seeing Mrs. Nance sitting on the edge of the bed, she asked over her still pounding head, "Did you send the wire?"

She nodded. Her face was grim. "The response just arrived."

Teresa tore open the seal, and read:

> *Tamar died last night. Come to Henry Adams if you can. Will wait to hear your plans before burial.*
>
> *Neil*

Teresa let the paper slip from her fingers. Turning her head away so Mrs. Nance couldn't see, Tamar's only girl child let the tears run freely down her cheeks, but she didn't make a sound.

Even though it was Saturday and the bank was closed, Madison was seated inside his office going over the ledgers. He knew that Tate had been anxious to get to Boston for the weekend, but he wished they'd spoken before his assistant departed because it looked as if fourteen more people had withdrawn their money and closed their accounts.

But he didn't blame Tate. He blamed himself. Had he not been so intent on spending time with Teresa, he would have been here, at the bank, and might have convinced those investors to keep their funds in place. He hadn't been, and the ledgers reflected the results. The future didn't look good. An infusion of cash from his own personal funds would make up the deficit, but he'd be left much poorer. Frustrated, he shoved the ledger in front of him aside and silently cursed Dawson Richards for bringing this about.

In the morning's paper had been a story detailing Richards's own woes. It seemed now two other women had stepped forward with their own certificates of marriage to him, bringing the number of total wives to three and the clamoring for his resignation seemed to be rising. A growing number of Republican Party politicians were trying to distance themselves from the scandal by calling for a full-fledged investigation, but under the best of circumstances, such things took time, and Madison knew he didn't have time. Even if Richards was forced to resign, there was no guarantee the defecting investors would return.

Madison hated to think what this meant. He was going to have to cease operations, and when that happened, the remaining fifty or so investors were only going to get a portion of their money back. The loans he had given out to businesses, homeowners, and entrepreneurs were still out there, and most weren't scheduled to come due for months. Ben Norton had stored some of his funds with his bank too, but most of his friend's fortune was downtown in the White banks, so Ben would undoubtedly shrug off the closure and tell him not to worry about it. But he knew that people like Charles Watson couldn't afford to lose even a dollar. And having to face the old chef wasn't something he was looking forward to. Of course, he could go to Ben for a loan to make up the difference and then owe Ben his firstborn, but he had never failed at anything in his life, and this was sticking in his craw.

At a knock on the door, Madison looked curiously out of the window. His curiosity turned to anger at the sight of Dawson Richards's smug face. "What the hell does he want?" Madison asked the silence around him.

He was sure that Richards had come to gloat. Going to the door, he undid the lock and opened it. "We're closed."

Richards smiled, showing off his perfect teeth. "Closing permanently, from what I'm hearing. Too bad. You're such an influence in the community."

"What the hell do you want?"

"Came to watch you weep."

Madison waited.

Richards grinned. "Now that you're headed to the poorhouse, maybe that little outlaw of yours will want to change horses. I'd love to watch her swallowing my dick."

The first punch knocked out two of Richards's perfect teeth, and before he could react, Madison was on him.

When it was over, Madison was staggering and breathing hard. He had a black eye that was already beginning to swell and blood was pouring from his nose, but he was still on his feet. Looking worse, Richards was lying at Madison's feet and out cold in the middle of the street. For the first time, Madison noticed the raucous crowd ringing them. Like a man waking from a dream, he stared around at all the eager faces. Seemingly out of nowhere, Charles

Watson appeared. He was grinning, and when he reached Madison, he quickly raised his arm to signal the winner, and the crowd roared. The weary Madison grinned too.

Later, when Madison entered his mother's parlor, Molly's and Teresa's eyes went wide, and his mother's hands went to her mouth. "My lord, son! What happened!"

Out of his one good eye, he viewed the concern on their faces then said to his mother, "I took exception to something Dawson Richards said, and so ... " His voice trailed off as if no further explanation were needed.

Molly went to his side. "Are you all right? That's a senseless question, I know, but—oh my goodness, Madison. Sit down, please. Emma! Bring some ice!"

"I've already done that, Mother. I'm fine."

Emma came in the room with ice in a bowl, but upon seeing Madison, she said, "I thought you wanted ice for a drink. Goodness. Look at you. What happened?"

"Fight."

"I hope the other person looks worse."

He nodded. "He does."

Satisfied, Emma went back to the kitchen.

Teresa was glad to hear he'd whipped Richards, but her heart had jumped into her throat when he first appeared. She'd been so mad at him last night. Now she felt only concern. "Are you sure you're okay? Did you break your hand?"

He looked at his heavily bandaged right hand and said, "I don't think so."

"What did Richards say?"

"I won't repeat it."

Teresa studied him. She had to be content with that for now. His entrance had momentarily distracted her from her grief, but now it was back and she needed to let him know that she'd be leaving on Monday's train. "Mrs. Nance, may I speak to Madison alone for a few minutes?"

The concern for her son was still on Molly's face, but she nodded. "Take all the time you need." She departed and closed the door softly.

For a moment silence reigned, then Teresa said, "I'm sorry about last night. I was drunk."

"Yes, you were."

She swallowed her retort and said instead, "Tamar died last night. I have to go home."

Madison felt that blow much harder than any of the punches thrown by Richards. "When are you leaving?"

"Soon as your mother hears back from the parole board agent, Singleton, I'll see about getting a train ticket. I don't think I can leave without him knowing. I'm hoping he'll say it's okay, but even if he doesn't, I'm going anyway."

He understood. "I'm very sorry for your loss, Teresa."

"Thanks." She took in his bruised face again. "Glad you got to whip Richards."

"Me too. He's been threatening some of the people with money in my bank and they've all closed their accounts. I'll have to shut down."

"Oh no."

He nodded.

"I'm sorry."

"No sorrier than I. I talked to my friend Ben after the fight. He's going to loan me the money I need to cover the rest of my clients' losses, but after that?" He shrugged.

Teresa shook her head sadly. It had been a bad day for them both. Two days ago their world had been filled with passion and light. Now? "I'm going to miss you, Madison."

"I'll miss you too."

There was a knock on the door.

"Come on in," Teresa called.

It was Mrs. Nance. "I finally got a reply from Mr. Singleton. You may go to Kansas, but you are still under court supervision, so I have to accompany you."

"Will you?"

"Of course, but I'd feel safer if Madison went with us."

Teresa didn't care who tagged along just so she could go. When she turned his way, he was watching her out of his battered face. She asked him, "Well?"

"Why not? It's not like I have a business to run."

His mother's face reflected her curiosity.

He told her the story.

She appeared both angry and heartbroken. "Oh, Madison. I'm so sorry. That Richards is a snake. What are you going to do?"

"For now, escort you to Kansas. After that? We'll see."

"You'll land on your feet," his mother said. "You always do."

He gave her a small smile. "In the meantime, I'll go

to the station and get tickets. I assume you want to go as soon as possible," he said to Teresa.

She nodded. "Yes, and after you get the tickets, I'll need to wire Neil so he'll know we're coming."

"I'll take care of that too. Just tell me where to send it."

Teresa was grateful for his assistance. She had no idea where they stood on a personal level, but was glad to have him at her back. The future would be what it would be.

They boarded the train on Monday morning. Ben had graciously donated his private car so Madison and the ladies wouldn't have their journey impacted by Jim Crow. He'd also driven them to the station to make sure there were no problems accessing it, and now that they were inside the sumptuously appointed car, Teresa gave him a big hug. "Thank you, Ben."

"You're welcome, Miss July. Sorry for your loss."

"Thanks."

He shook hands with Madison. "See what it looks like out there. Land. Business. I trust your instincts. If you see anything interesting, wire me."

"Will do."

They embraced, and after a good-bye to Mrs. Nance, the big man left.

As the train chugged west, Teresa was sure Tamar was with them on the journey because none of the problems that could have delayed the trip—like cars coming off the tracks, accidents with other trains, or blown boilers—occurred. The ride from Philadelphia to Chicago went well, as did the transfer of their private car to the Kansas Pacific Railroad at the station near Kansas City, Kansas. Molly spent the journey reading and watching the landscape change, Madison spent most of his time in the smoking car playing cards, and Teresa silently mourned her mother.

Now, standing outside on the small observation deck on the back of the train, she looked up at the night sky. She'd never envisioned a life devoid of the magical Tamar. Teresa had always believed Tamar would live forever. The magic in her crackled like lightning sometimes. Supposedly, Tamar was the last in a line of shamanlike women that stretched back to Africa, and whether she was frying tortillas or walking in her children's dreams, life seemed brighter with her around. Now she was gone, along with her lore and wisdom. In the July family, she was one of the last remaining Old Ones who had been born in the lush tropics of Florida, only to be forced to survive on the dusty and unforgiving soil of Indian Territory by the President of a country that never kept its word.

Tamar, I will miss you.

Teresa would miss her singing, her wisdom, and the arms that always held her when her brothers became too much, like the time they tied her to a post and used her for bow and arrow practice, or when they cut off her long hair to make false whiskers. She'd hated them all, all the time, it seemed, but Tamar would always punish them, and afterward would let her stay up late and tell her stories of the old times, and they'd look up at the night sky and count the stars.

It occurred to her that had she not been in prison, she might have been there when she died. But as it stood, Teresa didn't know if Tamar had been ill for

some time or if she'd died suddenly. Some daughter
I am, she said to herself again. The guilt was bad,
real bad, but she knew Tamar wouldn't want her to
feel that way. Tamar rarely looked back because it
wouldn't change the present. So Teresa resolved to
look forward, and to do that she would have to break
things off with Madison. She was pretty sure she was
in love with him and had been for a while, but the
two of them would never be one. Continuing to enjoy
his company was going to leave her with a broken
heart when he moved on, and she knew he would
because they came from different worlds, so it was
best to end things now, cleanly and finally, and with
her dignity and her heart intact.

Over the past four days, the bruising and swelling
on Madison's face had diminished considerably, but
traces of his altercation with Dawson Richards remained. Also remaining was his desire for Teresa, not
just physically, but for her companionship as well.
She'd been polite to him on the trip, but he sensed her
distancing herself. Most of it had to do with her grief,
but there was something else in her sad eyes, something deeper. He knew he hadn't been cheery himself,
if the truth be told. It could be she was simply react-
ing to his own distancing, which was rooted in the
mess Richards had made of his life.

That evening when he joined her outside on the
observation deck, he asked, "Want some company?"

"Sure."

He came and stood next to her and, like her,
leaned over the rail. The train chugged beneath their
feet.

Teresa told him, "Your mother's gone to bed, she said to tell you good night."

"I think she's enjoying seeing the country."

"I think so too. How was the game tonight?"

"Small pickings, but I enjoyed myself." He had won quite a bit of money playing poker while crossing the country. "How big is the town we're heading to?"

"By back East standards, not very, but for out here, it's big enough."

Madison knew the town was named Henry Adams because he'd sent the wire to alert her brother and sister-in-law of the time and date of their arrival, but he didn't know what to expect. The newspapers back East gave the impression that in western towns cowboys and outlaws rode up and down the streets shooting and raising Cain, and that there were saloons and loose women on every corner. "And your sister is the mayor?"

"Yes."

"How's that possible, when women don't have the vote yet."

"In some of our communities women can vote in local elections. In fact, women do have the vote in Wyoming, and have had it for a while, from what Olivia says."

Madison was surprised by that. "Is your sister-in-law White?"

Teresa stared. "Why would you think that? No. We're heading to a town full of people who look just like you and me."

Now he stared.

"Didn't I mention that?"

He smiled and shook his head.

"I'm sorry. Henry Adams is an all colored town. Folks from back East founded it back in the seventies."

"I've heard of the towns, just never thought I'd get to see one."

"Well, you will. Folks are real nice. It's where my brothers' trial was held." Teresa looked his way. Her desire for the two of them to go back to the way they were before was so strong she ached, but the fairy tale was over. Abruptly, she said, "I don't think you and I should be doing any more passion things together."

The night hid Madison's bittersweet smile. His head agreed with her words, but his heart was another matter. "I think you're right."

Teresa did her best to ignore the sadness creeping over her, but it was difficult. "We had fun, and I want to thank you for all you did, like taking me to the theater and on the boat ride, I'll never forget them. But when we get back to Philadelphia, you should get on with your life and I'll get on with mine. That way you can find that lady that you want so much." *He will give me strong grandsons.* Tamar's words from the dream echoed inside, but Teresa knew there weren't going to be grandchildren of any kind. "Besides, we went into this with our eyes open. No commitments or attachments. Correct?"

"Correct." But Madison didn't want the mythical *lady* she was referring to. In spite of their pledge of no commitments, he was as attached to her as he knew her to be attached to him. Being from different worlds was making this complicated. Add to the fact that he now had no visible means of income outside of what remained in his bank account and his poker winnings. Even if they were able to return to the couple they once were, he had no way to support her or take care of her. Not that she needed that. She was, after all, the indomitable Teresa July. But he was a man, and any man worth his salt wanted to be able to provide for the woman in his life. "When do you think we'll arrive?" he asked.

Teresa was glad for the change in subject. "Noon tomorrow. Hopefully."

"Good." He looked at her. "We did have fun."

"Yes, we did."

"I'm going on to bed."

"Okay."

They stared at each other in the dark.

"Good night, Teresa."

"See you in the morning."

Alone now, Teresa knew she'd made the right decision. So why did she feel like she'd been shot in the heart?

Chapter 15

Just as Teresa predicted, the train pulled into the Henry Adams station precisely at noon. Waiting on the platform were not only Neil and Olivia, but her other brothers, Two Shafts, Harper, and Diego as well! Forgetting her escorts in the excitement, Teresa ran to meet her family. She was engulfed. She felt their happiness, sorrow and their grief as they clung together, but most of all she felt home.

Wiping away the happy tears dampening her eyes, she looked at Diego, the brother she'd always loved best. His Comanche Seminole hair was as long as hers. "Where have you been? It's been over ten years!"

A smile split his dark face, showing off the patented July grin. "Yukon Territory."

"You couldn't write or wire?"

He shrugged. "I'm here now and I'm here to stay. We'll talk later." He gave her another hug. "Missed you, Teri. Glad you're out."

Teresa knew that her youngest brother had no idea how good it felt having him back, but also knew better than to become too emotional, so she backed off and stared in happiness at the men they'd all become, a happiness tempered by grief. "It's too bad it took Tamar's death to bring us back together again."

They nodded solemnly. She turned to Olivia, who was standing off to the side. The sister of her heart held out her arms to Teresa in welcome.

"Livy," Teresa said, moving toward her.

Tears in her eyes, Olivia enfolded Teresa, and as they rocked she whispered, "Welcome home, sister. So good to see you and so sorry about Tamar."

"Thanks." Teresa hugged her a moment longer, then pulled back and looked into Olivia's expressive eyes. She saw traces of pain. Olivia and Neil had been trying to have a baby since their marriage, but she hadn't been able to carry to full term. There'd been three miscarriages so far. Teresa hugged her again, hoping to give her some of her own strength so that her remarkable sister-in-law would stay strong. "Good to see you too. How are you?"

"I'm well. You look good. Almost the same way you did when you left."

"Much smarter, though."

Olivia grinned. "I knew you'd figure it all out eventually."

Her brothers surrounded her like mountains. None were shorter than six foot three inches tall. Later, she'd get the stories of the ones she hadn't seen in a while, like Harper and Diego, but right now she wanted them to meet the Nances. She looked back and saw them waiting on the platform. Madison's face was unreadable, and Mrs. Nance had a tentative smile on her face.

Teresa walked over and brought them forward. "Want you all to meet the folks I'm staying with in Philadelphia."

Introductions were made, and Teresa was proud of the politeness her brothers showed Mrs. Nance.

Madison was another story.

"Do you stay with your mother?" the green-eyed Harper asked.

Madison studied him a moment before saying, "No, but if I did, would that worry you, bother you?"

Diego crowed, "Whoa, he can speak."

Neil said, "Pretty good too."

"Thanks," Madison replied coolly. "Speaking 'pretty good' is fairly common where I live."

Two Shafts, Teresa's half-Comanche half brother, laughed. "Got some spine. I say we let him be. He either got that bruised face giving out a whipping or taking one. We'll find out soon enough."

Madison had been prepared for the ribbing. The men were Teresa's brothers, after all.

Teresa, on the other hand, wanted to sock the four of them. She could tell by Olivia's face that her sister-in-law wasn't pleased either, but what could they do? The July men were like a bunch of adolescent cougar cubs.

"Neil, darling," Olivia said, "you may take the inmates back to the asylum now. Teresa and I will get the Nances settled in down at Sophie's. I'll bring them home for dinner around six."

Her husband grinned and said to his brothers, "You all heard the warden, but before you go, shake Nance's hand and give him a welcome. Got a feeling we're going to be seeing a lot of him."

Madison met Neil's eyes. They were as black and as full of mischief as his sister's were, but Madison sensed purpose behind the smile, one that was harder, almost challenging. In response, he gave Neil an almost imperceptible nod, which Neil returned.

After the handshakes and the welcomes, the July men, walking abreast like the gang of outlaws they'd once been, departed to retrieve their mounts.

Once they were gone, Teresa said to Madison, "Sorry about that."

"It's okay. They're your brothers. I expected it."

Teresa asked, "Mrs. Nance, are you all right? You look a bit shaken."

Molly looked up at her. "You said there would be four of them, but I didn't know they were going to be so big. My goodness, I was afraid to move for fear I'd get stepped on."

Olivia cracked, "Big bodies and sometimes pea-sized brains. Come on, Sophie's expecting us. My wagon's over here."

Madison put Teresa's gang of brothers out of his mind as he stowed their wealth of luggage into the bed of the wagon and climbed in. His mother sat on the front seat with the mayor. Teresa tossed in her two carpet bags, then climbed in with him. She'd been wearing her leathers since the day they left Philadelphia, and all the way cross-country he'd had a hard time not staring at her shapely form and remembering.

Olivia signaled the team of horses, and they began the bumpy five mile ride to town. Madison divided his attention between viewing the flat golden countryside and the woman seated in the corner of the bed. The landscape was very different from the green he was accustomed to seeing back home. Kansas had

its own beauty, but it was the beauty with the onyx
eyes that had him entranced. Since they'd decided
not to do any more passion things, as she'd so accu-
rately described it, she seemed to be all he could think
about. Yes, she was unconventional, yes, sometimes
she gave him fits, but just looking at her mouth made
him crave just one more taste, all the while knowing he'd want a thousand more. He was in love with
this woman, plain and simple. What he planned to
do about it, he hadn't a clue, but finally admitting the
depths of his feelings was freeing. He respected her
grief, so he would give her the time he knew she'd be
needing, but afterward, because he knew how highly
passionate and sensual she was, he doubted she'd be
able to keep her leathers on for long if he asked her in
just the right way.

Teresa, seated across from him in the bed of the
wagon, had to look away from the intense gaze in
his eyes because her nipples were calling him. Although they had agreed to go on with their lives, her
body wasn't cooperating. Every time she looked at
him, sensual memories flooded her. She figured that
the passage of time would eventually be the cure, but
what was she supposed to do until then?

When they rolled into town down the unpaved
main street, Madison didn't see the gunslingers or
prostitutes but he did see a quaint bunch of buildings and plank walks lining both sides of the street. A
good number of people dressed like plain folks were
on the walks, and just as Teresa promised, they all
looked like him. He saw the sheriff's office, a livery,
and a mercantile with a large American flag flying on
a pole out front. There was a barbershop and a doc-

tor's office. Sharing the road with the mayor's wagon were other wagons driven by men in farmer's clothing, their bonnet-wearing wives seated beside him while their children laughed and giggled in the bed. Other wagons were packed high with bound bales of hay and what he guessed was wheat.

Taking all this in, Madison sensed a strange charge building inside of him that he couldn't name. This was a town established and governed by men and women of color, and Madison thought that an awesome achievement. It couldn't have been easy for the settlers that first year, or even in the years following yet this little town of Henry Adams, which appeared to be thriving, was going on twenty years old. Madison decided that what he was feeling was pride.

The mayor drew the team to a halt in front of a large building with an ornate sign that read: HENRY ADAMS HOTEL. It was grand, far grander than Madison had expected to find in such an out-of-the-way place. He shared his pleased look with Teresa, who held his eyes long enough for him to want to touch her.

"Teresa, this is a beautiful place," Molly said with surprise.

Teresa tore her gaze away from Madison's. "Hoped you'd like it."

"Oh, I do." Molly was looking up at all the windows and cornices. "It rivals some of the places back home."

"Wait until you see the inside."

Olivia said to Madison, "Mr. Nance, you can leave your bags in the bed. Sophie's staff will bring them in."

He nodded and followed the ladies inside, his eyes on Teresa's leather walk.

The Henry Adams Hotel was even grander on the inside. Beautiful frescoes graced the walls, and the chandeliers above their heads were ornate and stylish. A grand staircase done in red velvet led to the upper two floors, and a large dining room could be seen through an alcove on the right. The owner, Sophie Reynolds, had been in Henry Adams for many years. The beautiful Louisiana octoroon was in her late fifties, but her spirit was twenty-five.

When she came out of the back, she took one look at Teresa and threw her arms open. "Teresa."

They shared a tight hug, then parted as Sophie said, "Welcome back."

"It's good to be back."

"So sorry about your mother's passing."

"Thanks," Teresa said solemnly. She then made the introductions.

Sophie beamed. "Anybody willing to take this hellion into their home is all right by me. Want you both to be my guests while you're here. Teresa, are you staying here or out with Miss Olivia and your brother?"

Teresa looked at Molly, who shrugged. This hadn't been discussed, but Teresa felt it best if she stay with the Nances just in case. "I'll bunk here. Livy doesn't have the room anyway."

"No, I don't," Olivia conceded. "Your brothers are sleeping on everything but the stove top."

They all smiled.

A few minutes later they were in their third floor suites. Mrs. Nance and Teresa were sharing one, and

Madison was in a smaller one across the hall. Once they were settled and their luggage had been brought in, Olivia gave Teresa a parting hug. "I'll be back to pick you up for dinner. We'll have the service for Tamar after."

Teresa nodded.

Olivia left to return to her office, and Molly and Teresa took a look around their beautiful digs. The bathtub had gold fixtures and matching claw feet. The towels hanging on the gold racks were fat and thick. There was a sitting room complete with an embroidered robin's-egg blue sofa and matching chairs. There were ornate lamps. And the view from the windows overlooked the streets and the open prairie behind them.

Molly dropped onto one of the fancy chairs. "I'm glad we're finally here."

"Me too."

"Your sister-in-law is lovely."

"Thanks. Sophie's going to send up some food in a bit, then you might want to lie down for a while. It's been a long trip."

"Yes it was. A nap sounds like a good idea. I'm not as young as I think I am, but after you're done with your family responsibilities, I want to see as much of everything as I can."

"We'll do whatever you want. It'll be fun showing you around."

"I am so sorry about your mother. I truly wanted to meet her."

Teresa nodded. "You two would have gotten on well. She'll be missed." Because of the summer heat, Neil had had Tamar buried in Henry Adams's small cemetery, which meant she wouldn't even have a last look. That saddened her as well.

"And your father? If that's not an indelicate question."

Teresa shook her head. "It's not. He died about ten years back trying to cross the Rio Grande during a big storm. We think his horse lost his footing and he and Pap were swept away. Neil and Shafts found his body a few days later."

"I'm sorry to hear that."

Teresa shrugged. "We never saw him that much. He was a Seminole scout for many years and then he worked laying track for the railroads. He would come home every now and again, but Tamar raised us, even raised Two Shafts and Diego, and they weren't even her boys. Their mother Luella was Comanche. She died bringing Diego into the world." Teresa then smiled. "You know, it's funny. Neil and Shafts are twins. Even though they have different mothers, they were born on the same day."

Mrs. Nance blinked. "Really?"

"Yes, ma'am. That's why folks out here called them the Terrible Twins. In their day, they raised a lot of hell, um, I mean sand."

Mrs. Nance simply shook her head.

A knock sounded on the door.

"Food!" Teresa crowed, and quickly went to let the waiter in.

After lunch, while Molly rested, Teresa left the hotel and walked down to the sheriff's office. Chase Jefferson, an old friend of Shafts and Neil, had been the town sheriff during Neil's trial. While Teresa was jailed, he'd been taking care of something very close to her heart.

When she entered, the handsome former Buffalo soldier greeted her entrance with a smile. "Well, if it isn't Teresa July. I heard you were back."

"Hello, Chase. How are you? The family?"

"I'm doing well. We just had another son a few months back and he and my wife Cara Lee are doing fine." His voice turned serious. "Sorry about your mother's passing."

"Thank you. We'll miss her. I came to fetch my property."

"He's over at Handy's livery. He was real hard to handle at first, probably from missing you, but he's healthy and just as feisty as he was when Neil brought him here after your trial at Fort Smith."

Teresa grinned. "Thanks for boarding him at your place."

"No problem. With Neil being gone and Olivia not having the time, Cara and I were glad to be able to help. I made sure he got plenty of exercise."

"Thanks again."

Chase nodded.

As she walked back to the door, Chase called, "Teresa."

She turned.

"Glad you're out."

"Me too."

When Teresa walked down to the livery, she drew stares from some of the town folk on the walks, but nobody stopped her. Most knew her identity and had heard why she was back.

She found Handy out behind the livery feeding his stock of horses, and he grinned upon seeing her. "Teresa July?"

"In the flesh. How are you, Handy? How's my boy?"

"Ornery as ever. He'll probably kick the fences down when he sees you. Come on."

Handy led her to the paddock where her proud stallion was cropping grass. Tears stung her eyes. "Hey boy," she called softly.

Cloud's head went up. His ears went back, and as he met her eyes, he neighed loudly and reared. He reared again and again. She opened the gate and he galloped her way. She hugged his neck, and he rubbed his nose against her cheek. Laughing around her tears, she held him close and let the tears flow.

Borrowing a bit from Handy, she fit the apparatus over Cloud's magnificent head, then tossed a blanket over his back. She didn't bother with a saddle. Using the fence to aid her climb, she picked up the reins, turned the horse and headed him at a gallop toward the fence. When they reached it, the stallion sailed over the wooden slats with no difficultly, then he and Teresa were riding like the wind away from town.

As they rode across the countryside she spent the time talking to him, hugging his neck and trying to come up with a plan that would allow her to take him back East with her when the time came to return. She figured she could board him at the Constantines if they didn't mind, and she'd pay them for the privilege from the wages of the job she was determined to get once she got back. It was obvious he'd missed her as much as she had him, and when she finally turned the reins toward town, she was determined that they never be separated again.

She left Cloud with Handy and promised the liveryman she'd be back to claim him for good once she took care of the evening's family responsibilities. Seeing her mount again filled yet another hole in Teresa's soul, but not even her joy at being reunited with Cloud could fill the void left by the death of Tamar.

When she walked into the hotel, Madison was seated in a chair in the lobby reading a newspaper by the big fireplace. She crossed the carpet toward him and he looked up. Their smiles met, and she was glad he couldn't see her nipples standing up with their own welcome underneath her leather jacket. "Did you get some rest?" she asked.

He shook his head. "No. Too much going on, I think. Was just sitting here reading the paper. Is this the same *Cyclone* that the reporter who came to the house writes for? What was his name again?"

"Tom Kelly. Yes. It's the same one. It's out of Nicodemus."

"They've listed some businesses for sale I might want to look into while we're here." Madison could see the faint sheen of moisture on her brow. "Were you out riding?"

"Yep. Had to go see Cloud."

"And how is he?"

"In fine shape. I'm taking him back with us."

"Do tell?" he said, amusement lifting his thin mustache. She was the most unpredictable person he'd ever met.

"The way I figure, he can board with the Constantines, and I can pay them from the job I'm going to get when we get back. I'll borrow the money from one of my brothers to pay for his passage east. What do you think?"

"Sounds like a reasonable plan. I don't think the Constantines will mind."

"Can you wire them and ask?"

"Sure." Madison realized just how much he enjoyed pleasing her. He'd please her for the rest of their lives if she'd just let him.

Teresa was buoyed by his support. Being friends was nice, but the other relationship was better, she decided. Shaking herself free of that unwanted thought, she said, "I'm going to go wash up. Do you know if your mother is still sleeping?"

"I don't know. She hasn't come down, so I'm going to assume that she is."

"Do you have the time?"

He studied the face of the watch chained to his vest. "Four-thirty."

"Okay. Livy said six, so I have plenty of time to take a bath."

Madison didn't want to think about her in the bath, her skin glistening and dewed by the water, but the image rose anyway and so did his manhood. "I'll see you at six. I think I'll go take a walk, look around a bit."

"Sounds good. See you later."

She departed then, leaving an already aroused Madison to wistfully contemplate the sway of her sweet behind in those leathers.

At six that evening Olivia arrived to take them to dinner. Since her house was close by, they opted to walk. Olivia was a seamstress by trade. She ran her business out of the front of her house, and she and Neil resided in the rear.

As they walked the short distance, Madison looked around at the well-built houses and nodded in greeting to the people they passed. The town wasn't big by any means, but as Teresa said, you could see the sky, there was no cacophony of noisy traffic, and the air was sweet and pure.

Teresa put her nose up. "Somebody's cooking."

"Your brothers, no doubt," Olivia said. "They were in charge of the meal."

"Those giants cook?" Molly asked with surprise.

Olivia smiled. "Oh yes. When Neil and I got married, he had more cooking pots and pans than I. He's an amazing man."

"Smells good," Madison admitted.

Teresa boasted, "And it'll taste even better."

And she was correct. Madison and the others stuffed themselves on corn roasted in the husk, grilled steaks, spit-roasted chicken, and baked beans so good Madison groaned.

Hearing him, Teresa laughed, asking, "That good?"

"That good."

They were eating in Olivia and Neil's backyard seated at tables set out in the grass. When the couple married seven years ago, the area behind the house had been mostly open prairie. Now a few houses dotted the landscape, but none were close enough to intrude on the Julys and their guests.

Teresa could see that her brothers were enjoying catching up on what they'd been doing since the last time they saw one another, but the real reason they'd come together wasn't lost on them, and it made for a somewhat subdued gathering.

Madison, seated at the table with Teresa and his mother, asked, "Who's the oldest?"

"Neil and Shafts," Teresa responded.

"They're twins," Molly added knowledgeably. "They have different mothers but were born on the same day. Isn't that interesting?"

Madison nodded over his raised glass of lemonade. "Very." What he really wanted to know was why Neil seemed to be watching him. Every time Madison looked up, the black eyes of Teresa's oldest brother were directed his way. Madison figured he'd find out soon enough, but it was difficult not to be bothered by the silent scrutiny.

After the meal, Neil came over to their table. "You ready, T?"

Teresa nodded solemnly. "Yeah."

She and her brothers were going to the cemetery. Neil had held off on setting the headstone until the rest of his siblings arrived. Now the time had come.

As she got to her feet, she looked at Madison. "Not sure how long this will be."

"Don't worry about us," he replied quietly. "Mother and I will head back to the hotel. I'm sure we can find our way without getting lost."

She nodded. "I'll see you both later, or in the morning."

Molly added, "Like Madison said, you just go on. We'll be fine."

Teresa and Neil joined the others. Neil took Olivia by the hand, and the Julys walked off across the prairie.

At the graveside, Teresa looked down at the mound of fresh-looking earth and let the sorrow that had been trying to claim her since she received the news have its head. All of the sadness she'd ever experienced in her life when put together didn't come close to equaling what she felt at that moment. Tamar and her light had illuminated them all.

Teresa had no idea when the July burial tradition started or where it originated, but her family had been holding funerals this way since before the forced removal west. The ceremonial salutes that would be given always followed the birth order of the mourners, so Neil and Two Shafts were first. Neil saluted the grave with the bottle of wine passed to him by Olivia, then said in a firm, clear voice, "Tamar, as your eldest, I am the one who will tend your grave. That is my promise to you." He took a sip of the wine, then poured some of what was in the bottle onto the earth, and handed the bottle to Two Shafts.

Two Shafts said, "Tamar, you took me in and raised me even though I was not your blood. I will always call you Mother. That is my promise." He repeated Neil's actions, and after pouring a bit more of the wine onto the grave, handed the bottle off.

Harp followed. After thanking Tamar for stressing education for her children even though she had no formal schooling, he pledged to build a school on the land he owned in Montana and to name it for her.

When Diego stepped up, his eyes were wet. He said solemnly, "Tamar, the day after I was born, you took me in, and I became your son." He whispered, his voice thick, "I promise to always hold you in my heart."

Finally, it was Teresa's turn. The tears were threatening to spill down her cheeks. She wiped them away as she offered up the final words. "Tamar, I am your youngest child, and your only daughter. I will make sure the circle of our family continues. That is my promise." She poured the remaining libation onto the grave while her brothers looked on with pain. The caretaker of the cemetery had left shovels nearby. Each sibling tossed on a shovelful of dirt until the headstone was in place, and once the task was completed, a thick silence descended. Tamar was gone and the promises made. Now the Julys had to walk in a future without her.

For the next two days, Teresa buried her grief by showing Madison and his mother around the Great Solomon Valley, named after the Solomon River that ran through it. The valley was home to two all-Black towns. Nicodemus, the most famous, had been founded after the Great Exodus of 1879, when thousands of Blacks left the South to seek land and opportunity, and to escape the awful days of Redemption following the collapse of Reconstruction. Henry Adams was smaller and lesser known, but thanks to Olivia's successful lobbying, it had received the area's railroad spur instead of Nicodemus, and without access to the railroad, Nicodemus's future viability appeared uncertain.

Teresa and Madison spent the days being polite. Outwardly, they were committed to upholding the agreement they'd come to about no more passion things, but inside, both were finding the edict difficult to obey. Every time Madison looked her way, his need for her rose, and Teresa wasn't doing much better. Being near him made her remember his hands skimming over her body and the pressure of his kiss against her neck. Neither of them stepped outside of the boundaries they'd erected, but whenever their eyes met, they both felt the call.

Chapter 16

Madison was interested in investment opportunities. Mindful of Ben's last words, he'd made arrangements to rent a buggy from Handy's livery. Armed with the newspaper listings and a few leads from Olivia and Sophie, he planned to spend the day traveling the valley to evaluate land, farms, and businesses for sale, while trying to imagine what the Solomon Valley might look like in the decades to come and what kinds of new enterprises might prove profitable.

At the moment, however, he was in Sophie's dining room enjoying an early breakfast. Over the past few days, Molly and Teresa's sister-in-law, Olivia, had become fast friends. Drawn to each other by a mutual love of sewing, the two were spending every free moment discussing patterns, fabrics, and notions. With that in mind, he felt free to do his exploring, knowing that his mother would be safe and enjoying herself.

He had no idea what Teresa's plans were for the day. He assumed she'd be spending time with her family, and he didn't begrudge her that. Neil July was still watching him as if sizing him up for a coffin, but so far the former outlaw hadn't revealed whatever was on his mind.

Putting Neil aside, Madison stood and was paying his bill when Teresa sashayed into the dining room in a pair of brown leathers. Her flat crowned hat was hanging by a string around her neck, and her gun belt, complete with her big pearl-handled Colt, hung from her trim waist.

"'Morning," she said, approaching him, her ebony features sparkling with her smile. "What's got you up so early?"

"Going out to look at a couple of farms and a closed-up mercantile over in Nicodemus. They're supposed to be for sale." The sight of her brightened his day. "Where are you heading?"

"To get Cloud and go riding. You want some company, at least part of the way?"

"Sure. I have a map but you might be the difference between me getting there and me getting lost."

The town was quiet as they walked toward Handy's livery. Most of the businesses wouldn't open for another hour or two, depending on the owner. There were a few wagons moving up and down the street, bringing in vegetables and meats for the grocers and making deliveries to the mercantile, but for the most part, they had Main Street to themselves.

Madison said, "This quiet takes some getting used to."

"I think it's much better than all that noise back East. Out here you can hear yourself think."

He looked over at her. She was in her element here. In Philadelphia when she was first released she'd seemed a bit unsure of herself and how to fit in, but here she walked like the goddess that she was, gun belt and all.

The stop at Handy's took only a few moments. Now, out on the plains, he drove the buggy while she rode beside him mounted on Cloud. This was his first look at her fabled stallion, and the animal was magnificent. "Why'd you name him Cloud?"

Teresa shook her head with amusement. "You are such a city boy. Look at the horse, Madison, and you tell me."

The grayish white blaze that ran up from the horse's nose to between his eyes was so obvious the answer that even a city boy could see it. Madison had to chuckle at himself. "Forget I asked."

"It's okay." She stopped and raised herself in the stirrups. Looking west, she said, "Riders coming." Reaching into the worn brown leather saddle bag draped over Cloud's neck, she pulled out a spy glass and raised it to her eye. As she focused and the men's faces came into view, she cursed softly.

"What's wrong?" Madison asked.

She snapped the glass closed and put it away. "It's Sumner Booth. I used to ride with him. He's a real varmint. Got a glass eye."

Madison stood and turned his attention west. The men were now visible. They were riding fast. He turned to Teresa and saw that she was calmly putting bullets into her Colt. "Are you expecting trouble?"

"Maybe," she said easily. "Booth said he'd kill me if we ever crossed paths again."

Madison stared. "What!"

Teresa took a moment to check her aim. "He thinks I shorted him on a cut of a robbery five years ago. I told him I didn't, but he's chosen not to believe me."

Madison was speechless for a moment. He wasn't armed so he was of no value if something did occur. "Teresa?"

She gave him a cool smile, "Welcome to the Wild West, city boy."

That said, she placed the Colt across her thighs and waited for Booth to arrive.

Booth and the thin, dirty young man with him pulled their mounts to a walk as they approached. A tall Black man dressed in denims, old boots, and a worn plaid green shirt, Booth didn't appear to have shaved in days, if ever. The glass eye was fixed like a Cyclops, while the other eye evaluated Teresa and Madison. "Well, if it ain't Teresa July," he finally said. "Thought that was you in my glass but I had to come see to make sure." His chilly smile showed the gap of missing teeth. "When'd you get out?"

"Few months back. How you doing, Sumner?"

"Fine. Who's the pigeon?"

"Friend of mine."

Booth looked him up and down, "Nice meeting ya."

"Same here," Madison lied. He'd taken immediate offense at being called a pigeon, but kept his mouth shut because he knew to let Teresa lead on this.

"Where you from?" Booth asked

"Philadelphia."

Booth looked impressed. "City pigeon. He as rich as he looks?"

"Why'd you ride me down, Sumner?" Teresa asked coldly, putting an end to that conversation.

"Came to see if you had my money."

Teresa's jaw tightened. "There is no money. I gave Mooney your share. If it was short, take it up with him. How many times do we have to do this?"

"I talked to Mooney. He says the cut was short when you gave it to him."

"Mooney would lie about the color of grass, and we both know it."

That one eye impaled her. "I want my money or I'll take it out of your hide."

"Go back to Texas where that threat might work. It doesn't play here in the valley. And did I mention my brothers are in town? All of them?"

He stiffened.

"Thought that would get your attention. If something happens, you'd better hope I kill you, because if I don't, you'll go to your grave wishing I had. Now, good seeing you. Let's go, Madison."

As she and Madison moved away, Booth yelled, "This ain't over, bitch!"

Teresa ignored him.

After putting some distance between themselves and the glass-eyed Booth, Madison looked into her tightly set face and said, "You know some interesting people."

"Like I said, he's a varmint. Sorry about the name calling."

"I wasn't happy about it, believe me. Do you think he'll keep after you?"

"Oh, of course. He's been in my face for something or other ever since we met. He hates knowing there's a woman alive who can outshoot him, outride him, and outthink him. Sticks in his craw like a fishbone."

"What are you going to do?"

"Probably wind up shooting him."

Madison studied her.

She shrugged. "It's the truth."

"You'd risk going back to prison."

"If I shoot Sumner Booth, the jury will give me a medal. I'm not worried about that. Besides, you heard him threatening me. It'll be self-defense."

Madison couldn't believe how calm she appeared.

She told him, "Don't worry." The concern in his eyes touched her heart, but she could take care of herself. "So, where do you want to go first?"

His mustache lifted. "Back to Philadelphia. I feel a little out of place here."

She laughed. "Now you know how I felt being in Philadelphia."

"You are going to tell your brothers about Booth?"

She shrugged. "Probably."

"Probably?"

"I'm used to handling my own affairs."

"He threatened to hurt you, Teresa."

"He's not the first person to do that, Madison. I'll be fine."

Madison felt like a fish with a bicycle. He had no idea how to handle this but he knew that if Booth harmed her, Madison would be the one on trial because he'd hunt the man down. And if she didn't want to talk to her brothers, he would.

They spent the remainder of the morning looking at farms and studying the acres of land for sale. One of the lots had a small stream cutting through it and held one of the area's few stands of trees. It was about ten miles outside of Henry Adams. While walking across the open grassland, he noted the peaceful feel of the surroundings and could imagine someone building a house here. "Be a nice place for a house," he said to her.

Walking beside him, she looked around. "Land's not too low. Water's available. Trees. I'd say it was not only nice, but perfect."

"You know, the way the country's expanding, there probably won't be very many open spaces left like this, say in a hundred years."

"Don't say that. But then I'll be dead by then and won't care." The flippant remark brought up images of Tamar, and she went silent for a few moments as her grief rose then slowly subsided.

"Are you all right?"

"Talking about dying made me think about Tamar." She stopped, then looked out over the land again. "Maybe when I get my parole done, I'll buy this piece of land. Be nice for Cloud and me."

When she turned to gauge his reaction, he was already watching her. The memories of the good times they'd had together and the love that they'd made rose just like the images of Tamar had. Each had its own sadness. Not wanting him to read her eyes, she looked away.

"Teresa," he called softly

She kept her back to him. "Yeah?"

Next she knew, he was behind her and gently wrapping his arms around her waist. "I wanted to give you time to handle your grief, but this not holding you or being near you isn't working for me."

She whispered, "Me either."

He gave a soft chuckle and kissed the top of her hair. "So, what do you want to do?"

She turned in his arms and looked up. "No idea."

For a moment he fed himself on her eyes, then he reached up and tenderly stroked her cheek. "May I kiss you?"

"Please."

He smiled fondly, then lowered his mouth to hers. The kiss was made of longing, sweetness, and so much emotion they immediately pulled each other closer. It had been so long, and they'd wanted each other so much, that hungry kisses were soon roving over jaws and throats. His hands were exploring her leather-covered back, and hers his vest-covered chest. He undid the closures on her jacket, and hardened immediately at the sight of her having nothing on underneath it but the purple silk binding her breasts. He ran a hand over the yielding globes, then dragged the silk down and licked at one dark tipped delight. She groaned and arched. He lowered the other side, repeated the salute, and the sensations flared over her like flames.

They were out in the open, visible for miles, so they moved the buggy, Cloud, and themselves to the shelter of the trees. Once they were out of the sun and shielded from prying eyes, he pushed open the halves of her jacket to continue his masterful conquering. It didn't take long for desire to claim them both. His mouth on her set off a need in her core that only he could fill.

They wound up in the buggy with Madison on the seat and Teresa astride him. The penetrating rhythm of his hot hard strokes made her rise and fall in shameless response. He was unprotected, but she didn't care. The heat of him moving in and out coupled with his strong hands guiding her waist became her world, and she never wanted it to end. When the orgasm shattered over her and then him, their vocal responses were loud in the silence. The cadences of the union increased, and, growling and gasping, they rode their wild sweet love to completion.

It took them two more soul shaking bouts of uninhibited dallying to finally get enough, and when they were done, Teresa fell back against the seat sated, pulsating, and satisfied. Beside her, Madison was in the same state. The last orgasm had started somewhere down around his toes and kept rising until it blew off the top of his head. He didn't think his breathing would ever return to normal.

He turned his head on the seat and met her eyes. *Lord she was beautiful.* Beautiful, feisty, fearless, and because of their unprotected and overpowering lust, possibly impregnated with their child. He'd marry her, of course, but it was yet another potential wrinkle in their complicated relationship.

"That was nice," she said softly, and as if reading his mind, added, "And you don't have to worry about being roped into marriage. Out here there are herbs and seeds to take care of things like that."

He stilled. "What are you saying?"

"I'm saying," she echoed softly, "that you don't have to worry about being saddled with someone like me."

"Teresa?"

She placed a soft hand against his lips. "Let's not talk about this now, okay? I'm a big girl."

Madison's jaw was set angrily. "And if I want the child?"

"No child of mine is going to be raised back East."

"Why not?"

"Look around. Out here, or back there? No contest." She began righting her clothing.

Madison wanted to argue but knew it would only cause another rift, and they'd just found each other again. He knew that this was a discussion they were going to have, though, even if he had to tie her to a chair to do it. Herbs and seeds? Tight-lipped, he shook his head and started to do up his own clothes.

For two people who had only moments ago been each other's whole world, they rode back to town in silence.

After dropping off Cloud and paying Handy for the buggy's rental, they walked back to the hotel. When they reached their rooms, they stopped outside their respective doors and studied each other in the quiet for a long moment. Teresa tried to ignore the love in her heart, and said, "I'll see you later."

Madison had so much he wanted to say to her, but like most men, he didn't want his words to be slapped down, so he nodded tightly. She went inside and closed the door softly behind her.

Alone, he stood in the silent hallway a few moments longer, then he too went inside.

Teresa walked across the carpeted suite and saw a note lying on one of the tables. It was from Molly Nance, telling her that she was at Olivia's shop and would meet her in the hotel for dinner later. Teresa replaced the note, pleased to be alone. Stripping off her clothes, she padded naked into the washroom and started running water in the bathtub. The fading sensations of her spirited lovemaking with Madison continued to resonate, and she smiled bittersweetly. The conversation they'd had about a potential child resulting from their coupling continued to echo as well.

Being the youngest child, she knew next to nothing about raising babies; the only thing she knew for sure was that any baby would be better off being born to someone else. Hell, Neil knew more about babies than she did. Deep down inside, the idea of motherhood scared her to death. Babies couldn't talk, and as a result, couldn't tell you what they needed or what might be wrong. What if she gave it the wrong food, or carried it the wrong way? What if it caught something and got sick? Infants also appeared to need constant attention, and what if she wanted to go riding in the mornings, as she'd done every day before going to jail—who'd take care of it?

Maybe if she had a husband the possibility wouldn't be so daunting. But the last thing she wanted was for Madison to have to marry her because she was having their child. It would be a difficult way to start a life together, him being forced to make her his wife. He was a good man and deserved to be in love with the person wearing his name. There was also the issue of where they'd live. No way would she raise a child of hers around all that soot, grime, and noise of a big back east city like Philadelphia. Her childhood might not have been as privileged as his, but at least she could get up every morning and watch a true sunrise instead of the Philadelphia version that was hidden or bisected by roofs and tall buildings. The only way she'd live there was if someone put a gun to her head.

The bathwater was ready. She stepped in, sat and savored the warm liquid sliding over her love-worked limbs. Content, she leaned back and rested her head on the tub's high rim. The memories of the heated play of his kisses and hands on her body rekindled, and she smiled in response. In spite of the problems presently plaguing them, Madison Nance could make love like nobody's business, but if she had any sense, she told herself, today's lusty interlude would be the last.

After the reviving bath, Teresa dressed herself in a pair of snug denims, bound her breasts with a length of smooth black cotton, then shrugged into a worn flannel shirt. She was going to go over to Olivia and Neil's and hang around until dinner. The parole board had only granted her ten days leave in Kansas, but travel days weren't included, so she had plenty of time to stay and spend time with her brothers. There was no telling when she might see them again.

She left her room and knocked softly on Madison's door, to see if he wanted to walk over to Neil's with her. He didn't answer, so she went on her way.

Madison walked into the sheriff's office and found Chase Jefferson sitting behind his desk talking with Neil July. Once again Neil's eyes held his. Madison nodded. "Can I interrupt you both for a moment? Something I need to discuss with the two of you."

Jefferson waved him to a chair. "Sure. Come on in. Have a seat."

Madison sat in a chair next to Neil, aware of his scrutiny. "Sumner Booth," Madison said.

"Varmint," Neil spat.

"I agree," the sheriff said. "What makes you bring up his name?" he asked Madison.

"Teresa and I happened upon him on our way to Nicodemus this morning."

"I was wondering where you two had gone off to," Neil said.

"There was some land over that way I wanted to take a look at. She was kind enough to go along to make sure I wound up in the right place."

Madison couldn't read anything into Neil's closed expression, so he continued, "Booth threatened her."

Neil asked, "Is he still whining about that money?"

Madison nodded.

What money?" Jefferson asked.

Neil told him the story, and when he was done, Jefferson asked, "How much does Sumner think he's owed?"

"Four hundred dollars."

"That's a lot of money."

"Yes, it is," Neil concurred. "My baby sister may be a lot of things but she's no cheat. If she said she sent Booth his cut with Mooney, she did." Neil looked to Madison, "What did Booth say?"

"If she didn't pay up, he'd take it out of her hide."

"And he'll go to hell wearing the same clothes he was wearing if he puts a hand on her."

"We think alike," Madison stated.

He could see Neil assessing him. "You have feelings for her, don't you?"

"I do."

"She'd be lucky to get somebody as polished as you. Is she giving you a hard time?"

Although Madison was glad to hear the endorsement, he responded with a bitter chuckle, "Of course."

Neil smiled and shook his head. "She's a lot like that ornery stallion of hers. Independent. She's not going to come to the well willingly."

"Ain't that the truth," Madison said, remembering that afternoon's conversation.

Neil added, "Just hold onto your cards. Things will turn out. You'll see."

Madison wanted to believe him, but nothing was concrete where Teresa was concerned.

Teresa was striding down the plank walk on Main Street, on her way to Neil and Olivia's place, when she heard, "Hey, bitch!"

She stopped, turned, and saw Sumner Booth's dirty little sidekick sitting on his horse in the middle of the street. He had a superior-looking smile on his face. "You'd better get Sumner his money."

"Are you talking to me?"

"Yeah, bitch. I am. If it was me you owed money to, I'd already be making you work it off on your back."

Teresa stepped off the curb and walked over to him. "Where's your keeper?"

"Unless you have his money, why the hell do you care?"

Now standing beside him, without a word she reached up, angrily grabbed the front of his shirt, and snatched him out of the saddle. His surprised face exploded with pain as her punch broke his nose and sent him sprawling. Howling and rolling on the ground, he reached for his gun, only to have her powerful leg propel a kick into his sternum, cracking three ribs. He forgot about the gun, he was too busy screaming. She pulled him to his feet and snarled into his bloody face, "The next time you use that word, make sure you think about this!" The solid knee she sent into his groin made him sing like a soprano, then she dropped him back into the dust.

A small crowd was watching from the walk, including the sheriff, a smiling Neil, and Madison, who was staring at Teresa like he'd never seen her before. Seeing them, she called out, "He needed to be taught some manners."

The student in question was at her feet moaning and groaning, obviously in great pain. "Sheriff, you should probably get the doc," Teresa said. "I think this *desperdicio's* hurt."

The beaten man whimpered, "I'm going to kill you."

Teresa's reply was cold. "Only if you ever walk again. Until then, adios." She left him lying there and continued the walk to her sister-in-law's house.

Neil, Chase, and Madison watched her stride away. They'd heard the kid's loud slur in the office and had come outside to investigate just in time to get a ringside view of the main event.

Jefferson asked, "Think he'll watch his mouth next time?"

Neil cracked, "I think he'll run in the opposite direction next time."

A still amazed Madison chuckled. "I know I would."

He and Neil shared a look, then headed off to his house, leaving the sheriff to pick up the *desperdicio* still moaning in agony in the street.

"What's *desperdicio* mean in English?" Madison asked.

"Garbage."

"Ah."

When Olivia poured the iodine onto Teresa's busted knuckles, her curses turned the air blue.

Molly gasped, "Teresa!"

"Hell, it hurts. Sorry. Heck, it hurts!"

The three July brothers laughed.

Olivia simply smiled and mopped at the small bits of blood with a clean rag. "At least you taught that cretin a lesson."

"Yes, she did," Neil announced as he entered the yard with Madison. "She did herself proud, boys. Didn't she, Madison?"

He met Teresa's gaze. "She definitely didn't need any help."

Two Shafts asked, "This was a kid riding with Sumner Booth?"

Teresa tore her attention away from Madison's concerned eyes. "Yeah. Sumner's still griping about the money I supposedly owe him."

She related that morning's meeting with Booth to Harper and Diego, because they didn't know the story.

Diego's face was hard. "He'll go to his grave still crying about that money if he isn't careful. We may be reformed but we're not that reformed."

Chuckles followed that.

Teresa's hand was bandaged, and Olivia put away her doctoring supplies.

They were just sitting down to dinner when Chase Jefferson came around to the back of the house. Olivia stood. "Is something the matter, Sheriff?"

"Telegram just came in for Teresa from Judge Parker. Thought she'd want to see it right away."

Teresa was scared of what it might say. Was Judge Parker mad that she'd been allowed to attend Tamar's service? Did he think ten days too long a stay and wanted her back in Philadelphia on tomorrow's first eastbound train? All manner of questions filled her mind. Confident in the knowledge that she'd face whatever this might turn out to be, she took the envelope holding the message and ripped it open while everyone looked on tensely.

Her scream of joy startled them. She jumped up and down and flung the message into the air. "I'm free! I'm free!"

Neil hurried to pick up the paper so he could see what had set her off. Teresa was in another world, bent over, dancing and singing joyfully in the old tongue. Her brothers looked on in happy confusion. Against the sound of Teresa's voice now warbling the Seminole victory chants, Neil read aloud: "'Dear Miss July. On this day the second of September in the eighteen hundredth and ninety-fifth year of Our Lord, I, Judge Isaac Parker, do hereby grant you pardon of all charges...'" A wide-eyed Neil stared around.

The brothers took up her celebratory cry, then guns started firing, much to the sheriff's amusement and Olivia's dismay, but the Julys didn't care. Their baby sister was free. No more parole, no more living back East.

In the midst of the celebration, Neil's eyes met Madison.

Madison was pleased for Teresa, very pleased, and his look imparted that to Neil. Inside, however, all he could think was, Now what?

Chapter 17

Teresa ran over to Madison and Molly. "Isn't this wonderful?"

Madison couldn't help but enjoy her happy excitement. "Yes it is."

She gave Mrs. Nance a strong hug. "Thank you for all you've done for me. Thank you so much," she gushed.

Molly held her tight. "You're welcome, dear."

Harper declared, "I say we move this celebration to the nearest water hole."

The brothers shouted agreement like raucous Vikings.

Teresa asked Madison, "Do you want to come? You're welcome to."

He shook his head. "No, you go on with your brothers and have a good time."

"Are you sure?"

"Positive. I'll see you tomorrow."

"Okay." She gave him a fleeting look, then ran to catch up with her siblings.

On their walk back to the hotel, Molly and Madison were silent. Only when they got to Molly's suite did she speak. "I guess we're going to lose her," she said sadly, taking a seat on the pale blue sofa.

"Looks that way."

"I'm going to miss her so much."

"I know you will."

"It's wonderful news for her, though."

"Yes, it is." And it was. It was yet another complication, but he was happy for her.

"Oh, I almost forgot," Molly said, getting back to her feet. "I received a letter from Emma today, and she included something you need to see." She hurried into her bedroom and came back to hand him a small folded newspaper article.

Madison opened it and read the headline:

REPUBLICAN PARTY BOSS RICHARDS KILLED

Stunned, he scanned the story. Richards had been shot to death by Charlotte Richards, the Louisiana-born mother of his three children. According to the article, Richards arrived home one evening last week accompanied by "a young female from Memphis visiting the city." Mrs. Richards—the article mentioned his other two wives—was lying in wait and opened fire, killing him and superficially wounding his lady friend. Apparently, Mrs. Richards was sent over the edge by the delaying tactics used by Richards and his attorney to keep the case from going to court. The story ended with the news that Mrs. Richards was being held in the city jail and charged with open murder.

Madison shook his head.

Molly said, "You tried to warn that silly Paula. Sounds like she was lucky to escape with her life."

Madison read it over again. "I hated the man, but I certainly didn't wish him dead."

"Apparently his wife did. I hope she has family able to care for the children."

Madison hoped so too.

Molly looked at him and asked, "So, what are we going to do about Teresa?"

"What do you mean?"

"You're in love with her, Madison. Have you told her?"

He didn't respond.

"Don't try and deny it, it's very apparent ... so have you told her?"

He shook his head. "No."

"Do you plan to?"

"No."

"For heaven's sake, why not?"

"That's between us, Mother. Please don't meddle."

She pursed her lips and then sighed with resignation. "All right. I'm sorry. I'm just— Never mind. I'll stay out of it."

"Thanks," he said with a smile. "In the meantime, we're still leaving as scheduled, so keep that in mind."

"I will."

"You sound disappointed."

"Just when I'm starting to get the hang of things here, it's almost time to return home. Do you know that they have both a literary society and a historical society here? There are even plans to start a lending library. I see what Teresa meant now. There's a freshness and an excitement here that I don't feel in the city."

"Next, you'll be wanting to stay."

"Don't think I haven't considered it."

That startled him. "You're joshing, right?"

"No. I'm serious. Everyone here looks like me, and you, and Emma, and Rebecca. The town is bustling and the trains run on time. What more can one ask? The pace is a bit slower, yes, but I'm in my sixties. My days of fast living are over."

"You're serious, aren't you?"

"I am. You may be between funds right now, but I'm not. I can afford to live anywhere I choose."

She was right, of course. Molly's father Cecil had accumulated quite a fortune as a caterer to Philadelphia's wealthiest citizens before and immediately after the war, and the wise investments made by many of those White clients on his behalf continued to fatten his mother's bank account. Couple those funds with the monies left to her by his father, Reynolds, and his mother had no wants. Except maybe grandchildren. He put that thought aside. "So do you want to delay going home?"

"I do, but there are two of us here. If you wish to honor our tickets and leave, that's fine with me, but I'm going to come back here in the spring just to see if I feel the same way."

"Fair enough. I've been bitten by this place too, in a way." With his business no longer viable, he could pick up and start over wherever he chose, and why not choose here, where the race was accomplishing remarkable things and opportunity depended on nothing but one's own entrepreneurial spirit and know-how? Of course, if Teresa decided to live in Henry Adams instead of returning to her home in Indian Territory, that might present a problem. "I'll think about all this and let you know what I decide."

She nodded.

"Now, I'm going to my room. Will you be okay here alone? If Teresa comes back at all tonight, it's likely to be very late."

"I'll be fine. I've some decorations to work on for the dance the town's having in a few days, to benefit the school, so that should keep me occupied until bedtime. You should ask Teresa to go with you."

"You're meddling, Mother."

"No, I'm not."

He grinned. "I'll see you at breakfast."

She grinned too. "I didn't ask about your foray this morning. Did you find anything to invest in?"

He thought about the land he'd seen with the trees and water. The perfect place to build a house, Teresa had declared. "A few."

She nodded. "Okay. Good night, son."

"'Night, Mother."

Alone in his suite, Madison looked into the mirror hanging on the wall and stared at his reflection. *This is ridiculous.* He wanted Teresa, Colt and all, lady or not, pregnant or not. He couldn't see not having her in his life for the rest of his life. His mother was right. He needed to do something about Teresa, and he needed to do it soon.

The Julys were seated at a large table inside of the Liberian Lady, the big fancy saloon on the edge of town. There weren't many people in attendance, but the piano player's tunes were lively enough to make the place seem full.

Harper held up his drink. "To Teri," he said in salute. "May she be smart enough to stay out of jail from now on."

The brothers raised their glasses. A happy Teresa shook her head but relished the tribute. She raised her own shot glass. "To the best brothers an outlaw woman could have."

They all downed their drinks, and when their glasses were empty, they bought more. Teresa limited herself to one small shot. Last week's hangover in Philadelphia was still very vivid. She didn't want to ever spend another morning lying on a washroom floor. She was also a bit melancholy.

As the evening progressed and the Lady began filling up with customers, her brothers eventually drifted away from the table to sit in on poker games, play pool, and flirt with some of the saloon's girls. She and Neil were left sitting with each other, watching the fun.

Neil asked, "Can I get you another whiskey?"

"No, I'm okay."

He leaned over and peered into her face. "Are you sure you're my little sister. Not like you to forgo a celebration."

She told him about her last tequila encounter.

He nodded his understanding. "Not like you to be sick after a night of drinking either."

"I know, but it put me on the floor the next morning."

Neil studied her.

"Why're you staring?"

"Just looking at you all grown up. Trying to see what's different about you and what's the same."

"I'm still me, but what's different is that I won't be stealing anymore. Learned my lesson."

"So have I. Working for the railroad's not been as bad as I thought it might be. They pay well. Want me to put in a word for you?"

"Sure," she said, shrugging. "Why not? I'll be needing a job now that I'm staying." The idea of not having to go back East made her extremely happy, but the knowledge that she'd more than likely never see Mrs. Nance or Madison again left her unsettled.

"What's the matter?"

"A little unhappy about having to leave Mrs. Nance. She's been like an angel. I'll miss her a lot."

"And her son?"

Teresa met Neil's eyes then slowly looked away. "I'll miss Madison too. He's been very kind." Thinking about him and all they'd shared, she added softly, "Very kind."

"Do you have feelings for him?" he asked gently.

She nodded. "I do, but nothing's going to come of them. Two different worlds. Where he's from, women don't get drunk on tequila, or fight in the middle of the street."

"So you think you're not good enough for him?"

"Of course I'm good enough, I'm just not right for him. There's a difference."

"Have you told him how you feel?"

"Sort of, but like I said, it doesn't matter. He's going back to Philadelphia and I'm staying here. End of story." Only fairy tales had happy endings.

Neil placed a brotherly hand over hers. "It'll work out."

"I know, but it probably won't be in the way I wish."

"You never know. Who'd have ever thought I'd fall in love with a real lady like Olivia?"

Teresa rolled her eyes. "I'm not in love, Neil. I saw what love did to you, and I don't want any part of that."

He sat back and folded his arms. "Oh really?"

Teresa snorted. "Love? Please. I don't mean any disrespect, but there is no way in hell I would have put my life in Judge Parker's hands because I was in love with some man."

"No, you put your life in his hands because you were a hot-headed know it all, and where did it get you?"

She evaded his mocking eyes.

He told her, "At least my reasons were sincere. Olivia was and is the best thing to ever happen to me. I thank the Ancestors for her love every day. Maybe if you're lucky, you'll get to feel that way about someone too."

She felt an inch tall.

Pleased that he'd made his point, he drained his glass. "Now, I see Diego taking a seat at the poker table. Think I'll join the game and help Shafts and Harp clean out his big fat billfold."

"Big fat billfold. Diego rob a bank?"

"Nope. Baby brother owns a Yukon gold mine."

"*What?*"

But Neil was already moving away, and she was left with her mouth hanging open. Teresa knew better than to demand an explanation while her brothers were playing cards, and for sure Diego wouldn't take kindly to having his business aired in the middle of a saloon. But a gold mine! She made a mental note to collar him later.

In the meantime, she sat and brooded. Neil had a way of cutting a person so smoothly they didn't even know they were bleeding until after he'd gone, and that's how she felt. He'd sliced her up in his gentle big brother way, leaving her to deal with the aftermath, which for her was to acknowledge that what he'd received in return for his capitulation to Judge Parker far exceeded her own. In exchange for turning himself in, Neil had been sentenced to work for the railroads, which meant he didn't have to go to jail and maybe lose his beloved Olivia while he was gone. She, on the other hand, had not only refused to work for the railroads, period, but went back to robbing trains soon after Neil's trial, all but daring the authorities to hunt her down and bring her in. They had, of course, and where Neil's reasons had been sincere and genuine, hers were rooted in hubris.

He has the silence inside that you need.

The words of Tamar haunted her and turned her thoughts to Madison. Everything about him made her smile, from his buttoned-up suits to his scandalous use of orange marmalade. Was he her silence? Olivia was definitely Neil's silence. A person only had to know the Neil of before to see how being in love had affected both his personality and outlook on life. Now, she wondered if Madison or someone like him could do the same for her, and if maybe this whole love business wasn't so loco after all.

Sumner Booth stepped into the saloon, and all the Julys looked up. Eyes followed him as he walked over to the bar, ordered from the barkeep, and took his glass. He turned toward Teresa, who was now standing a few feet away making small talk with Handy from the livery. Booth quickly tossed his drink down and slammed the glass down on the bar top. "Teresa, that was a terrible thing you did to young Anderson."

"Was that his name?" she asked calmly. "He was so busy calling me out of my mine, I never caught his."

"He's got a cracked sternum, three busted ribs, and lost a bunch of teeth. Doc said he'll be drinking from a straw for months."

"Well, good. Tell him I send my regards." She turned away.

"I want my money, July."

She sighed. "Sumner, if you tell me that one more time, I swear I'm going to plug you."

"You shorted me."

"Dammit, I did not. Even if I did owe you, I'm flat broke. I just got out of jail, remember?"

He paid for another drink. "Your fancy boyfriend and his mama look pretty flush. Get it from them."

Teresa held onto the last of her temper. "First of all, he's not my boyfriend, fancy or otherwise, and second, if you go anywhere near them, I will shoot you—on the spot."

He downed his drink and slid the glass to the keep. "This ain't the end. I'm getting my money, one way or another." He looked out at the Julys staring his way with hard eyes, and said again, "One way or another." Then he walked out.

* * *

The next morning when Teresa got out of bed, Mrs. Nance had already left the suite. Teresa had gotten in pretty late and was still a bit bleary-eyed. The note she found on one of the front tables said Molly and Madison were at breakfast and that she was welcome to join them if she cared to. She appreciated the invite and thought that if they were still in the dining room when she got downstairs, she'd sit and have some coffee. Since returning here last week, the hearty breakfast she was accustomed to eating each morning seemed to upset her stomach. The only thing she could attribute it to was maybe the change in locale and altitude, but she figured whatever the distress was related to, it would be made right eventually.

Madison and his mother were still eating when she walked into the dining room. "'Morning, everybody."

Madison gestured her to a chair. "Join us."

"Thanks. How are you two?"

Molly took a sip of her coffee and then set the cup down. "We're fine. Did you have fun last night?"

"I did." Her eyes were on Madison and his were on her. "Are you looking at properties today?"

"Yes, but in town. The mercantile down the street. Sophie says the owner is looking to sell. What are you doing this morning?"

"Riding. How about you, Mrs. Nance?"

"I'm going to help Olivia and her committee finish up the decorations for the dance tomorrow evening."

Teresa asked, "Is this the one for the school?" She'd seen the posters tacked up around town.

"Yes. Are you going?"

She shrugged. "Hadn't thought about it, really."

"Madison is looking for someone to escort."

Madison choked on his coffee. Shooting daggers at his lovable but meddling mother, he picked up his napkin and wiped his mouth.

Witnessing Madison's reaction, Teresa was sure Mrs. Nance was playing matchmaker again, so she asked him, "Is that true?"

"Yes, it is," he lied. The time had come to put his cards on the table. He was determined not to lose her. "Would you like to go?"

Teresa sensed he was up to something, but she didn't know what. "Okay, I'll bite. Yes, I'll go. I'll even wear one of the fancy gowns your mother insisted we bring along, and you can pick up my brothers' eyeballs."

He chuckled. "You have a deal."

Molly asked, "Did Madison ever teach you how to waltz?"

Teresa eyes were still on Madison. "No."

"Well, you should learn between now and the dance."

"Fine."

Madison asked, "Shall we meet here around two and practice?"

"Okay." She stood. "I'll see you then. 'Bye, Mrs. Nance."

After her departure, Mrs. Nance said, "See how easy that was?"

Madison shook his head at her antics and poured himself more coffee.

* * *

The price the owner wanted for the mercantile was reasonable, but Madison wasn't sure if Ben wanted to own a general store. Of course, he could hire one of the locals to run the place for him, so he added the store to the list of other prospects. He'd notified Ben by wire about what he'd found and was waiting for his reply.

At two that afternoon he knocked on the door to the suite Teresa and his mother were sharing. Teresa opened the door. The sight of her dressed in a skirt and blouse threw him for a moment. She looked like she'd look back home.

Noticing his reaction, Teresa looked down at herself and said, "I figured if I'm going to be wearing a gown to the dance, I should probably practice in this instead of my leathers."

Seeing her dressed that way made the memories of her in his bed rush back. "That's a good idea," he managed to say evenly. "Are you ready?"

"Yeah. Come on in." She stepped aside and he entered.

"Is Mother here?"

"Nope. I left her over at Olivia's. She put my brothers to work cutting out doilies for the tables. They were not happy about it."

"I'll bet they weren't."

For Madison it was good being alone with her again, in spite of the issues between them; issues he wanted resolved so they could move on.

"How do we start?" Teresa asked. Being alone with him was so heady, her heart was already pounding.

"Like this." He placed one hand lightly on her

waist, and with the other took her hand in his and raised it in the air. He then walked her through the steps. "One, two, three. One, two, three."

It wasn't complex and Teresa caught on quickly. As he increased the pace, she said delightedly, "This isn't hard at all."

"No, it's not."

So they waltzed all over the suite, back and forth, past the windows and around the furniture. Their gazes were locked, their steps in perfect sync. He then taught her the waltz glide, which was the Negro version of the dance. The steps were basically the same, but it was a bit more rhythmic and a lot less stiff than the original.

As they practiced the glide, Teresa could feel his hand burning her waist through the fabric of her skirt and could smell his cologne. Although she had denied being in love while talking to Neil last night, she'd already admitted the truth to herself, she just hadn't wanted to acknowledge it. She was a lady outlaw, or at least she used to be, and women like her didn't confess to having a weakness for any man. But her weakness toward one Madison Nance was turning into the damnedest experience of her life.

The sound of a key in the lock slowed their steps, and when Mrs. Nance entered, Madison's hands were still positioned.

She smiled their way. "Good. I see you two are practicing. How are things going?"

"Just fine," Teresa said, feeling Madison's hands drop away and wishing he were still holding her.

He asked, "Done with the decorations?"

"No, my doily cutters staged a mutiny. Olivia

wants everyone to come to dinner so we can finish it all after we eat."

"How much is left to do?"

"There's still a bit. I came back here to change my skirt. I've paint all over the front." She showed them the big black splotches.

"How'd it happen?" Teresa asked.

"Your brothers, of course."

Teresa echoed with resignation, "Of course."

"Diego and Shafts were flicking brushes at each other. It was all good-natured fun, but I was caught in the cross fire."

Teresa said, "Let me change out of this skirt and we can walk over together."

"Good idea. I'll get out of this paint-stained one and be right back."

After Molly disappeared into the bedroom, Teresa looked up at Madison. "You didn't have other plans for the evening, did you?"

"Nope."

The look in his eyes was making her nipples stand. "I'll go change."

"I'll be here."

After yet another satisfying dinner courtesy of the July brothers, they were spread out all over the house and in Olivia's dress shop in front, working on the decorations, when they heard from the street, "Teresa July! Get your ass out here!"

It was Sumner Booth, and he sounded drunk.

Teresa, in the kitchen working with Harper and Madison, looked up from the stack of doilies she was counting, and she was sure steam could be seen pouring out of her ears. She'd had it. Getting to her feet, she snatched her gun belt off the table and headed to the door.

Harper said calmly, "Put the gun belt down."

"I'm going to settle this once and for all."

"Put it down, Teresa," Madison echoed.

Teresa left the kitchen and stalked into the parlor that led to Olivia's shop at the front of the house.

In the parlor, Neil looked up. "Where the hell you think you're going?"

She kept walking.

By then the massive frames of Two Shafts and Diego were blocking her exit.

"Get out of my way," she told them.

Of course they didn't. "Put the belt down and we will," Two Shafts told her.

"Step aside," she demanded.

From outside, Sumner hollered again, "Damn you, July! Come out or I'm coming in."

Standing in the door of the shop and looking out at him, Olivia said over her shoulder, "He's so drunk he can barely sit his horse."

Neil shook his head at the fire in his sister's eyes. "Teri, put the belt down. Booth's not worth going back to prison for."

Madison and Harper had followed her into the room, and seeing Madison's tensely set face, Neil said, "Would you hurry up and marry this woman so we can turn the reins over to you? We're getting too old for this."

"Hey," Harper chimed in. "Speak for yourself."

Teresa was staring at them as if they'd lost their minds. "Madison isn't marrying me."

"Sure I am."

Her eyes narrowed. "No, you're not."

"Yeah, I am. I love you, Teresa." Madison knew this was neither the time nor the place to do this, but he didn't care. "Marry me."

Teresa shook her head. "The only reason you're saying that is because you think I might be carrying."

In unison, the July men shouted, *"What?"*

Wrong thing to say.

Madison found himself under intense scrutiny, but he ignored them and spoke to Teresa. "My reasons for wanting you to be my wife have nothing to do with that."

"Teresa July!" Sumner called out drunkenly.

Neil snapped, "Will somebody please take care of that yahoo so we can get this settled?"

Shafts smiled coldly. "Thought you'd never ask," and he left the room.

Madison walked over to Teresa and looked down into her sullen face. "Marry me, Angel."

The last word resonated through every inch of her body with such power it melted her anger. "You know that's not fair."

He smiled fondly. "Have to use what I can."

"I'm not marrying you, Madison. You want a fancy lady."

"No. I want you."

Teresa could see everyone staring shamelessly. She shook her head again. "No."

Neil had had enough. "Dammit, girl, the man just proposed. Who else is going to be loco enough to want to give you their name?"

A snarling Olivia snapped, "Stay out of this, Neil July."

Diego said, "But Neily's right, Livy. It's not like she's got a barn full of suitors begging for her hand."

Harper drawled, "She going to give him fits, but I'm putting my money on him."

"Would you all shut the hell up!" Teresa demanded, fire in her eyes. Wishing she'd been born an only child, she looked up at Madison. The humor in his eyes didn't help.

He said again, "I love you, Teresa July. I really and truly do."

She was totally unprepared for any of this. Did he really love her? He certainly looked sincere. She looked over at Molly, who had tears in her eyes. Teresa turned back to Madison. "Give me a few days to think about this."

"So you can talk yourself out of how I know you feel? No. I need your answer, now. In a few days, I'll be heading back to Philadelphia."

Teresa thought about not having him in her life. Could she stand it? She knew she loved this man more than she loved Cloud, walking trains, and her dumb-butt brothers, but could a marriage between such different people really work? Once again she thought about a life that didn't have him in it, and knew what she had to say. "Okay, city boy. You got yourself a wife."

Cheers went up. Not caring who watched, a happy Madison pulled her close and kissed her until she saw stars.

Two Shafts came back inside, and hearing all the noise, asked, "What did I miss?"

Neil said gleefully, "Brother, we're having a wedding."

Shafts looked at the happy Madison and then at his baby sister and grinned. "About damn time."

Olivia asked him, "What did you do about Sumner Booth?"

"Grabbed him off of his horse, tied his shirt around his face, put him back in the saddle, and slapped the horse's rump. He's probably halfway to Topeka by now."

Molly stared.

Olivia saw the look. "Molly, if you're going to be family, you're going to have to get accustomed to the way the Julys play with their prey."

Molly still looked stunned.

Teresa added, "And don't worry. We never play with family."

Everyone laughed, and Madison hugged the smiling Teresa close to his side. Things were going to be all right from now on.

Chapter 18

Later, after everyone had calmed down, Teresa and Madison stood alone in Olivia's backyard, enjoying the night, the decision they'd made, and each other's company. As he held her close against his heart, she still found it hard to believe he loved her. She looked up. "Do you really love me?"

"More than I do dividends."

"That much? Well, I love you more than Cloud."

"I'm honored."

With her cheek against his heart once more, and relishing the feel of being close to him, she couldn't imagine not having him in her life even if he was a city man. "So when do you want to have the ceremony?"

"Today, tomorrow. Yesterday."

His words filled her heart. "How about tomorrow? I'm sure Sheriff Jefferson can marry us in his office."

He shrugged. "The sooner I can have you with me all day and all night, the better."

"Then tomorrow it'll be. Let's go in and tell everyone."

Madison thought that an excellent idea. They still had issues to discuss, primarily where they were to live, but he was certain they'd figure it out.

When Teresa and Madison came back inside the brothers clapped.

Smiling, Teresa announced, "We're getting married tomorrow. I'll ask Sheriff Jefferson if he can marry us at his office. You're all invited to join us."

"No," Molly said.

Teresa turned. "What do you mean, no?"

"No. This is a life-changing event. My son, and the daughter of my heart will only do this once, so I want it done with pomp and circumstance."

Madison sensed the nice quiet ceremony he and Teresa had planned was about to unravel. "Mother … "

"The groom shouldn't see the bride until the wedding day, so Teresa, you and I should head back to the hotel so we can get you ready."

Madison tried again. "Mother, Teresa and I—"

"Son, I know you and Teresa have things to discuss, but as the mother of the groom and quite possibly the grandmother of your child, you will simply have to put up with me. We will have this wedding tomorrow afternoon and it will be done correctly. You'll both thank me later."

Madison didn't think so, and Teresa didn't appear to be buying it either, but they loved her too much to put up a fight.

Neil asked Teresa, "You will be here tomorrow for the wedding, right? You're not going to bolt and ride off in the middle of the night?"

"No, Neil."

"Good. Then I won't have to have Shafts and Harp camp outside your hotel to make sure."

Teresa looked up at her groom-to-be with love in her eyes. "Not necessary. I'm really going to marry him."

Madison grinned.

She looked over at her sister-in-law. "Livy, will you stand up with me at the ceremony?"

"I'd be honored."

"Thanks." Teresa held Madison's eyes for a moment. She didn't want to leave him tonight, but she didn't want Molly to toss her in a bag and drag her away, so she leaned up, gave him a soft kiss, then said to Molly, "Okay, Mrs. Nance. I'm ready."

Molly smiled. "We'll see you all tomorrow. Olivia, will you make arrangements with the reverend?"

She nodded.

Molly's next words were for the brothers: "Be well dressed, gentlemen, and don't be late."

After their departure, Neil looked over at Madison and said to him, "You'll be good for her."

His brothers voiced their agreement.

Madison appreciated their endorsements. He thought he would be too. A few minutes later he headed back to the hotel too.

Teresa and Molly entered their hotel suite and Teresa dropped down into a chair. What a day! By this time tomorrow she was going to be married—she, who once held the title of the Most Wanted Woman in the West, and to a city boy from Philadelphia, of all places. *Dios!*

Molly came over to her and said, "Do you have any idea how happy you've made me today?"

Teresa saw the tears in her mentor's eyes. "You've been so good to me."

They embraced, and both were teary. "I plan to make you the best daughter-in-law ever."

"And I'll be a stellar mother-in-law."

Teresa had no doubts about that.

* * *

The quiet was suddenly broken by the sounds of pounding on the door across the hall and the deep rumble of male voices. Mrs. Nance looked toward the door.

Teresa said, "It's probably just my brothers arriving to initiate Madison into the July brotherhood."

Mrs. Nance looked concerned.

"Don't worry. No matter how drunk they may get him, they'll have him at the ceremony on time, even if they have to put him on Shafts's back to do it."

Mrs. Nance looked even more concerned after hearing that, but Teresa simply smiled and turned back to the window.

Across the hall, Madison heard the loud knocks, and when he opened the door there stood his grinning brothers-in-law. In their hands were bottles of whiskey and glasses. He said, "Since you'd probably just kick the door in if I refused you entrance, please come on in, gentlemen," he said, gesturing.

Shafts grinned. "I'm liking him more and more."

"Me too," Harper concurred.

Once they were all inside, Madison asked, "What can I do for you?"

Neil replied, "Thought we'd spend your last night of male freedom with you. It'll help us get to know you better, and you can do the same."

"Fine."

"You play poker?"

"A bit." He saw the brothers turn knowing eyes to each other, but Madison kept his features placid. "Did you bring a deck?"

Diego smiled, "Oh, yeah."

"Then shall we?" Madison said, gesturing to the chairs and sofa. Harper pulled a long end table close, and as they circled around it, Madison knew they thought they were about to pluck a pigeon.

It took the July brothers a few hands before they realized Madison knew his way around cards the way they knew their way around train robbing. He'd played cautiously at first, lulling them to sleep while he assessed their individual games. However, once he realized they were good but not as good as the professional card sharp he once held title to, the Julys were in trouble.

As he won the fourth, fifth, and sixth hands, Neil threw in his cards. Eyeing Madison, he announced, "Boys, I think we got us a wolf in sheep's clothing here."

Shafts wasn't happy either.

Harper asked suspiciously, "How do you make your living?"

"Banking."

Diego, who had bet and lost the most money so far, asked, "And before that?"

Madison picked up the deck of cards and proceeded to give them the fanciest thirty-second card shuffling show they'd ever seen. When he set the deck down, he said with a smile, "Gambler."

A few good-natured curses followed this confession, and Neil flat out laughed.

Shafts shook his head, then leaned over and held out his hand to Madison so they could shake. He said with amusement, "Welcome to the family, Madison."

Madison shook the big Comanche's hand. "Thanks."

"I'll be damned," Harper said, studying Madison's face and clothing. "And here we thought Teri was marrying a goody goody. You had us fooled, I have to admit." He offered Madison his hand too.

So now the brothers started over with their soon-to-be brother-in-law. They spent the rest of the night playing cards, laughing, and telling stories.

Neil asked his siblings, "Remember the time we used Teri as target practice?"

Madison choked on his drink, and the grinning Harper slapped him hard on the back.

Harper added, "And the switching Tamar gave us when she found out."

They all laughed.

"Then the next day, we cut off her plaits because we needed the hair to make whiskers."

Madison couldn't help it—he roared.

Diego, chuckling, said, "Teri hated us twenty-four hours a day, 365 days a year."

Over the course of the evening, Madison learned all about his new brothers. Shafts lived in the mountains of New Mexico, and Harper owned a saloon in Montana. The most surprising piece of information was Diego's Yukon gold mine.

Diego explained, "After me and Pa had that fight, I didn't stop riding until I reached the Canadian border up near Washington. Ran up on some no goods beating this poor old man to death, so I intervened. Found out later he was a prospector, and when he asked me if I wanted to help him mine gold in the Yukon, I said sure, why not?"

"And you got rich," Neil stated.

"As Midas. Of course I'm a lot poorer now thanks

to our new card sharp brother over there, but if anybody needs some gold, just let me know."

Four sets of hands shot up, and they all laughed.

It was dawn when the brothers finally left the suite. Lying in bed as daylight chased the shadows out of the bedroom, the slightly drunk Madison felt good. He'd never had siblings before, and now he had four. Four of the wildest and craziest men anybody would ever want to meet, but they'd made him feel like family, and that made him smile. He turned over to get more comfortable, and his thoughts settled on his soon-to-be bride. By nightfall he would be married to the most sensual, fiercest woman in the country. He just hoped she didn't shoot any of her brothers during the ceremony. Laughing softly, he drifted off to sleep.

When it came time for Teresa to get dressed for her wedding, her first thought was to put on her leathers. The second thought was that both Olivia and Molly would probably keel over if she did, so she took down the midnight blue gown she'd worn to the Academy of Music. Because of the deep-cut bodice, binding her breasts wouldn't work, so she struggled into the corset. Just like the day she went to jail, she refused to speculate on what the day and the future would hold. Instead, she decided to take each moment as it came.

"My goodness, Teresa!" Olivia gushed when she stepped out of the bedroom. "Look at you. You're beautiful!"

"You think so?" she asked, smiling.

"Oh, yes, ma'am. Your brothers are going to faint."

Molly added, "Yes they are."

Because Teresa knew nothing about styling her hair, she'd pulled it back, twisted it into a chignon, and pinned it down, unaware that the simplicity added to her elegance.

She had to admit she did feel pretty good all spiffed up. The dress had a lot of nice memories tied to it from the night at the Academy and she guessed that was why she felt more comfortable in it than she'd anticipated. "So, where's the wedding going to be?"

"Downstairs in one of Sophie's salons," Olivia responded. "She's providing food and drinks."

Teresa would have to remember to thank the hotelier for her many kindnesses. "So, are we ready?"

"Almost. Neil's going to give you away, and as soon as he arrives, we'll head down."

Neil showed up fifteen minutes later decked out in a new blue suit. He gave Olivia a kiss at the door, and then, upon seeing his sister, stopped in mid-step and said, "*Dios!* Who are you and what did you do with little Teri?"

Hand on her hip, she shot him a smiling look, then turned around slowly so he could get the full effect.

"You look like gold, Teri."

"Thanks, Neil. You clean up pretty well yourself."

His voice turned serious. "Learned a lot about Madison last night. He's a good man, Terecita. We are proud to add his line to ours."

She nodded. "He is a good man." She looked over at Mrs. Nance. "His mama's pretty special too."

Molly smiled around the tears standing in her eyes.

Olivia handed her a handkerchief. "Stop that, Molly, before you have us both bawling," she fussed with amusement. "Save it for the ceremony."

The laughing Molly wiped her eyes, then Neil escorted the ladies out.

An uncharacteristically nervous Madison consulted his watch for seemingly the fiftieth time while waiting in Sophie's salon. The ceremony was supposed to start at two, and it was now five minutes till. Would his lovely bride show up, or were she and Cloud on their way to the border? Two Shafts kept reassuring him that everything was on schedule and that Neil was even now bringing Molly and Teresa downstairs, but Madison knew he wouldn't relax until he saw Teresa with his own eyes. The Reverend Whitfield had arrived a few short while ago and was standing off to the side, talking quietly with Sophie and his wife Sybil. Unlike Madison, they didn't seem worried, nor did any of the others in attendance. It appeared as if half the residents in the Valley had shown up. How they'd gotten wind of the nuptials was a mystery, but Madison didn't have time to delve into the answer, he was much more concerned with the arrival of his bride.

When Neil walked over to ask Madison and then Reverend Whitfield if they were ready, they all answered, and Neil went out again. Sophie cued the piano player, who was also the church's organist, and as the woman began to play a soft hymn, Neil entered solemnly, with Molly on one arm and his wife Olivia on the other. Madison could see the tears in his mother's eyes, and her happiness moved him.

Neil escorted them to their seats then went back out of the room.

He came back with Teresa, and Madison's emotions stuck in his throat seeing how beautiful she looked. He remembered the gown, the one she wore to the Academy of Music, and how lovely she'd looked when she slipped out of it so he could make love to her. She met his eyes, and her soft confident smile made him beam inside.

Neil was walking her slowly to the front of the room. Madison was standing up with the remaining Julys who were all spiffed up for the occasion. Madison heard Diego gush quietly, "*Dios!* She looks like a woman."

Harper drawled, "She is a woman, nitwit. Now hush up before you embarrass her."

Neil and Teresa halted just a few steps away from the kindly face of the reverend, who raised his voice and asked, "Who gives this woman?"

The July men and Olivia shouted, "We do!"

The thundering voices set off titters in the crowd of uninvited guests. Neil walked Teresa to Madison's side, and while the two locked gazes on each other, he quietly withdrew and took a seat next to Olivia and Molly in the front row of chairs.

Teresa and Madison turned to the reverend as he began the words, and when Madison gently took her hand, Teresa threaded her fingers with his.

When he awakened that morning, Madison had a sore head because of last night's drinking, but one look at Teresa cleared his mind, and the world was now crystal clear.

Whitfield went on with the reading, then raised his

voice again and asked, "Is there any reason why these two should not be united in holy matrimony? Speak now or forever hold your peace!"

Diego whispered out of the side of his mouth, "I'm shooting anybody that stands up."

The reverend coughed to hide his laughter. When no one responded to the question, he cleared his throat again and carried on.

The ceremony took less than ten minutes. Getting dressed had taken longer, Teresa noted to herself.

The reverend closed his Bible, smiled at the couple and said, "I now pronounce you man and wife. You may kiss your bride, Mr. Nance."

Madison looked down into Teresa's smiling face, slipped an arm around her waist and kissed her while her brothers cheered loud enough to be heard in Philadelphia. When he turned her loose, Teresa was so dizzy she had to blink a few times to restore her equilibrium and to remember where she was. She said beneath the cheering and applause, "Now that was a good one."

"And there'll be more where that came from, soon as I get you back upstairs and out of that dress."

"Do you think Sophie has any marmalade?" she asked him provocatively.

"We can always ask."

As they turned to greet the well wishers now lined up to shake their hands, they shared one last look and knew that no matter what lay ahead, they would work it out. Together.

But before Madison could get Teresa alone and out of her dress, they had the rest of the day to get through. Sophie set out a fabulous meal for the family. Molly, who'd cried through the entire wedding, had finally recovered, and to Madison's amusement offered up the first toast.

"To Madison and Teresa. May their union be happy and may I have many grandchildren!"

The brothers cheered.

Teresa grinned, but when she saw a distressed-looking Olivia get up from the table and hastily leave the room, a heartbroken Teresa met her brother's eyes. Neil hurried out after his wife. Luckily Molly and everyone else were too involved with the ongoing toasts to witness the incident, because Teresa knew how mortified the kindhearted Molly would be to learn that her toast for grandchildren had inadvertently triggered Olivia's despair over not being able to bear a child. Teresa made a silent promise to speak to Livy later.

The night's benefit dance at the town hall also became the wedding reception. They danced, played parlor games, and, thanks to Diego, raised quite a good sum of money for the Henry Adams school. Olivia and Neil came in about an hour after the dancing began. Olivia looked to have recovered, but Teresa could still see the remnants of sadness in her eyes. After waltzing with Handy from the livery, Teresa told Madison, who was taking his mother out onto the dance floor, that she was going to talk with Olivia for a moment, then went looking for her.

Of course, the mayor was busy. She was cutting cake and giving directions to the ladies restocking the punch table. Teresa wondered if the woman ever slept. "Let's go get some fresh air," she said to her. "I'm roasting."

Olivia shook her head. "Not right now. I need to—"

"You need to take a break. Now. Come on."

Olivia sighed but put down the cake knife, wiped her hands on her apron, and followed Teresa outside. The chirp of the crickets were like background music against the quiet night, and the soft breeze felt good after the heat inside the hall. "Lovely night," Teresa said.

"Yes it is."

"I'm sorry Molly's toast hurt your feelings. She doesn't know."

"I know she doesn't. I'm not holding anything against her. I'm just so frayed and frazzled." She went silent for a moment, then confessed, "I'm carrying again, Teresa, and I'm scared to death I'm going to lose this baby too." Teresa turned to her in the dark and saw her hands nervously worrying the front of her apron. "I want this baby so much."

Teresa pulled her into her arms and held her while she cried. As if suddenly realizing what she was doing, Olivia backed away and said, "Lord, I'm a mess. Crying all over your gown."

"I don't care about the gown, but I do you. Have you told Neily yet?"

"No. I don't want to get his hopes up." She added, "He's been so kind through all of this. Falling in love with him was the best thing that ever happened to me."

Teresa's memories of her talk with Neil rose. "He says the same thing about you."

Teresa sensed Olivia's smile.

"Your brother, for all his outlaw past and ways, is a good man. I'm proud to be his wife."

"Does the doc have some kind of special medicine you can take to hold onto the baby this time?"

"Delbert said resting up more might make a difference, but I have a town to run. There are meetings in Topeka I have to attend, landowner disputes to settle, town council members to wrangle with. Who'll take care of all of that?"

Teresa turned and stared. "Are you telling me that all you have to do to maybe keep this baby is to rest?"

"Well, yes, but—"

"But, my butt. Olivia July, you are the only sister I have in this world—well, Harper is supposed to be married, but nobody's ever seen her so we're not sure she really exists—but what I'm saying is this: If the doc tells you to lie down, that's what I expect you to do. You're supposed to be the smart one in the family. Appoint a deputy mayor or something. There's got to be somebody in town who can run the place without anything blowing up."

When Olivia didn't respond, Teresa said, "And I'll bet the real reason you haven't told Neil is because you don't want him to know what the doc wants you to do."

More silence.

Teresa smiled. "If you weren't carrying my niece, I'd box your ears."

"Niece?"

"Yes, niece. If those dumb brothers of mine think they're going to have nephews first, they are wrong."

"Do tell."

"Tell. If I'm carrying, I'm having your niece and you're having mine."

Olivia began to laugh. "Teresa, to achieve that, I will lie down until Christmas."

"Good, then let's make a deal." Teresa stuck out her hand. "Girls."

Olivia grasped it and they shook. "Girls."

Olivia embraced Teresa and they held each other for a long moment. When they separated, Olivia said, "I'm so glad you're my sister. You always give me good advice."

"Good. Now it's your turn to give me some."

"My advice is to love him as much as he loves you. I know how independent you've always been, but you and Madison are as evenly yoked as Neil and I. Stop trying to pull ahead all the time."

Teresa sighed. "I am trying."

"I know you are, and the bumps in the road will smooth out, they truly will."

"I'm holding you to that, and to the promise that you're going to follow the doc's advice. I won't say anything to Neil because it's not my place."

"I promise."

They both held their own thoughts as the breeze came up and the night songs of the insects echoed over the plains. Teresa finally asked, "Are you ready to go back inside?"

"Yes, and then I'm going to take off this apron and dance with my Neil." Her voice turned serious and sincere. "Thank you, Teresa."

"No problem."

When she returned to the hall, Teresa found Madison dancing with Sophie. He winked at her when they waltzed by, and she grinned.

After the dance, he came over and said, "How about we head back to the hotel."

"Thought you'd never ask."

They spent a few moments making the rounds to say their good-byes. Molly gave them both a hug. She planned to stay and help with the clean up, and the July brothers promised to make sure she got back to the hotel safely. With that taken care of, the newly wedded Mr. and Mrs. Madison Nance made their exit.

Once they were in the buggy, they sat in the silence for a few moments, then he turned to her and said, "I love you very much, Teresa. Thank you for marrying me."

"Do you, really?"

"Yeah. For some time now."

She sat back against the seat and felt her world go bright again. Looking his way, she said, "I love you too. For some time now."

"I asked the chef about the marmalade."

She laughed. "And what did he say?"

"It's in my room even as we speak."

"Then we need to get moving."

"Yes, ma'am, but first, this … "

He leaned over, kissed her soundly and thoroughly, then set the buggy in motion.

At the door to his room, they shared another long kiss, then Madison hoisted her into his arms and carried her inside. There was just enough light in the suite to allow them to follow the shadows to the bedroom. He set her down gently on her feet in the front room, and their wedding night, complete with marmalade, commenced.

Madison gazed down at the beautiful woman in his arms. She'd been his bane but was now his love. "I want to look at you for a moment, just to make sure I'm not dreaming."

She smiled up. "This may turn out to be a nightmare, you know."

He slowly traced her lips. "Never."

Placing her head against his heart, she savored the feel of his arms wrapping her tight.

"Teresa, I promise to love you, to be faithful, to provide for you. I'd promise to protect you, too, but you already have that in hand." His humor-filled eyes met hers.

"Yeah, I do, don't I?" She then turned serious. "I'd never harm our baby. All that talk about herbs and such was just that—talk and me being scared."

"Of what?"

"Babies."

"Why?"

"Can you imagine me as a mother?"

He nodded. "I can. You'd do a good job, too, but then again, if we do have children, Mother's never going to let us see them anyway so..." his voice trailed off.

She grinned. "You do have a point."

He eased her against him again. "Thanks for straightening that out for me, though."

Glad to have that off her chest, because she knew her boast of harming their child had worried him as much as it had her, she replied, "You're welcome."

Savoring the feel of her silk-gowned warmth and again glad she was his, Madison kissed the top of her head. "You have on entirely too many clothes, Mrs. Nance."

"I think so, too. Would you do the honors?"

His brown eyes were now lit with desire. Leaning down, he kissed her. "Eventually...."

In the aftermath of the humid kisses and the languid disrobing that followed, she was left pulsating and crooning while standing in the center of the silent, low-lit room. Aroused by the passion playing over her face, he teased marmalade over the straining dark points of her breasts, then brazenly licked and sucked her clean. He anointed the caps of her bare shoulders, the hollow of her throat, and the nook of her navel, working his way down her shuddering ebony body while enjoying her like a sweet sticky treat. When it became time for her to widen her stance so he could feast there, too, her legs shook, her body on the edge of shattering. "Madison," she breathed.

"Are you close?" he asked, already knowing the answer and loving the rictus of passion showing on her face.

"Oh my, yes."

Smiling, he parted her gently, then leaned in.

She growled her delight. He was magical, wicked, and so overwhelming, it didn't take long for his erotic ministrations to send her over the edge. Shuddering and convulsing, she was still in the eddy of the orgasm when he picked her up and carried her into the bedroom.

Chapter 19

That morning, Madison and Teresa were sleeping soundly after their night of loving when they were awakened by pounding on the door.

Teresa said sleepily, "It's just my brothers. Ignore them."

But the thundering continued, accompanied by Neil shouting Madison's name.

Teresa swore. Throwing back the sheet covering them, she got up and stuck her arms into her robe. "You go back to sleep. I'll take care of them."

Half asleep, she stumbled through the suite and snatched open the door. "What!"

"Molly's missing," Neil said grimly.

"What? What do you mean, missing? Come on in." She turned and called out, "Madison!"

He appeared a moment later and asked sleepily, "What's the matter?"

"Your mother is missing?"

His eyes widened.

Neil said, "You two get dressed and I'll tell you on the way. Sumner Booth has her."

"Dammit!" Madison swore angrily. He and Teresa

hurried away to get dressed, and as they left the suite, Neil told them the story.

According to Neil, after Teresa and Madison left the dance, the celebrants also began leaving. Molly had volunteered to help with the clean up, and Diego stayed with her to escort her home. Once the major things were done, Molly sent the rest of the women home and stayed behind to take down the decorations. She put everything in a crate, and Diego took the crate outside to put it in the buggy, but he never got the chance to go back inside because he was ambushed.

By the time Neil related the story, he, Madison, and Teresa were halfway to the sheriff's office.

"Is Diego okay?" Madison asked, though he was more worried about his mother.

"Yeah. Booth hit him over the head with something. Knocked him out cold. He came to this morning tied up in the town hall privy."

Teresa shook her head at the troubling turn of events. "How do you know it was Booth?"

"He left a note on Diego's lap."

Madison cursed.

Jefferson, the remaining brothers, and a tight-jawed Olivia were in the sheriff's office.

Diego, looking furious, said to Madison, "I'm sorry. I didn't know Booth was hanging around."

"No one did," Madison replied. "We'll get her back. May I see the note?"

Jefferson handed it over. The hastily scrawled words asked for seven hundred dollars and said to bring it to a place called Red Cloud.

"Where's Red Cloud?" Madison asked.

"About a two-day ride north," the sheriff told him. "It's on the other side of the Nebraska border."

Teresa said, "He has family there. We holed up there a few times when I rode with him."

Jefferson said, "I've wired the county sheriff, but he only has one deputy, so I'm going to swear you all in. In the meantime—"

"In the meantime," Diego interrupted, "deputize us now so we can ride. I'll pay the ransom because it's my fault she got snatched. After we get her back, I get first dibs on kicking Booth's ass."

Jefferson agreed to deputize the July brothers and Madison, and the posse set out. Teresa rode Cloud, and Madison was given one of Handy's best mounts.

Madison had no problem keeping up. He was as angry as he was concerned. What kind of place was this, where people took out their revenge on innocent old women? Diego was going to have to stand in line, he vowed to himself, because he wanted a piece of Booth first.

They rode hard most of the morning, stopping only to water the horses, and then pushed on. By evening their mounts were tired and so were they, so they made camp. No one wanted to stop, but without fresh horses, going on was impossible. As they ate beans around the fire, Madison reflected on the day and worried about his mother.

Teresa was seated at his side. "How are you holding up?"

"I'm okay. Worried, though."

"Booth has no idea what he's in for. He's as stupid

as he is ugly if he thinks we're going to take this lying down. His beef is with me, not Molly." She added, "I'm sorry she got mixed up in this."

"So am I."

The terse reply tightened Teresa's jaw.

He said, "And you want to raise our child here? No."

"Let's get Molly back first, and then we'll fight, okay?"

"Agreed."

Teresa knew his mood was tied to his concern for his mother, but bickering was not going to be helpful. She wanted to shoot Booth for what he was doing to Madison and for impacting her day-old marriage.

The next morning, they headed out at dawn. Still riding north, they crossed the Kansas-Nebraska border around noon, and turned toward Red Cloud. Madison hadn't had much to say to Teresa since their short conversation the previous evening, but she didn't take it personally. She loved him and knew that underneath his apprehension and anger, he loved her as well. She was sure that once they found Molly, things would be better.

Red Cloud was a tiny little plains town that made Henry Adams look like Philadelphia. The Julys and Madison rode slowly abreast down the main street, ignoring the alarm on the faces of the people staring on. They looked like the gang of outlaws they once were.

A man standing in the doorway of a storefront with a sign showing it to be the undertaker's office seemed to agree. He called out, "We ain't got no bank!"

Teresa called back, "Does Hank Booth still live nearby?"

"Ten miles east."

She touched her hat in thanks, and the grim-faced riders sent their horses into a gallop.

Madison felt as if time had slowed because the ten miles seemed to take forever. He looked over at Teresa riding beside him on her big stallion. He owed her an apology for having been so unapproachable since last night, but he couldn't help it. He didn't know if his mother were alive or dead. Molly Nance was a kind Christian woman from Philadelphia; she didn't know anything about life out here on the plains. He remembered how excited she'd been while talking of moving out here, but after this, she probably never wanted to leave the safe city confines of Philadelphia again, and he wouldn't blame her.

A soddie appeared up ahead.

"That's it," Teresa called out.

They reined their mounts to a halt. The soddie was out in the middle of nowhere. There wasn't a tree or a place to conceal themselves from view for as far as their eyes could see.

Madison stared at the soddie. "Is it made out of grass?"

Teresa nodded. "Pretty common in these parts. No trees."

Diego said, "Come on, Madison. Me, you, and Teri will go see what's what."

Neil and the others took out their rifles. "We'll cover you."

The three of them moved their horses forward at a walk. Madison was tense. Teresa looked at her husband. The worry on his face broke her heart. "Just a few moments more and we'll have her back." Teresa hated the idea of paying Booth even a dime, but with Molly's safety on the line there was no other choice.

When they got within fifty yards, Booth stepped outside. From behind a raised rifle he yelled, "Hold it right there!"

They stopped.

"You got the money?"

Diego held up a leather pouch. "Gold!"

They saw the smile split Booth's bearded face.

Madison snarled, "Let me see my mother!"

Booth turned, said something, and Molly walked out.

"Here she is!" he said, facing them again.

Molly looked tired, but her anger was plain. Also plain was the large cast iron skillet that she brought out from behind her skirt and crashed down on Booth's head. He keeled over like a tree, out cold before he hit the ground.

A wide-eyed Teresa met Madison's equally wide eyes and they began to laugh. An ecstatic Diego threw his head back and yelled the Seminole victory cry, while the rest of the brothers came riding up to find out what had happened.

More proud than he'd ever been in his life, Madison watched Molly toss the skillet aside, step over Booth's prone body, and walk out to meet them. Madison dismounted and ran to her. Snatching her up, he held her tight. "God, are you all right?"

She was crying happy tears. "I'm fine, son. I'm fine."

By then they were surrounded by the smiling Julys. Once Madison turned her loose, it became Teresa's turn, and she hugged her mother-in-law as tightly as Madison had. "Did he hurt you?"

"No. In fact he was very respectful. Kept apologizing and saying if you had paid him, he wouldn't have taken me."

Teresa rolled her eyes.

Molly said, "I know, dear." She looked at Diego. "Are you okay? I figured he must have done something to you when you didn't return and he walked into the hall."

Diego said, "I'm so sorry I didn't protect you."

She waved him off. "This was so exciting! When Booth stepped outside and left me alone for that moment, I grabbed that skillet."

Two Shafts chuckled. "I'm liking her a lot too."

"Me too," Harper said.

Neil asked, "So you're all right?"

"Yes, Neil, I am. I'm a July now. It'll take more than a varmint like Booth to put a scare in me."

They all fell out laughing.

Madison laughed too, all the while staring at her as if he'd never seen her before. "Mother?"

"Oh, Madison. I don't care what you and Teresa decide. I'm moving here. I've never felt so alive. And wait until I get home and tell Rebecca I was taken hostage and held for ransom. She is going to be so jealous!"

Teresa laughed so hard she had to sit on the ground.

Afterward, the brothers took a moment to tie up Booth, who was still out cold, and cuff his hands behind his back. They also put a gag in his mouth, because no one wanted to hear him complaining on the ride back when he woke up. Two Shafts found two horses grazing in back of the soddie and threw Booth over the saddle of one. They put Molly on the other and headed back to Henry Adams.

Their return was greeted by a happy Olivia and a pleased Sheriff Jefferson, who took the angry but still gagged Booth into custody.

Two Shafts told him, "You really should let us play with him before you lock him up."

Jefferson, chuckling, shook his head. "Oh no, that's going to be the judge's job."

So, Chase pushed Booth toward his office and the Julys went on their way.

That evening, while Molly slept off her adventure in her bed, Teresa and Madison were out on the blue sofa enjoying both the solitude and having Molly back safe and sound.

"Your mother's quite a woman," she said. "Booth had a knot on his head big as my fist."

"And well deserved, I might add."

"When she knocked him over the head, I almost hurt myself laughing."

Madison was certain he'd take the memory of the incident to his grave. "Amazing."

Teresa looked up into the eyes of the man she loved so very much and said, "Well?"

He turned her way and stroked her cheek. "Well, what?"

"We have one last issue to take care of. Where are we going to live?"

He smiled. "Here."

Her eyes widened. "Truly?"

He nodded. "Between you and my mother, I'm not going to win. And besides, if my sixty-two-year-old mother can take care of herself out here on the plains, our children will be able to do so too."

Teresa threw her arms around him and began kissing him all over his handsome face. "Thank you! Thank you! Thank you!"

"You're welcome," he said, laughing. "We'll have to go back to Philadelphia and sell the houses and see if Emma wants to come out, but after that, Henry Adams will be home."

Teresa worked her way onto his lap, and he held her close. He asked, "Remember that land we were looking at?"

"The one with the trees and water?"

"Yep. Think I'll buy it and build us a house. Now that I own a twenty percent interest in a Yukon gold mine, I can afford it."

Teresa leaned back. "A twenty percent interest in a gold mine?"

"Yep. Won it from Diego playing poker the night before we got married."

She placed her head on his chest and laughed. "You are something," she told him.

"So are you."

Teresa met his gaze and said softly and with feeling, "I love you, Madison Nance."

"I love you too, Teresa. As much as I love breathing."

A gleam of mischief sparkled in her eyes. "You

know, Molly's probably going to be sleeping for a while. "Do we have any marmalade left?"

He grinned. "I think so."

Her voice sultry and playful, she said, "Shall we step across the hall?"

"Thought you'd never ask."

In the spring of 1896, Olivia and Neil welcomed their first child into the world. Teresa and Madison's baby was born later that summer and drew its first breath in the bedroom of its parents' new home. True to their pact, the sisters-in-law gave birth to beautiful baby girls.

Author Note

During an event for the Lincoln branch of the Peoria Public Library, Angel Carson approached me with an idea for a book. She wanted a story involving a female outlaw. I paused to consider the idea. Recently, she confessed that she thought my pause meant she'd offended me, but that was not the case. Out of that encounter came Teresa July, who made her first appearance on the BJ stage in *Something Like Love*, published by Avon in 2006. Madison Nance made his debut in *A Chance at Love* (Avon 2002) and played a small but pivotal role in the story featuring lady gambler Loreli Winters.

I had a good time bringing the irrepressible Teresa to life in SLL, but had no idea who to pair her with until a talk with another sistafan, Dee Dee Graves, solved the problem. Many thanks to both Angel and Dee Dee for helping bring *Wild Sweet Love* to life.

One of the most famous female outlaws in the Old West was Belle Starr, who, according to sources, wore "buckskins ... tight black jackets, a man's Stetson with an ostrich plume and twin holstered pistols." She managed to elude the law for many years but was finally brought to trial for robbery, and sentenced by Hanging Judge Isaac Parker in 1883. Belle served her time in the House of Corrections in Detroit, Michigan. She only served nine months, however, having earned a reprieve for good behavior, and returned to her home in Indian Territory. For the next six years she continued her outlaw ways, but a shotgun blast to the back ended her life on February 3, 1889, two days short of her forty-first birthday.

I chose Philadelphia as the setting for *Wild Sweet Love* because of the important role the city played in the race's history. The battle between the Radicals and the Conservatives was very real and ultimately led to the formation of the NAACP. For more information on the issues and events of the day, please consult this partial list of sources:

W.E.B. Dubois. *The Philadelphia Negro: A Social Study*. University of Pennsylvania, Philadelphia, Pennsylvania, 1899.

Mitch Kachun. *Festivals of Freedom: Memory and Meaning in African American Emancipation Celebrations, 1808–1915*. University of Massachusetts Press, Amherst and Boston, 2003.

August Meier. *Negro Thought in America 1880–1915*. Ann Arbor Paperbacks, University of Michigan Press, Ann Arbor, 1963.

Lane, Roger. *William Dorsey's Philadelphia and Ours*. Oxford University Press, New York, New York, 1991.

In closing, let me say thanks again to my readers for all the support, love, and prayers. Without you all, I'd be nothing. The best way to get in touch with me and to receive a response is to e-mail through my Web site at www.beverlyjenkins.net. Until the next time, stay blessed everybody.

Sincerely,
B.

Next month, don't miss these exciting
new love stories only from
Avon Books

The Viscount in Her Bedroom by Gayle Callen

An Avon Romantic Treasure

Simon, Viscount Wade, leads an orderly life. Then he meets
the vivacious, witty, and beautiful Louisa Shelby and everything is turned upside down. Suddenly, Simon finds himself drawn into the mystery of Louisa's past . . . and dreaming of a future in her arms.

At the Edge by Cait London

An Avon Contemporary Romance

A powerful empath, Claire Brown has learned it's much
easier to live in solitude than constantly be exposed to the
pain of others. But when a desperate man moves in next
door, she finds herself powerless against his pleas for
help—and unable to stop him from breaching her carefully
erected walls.

The Templar's Seduction by Mary Reed McCall

An Avon Romance

Spared a death sentence, Sir Alexander must impersonate an
earl if he wishes to stay on the king's good side. But his task is
made all the more complicated by the earl's lovely—and suspicious—wife, who is starting to believe that the miraculous
return of her husband is not all that it seems.

A Dangerous Beauty by Sophia Nash

An Avon Romance

Rosamunde Baird has sworn off adventure and temptation.
That's what makes the mysterious Duke of Helston so dangerous—and compelling. And now, to hold on to the love he
never expected, the duke must reveal a past he has so desper-
ately kept hidden.

Visit www.AuthorTracker.com for exclusive
information on your favorite HarperCollins authors.

REL 0507

Available wherever books are sold or please call 1-800-331-3761 to order.

Avon Romances
the best in
exceptional authors and unforgettable novels!

Avon Romantic Treasures

Unforgettable, enthralling love stories, sparkling with passion and adventure from Romance's bestselling authors

TEMPTING THE WOLF   *by Lois Greiman*
0-06-078398-2/$6.99 US/$9.99 Can

HIS MISTRESS BY MORNING   *by Elizabeth Boyle*
0-06-078402-4/$6.99 US/$9.99 Can

HOW TO SEDUCE A DUKE   *by Kathryn Caskie*
0-06-112456-7/$6.99 US/$9.99 Can

A DUKE OF HER OWN   *by Lorraine Heath*
0-06-112963-1/$6.99 US/$9.99 Can

AUTUMN IN SCOTLAND   *by Karen Ranney*
978-0-06-075745-8/$6.99 US/$9.99 Can

SURRENDER TO A SCOUNDREL   *by Julianne MacLean*
978-0-06-081936-7/$6.99 US/$9.99 Can

TWO WEEKS WITH A STRANGER   *by Debra Mullins*
978-0-06-079924-3/$6.99 US/$9.99 Can

AND THEN HE KISSED HER   *by Laura Lee Guhrke*
978-0-06-114360-1/$6.99 US/$9.99 Can

CLAIMING THE COURTESAN   *by Anna Campbell*
978-0-06-123491-0/$6.99 US/$9.99 Can

THE DUKE'S INDISCRETION   *by Adele Ashworth*
978-0-06-112857-8/$6.99 US/$9.99 Can

Visit www.AuthorTracker.com for exclusive
information on your favorite HarperCollins authors.

RT 0207

Available wherever books are sold or please call 1-800-331-3761 to order.